# Child of
# a Hidden Sea

ALSO BY A. M. DELLAMONICA

*Indigo Springs*
*Blue Magic*

# Child of
# a Hidden Sea

A. M. DELLAMONICA

A TOM DOHERTY ASSOCIATES BOOK
NEW YORK

CHILD OF A HIDDEN SEA

Copyright © 2014 by A. M. Dellamonica

A Tor Book
Published by Tom Doherty Associates, LLC
175 Fifth Avenue
New York, NY 10010

www.tor-forge.com

Tor® is a registered trademark of Tom Doherty Associates, LLC.

The Library of Congress Cataloging-in-Publication Data is available upon request.

ISBN 978-0-7653-3449-7 (hardcover)
ISBN 978-1-4668-1235-2 (e-book)

Tor books may be purchased for educational, business, or promotional use. For information on bulk purchases, please contact Macmillan Corporate and Premium Sales Department at 1-800-221-7945, extension 5442, or write specialmarkets@macmillan.com.

First Edition: June 2014

Printed in the United States of America

0  9  8  7  6  5  4  3  2  1

*For Jessica Reisman, who navigates the same stormy waters*

# ACKNOWLEDGMENTS

*Child of a Hidden Sea* could not exist if I weren't blessed with an abundant network of generous and inspiring people. Always at its heart, and in mine, is my wife, Kelly Robson.

I owe much to my family—the Tuckers, the Millars, and the Robsons, and to my wonderful siblings: Michelle, Sherelyn, Susan, and Bill. My friends do everything from reading drafts, explaining research concepts, and providing moral support when I am flailing: thanks are due to Ming Dinh, Denise Garzón, Nicki Hamilton, Elaine Mari, Ginger Mullen, Dawn-Marie Pares, Ramona Roberts, and Matt Youngmark.

I am grateful to my agent, Linn Prentis; my editors, Jim Frenkel, Stacy Hill, and Marco Palmieri; the staff at Tor.com and all the editors, writers, and mentors who've guided me, including: Camille Alexa, Ellen Datlow, Don DeBrandt, Gardner Dozois, Claude Lalumière, Jessica Reisman, Nancy Richler, Harry Turtledove, and Jeremy Zimmerman.

Even a book about magic needs the occasional fact. The wonderful people at SF Novelists helped with everything from research details to brainstorming titles. Mark Bowman and Gordon Love checked my scuba-diving details, while Peter Watts has shown extraordinary patience over the years with my arty, drama-geek approach to physics. Walter Jon Williams got me started on resources for tall ships. Any errors in what passes for science, language, or sailing procedure within this book are mine.

I am one of those people who do much of their creative work out in a café environment, and all of the Stormwrack books were drafted in the remarkable Caffe Calabria on Commercial Drive in Vancouver. I'm not the first to note that space made available to writers (along with everyone else in the neighborhood) by the Murdocco family was like a second home to me. It was a privilege to work there.

You all made it possible for me to embark on this journey, and I owe you.

# Child of
# a Hidden Sea

CHAPTER 1

Sinking.

Sophie Hansa had barely worked out that she was falling before she struck the surface of an unknown body of water.

First, there'd been a blast of wind. A tornado? Rushing air, pounding at her eardrums, had plucked her right off the ground. Howling, it had driven her upward, pinwheeling and helpless, over the rooftops of the houses and shops, carrying her up above the fog, in a cloud of grit and litter, trash can lids, uprooted weeds, discarded heroin needles, and a couple very surprised rats.

She remembered pain as something tangled and wrenched her arm. Then the upward thrust of wind blew itself out, taking with it the sunlight above. One second she was flying and sunblind. The next, she was plummeting, dead weight in the dark.

Terror jolted through her. She drew breath to scream, only to feel the spank of the sea, a wet fist of concrete between her shoulder blades, stinging even as it slowed her fall. She plunged beneath the waves, headfirst.

This, at least, was her element. Despite the fear and disbelief—*the ocean? I made it to the water?*—she instinctively held her breath as she went under.

Reaching out with the grace of long practice, arms extended, her body twisted to break her downward momentum.

A jerk—the arm—brought the motion short. Weight pulled her downward. The nylon strap of her camera case, looped around her wrist, had snagged something heavy.

She tried to slide it off, but there was no slack. Instead, she yanked up her skirt with her free hand, clearing her legs and scissor-kicking for the surface. *One, two.* For a frightening moment, she made no headway. Then she, the camera case, and whatever it had hooked all started moving upward. Sophie broke water, blowing to clear her nose and mouth, inhaling deeply.

*Taste of salt, definitely not some lake . . .*

"Help," she shouted. "Hello?"

No reply. She kept treading, reeling in the tether on her wrist, creating slack so she could slip it off her arm.

The night sky was clouded over but something—a million somethings—twinkled above her, forming an oscillating, multipoint strip of light.

*. . . shouldn't be night; it's three in the afternoon. Could I have hit my head? How far did the wind carry me? I was inland. Water feels too warm to be the Pacific . . .*

*What happened? Where am I?*

One thing at a time. She tugged again on the nylon tether and saw a hand just below the surface.

"Nyuhh!" She got a good grip, wrestling the weight of the unconscious stranger. A woman's upper body rose from the water, head lolling. Water dribbled from her lips.

*Don't be dead.* Muscling her onto her back, Sophie supported her neck, letting her head drop behind her and fumbling to open her mouth and check her airway.

She was breathing. Relieved, she tried stabilizing the woman in a supported float—only to get swamped by a wave. Warm brine sheeted over her mouth and nose.

Spitting, she kicked harder. One foot caught solid meat . . . a fish? The sensation was like kicking a slimy two-by-four. She surfaced again, spitting.

"We're good." She coughed out the words. "I've got you, it's okay."

No answer. In the dim, cloud-filtered moonlight, the woman's skin was the color of pewter, her lined face as still as an engraving. Then Sophie noticed the dagger, buried haft-deep under her breast.

Daggers. The alley. A couple of men had attacked the woman.

*And I piled in,* Sophie remembered, *swinging the only thing I had, the camera case. The strap snagged her, I guess, in the wind. Or she grabbed it. I saw something go flying . . . a pocket watch?*

The initial rush of fighting, falling, gonna-die terror was wearing off now. In its wake, she felt fatigue building in her muscles. Pain, too—the shoulder and wrist were throbbing. Sprained? She'd been lucky, she supposed; nothing was broken. She could have snapped her neck, hitting the water like that.

*Just tread, Sophie,* she told herself. *Catch your breath, look around.*

Fumbling to adjust her grip on the woman, she scanned the surface of the water. The breeze was light and the swells weren't big—maybe half a meter high. Eddies near the surface and movement below, near her legs, hinted at more fish.

One of the aerial fairy-lights dropped out of formation, spiraling down to splat beside her like a fat purple-gray snowball. It was a bioluminescent moth, quivering feebly, in its death throes.

*What the—I don't recognize that species,* Sophie thought. She wasn't merely seizing on an ill-timed distraction—if she could identify the insect, she might at least know where she was, which ocean.

The moth's wings had fanned out in the water: it was about five inches long from end to end. The posterior tip of its abdomen was aglow, but the light was fading as it died. Around her, more were falling, a sparse glittering snowfall.

Another fish bumped her treading legs, catching the edge of Sophie's skirt as it lunged around her knee, spaghetti-slick and weighty, its open mouth crammed with jagged teeth. It gulped down the moth and vanished, leaving a wing drifting on the surface.

"Some kind of prey bonanza," she said. "The moths are . . . migrating? This is incredible! I can't believe I don't recognize the species."

A wave washed the wing against her wrist. It clung stickily. The injured woman's chin dipped into the water.

*Am I tiring?*

"Wake up, please, wake up." Kicking against the next surge, she tightened her grip.

Another moth drifted into view, wings beating furiously as it tried to stay aloft. As Sophie watched, it glided a foot, fluttered up a couple inches, then dropped down into another ready mouth.

It was easy to imagine the same thing happening to her. Tiring under the weight of the unconscious woman, wearing out, sinking below. The two of them breaking into anonymous nutrients, feeding the ecosystem.

"Not gonna happen," she told herself. "Come on, focus on something else . . . like why isn't it afternoon?" Talking to herself provided a check on her breathing. If she could speak, at least in short bursts, she wasn't too exhausted.

Higher up, past the moths, a layer of cloud obscured the stars. It was bright nonetheless. The edges of the clouds were silver; edged in bone-white, lacy wisps backlit by moonlight. The full moon was ten days away. Could she have lost ten days?

Another swell lifted them, and she got her arm properly snugged around the woman, below the slender neck, braced above the knife. The lolling head rested against her shoulder. Now she felt secure enough to use her free hand to adjust her skirt, tucking it higher into her waistband, further clearing her legs.

"You got lucky there," she told the woman. "I dressed up to impress you. No way could I have kept us both afloat if I'd been wearing jeans. You'd have drowned before I got them stripped."

She was easing into what Bram called "diving mode" now, scanning the waves for threats, or anything she might use to improve their situation. She groped for the bobbing waterproof camera case, still bound to her wrist.

"Every bit of buoyancy, right?" Raising her face to the sky, Sophie aligned herself with the moths. Kick, kick, breathe. "Hope you're headed for land, guys."

The moths didn't answer. They glimmered above, a streamer of pinpoints aswirl on windy gusts. Their bodies kept falling, more and more of them, blanketing the water, so many that Sophie could observe there were lots of big ones and a lesser number of smaller individuals. Females and males?

They were noisy, too. Between the splash and murmur of the waves she could hear . . . was that cheeping?

"Oop." Embarrassment flared, though nobody was around to witness her mistake. "That's not the moths, it's—"

The woman coughed, spitting blood onto Sophie's hand.

"Please wake up," Sophie said. "Where are we?"

Something big broke the water, maybe twenty feet away. Anything might be coming from the depths, surfacing to feast on the fish that were here for the moths. Orca, sharks . . .

"Stay with me, okay?" she said. "Don't die."

A long sigh that might have been a groan.

"You kind of owe me. You'd *so* be dead if I hadn't jumped into that fight with the guys who stabbed you. Besides, I think maybe you're Beatrice Vanko's sister. And the thing is, Beatrice is my biological mother . . ."

*And apparently she hates me.* "If I'm right, that would make you my aunt. I'm family. Maybe I didn't exactly save your life, but you can't die on family, right?"

Silly argument, but she pushed on.

"I know I shouldn't have just turned up at Beatrice's house. I should have called. I meant to drive by her place, get the lay of the land, you know? But she came down the street and I got excited. Seeing what I might look like when I'm middle-aged—"

So she'd done what felt right, as usual, without thinking it through.

"I'm sorry. You're in shock, and I'm babbling. Suboptimal behavior, my brother would say."

Kick, kick, breathe. "I guess after twenty-four years, I figured she'd want to know her daughter was alive. But that's stupid, isn't it? She got rid of me. I should have known she'd blow me off."

*Should've known she wouldn't see anything worth getting to know.* "Anyway, I saw you—" She skipped the part where she'd slept in her car for three days while watching Beatrice's house. She wasn't about to admit—even to an unconscious maybe-aunt—to practically stalking her biological mother. "I thought I'd try again. But those guys attacked you, in the alley—what was that about?"

*You snapped,* said a calm interior voice. *The terrible things your bio-mom said drove you over the edge. All of what happened afterward— watching the house, weird guys attacking this unnamed maybe-aunt—it's a nervous breakdown. Or do they call them psychotic breaks?*

Kick, kick, breathe.

*Maybe when your advisor called and tried to push you into setting a date to defend your thesis, you couldn't deal. Finding Beatrice, the mugging and now this . . . maybe it's all a delusion.*

"If I'm insane, I'll wake up in a clean, safe hospital sooner or later," she said. "My family will come, I'll take some antipsychotics and doctors will promise us it's gonna be okay. Right?"

A furious, inhuman cheeping. A bedraggled moth had landed in the hollow of the woman's belly. A small shadow splashed after it: one of the bats Sophie had heard earlier. It came up, triumphant, in the puddle of brine and blood, with the insect caught in its jaws.

The bat hitched itself past the knife, across her aunt's breast, over Sophie's wrist. It continued up her sore arm, climbing from the unconscious woman's face into Sophie's hair, pulling itself to the highest point it could find.

The bat settled on her head, munching on its catch and preening seawater out of its wings.

Sophie groaned. If this *was* a delusion, her subconscious mind was going all out to make it seem real. Pieces of carapace and drops of wet bug juice pattered on her forehead.

*Just don't crap on me, Dracula,* she thought.

And then: *I don't know this species, either.*

"See, that's proof! Seagoing bats, glowing moths—come on! I don't care how real it feels, it has to be a delusion."

Munch, munch, munch.

"This is profoundly mediagenic. Somebody would have shot this. I'd have seen those moths migrating a thousand times. On IMAX, no less."

From the bat, a spitting sound. The glowing tip of the moth's posterior bounced down her face.

"I've never lost anyone—not on a climb, not on a dive," Sophie said. "I've been in trouble before. You'll make it."

The body in her arms stiffened, then coughed.

"Those moths are going somewhere, and I'm rationing my energy. The sun's gonna come up and I'm going to make it to shore. Some shore. With you, maybe-Aunt. That's a promise."

The woman's eyelids fluttered. A second later, her weight shifted, lightening the load. Sophie felt a burst of acceleration; she was kicking.

"I don't know for sure," she said, "but I think that might make you bleed faster. Just float, okay?"

The woman sputtered some more; the kicking stopped. Her hand crawled to the knife, probing. She hissed, obviously pained.

"Dinna seyz Fleetspak?" she mumbled.

"What?"

"You speak Anglay . . . ?"

"English."

"Thought I'd imagined—Anglish only?" Her voice was thready.

"I can do Spanish, I guess, or a little Russian—"

"Who are you?"

"I'm—ow!" The bat on Sophie's head had taken wing, yanking hair as it launched itself at the flying buffet above. "Hey, is that land?" The trail of lights in the sky was accumulating into a bright mass on the horizon.

"Stele Island. Moths . . . lay . . . eggs on the cliffs."

"I don't know Stele Island—is this the Caribbean? The Mediterranean? The Gulf?"

"Stele Islanders," the woman repeated. "Boats'll be out. The moths bring up deepfish . . . swim another mile or so, they'll catch us."

"Only a mile?" Sophie felt a surge of relief. "No problem."

"Who are you?" the woman repeated.

*Okay, Sofe, for once in your life don't blurt out everything at once. Keep it simple.*

It was what her brother, Bram, would have told her. Sophie blinked back tears as her detachment shredded. "I'm Beatrice's daughter."

*Don't go all motormouth on her, she's injured . . .*

"Daughter, Beatrice?" The woman's face pinched; her mental processes probably muddled by pain or blood loss. "No. That daughter? How old are you?"

"Twenty-four. I didn't mean any trouble, I just wanted to meet her. My parents are traveling and I wanted to track down my birth family while they were gone. Without hurting them, see? But Beatrice went mental when she saw me."

"'Trice can be . . ." the woman mumbled. "High strung."

"I kinda noticed. I told her, 'Fine, I'll go. Just tell me about my dad and I'll bug him instead.' That was when she lost it."

"Your. Dad."

"Do you know him? Did he die tragically or—" Sophie quailed from a picture-perfect memory of the horror on her birth mother's face.

*Beatrice recoiling, like I was poison . . .*

She couldn't quite ask—had her biological father been a rapist? Instead, she changed the subject. "Then those guys jumped you."

The woman eyed her dully.

*Told you, Sophie. You always feel this need to overshare.*

Deep breath. Try again. "Sorry, miss—you are my aunt, right? I mean, you look like Beatrice."

"Gale, child . . . name's Gale."

"I just wanted to know where I came from. Gale."

A cough that was very much a laugh. "And here we are."

"What do you . . ." But Gale had passed out, once again becoming dead weight.

*Just swim, Sophie. It's a delusion, remember? Kick, rest, kick, all in your mind, Kick, kick, rest. An aunt who's a street-fighting ninja? Wizard of Oz windstorms that dump you in the ocean? Has to be a delusion.*

*Please, let me wake up in the hospital. Is that a bedsheet?*

No such luck. She'd caught a thread of seaweed with her arm.

She pulled free.

Another tangled her feet.

The weeds were moving.

Up and down the glimmering path of winged bodies on the water's surface, green-sheathed bubbles were rising, bean-shaped floats dotting a growing thicket of stems. Seaweed: it formed a carpet, highway-wide and blistered with the buoyant, air-filled pods. Bristly stems clung to Sophie, winding around her legs, around Aunt . . . Gale?

The weeds raised both women, the camera case and all the fish who'd come up to feast on the moth migration. Water streamed out of Sophie's hair and her dress and she shivered, suddenly chilled. Gale's weight came off her arm. The pain in her shoulder ramped up a notch.

The fish, lifted out of water, thrashed as they suffocated. A pelican landed on the cushion of weed and plucked one of them up.

*Brown pelican,* Sophie thought, pelecanus occidentalus, *perfectly ordinary. Maybe this is the Gulf of Mexico. But how?*

Entangled, afloat, apparently safe, Sophie stared at the tons of gasping fish as insects dropped in a twinkling rain around her and bats chittered above.

A jerk—something was towing them.

She kept her good arm locked around Gale, in case any of this was real. The way things were going so far, whoever was reeling them in would probably decide to throw them back.

CHAPTER 2

The first thing their rescuers said to Sophie was the same thing as Aunt Gale: "Sezza Fleetspak?"

They were out in small wooden sailboats, rickety eighteen- and twenty-footers with patched sails, whose crews were frantically hauling in the rising seaweed and its catch. A bucket brigade of adults sorted the thrashing fish; anything shorter than arm's length went over the port side. The larger ones they clubbed to death and transferred below.

Preadolescent kids clad in undyed, lumpy sweaters worked at stripping the moths' wings, trimming off their glow-bulbs and dropping the bodies into vats that stank of hot vinegar. Guttering motes of chitin flickered at their feet, which were mostly bare. A third group sliced the seaweed into arm's-length strips as they hauled it up, popping off the floats and storing them in crates. Nothing was wasted.

*No garbage,* Sophie noticed. The dense mattress of vegetation should be full of plastic grocery bags, water bottles, and other refuse; the oceans were full of floating and submerged trash.

"Fleetspak? Sezza Fleetspak?"

The grizzled woman directing these words at Sophie was already examining Gale's wound, tearing her jacket and shirt aside to reveal the knife, embedded just under a rib.

"English," Sophie replied. "Español? Français? Russki? Anyone?"

Blank looks all around.

"Guess we can't communicate." She crouched by Gale, taking her hand. The knife had a leather-wrapped handle, she noticed, and a familiar brand name.

The woman—the ship's skipper?—barked orders. One of the crew vanished below, reappearing a minute later with a threadbare blanket and a steaming cup. Sophie let him drape her—the wind was icy—and took a careful sip of what turned out to be hot fish broth, flavored with dill.

By now, the skipper had improvised a pressure bandage for Gale's wound. She picked through her pockets and found a small purse, made of reptilian-looking leather and worked with unfamiliar letters.

At the discovery, the woman stiffened: whatever the thing was, it was bad news. She looked at Sophie before removing it—as if seeking permission? Sophie nodded, holding out a hand. The woman passed it over.

"Looks like it might be watertight," Sophie said. The pouch had a clamshell shape and pursed lips with interlocked zipper teeth. Sophie ran her finger over the closure, looking for a tab, and the zip separated, releasing with a sound that was almost a sigh.

She could feel the crew's eyes on her as she reached inside.

The first thing she pulled out was a badge.

It had the look of a police badge: shield-shaped, with a stylized sun stamped on it. It was made of an unfamiliar substance; it had the weight and hardness of metal, but looked like a polished piece of wood—fir, maybe, or birch. Ordinary Roman letters were pressed or carved into it. A couple of the words looked familiar—*arrepublica, athoritz*. Republic? Authority?

The sailors' attitude, already disapproving, seemed to darken.

*At this rate, they'll chuck us overboard.* She turned her attention to the next item, a silk scarf so fine she could see through it, like a veil. It was an oceanic chart—currents and islands were printed on the almost weightless fabric. There were no familiar landmarks, no X to mark any particular spot.

There was a USB flash drive.

"Any chance there's a computer aboard?" she asked, but the skipper looked at the disc key without recognition. Sophie swapped it for the biggest thing in the purse, a cell phone, charged up and flashing "No Service." She held it up and, again, got blank expressions.

The bottom of the pouch held some golden coins and a platinum Amex card bearing the name *Gale A. Feliachild.* There was a laminated picture of a younger Gale, standing with Sophie's birth mother and a teenaged girl. A cousin? Half sibling?

Beatrice's words came back: *Get out, go now—you can't be here—get away from me, you viper. No, I won't calm down, I'm not answering questions. Go, go and don't come back!*

"Is my being here something Beatrice did—she sent me away?" Nobody answered her.

*Right, and how would she do that?*

*How much time have I lost?*

*Where on earth am I?*

She fought down the panic by focusing on the pouch again. The last thing in it was a dried chrysanthemum, carefully wrapped in waxed paper. More than half of its petals had been plucked.

She opened the paper, catching a faint whirl of peppery scent and dust. Just a flower, then.

"No answers here." She replaced everything but the cell phone, taking one last look at the photograph as she closed the flap of the watertight leather satchel . . .

. . . which promptly chomped itself back together.

Sophie let out a little squeak as the ivory zipper teeth sealed, the leathery lips of the purse tightening over them. She nudged her finger between them again, feeling for wires, and the movement reversed. It sighed, again, as it flapped open.

She closed the purse, and it zipped itself shut.

"Oh, wow. You guys seeing this?"

Sullen glares from the sailors. They were probably deciding whether to tie the anchor to her ankles or her head when they dropped her in the drink.

At least they'd fed her first. She tightened her grip on the blanket, and drank more of the broth. Her shoulder and wrist were working up a deep ache that matched the rhythm of her heartbeat.

The skipper reached a decision. She clapped her hands and the ship disentangled itself from the fishing effort. A teen used tattered white flags to signal to the next ship. Turning to port, they set sail for the island, whose cliffs were outlined in starry white by the survivors of the moth migration.

They made good speed—the wind, at their backs, was rising.

Sophie tucked the clamshell pouch into her camera bag, and held Gale's limp hand. Her pulse was faint but steady. She fought back a sense of wrongness as she did so, a weird feeling of falseness, as if she was pretending to be attached to this woman and all these people knew better. Head down, she rested, breathing slowly, monitoring her surroundings and not quite dozing. The ship sailed around the moth-starred edge of the escarpment and into a shallow bay.

Sophie's relief at being in port—despite all evidence to the contrary, she had been imagining a hospital for Gale, phone service and Internet access—was short-lived. The people coming out to meet them looked as emphatically poverty-stricken as the sailors. Their village—a collection of shacks made of scavenged ship beams and driftwood, mortared with seaweed-colored muck—ringed the rise of land sheltered by the bay. There wasn't a single electric light or cell tower; what illumination there was came from crude torches. Gaps and breaks in their teeth suggested they had little access to modern medicine.

The skipper had Gale transferred to a lifeboat, and gestured to indicate that Sophie should follow. The others were unloading, packing seaweed, fish, and barrels of brined moths into other boats. They were careful but hurried, moving with an air of urgency.

Sophie didn't need to speak the language to know they were spooked by the storm—it was blowing up out there—and concerned about the other fishers. The kids were ordered ashore. A couple protested, and were overruled.

Hostility brimmed in the glances everyone was giving her.

The skipper grasped Sophie's hand briefly before she clambered aboard the rowboat. "Feyza Stele kinstay," she said. Gibberish, but her tone was reassuring.

"Thank you," Sophie replied. She put her hand on her heart and the message seemed to get through. Straightening, the captain replied with a formal-looking bow. Then she was on the choppy waters of the bay, in a rowboat with her injured aunt and four burly sailors.

"Do you want me to . . . ?" Tapping the nearest sailor, Sophie mimed a willingness to row. He pointedly set his foot on the spare oar.

*Face it, Sofe, nobody wants anything from you.*

"Be that way. My arm's hurt anyway." Behind them, the preteen kids were rowing themselves ashore. People were waiting, on the beach, to meet them.

They pulled up onto the sand, the sailors leaping out to tow the rowboat up beyond the reach of the waves. The biggest of the men lifted Gale like a baby.

"Watch her injury—" But one of the others had clamped onto Sophie's elbow, manhandling her in the opposite direction.

"Ow! I want to stay with her! Where are you taking me?"

No answer. He hurried her along, up to a boardwalk, then a crude staircase cut into the rock. His grip on her elbow was like a granite cuff; struggling just ground her bones against each other.

*What now?*

Not drowning had been such a relief she hadn't even thought about who her rescuers might be, what they might want. She fumbled for Gale's pouch—*if I flash that badge, or offer him the coins . . .*

She stumbled as her escort jolted to a stop in front of the biggest of the shacks.

"Bastien," he boomed.

Sounds from within. A willowy man with limp flaxen hair and gapped, soft-looking teeth opened the door, spilling candlelight out into the rising breeze.

The man looked from the sailor to Sophie, then past them to the sky, the signs of the rising storm. He uttered a single phrase, in a soft voice, and the sailor let Sophie go.

She didn't wait for an invitation, plunging past them both on shaky legs, collapsing onto a bench on the far wall. The men conversed in the doorway; then the sailor left, and she was alone with the blond.

*Him I can fend off.* Even by the starved standards of these islanders, he was twig-thin, unhealthy-looking, pale where they were weathered.

He looked at Sophie, assessing her. After a moment he opened a trunk, pulling out a slate and a piece of chalk.

"Bastien," he said, pointing at himself.

She felt a trickle of relief. "Sophie."

"Bastien," he said again, and now he wrote it: "Bastien Tannen Ro."

He offered her the chalk.

Sophie wrote her first name.

"Sophie . . . ?" He tapped the two names after his first.

"My whole name?"

He tapped again. "Zhillscra."

Feeling stupid, fighting tears, she wrote: Sophie Opal Hansa. *Age twenty-four, lost at sea,* she added mentally.

"Tanke, Sophie," he said. "Din sezza—"

"No, I don't know your damned Flitspak," she snapped. "I've got three languages, bits of anyway. You can't speak any of 'em? I mean, you look like you're the educated guy, right? Teacher? Scientist? You should be speaking English and applying for foreign aid and . . . I'm ranting now, aren't I?"

*Why not rant?* She wasn't in danger of drowning anymore. She was lost, miserable, and, apparently, a prisoner. Gale might be dying.

Outside, the wind howled, louder now.

"Seriously. You need Yankee dollars," she told him. "Those leaky, scavenged-wood tubs . . . nobody should be out chasing fish in this weather."

He gave her bad shoulder a sympathetic pat, then threw a brick of what looked like pressed kelp on his smoky, makeshift hearth. He made a thin tea, putting it before her in a shallow black bowl.

She took a sip. Whatever it was, it was bitter enough to make her sputter and spit it back. Bastien promptly took it away, setting the bowl on a marble table next to his trunk.

"Look, I—"

He held up a hand—wait. Then, opening a tiny larder, he came up with a carved wooden cup of water and an earthenware jar of pickled moths.

Sophie shook her head. "Not hungry."

He pointed at a rough bed in the corner. "Fezza dorm?"

She retreated there, curling up near the stove. Bastien fussed with her confiscated tea, dropping in dust from a vial of saffron-colored powder, then grinding golden, beeswax-scented granules into the mix.

*Could be worse. He doesn't seem to want to "fezza dorm" together.* She checked the cell phone she'd found in Gale's purse. Still no service. She punched in Bram's number, an oddly comforting ritual, and composed a text message:

*Losing my mind. Send doctors with straitjackets and Haldol. LOTS of Haldol. Sofe.*

The phone generated an immediate reply:

*Message will be sent when you return to service area.*

She'd last seen her brother five days ago, after the two of them put their parents on a plane to Italy.

Sophie had decided their vacation was a chance to take another good look through Mom's stuff, to see if she could find any clues that might lead back to her birth family. She had assumed Bram would want her to drop him off so he could go dive into the latest pile of research.

Instead, he'd just finished a paper and was restless.

Bram in a mood to play was too much of a temptation to pass up. They'd gone for burgers, and then he'd wanted her opinion on a mountain bike he was thinking of buying, and by the time they'd chewed over the pros and cons of that he'd run into a couple friends who were doing a stand-up comedy show as a benefit for a neighborhood family who'd lost their house in a fire.

The two of them had agreed to be the comedy test audience for the show's final rehearsal. That turned into Sophie getting pressed into providing musical backup—she'd taken guitar for a while, in school. They were at the comedy club all night, with her strumming and Bram alternately waiting on tables and "playing" the tambourine.

Wind slammed the flimsy wall of the shack with the strength of an angry bear, jolting Sophie back to the here and now. The storm was building.

She traced a finger over her case. There was no point in taking the camera out: the light was bad. She could click through her shots from the past three days, two hundred stalker pics of Beatrice, her husband, and Gale. But that would waste battery power. Tomorrow—if she didn't get put to sea in a raft or forcibly married to the King of the Starvelings—she might get a shot of one of those moths in its pre-pickled state.

*Power down.* Years of hiking, sailing, caving, and climbing had taught her to catch up on her rest when there was nothing else useful she could do. She closed her eyes, made a halfhearted attempt to meditate, and drifted into dreamless sleep.

Clinking woke her. She opened her eyes to see Bastien had finished measuring and mixing the contents of his tea bowl. He flipped an hourglass-shaped timer and stared at the chalkboard with Sophie's name on it. Humming, he sketched letters from the unfamiliar alphabet below the letters of her name. Translating it? His lips moved as he worked. "Zooophie. Nuh. SSSSohhhfeee."

When he was satisfied, he dug in the trunk, this time coming up with a conch shell about the size of a softball and a tool—was it made of ivory?—that reminded her of a dentist's pick. He lit two lanterns, brightening the room around the table. Then, taking a deep, meditative breath, he began to carve.

*Great. Now it's hobby hour?*

"Bastien—"

"Shhh!"

She took out Gale's purse again, touching the zipper and watching it open itself. She dumped its contents, examining the seams, looking for wires or magnets, feeling the weight of it, listening to the purr of its teeth locking together. She'd have to cut the thing up to figure out how it worked.

She examined the gold coins. They were a set, of sorts—each had a ship on one side and an unfamiliar flag on the other. Words, too, in the Latin alphabet: Sylvanna, Tiladene, Redcap, Ualtar, Wrayland . . .

*Land*, she thought. *Names of states? Towns?*

Places she hadn't heard of. Coins she'd never seen before. They had the weight and softness of real gold, but who minted with gold these days? How remote would these places have to be—Viemere, Tiladene—for her to have never heard of any of them?

, There was so much here she didn't recognize—wildlife, cash, these place names, if that's what they were. She knew what Sanskrit looked like, and Arabic; she could recognize Cyrillic text and Chinese characters even if she couldn't read them. But Bastien's alphabet—the one stamped onto the satchel, the alphabet he was using, even now, to score beautifully calligraphed words onto the conch shell—she'd never seen those characters.

She saw he'd inscribed the translated version of her name onto the shell.

*That can't be good.* Maybe it was a bridal gift. She eyed the flimsy wooden fork he'd stuck into the jar of moths. That nice sharp pick might make a better weapon if she had to defend her virtue.

It was a silly thought. Frail as he was, one good swing of the camera case would snap him in half.

*These people are poor, but the stuff in his trunk, the hobby tools, they're finely worked—expensive.* She looked at the purse. *The weird alphabet goes hand-in-hand with premium stuff.*

Which was maybe a decent observation, if it proved out, but what did it get her?

The outer surface of the conch shell was brown, a complex mix of sand

and driftwood hues. Bastien had scored through to a deeper layer, revealing creamy calcium beneath.

Sophie closed the satchel, watching it zip itself yet again. What could do that? Nanotech? Robots? That was the stuff of science fiction. She opened it, stuck her fork half in and half out of it, and tried to close again. Its lips curled, closing on the stem, delicately pushing it out onto the table. Then it clamped shut.

Bastien scraped at the shell, *scritch, scritch*. It seemed to be getting louder.

*Everything* was getting louder. The creak and the groan of the wood walls of the shack as it shuddered in the wind were multiplied. She realized she could hear the shack next door rattling, too—and the one beyond that. Sand grains gristled, rubbing each other as they passed through the neck of Bastien's egg timer. His breath gurgled.

Outside, stones clattered, thrown up the beach by the surf outside. She heard the whispers of mothers, comforting their children, the whimper of a storm-scared dog, air popping in lantern wicks. Out in the insufficiently sheltered bay, a ship's sail was tearing.

And now a light, squeaky rub—Bastien was polishing the shell with fluid from the black bowl. The liquid he'd mixed was a waxy yellow substance, and the carved letters glowed copper as he filled them. The surface of the shell buffed up to a deep walnut glow.

So much sound.

Sophie touched Gale's pouch again and the reptile-leather lips over the zip pulled back, like muscles flexing, no wires, and the thought she'd been holding back broke through: *It's magic, has to be magic, you're not in Kansas anymore, Sofe.*

She pushed the pouch away, clutching her camera case and Gale's cell phone, hugging them to her chest, as if they could help.

Bastien finished rubbing in the last drop of lambent beeswaxy ink. The text on the conch shell glowed. The cacophony cranked up another notch. Sophie heard shouts and the bustle of sailors, far out at sea, the fishing fleet trying to get their ships in, fighting to save the crew of one rattletrap boat that had already gone under. "Grab this, grab this!"

It hurt. She closed her eyes, breath hitching in a sob.

Then the cries—all the noise but for the storm outside and the crackle of the fire in Bastien's clay stove—faded.

"Kir Sophie? Do you understand me now?"

Her eyes flew open. "You bastard! You do speak English!"

*Magic.* She clapped her hand over her mouth. What had come out of it, in an enraged yelp, was this: "Zin dayza Anglay!"

"No, no, it's you," Bastien said unnecessarily. "I've taught you Fleetspeak."

## CHAPTER 3

She understood him. It wasn't English, or Spanish: Bastien was speaking the same language he'd been using all night, and now Sophie understood every word.

She leapt to her feet, quivering, torn between outrage—*this snaggle-toothed stranger has rewired my brain!*—and excitement—*that is so cool*—when he spoke again. "Zophie, Sophie, yes? I apologize for inscribing you, but we must talk."

"Yes, of course. Right. You're right. Wait—inscribing?"

Before Bastien could say more, there was a quick tap at the door. A bent, rain-drenched woman let herself in.

"This is Dega," he said. "Our herbalist."

"Hi," Sophie said. At first glance, Dega seemed ancient, but as she shed her cloak, Sophie decided she might be no older than forty. Maybe she'd been prematurely aged by hardship. Sanded down.

"You guys have magic powerful enough to teach me a language," she said, "But it must have serious limits, or you wouldn't be living on pickled moths."

"Stele Island is no wealthy nation," the woman agreed.

"We keep our place in the Fleet," Bastien added with an asthmatic wheeze. He sank down by the stove, shivering, and Dega handed him the hunting knife that had been in Gale's chest. He examined it with an expression of deep concern.

"You're the doctor, Dega?" Sophie said. "Can you tell me how my aunt is doing?"

"The Verdanii is your kinswoman?"

*What's a Verdanii?* "She's my mother's sister." Sophie waved the magic satchel. "The name on her Amex is Gale Feliachild."

Dega scowled. "That is a government courier pouch."

"It's Gale's. Can't you tell me if she's okay?" *Maybe I just think I understand them. Maybe I'm standing here jabbering.*

Dega said: "You hold the Feliachild pouch?"

"You can see I am," Sophie said.

"It opens for her," Bastien put in.

"Will she live?" Sophie demanded.

The woman's expression softened. "It's not certain yet, I'm sorry. As her kinswoman, you may have to say whether Bastien should scribe her. If she worsens."

Kinswoman. That sense of being dishonest, an impostor, washed through her again. "Bastien can heal her?" Why were they even asking? "Would that be a problem?"

"If she can recover normally, it is better."

"Why?" A dozen questions occurred to her, among them, *OMG, seriously, magic?* But she made an effort to stay on point. "Does magic have . . . side effects?"

Dega nodded, as if this was obvious.

"One can only bear so much intention," Bastien said.

"There's a limit on how much you can take?"

"Yes."

*Magic with a . . . would you call that a load limit? Wow.* "This is why you apologized for . . . scribing me, was that what you called it?"

He set the knife aside gingerly. "This is an emergency."

She thought that over. "It was a first for me."

"You've never been scribed?"

"I'm not from around here," she said, adding the worrisome question of magical limits and side effects and how soon could she get an MRI to a growing list of things to follow up. "But you think Gale has been? Scribed? And if you heal her—"

"We can't know unless she wakes and tells us. And there are other urgent matters," Dega said.

"Matters?"

"I must assist the others." Bastien had brewed himself a hot drink. He broke a white egg with dark brown speckles into it and gulped the whole thing down. Taking his tools and a small, leather-bound book, he wrapped himself in Dega's sailcloth poncho and disappeared outside.

As he closed the door, Sophie settled at his ramshackle table. "What's the issue, Dega?"

"Who stabbed Kir Feliachild?"

"You don't think I stuck that—" she indicated the hunting knife "—in her chest?"

The woman shook her head. "If you wanted her dead, you'd have let her drown. What happened?"

"Two guys attacked her about a block from my mom's place—"

"On Verdanii?"

"Uh. San Francisco."

Blank expression.

"Not the point, okay? There were two of them, both Caucasian. I noticed their clothes first: they were cut like medical scrubs, almost institutional, but the fabric was heavy and their pants were pressed. Good quality, you know?"

"I don't know scrubs, or Caucasian. They were wealthy, these men? That blade . . . it is outlander material, I think."

"It's just steel."

Dega shuddered a little, as if Sophie had said "radioactive." "Did the ruffians say anything?"

"Not in English." Sophie shook her head. "I caught a few words. "Tempranza . . . Yacoura? And Gale laughed. That's when everything got all brawly."

"Yacoura is lost." The woman looked outside. The storm had abated as suddenly as it began. "You should rest. I'll come for you if she wakens."

Sophie eyed Bastien's filthy-looking cot and then checked her watch. It was barely evening in San Francisco. "Isn't there anything I can do to help out?"

"Our fishers were caught in the storm. We're sending boats out to assist them."

"I can sail. I can row. I'm a great swimmer."

"No, Kir. Your aunt may want you."

*Fat chance of that,* Sophie thought. "I can gut fish, cook, tie nets, gather specimens, pound nails . . . um, hang-glide. Come on, you're in a jam. You must need able bodies."

At length, Dega nodded. "Come with me."

She led Sophie down to the mudflats by the beach. The teens they'd put ashore earlier were prepping a flimsy-looking fishing boat for launch, loading up tools, rope, and buckets of steaming violet-colored goo—to patch leaks, Sophie guessed. As she and Dega appeared, their already sober conversations stopped. Silent anger raked at her.

"Ralo!" Dega summoned a stringy teenaged boy with a leg splint and crutches. "This is Kir Sophie Feliachild of the Verdanii."

"Actually, I'm not sure—"

"She's to help you today. San can go out with the boat."

"Zophie," the boy said. Sophie noted, with a thread of amazement, that he sounded to her ears as though he had an accent. Did she speak better Fleetspeak than he did?

"Go with Ralo, Sophie. He's in charge, nuh?"

"I understand."

"I'll fetch you when your aunt wakes." With that, Dega toiled away.

*This is me, pitching in.* Sophie gave the boy a bright smile. "So—Ralo. What are we doing? Coordinating the rescue boats? Signaling for assistance? Breaking out the emergency supplies?"

"Over here," Ralo said. He led her down the beach, over the wrecked remains of driftwood houses and the storm-thrown flotsam on the sand. Gulls—mining for edible bounty—swirled and scolded as they passed.

They reached an open hut that was as ragged as all the rest. The seaweed weave of its roof had been shredded by the wind. In the shade of the one relatively intact corner, a young woman rocked a bundled infant. A quartet of heartbreakingly thin little kids, maybe three or four years old, ran up and down the beach under her supervision. The children were scavenging, competing with the seagulls for whatever protein had washed up on shore.

"San," Ralo called. He gabbled incomprehensible words.

Was the Fleetspeak spell wearing off? Did that happen? No, she decided; this must be a local dialect. The language Bastien had taught her must be a trading language . . . something sailors and merchants might use?

She hoped that was a good conclusion, and not merely wishful thinking.

The woman handed Sophie the baby, then stalked back to the wharf. The child immediately began to scream.

"We're babysitting?" she said. Its mother didn't turn back.

"You, me, we watch littles," Ralo agreed. He started gathering the broken pieces of the shelter roof.

*This is what I get for saying I'd do anything,* she thought glumly. "I don't think this kid likes me."

"Walk with him," he said. "Bounce."

She did as he suggested, snuggling the tiny body against the shoulder that didn't hurt. "You don't scare me," she whispered. "I've done dives in sharky water."

Baby notched up the wails. Sophie put more *boing* in her step, pacing the beach, making what observations she could, if only to stop her inner monologue from running *where am I, where am I where the hell am I?* in an endless, anxiety-cranking loop.

The kids first: They were tanned, and their hair ran the gamut from nearly blond to strawberry roan. No blue eyes; she'd characterize their skin as olive.

She'd seen children elsewhere in the developing world, in places as poor as this one seemed to be. They'd been clad in T-shirts provided by aid workers, their little bodies serving as billboards for donor NGOs or Coca-Cola or, lately, trendy cartoon characters. But these kids wore hempy-looking tunics, clothes hand-woven from unbleached, undyed fabric, same as the sandpapery blanket the baby was wrapped in.

The baby who was, finally, quieting.

If someone out in the wider world was giving aid to these islanders, there was no obvious sign of it, Sophie thought.

She bounced her way to a tidal pool. It held two familiar-looking hermit crabs and a proliferating anemone. She could identify one broken piece of coral—*large polyp stony coral*, she thought.

There was a second anemone species she didn't recognize, but that might not mean anything. She'd dived a lot of reefs, but that didn't make her a search engine.

Across the water in the direction the boats were taking, the sun was just clearing the horizon. Sophie turned her back on it, studying what she could see of the darker sky to the west. The sun was just high enough to have blotted out the stars.

But it had been light last night; Sophie remembered wondering about the moon as she hauled Gale through the waves.

As if they'd caught her thought, the thinning clouds separated, revealing a pale, familiar disk.

Tears pricked her eyes. "There's the Sea of Tranquillity."

However far off the beaten path she'd come, whatever magic had been used to move her here, she was still the same distance from the moon. The thought was comforting.

"I wish Bram was here," she whispered.

The baby had drifted off. She returned it to its pallet. Ralo was plaiting dried seaweed into rope.

"I could help with the roof," she said.

He shook his head: Why would he believe she was capable when nobody else did?

"Just watch them." He indicated the little ones, who were running up and down the beach turning over branches and scooping up the occasional mollusk.

Sophie opened her camera case. It was shockproof and waterproof: A fine scratch marked the path of one of the daggers across its surface, but smashing one of Gale's attackers across the face with it hadn't done any real harm.

She'd never been in anything resembling a fight before.

*That wasn't a fight, it was attempted homicide.*

It was the fight that had caught her attention. She'd seen Gale go into Beatrice's house and hadn't noticed the two older women's resemblance; hadn't thought much of her at all. Even when she'd spotted the two men loitering across the road, watching the house and muttering, it was Beatrice and her husband she'd worried about.

She was debating whether to call the police, was imagining explaining to a 911 operator: *Hi, I've been parked outside my birth mother's house for a couple days. Now someone else seems to be stalking her, too . . . and I hate competition.*

When Gale had come out, heading down the street, the two guys had perked up and begun following her. It had been an *Aha!* moment: *Hey, that woman looks like Beatrice! And hey, those guys are after her!*

Knife-wielding, grim-faced men . . . She shuddered.

"Don't obsess," she muttered. "Stick with the here and now."

The DSLR camera inside the case was undamaged, as was the housing that let her shoot underwater. Easing it into the housing, Sophie tipped the lens into the tidal pool, taking a few shots of the unfamiliar anemone. The snapped-off bit of coral went into the case itself, next to Gale's magical courier pouch. She shot an image of the moon and then the mud village.

*Look at the beach, Sofe! Not one candy wrapper, no plastic bottles or grocery bags, not even a scrap of a condom.*

How remote would this island have to be for there to be no litter, no SAT-phones? Her battery warning came on and Sophie powered off the camera immediately. The spare was in her car, recharging. She'd shot over two hundred frames of her birth mother, and suddenly she regretted them all.

She'd have to restrict herself to species she didn't recognize; if she was careful, she might coax thirty more shots out of the battery. She took one frame of a bat sea star, because it had a fine spiderweb pattern in black on its back, something she hadn't seen before in *Asterina miniata.*

"If I wanted one of those moths, would I be able to get one?"

"You're hungry?"

"Hungry? Oh, the pickles. No, I want a live one."

"They're sour when they're fresh."

She wasted a few seconds of battery power to show him the photos she'd taken so far. The little kids crowded around, asking questions.

"They ask if your lightbox is magical." Ralo indicated the camera.

"It's a machine."

"Mummery?" Ralo said.

At the word, two of the eldest kids stepped back, putting some space between the camera and themselves, and tugging on the younger children. The expression of distrust on their faces was much like Dega's had been, when she was eyeing up the steel hunting knife.

"It's a completely safe and pretty cool machine, as it happens," Sophie said. Was it silly to be insulted?

"Then you're not a spellscribe?"

"What? Like Bastien? No."

"Or Sylvanner?"

"I don't know what that means."

A little kid tugged on her skirt, offering her an ordinary clamshell and pointing at her camera.

"Only if I don't recognize it," Sophie said firmly. "That's a ribbed limpet."

"Children don't Fleetspeak." Ralo said a few words and the children sprinted back to the beach, chirruping and scanning the sand.

*Suddenly I've got an itsy bitsy research team,* Sophie thought. "Ralo, can you explain about . . . Sylvanner?"

"They like to write new spells," he said, swinging a repaired mat of thatch onto the shelter roof. "Earn coin."

"They're a . . . people? A corporation?"

"Sylvanna is one of the great nations."

"Oh! Dega asked if I was Verdanii. Is that another nation?"

He nodded, clearly amazed at her ignorance.

Nations she'd never heard of. She pondered that. If Stele Island and Sylvanna and the others were part of an archipelago of small islands, tucked into . . . which ocean was most likely? She wouldn't have believed they could escape notice, but for the magic.

*They must use it to conceal themselves. That's why I don't know where I am.*

It was a strangely reassuring thought, one that made her feel as though she might not be that far from home after all.

A cry of triumph from the kids. One skinny four-year-old dashed up, holding one of the float pods for the ubiquitous seaweed. Inside the pod was a crimson eel, barely wider than a strand of spaghetti, and it was brooding over a clutch of red granules. Eggs?

"Good!" Sophie set it up so the sun was shining through it, exploiting the natural light, and took a macro shot. She let the kids look at the resulting image for three seconds before shutting the camera down again.

"So Sylvanna does . . . they research new magical spells?" Sophie asked Ralo.

"Yes."

"This is bad because—"

"They are crooks," Ralo said. He pointed at the sea pod, struggling with either the concept or the translation. "This eel are ours. If they uses them in a new scrip, the scribing, they should pay."

If this was a delusion, it was getting complex. International politics and conflicts about resource use? And magic that seemed to operate under something like patent law. "Could any of this be tied to the attack on my aunt?"

Ralo gave a peculiar little shrug, indicating, she figured, indifference.

The morning passed. The kids found her a shell with an interior that was crimson-colored mother-of-pearl. She set it on a board next to the body of a seagoing bat, collecting specimens she could photograph in a group. They led her to a stand of delicate orange flowers that looked like miniaturized helliconia. Using signs, she asked them about the moths. They pointed at the cliff tops. Too far away.

At midday, Ralo broke out bowls of seaweed and fish broth, carefully dividing the mushy lump of one cooked dumpling among the children. He and Sophie got the soup without dumplings. If anything, the broth made her hungrier.

The woman, San, returned to nurse her baby. She looked half dead with exhaustion. She spoke to Ralo in the islanders' dialect, pointedly excluding Sophie.

Sophie gave them some space, sitting in the sun with one of the kids. If she could get home, she'd pick up some proper equipment—her diving rig, the video camera. She could give her little collection of shells to one of her bioscience buddies—maybe the USC team, or the guys at the Scripps Institute.

She wondered if the rest of these magic users were as backward as the people on Stele Island.

That wasn't likely, was it? The scarf in Gale's pouch was a fine silky fabric, and there were the gold coins. Wherever this subculture was hidden, it had its rich and poor, same as anywhere else. *Sylvanna*, Ralo had said. *A great nation. Scientists. Crooks.*

She turned the shell over in her hands. The possibilities for exploration were mind-boggling even before you got to the existence of magic.

Magic. Every scientist on the planet was going to freak out. Bram was going to lose his mind.

Ralo broke into her thoughts: "Dega's calling you."

Sophie scrambled to her feet and ran to Dega, saving the older woman the effort of crossing the distance between them.

"Your aunt is awake, Kir Sophie."

"Just Sophie's okay," she said.

"If you wish." They crossed the wharf, where a crowd of villagers had gathered around four bodies, fishers who'd been recovered from the sea. They glared as Sophie passed.

"Am I bad luck or something?"

"The storm was unexpected."

"It's weather."

"Kir Feliachild was nearly murdered," Dega said. "You're Fleet Couriers; the storm pursuing you was unnatural—"

"The storm might have been magical? Seriously?"

"The moths migrate on windless nights, always windless." Dega ushered her into a shack that seemed to serve as their infirmary. "Kir Feliachild, your niece is here."

Gale looked about ready to expire—she was pale, her chest was bandaged, and her breathing was raspy. She opened her eyes, took in Sophie, and closed them with a pained expression.

*Nobody* was glad to see her. Exploring the beach with the adorable moppets had cheered Sophie, but now rejection by her birth family struck again with the force of a slap.

She perched by Gale's bedside. It was little more than a pallet covered in shreds of grubby blanket. "They said they can . . . spellscribe you if you aren't healing."

"No scrips!" Gale looked past her to Dega. "There must be ships coming to assist you."

"Our light is signaling for help. Someone might arrive tomorrow, if winds are fair."

"You want to be rid of us; we want to go," Gale said. "The girl's to catch the first respectable ride to the Fleet."

"Yes, Kir. And you?"

"Give my ship, *Nightjar*, until tomorrow evening. If she hasn't arrived, send me to Erinth, whether I'm conscious, half dead, or a corpse."

"Understood, Kir Feliachild."

"Well, I don't understand," Sophie said. "How can you send me off on my own?"

"I'll leave you." Dega bowed and let herself out.

Gale struggled for breath. "I must get you back to your home world—"

"World?" Sophie interrupted.

She'd broken her aunt's train of thought: She got a blank stare.

"It's not another world," she said. "The moon's the same."

"You must go home," her aunt repeated.

"Eventually, yeah. But you're hurt—" Her mind was spinning. *World? Another world?*

The older woman shook her head. "You can't stay."

"Someone tried to kill you," Sophie said. "These islanders think they'll try again. You can't sail off by yourself."

"You're my bodyguard now? What do you do back on Erstwhile—are you a cop?"

"Well, no. I'm . . ." She felt a rush of embarrassment. She'd spent the past four years bouncing between teaching diving classes, guiding mountain-climbing gigs, and going on short-term video shoots aboard scientific research vessels.

Adventuring, her brother called it. Frittering, her father said.

"I guess mostly I'm a marine videographer."

"I feel so much safer," Gale wheezed.

"You need help," Sophie insisted.

"If they come after me, what can you do, besides get hurt?"

"I don't know. Make some burly sailor guard your cabin door? Scream my head off?"

A weak smile. "They'd have killed you, girl."

*Don't thank me or anything.* Sophie bit her tongue. "Okay. Yes, those guys scared the crap out of me. I don't want to be in another brawl. If something's gotta try to kill me, I prefer it to be an avalanche or . . . I dunno, hantavirus."

"Something impersonal."

"You're helpless. I'm responsible for you."

"Responsible . . ." Gale closed her eyes, long enough that Sophie wondered if she might have passed out. Then she spoke, voice cold. "You saw the bodies, the drowned fishers?"

Sophie nodded.

"We brought that on them, you and I. They lost villagers, and half of a critical harvest. Even with aid, they're going to have a terrible year."

"That's on the guys who tried to kill you."

"You prevented the assassination, child. You kept me afloat. You meant well, but had I died in San Francisco there would have been no storm here."

Hot tears burned their way down her face.

"If you stay in Stormwrack, Sophie, you'll bring trouble to your closest kin. Beatrice, me, your sister Verena—"

"I have a sister?"

Gale closed her eyes. "You are going back to your own world—to Zan Francisco—on the fastest ship I can hire. You cannot ever come back."

## CHAPTER 4

"Zophie," Bastien said. "We've found a ship for you."

He was calling from the base of a low escarpment, one of the ridges that bordered the bay and essentially formed the boundary of the village. The surface was pocked but solid, an easy free-climb, and she'd scaled about thirty feet to peer into a series of deeper pits and notches that riddled the stone.

It was a spectacularly beautiful morning. She had awakened from uneasy dreams to find the sun bursting over the horizon, edging a postcard-perfect backdrop of long wispy clouds with gold and orange. The tide was out, revealing a stretch of beach with sands the consistency and color of brown sugar. Ralo and the little kids were already out there, scavenging for crabs and other treasure: things they could eat, things they could make into tools.

So much had happened since she'd been rejected by her birth mother; Sophie's mind had been chattering even before she was fully awake. It circled her memories of the fight in the alley: the men with hunting knives, Gale getting stabbed. Remembering the shock of a man's nose crunching under her camera case made her wince. A pocket watch flying out of Gale's hand, bouncing behind a Dumpster and the blast of wind, lifting her into the air . . .

Finally, Sophie had made for the rock wall and begun hoisting herself up.

Free-climbing quieted the interior gabble, forcing her attention back to the present. She checked her holds and balance points one after another, remembering that every foot she hoisted herself upward was another foot she'd fall if she screwed up.

A vertical climb didn't leave space in the mind for *OMG I could've been killed!* or *How could a different world have the same moon as Earth?* or *Why don't these women want to know me?*

She'd gone up the rock wall, come down again, and then tried meditating—she'd never been great at it, but she knew the signs of trauma, and it was the only treatment she could think of. When the edge of anxiety faded, she went asking for jobs. Nobody wanted her help.

She'd finally rejoined Ralo on child care duty, despite a clear "don't need you" vibe from him.

But watching children left plenty of energy for chasing the question of magical loads and the possible side effects of having the brain rewired by third-world mystics. Within an hour, she was obsessing again: *How could a different world have the same moon? Maybe Gale misspoke. Maybe she doesn't understand how we got here. Wherever here is. Another world? No, can't be—*

*Okay, Sofe, you're freaking out. Back to the cliff.*

She'd been halfway up, that second time, when Bastien had spotted a lizard above her and gone into a frenzy. He was excited, not freaked out—he clearly coveted the thing.

Specimen collection was a definite step up from babysitting. Sophie had climbed down and asked about fifty questions: Does it bite? Is it poisonous? How do you usually catch it?

It wouldn't make up for the drowned fishers or lost harvest, but the thing was obviously valuable.

She was beginning to feel more centered as she started up the rock face for a third time.

Now she peered into one of the holes and was rewarded with a shock of eye contact.

Taking a slow breath, she checked her footholds again before plunging her right hand into the hole. She caught the lizard behind the head. Cool scaly flesh writhed under her palm. For an instant it seemed as though it might wiggle free, but no—she had it.

"Zophie, you must come down."

Moving gently, so as not to scrape the still struggling creature on the edges of its bolt-hole, she drew it out into the light.

It was eighteen or so inches long and had many of the characteristics of an iguana: the same stocky trunk and pit bull proportions, the dewlap, the long toes, which even now were digging into her fingers, working to break her grip. But its coloration was entirely different, its skin a mottled pattern in two browns, one the same mahogany shade as the stone escarpment, the other the lighter, sugary shade of the beach.

It opened and shut its mouth, glaring at Sophie with yellow eyes as she took it in, a marvel, an alien, a fistful of life. The breeze ruffled her hair and she caught a whiff of flowers from somewhere.

Gently, she lowered the lizard into a nylon bag from her camera kit. Its weight pulled the drawstring shut, trapping it.

Shaking out her wrists, one after another, she worked her way down the escarpment.

"It is a male," Bastien said, when she had descended to ten feet or so. "Big."

"He looks healthy to me." It was squirming at her hip, not enough to throw her balance off, but with enough zeal that she couldn't entirely tune out its presence. "Is it for magic?"

"I use the shed skins to scrip fishers and sailors with better vision."

"For trade?"

He nodded. "It's been some time since we had a village lizard. People will come to me, for the scribings. They will pay. Thank you."

"Think of it as a going-away present." She stepped down to solid ground again and handed him the sack. It felt good to have made herself useful.

"Your boat is here," he said.

Sophie nodded. Every time she had awoken, Gale made it clear that her conviction that Sophie had to leave—and leave immediately—was unshakable. When it was obvious there was no changing her mind, Sophie had changed tacks, insisting that Gale come visit her at home. "You obviously come to San Francisco to see Beatrice," she'd argued, just the night before. "You can see me, too."

Maybe it wasn't fair to badger an injured woman, but Gale had agreed. They would meet.

*She'll see I'm not dangerous, and I'll get her to introduce me to my sister—half sister, she said—and I can get her to explain in detail about this whole "you must go!" issue. It'll take time, but I'll change her mind.*

Her stomach grumbled, trying to quash the little sprout of optimism. All they had for food here was fish broth and pickled moths. Sophie didn't ask for more. The islanders had to live on this, year in, year out.

Because of the storm, because of her and Gale, they'd missed their big annual fish harvest.

She followed Bastien to his place, where he put the reptile in a wicker cage, murmuring reverent words over it. Then they trooped to the healer's hut, where Gale was resting. By day it seemed even more ramshackle: The seaweed bundles that made up its roof had patches of rot here and there, and the mud seals between the pieces of driftwood were flaking. That much was true of many of the structures, especially those on the southern edge of the village, which had less shelter from the wind. But the door frame of Dega's shack had a bent, cracked look to it that made the whole thing look dispirited, ready to fall.

She'd hoped to find Gale awake, but she was fast asleep. Her breathing was steadier than it had been a few days before, her face less pale.

"There's great strength in her," Dega whispered. "She will live."

Sophie nodded. *She'll make it, and she'll come to San Francisco, and I'll talk her 'round . . .*

Bastien shifted behind her, not so subtly hinting that they should go. Sophie kissed her unconscious aunt's forehead, then followed the spellscribe.

"Your things." She already had the camera bag with her, but Bastien handed her a rag-woven bag containing the handful of biological samples she'd collected. The conch shell he'd used to teach her Fleetspeak was nestled inside.

"Thank you."

"Take care, Kir." He escorted her to a rowboat and gave her a whisper-frail hug before telling the sailor: "She's to go to Convenor Gracechild."

The little harbor was busy: A number of sailing ships had arrived to give aid to the islanders. The seascape looked like a painting from the Napoleonic Wars. *Horatio Hornblower,* she thought, as they rowed out to meet them. Her head was throbbing. Now that she was sitting, fatigue from the climb was combining with hunger to leave her a little dizzy.

At least she'd caught up on her sleep.

An incoming boat passed on their starboard side.

The boat bore, as its passenger, one of the most attractive men Sophie had ever seen. He was perhaps thirty, with skin the color of a walnut shell, glossy black curls and a full mouth that made her think, in her hunger-addled state, of ripe plums. His expression was sober and intensely focused.

Her hand drifted to her camera.

One of the rowers saw her looking. "Captain Parrish, of *Nightjar*. Pretty, no?"

"*Nightjar* . . . Gale's ship?"

"The cutter." He pointed it out, a gray, somehow frumpy-looking ship.

"Is that where we're going?" Maybe she'd misunderstood; maybe Gale would take her with her after all.

"No, Kir, we're for *Estrel*."

Sophie had spent considerable time at sea on various dives, but had only been aboard a proper tall ship once. Now, as she climbed to the main deck under the watchful eye of her sailor escort, she saw this ship wasn't quite the Age of Sail relic it seemed. The same letters that glowed on her Fleetspeak shell had been carved into the ship's wheel. It and the masts had a sinewy, organic sheath; the spokes of the wheel reminded her of a bird's talons. *Estrel*'s sails were embroidered with gray thread, long gray stitches that gave them the appearance of feathers.

The figurehead itself was a bird of prey, one Sophie didn't recognize.

"More magic?" Excitement pipped, like a newborn chick, over the physical distress. She ran a hand over the rail. It was polished to a high shine and, at first glance, also seemed to have a feathery pattern to it, but under her fingers it felt like varnished wood.

"Scribed for speed." A woman—the captain, presumably—answered her unvoiced question. "*Estrel*'s uncanny good at finding the breeze. We'll get you to the Fleet in a week."

Sophie made herself smile. There were still things to see here, observations she could make.

*Lots of opportunity if you take it.* It was what Bram would have said.

"Are you all right, Kir? Seasick?"

*Starving.* "Just . . . missing my brother."

"I'm Captain Dracy," said the woman.

"Sophie Hansa."

"Of the Verdanii Feliachilds, I understand?"

"Um . . . I guess that's technically true."

"A Verdanii princess, eh?"

Sophie turned. The man who had just come up from below was dressed like the hero on the cover of a romance novel. Tanned, with flowing golden hair and a toothy grin, he wore an open-collared peasant shirt and tight tan breeches.

"No princesses here," Sophie said. *And what are you, the ship's gigolo?*

Dracy cleared her throat. "This is Lais Dariach of Tiladene . . . another passenger. Lais, Kir Sophie Hansa."

"You must be somebody, Kir," he said. "We're dropping everything to rush you to the Fleet—"

"All that makes me is inconvenient," she said. "To my aunt, to the islanders, and apparently to all of you. Believe me, if I'd known chasing my past was gonna drop me in a fantastic new ecosystem that I'm not allowed to explore, I'd have stayed home and rewatched *Veronica Mars*."

Lais rocked back on his heels, seeming baffled. "Beg your pardon, Kir."

"It's okay: I'm joking, sorta." Sophie upended the rag bag onto the deck, shaking its contents free so she could toss it down to the departing rowers. The Stele Islanders were so poor that even a woven bag was a sacrifice.

Lais caught her conch before it could bounce across the deck. "Careful, Kir! You don't want to break the intention."

"What? If it breaks, I won't understand Fleetspeak anymore?"

Dracy and Lais exchanged a look.

"I'm not from around here, okay?"

"Well . . . yes," Lais said, bemused. "The purpose of the spell lays within the inscription."

She bundled it in her skirt. "I've been keeping samples in it."

"We'd better lock it in your cabin." Dracy picked up Sophie's collected bits and pieces, leaving her the camera case, and led her aft.

Sophie followed, automatically falling into walking with, rather than against, the rhythm of the ship's movement. "You came to help the islanders?"

"As we're able. We gave them some salted fish and a few barrels of preserved onions. I'm leaving my diver behind to see if they can raise one of the downed ships. We'll pick up more food and swing back, after we've dropped you off."

*Estrel* had already caught a fresh breeze. Her sails filled, and she made for the open ocean beyond the bay.

"Were you caught in the storm?"

"Skirted it," Dracy said. "We were headed out toward Zunbrit Passage with Lais. It was an evil clash of winds, Kir. My mate and cook saw towers of lightning, spun between the water and cloud. It blew up of a sudden and was gone just as fast."

"But you're okay? No damage?"

"*Estrel* saw us through," Dracy said, laying a hand on the bulkhead with obvious affection. "And here we are."

"Home sweet home, huh?" The cabin was small, a triangular closet, well aft, with a peculiar, heavy portal. Its substance was glassy, but it was thick and its texture was rough. It was more translucent than transparent, with a dark tint.

"Is this obsidian?"

"Yes, from Erinth. Stow that scrip here," Dracy said, opening a small locked cabinet and offering her a linen handkerchief to wrap the conch shell in.

"It's not that fragile."

"It names you, Kir." Dracy explained. "A certain amount of discretion is . . . customary."

"Meaning what? Someone needs my name to do a spell on me?"

"Exactly. Lais and two of my crew have seen it already, as have I. You should conceal it from now on."

Sophie ran a hand over the glowing copper script on the shell, fighting a momentary urge to dash the thing against the wall. It was hardly worth it to know Fleetspeak if she was being packed off home.

*That's not true.* The inner voice, the one that sounded as much like Bram as herself, argued. *The language itself is an artifact. A good linguist might make links between Fleetspeak and the tongues of home.*

Not to mention that the shell could serve as a sample of the magical writing. Cheered, she locked the conch in the cupboard.

"Perhaps, too, since you're an outlander . . ."

What else had she done? "Yes?"

"Lais Dariach . . . he's from Tiladene."

Tiladene. That word was on one of Gale's coins. "You said that. So?"

"They're somewhat . . . promiscuous."

The significant look on Dracy's face made her want to giggle. "You mean sexually promiscuous?"

"They don't believe in marriage—in faithfulness."

"Okay, got it. Your other passenger—"

"Lais."

"Lais is from Friends with Benefits Island." *Planet of the Polyamorous Sluts,* she thought, lightheaded. *Didn't the* Star Trek *guys used to go somewhere like that for shore leave?*

And then: *A little shore leave wouldn't be the worst idea I ever had. And he is cute.*

*Not as cute as that guy in the rowboat.*

"Is there anything else I can do for you?"

*Artifacts. Samples. Lots of opportunity to learn.* "I'd love to see some charts. I don't know this area."

"Of course, Kir. This way."

Still carrying the camera case—she figured her battery might be good for another fifteen shots—she followed Dracy up to the pilothouse, where she unrolled a map of currents and islands.

"This is our position and bearing. Stele is here . . ." She indicated a small hump to the north-northeast.

"We're making for the open ocean?"

"The Fleet is on its spring tour to the islands of Greatwater; we'll rendezvous around here." Dracy tapped the map.

*Spring. It's spring at home, too.* "How many days until the equinox?"

"Seventeen."

She bent over the chart. Since recognizing the moon, Sophie had been convinced that seeing a good map would orient to the geography of the area her aunt had called Stormwrack. This was some little unheard-of archipelago of islands, had to be. Yes, she'd been flung across the planet in the blink of an eye, and yes, there were some animal species she didn't recognize. But another world? Come on.

*Same moon, same gravity, same pelicans, same Earth. Gale's wrong.*

She knew magic existed: It made sense that the Stormwrackers kept themselves hidden.

None of the landmarks on this map matched anything she knew, though.

"Do you have anything with a smaller scale?"

"A world chart?"

"Exactly."

Dracy's brow knitted. Rummaging in the cupboard, she found a page the size of a place mat, colored with a crude enthusiasm that hinted it was a kid's school project. "Does this help?"

"Yes, thank you," Sophie said, but she was lying. There were continents at the north and south poles, all right, but the oceans between them were massive, laced with fairy-rings of islands, small and large. The biggest of the landmasses wasn't quite as big as Australia. And Europe, North and South America, Africa . . . *where the hell are they*?

"Kir Sophie?"

"I'm sorry. It's just—I've seen projections of land losses to global warming. In one, the water rose two hundred meters, and I could still make out the continents. Where's Asia? Where are the Rocky Mountains?"

"I don't understand 'Asia,' I'm sorry."

"*You* don't understand?" She fumbled out the camera and photographed the map. The battery light blinked at her, dying, dying. Shutting off the camera, she gaped at the map again. "Okay, maybe we're not in Kansas, Toto."

"I don't know Kansas. This is the Northwater." Dracy stubbed her finger down on the northwest quadrant of the page. "Our position."

Sophie took a moment to put her camera away, fumbling the case open, shoving Gale's courier pouch aside—she'd forgotten to return it.

*Ask for some food, Sofe.* Bram's voice again. *Your mood's swinging like this because you're being an idiot.*

She didn't deserve food. She'd drowned those islanders.

"Northwater. So . . . north?" She tapped the top of the map. "South, down here? East, west?"

"Yes, of course. But that little chart's no use for day-to-day navigation," Dracy said gently. "If you want it . . ."

"It's almost all water," she murmured. The child's rendering of the map showed chains of islands, hundreds of them, and no real continental masses at all. Even the biggest landmasses were mere lumps at this scale; if this was even somewhat accurate, there wasn't an island on this world that had even the area of Australia.

"Thanks," she said. And then, just to change the subject: "Where were you taking Lais?"

"It was a speculative venture, Kir—we're a salvage ship. He hired us to help recover some stolen goods."

"Transporting me's messed that up?"

"It's not just you. His goods are sunk, and I loaned my diver to Stele."

"Sunk at what depth?"

"Forty, fifty feet down."

She paused, toying with the map that made no sense and looking at a shell someone had nailed to the wall of the pilothouse. It had the reptilian pattern and texture of tortoiseshell, and the shape of a clam.

*What the hell. I can't go yet, not if—* "Forty feet . . . a person could freedive that, if she knew what she were doing."

"We're to take you straight to the Fleet," Dracy said.

"The dive site's not even remotely on the way?"

"Perhaps a day or two out of it." Her eye fell on something in Sophie's camera bag—the courier pouch. "Could you override our orders, Kir?"

"Why not? I didn't mean to screw up your plans."

Dracy brightened. "We'll discuss it with Lais over dinner."

"Dinner?"

So much for playing it cool: The captain looked as though a flashbulb had gone off in her face. "Oh, Kir Sophie. I should have thought."

She went on another rummage through the cupboards, this time coming up with an oilcloth packet that smelled faintly of bacon.

Sophie's stomach growled audibly as Dracy handed it over. Inside was a pressed cake that looked like it was made of unidentifiable fish, seeds, and bread—a salted ball of oil, protein, and crunchy flour.

"Slowly," Dracy said. "I'll have the cook get onto a meal right away. Milk, soup."

Sophie nodded, forcing herself to chew. The seeds tasted like sesame; after days with little but broth, the flavors seemed amplified, so intense they all but burned her mouth.

"Come," Dracy said. "We'll dine early and the Tiladene can tell you his troubles."

## CHAPTER 5

The story on Lais—besides his apparently being some kind of bisexual Lothario—was that he worked for a cooperative of horse breeders whose prize stallion had recently retired from an inter-island racing circuit.

"We mean to put him out to stud, of course. I'd set up his first pairing with a very exalted mare. But he's suddenly grown . . ." His eye wandered to Captain Dracy. "Docile."

"Like a gelding?"

"Like a lamb."

"I don't suppose maybe he's having trouble adjusting to retirement?"

"We got a ransom note two weeks ago," Lais said. "Silesian has been scripped infertile."

"Scripped. Someone learned the horse's name, then wrote up a magical . . . intention, was it?"

"Intention, yes," Lais said.

"And now Silesian can't get it up?"

"Better him than me," Lais said.

Dracy clattered a saltshaker and cleared her throat. The message was clear: *No flirting.*

They were finishing off the remains of a cod and mussel stew and a dish of roasted, buttery fava beans, wiping up their plates with the remains of a hearty rye bread. Every bite had lifted Sophie's spirits. She felt like her best self again: calm, optimistic, able to deal with whatever came her way. "The bad guys are holed up in this Zunbrit Passage?"

"No, they're long gone. We paid the ransom and they gave me the scrip's location. It's sunk near one of the Zunbrit sea mounts."

"You paid, just like that?"

"Silesian's appointment with Balletic is soon."

"Balletic's the mare?"

He nodded. "We didn't want to lose face by breaking contract, so paying the ransom seemed expedient. The more so because I wanted the issue resolved quickly. Horses are the family business, but I have a side project."

"Problem is, I loaned my diver to Stele," Dracy said.

"Dracy says you can countermand the diversion," Lais said. "And if you can, as you say, free-dive . . ."

"I do have to go home," Sophie said, trying to deploy her nonexistent poker face. "My brother'll notice I'm gone eventually. But . . ."

"Yes?" Lais slid a tray of what looked like cream puffs across the table at her.

"Not to be rude, but you're rich, right?"

They both seemed taken aback, but she pressed on. "You paid this ransom, you've commissioned Dracy, and you're in a hurry. This is kind of a big deal for you."

"True."

"If I get this scrip back for your horse," Sophie said, "could you buy some food for those islanders, once I've gone home? I'm not asking you to beggar yourself, just to do whatever you can. The storm . . . Someone was after my aunt; their harvest is lost and it's our fault."

Whatever breach of etiquette she'd committed, the request seemed to amend it: Both Lais and Dracy relaxed.

"My word on it, Kir," he said. "Whether you succeed or not."

"I'll pull it off." She accepted the cream puff at last, raising it in a mock toast. "Let's divert the ship."

That night, she lay in the confines of her small cabin, swinging in the hammock—which was vastly more comfortable than the pallet she'd borrowed on Stele Island—and trying to will her camera battery back to life. She'd used the last of her juice shooting a dusky gray-purple seabird, and a spidery crab the crew had hauled up from the depths. Now she'd been reduced to taking bad pictures with Gale's phone, queuing them up to send to her e-mail account at home. She was still firing off the occasional text to Bram, too, just to jolly herself up:

*Bad news, Bro: UR gonna have to maybe rethink some physics.*

*Message will be sent when we return to service area,* the phone replied.

*OTOH, Good news: I'm not as crazy as initially reported.*

Bram might disagree with that one. He had had enough therapy over the years to come away with the idea that everyone was fundamentally neurotic.

Her brother was a bona fide kid genius. He'd finished high school when he was twelve and had been working on his second undergraduate degree, two years later, when he came out to their parents. Dad had decided a teen whiz kid who was also gay was someone with too much to cope with, and packed him off to a doctor to talk it all through.

If she could only have one week on Stormwrack, Sophie wished Bram could have been around to share it. The magic would offend his sense of an ordered universe—at heart, her brother was an engineer. But he might have some idea why Stormwrack's moon was the same, so indisputably, Earthily familiar, when its landmasses were jumbled beyond recognition.

*I'll get back. Gale's already promised she'll get to know me. We'll talk her into letting us have a proper look around, him and me. So little land-mass, and it sounds like it's mostly one country to an island . . .* She dozed off contemplating the map, falling into thick, dreamless and restful sleep.

A tap at the cabin's hatch woke her. "Zunbrit Passage, Kir."

She made her way up to the main deck and found that *Estrel* had dropped anchor. To the stern, the water was pewter and foam, the waves breaking over a series of jagged rocks that extended eastward in a wind-ing, dangerous-looking line. Most of the rocks were scoured bare by the water. One was just big enough to host a few dozen petrels.

Her pulse raced as she looked at the birds. They resembled Leach's storm petrel, a species she'd filmed in New Zealand. There was another bird, almost identical to the Leach's, that had recently become extinct.

Which species was this? Any number of organisms that had died out at home might survive here, wherever here was. The thought was so ex-citing it very nearly hurt.

One of the birds dropped off the sea mount and started dabbling in a stretch of shallow water at its base, almost dancing on the water's surface as it fished.

"Sophie?"

She shook herself back on task. "Just thinking."

The crags and islets were the tip of a great mountain range. They were mostly too small to sustain larger animals; they wouldn't be good for much besides wrecking ships. Sophie thought: *I can see why they used it as a ransom drop. Lots of cracks and crannies.*

"Captain, do you have a dive locker? Equipment?"

"After a fashion." Dracy led Sophie amidships and down. The room was all but empty. "I left the best of our salvage equipment on Stele with Boris, my diver," she explained, apologizing.

"You must have something—a snorkel?"

"Don't usually need 'em," Captain Dracy said. "Boris is a merman."

"He breathes water? Are you serious?"

Dracy nodded.

"Wouldn't that have been something to catch on video?"

"I don't know video, Kir."

*Hell with whether Gale wants me, I will get back here,* Sophie thought.

She quashed the urge to ask five thousand questions about mermen and magic, instead looking over what was left in the locker. Tanks and a regulator would have been too much to ask, but there was a decent mask—it appeared to be made of a dried sea jelly—and a pair of flippers that might have been carved from the cartilage of some massive creature. Plus plenty of rope, floats, and flags.

The fins were short—not quite right for a free dive, but they'd do. She scooped them up and headed topside.

"My heroine," Lais said, as she emerged. "Savior of my honor."

"Your horse's honor, anyway," she said, leaning against the rail so she could put the flippers on.

"The studs of Tiladene will neigh your praises for five generations."

She laughed. "I haven't succeeded yet."

"Remember," Dracy murmured. "Promiscuous."

"I promise not to get my heart broken," Sophie whispered back. "Have you found the sea mount, Lais?"

"They marked it." He pointed out a mossy hump of land, barely bigger than an SUV, pocked and covered in puddles, and covered in seabird droppings. A post had been driven into its peak, an old ship's mast from the looks of it. A strip of red cloth fluttered from its tip.

"The scrip is supposedly sunk and weighted about forty feet from that mount's northern point," Lais said.

"What do you know about the currents around here?"

"They can be treacherous during high tide, but that's not for . . ." Dracy checked. "Six hours."

"Great! I'm not drowning for a horse, so if anything looks off—"

"No, of course!" Lais nudged Dracy. "Captain?"

With obvious reluctance, Dracy produced what looked like a miniature birdcage, covered in thick black leather. "This will help."

"What is it?" Sophie removed its cover, finding a shuttered, waterproof lantern inside. Something glowed within, bright enough to illuminate it, even through the shutters. A shape, inside—

"That's—" Sophie said. "That's a skull."

"It's my father," Dracy said. "He had his teeth scripped to shine as the sun. The intention survived his death."

"Was it literally sunshine?" Sophie's mind spun through implications. A constant flood of solar radiation in the mouth—hadn't it burned? Could he give others sunburn, then? Did he die of cancer? Couldn't they have just made a magic lantern? Had Dracy kept it for sentimental reasons?

Dracy replied with a gesture that was less than a shrug, more than a twitch. Sophie was coming to realize it came standard issue among these people: It meant "Don't know, don't care."

She added magical solar radiation and *Can a whole people be fundamentally incurious?* to the continually growing list of things she had to find out, and then eased herself overboard. It was cool but not cold. She'd borrowed a light tunic to swim in; it stuck to her body but didn't constrain her movements.

It was good to be back in the sea; she dipped her head underwater, letting salt water run through her hair. The ocean felt like silk on her skin. Dipping the gelatinous mask in the water to moisten it, she laid it over her face. It had the texture of silicone, sort of. She thought briefly of breast implants and giggled.

There was no strap, but once she had it laid over her skin, the mask clung, flesh to flesh, leaving small pockets of air in front of her eyes. The visibility was sharp; unlike a plastic mask, it seemed to have no blind spots.

She experimented with it, adjusting the fit around her nose, figuring out how to equalize the pressure.

"Careful with this." Lais handed down the lantern. "It's precious to Dracy—I had to pay extra."

*It's her dad's* head. *Of course she charged extra.*

Tying the lantern to the float, she swam out to the sea mount. The land rose to meet her: She ended up wading more than half the way. After picking her way up the slicks of seaweed on its rocks, she stood atop its peak, leaning on the improvised flagpole and peering down. The downward slope of rock was furred in normal reef vegetation—polyps, anemones, a sea star or two.

Glancing at her watch to confirm the time, she drew several deep breaths, purging as much carbon dioxide from her bloodstream as she could. Then she swam downward, picking her way along the descending slope of the underwater mountain. She was twenty feet below the surface in fifteen seconds. There was no sign of anything man-made in the water.

A long stroke took her to thirty feet. It was dimmer now, the water murkier; she unshipped the lantern. In the dark, she could just see the seams of its shutters glowing. She opened one a crack and a searing shaft speared the gloom.

A swirl of crabs shifted as the light hit them, then went back to worrying at a carcass on the floor. *Dead shark,* Sophie thought, *looks like a mako.* An orange tentacle that had extended across the reef pulled back under a low rock shelf; from underneath it, a single octopus eye regarded her with peculiar intensity.

Sophie checked her watch. She'd been under for one minute. There was no sign of an inscription. She swam deeper, and another minute passed.

*There.* Ten feet farther down she saw a jagged hole, an opening in the rock.

Her heart had begun to thump, protesting the lack of air. But she'd done some breath holds since yesterday, watching her stopwatch, checking her capacity: She still had time.

She swam closer, poked the lantern into the hole, and took a good look. The extortionists had wedged a tube—it looked to have been made of their hard-as-metal wooden substance—into a cave about the size of a walk-in closet.

Sophie untied her ankle, looping the end of the rope around a rock outcropping near the cave entrance. Then she pointed herself upward. Rising calmly, she closed the lantern hood and surfaced, gulping air and treading.

Lais had, by now, rowed out to the sea mount in a dinghy. "Find it?"

"Yes. I should be able to get it in another breath. Be easier if someone else held Dracy's lamp. You up for a swim?"

He nodded, peeled off his shirt and unlaced his boots.

"Pass me another length of rope," she said. This time she tethered him—to the dinghy. "Do you know any diving signs? Up? Down? I'm in trouble?"

"I think I understand." He imitated her moves. "Up. Down. Help."

"I'd rather grope my way to the surface than have to save you, so if you get light-headed, come up. But if all goes well, we should be up again pretty quick with your watchamacallit."

"Inscription," he said, easing into the water. His legs were well formed and a bit thick at the thigh: *Rider's muscles,* Sophie thought, enjoying the view. He had tied back his hair to keep it out of the way. She watched him tread for a minute. He seemed comfortable enough in the water—no nerves, and they weren't going very deep.

By now, she'd caught her breath. "Okay, you're attached to the boat. The line attached to the float leads to where we're going. Don't get the two tangled, okay?"

He nodded. She half raised herself to the dinghy, grabbing for a thirty-pound weight she'd borrowed from the ship. With her other hand, she groped for Lais.

"Big breath!"

The weight pulled them straight down. Lais deployed the light. They hadn't really needed the float line—the cave entrance was visible—but she wanted to save every second she could.

*Okay, no problem, just a little hole.* She took a second to show Lais where she wanted the light focused, and then wiggled through the gap in the rock. It was easier than it would have been if she'd been wearing tanks.

The case had been wedged under a couple big rocks, loose, flat stones that were easily pushed aside. It popped up like a cork, bouncing off the ceiling of the cave, but she grabbed it on the second bounce; she'd always had good reflexes. Then it was just a matter of pretzeling herself around so she could come out of the cave headfirst.

She had just reached the entrance when her light went—Lais must be out of air. She checked her watch: She'd been down for two minutes, forty-five seconds.

*Time always goes faster.* Feeling her way, she found the float rope and detached it from the rock, looping it back around her ankle out of habit as she kicked up.

The light returned: Lais, coming back down, half blinded her.

Snugging the casket under her arm, she made a sign: *UP!* Lais churned water as he changed directions. Sophie kept ascending, taking it slow now, lots of time, all the air in the world was up there, waiting, waiting.

The surface felt closer than it was. Her head broke the water and she gasped.

"I dunno—how pearl divers—did it," she said.

Lais just sputtered.

They climbed back into the dinghy, lying against each other until they had their breath again, their bodies warming where they touched. Then they rowed back to the *Estrel*. Dracy leaned out, reaching for the skull, reclaiming Daddy.

"Please tell me this is it," Sophie said, holding out the stumpy tube to Lais.

He produced a small key that hung from a chain around his neck. "This is the key the extortionists sent," he said. He searched the outer edge of the case until he found a lock. He jiggled it. There was a click.

"Hooray for that," Sophie said.

He unscrewed the cap and, peered inside, reaching with a finger and tugging. "There's a plug."

Tug. Tug. The "plug" popped out with a thump.

Sophie felt a kick go through her whole body, a jolt of terror.

"Is that . . . a metal?" Dracy asked.

"Down, get down!" Sophie snatched the grenade—*grenade, dammit grenade, don't go off!*—from the deck and hurled it as far from the *Estrel* as she could.

"Teeth, Sophie, what are—"

She grabbed Lais by the ankle and flipped him on his back.

There was a bang. A tremor thrummed through the ship: shock and a chattering as shrapnel and water clattered off the starboard hull.

The birds, as one, took off, shrieking reproachfully.

*Bet there's some petrel feathers in the water now,* Sophie thought, a little stunned. *I could grab 'em for DNA.*

"Is everyone all right?"

She could see they were. Dracy had curled protectively around her lantern; a piece of flying metal had winged her arm, opening a gash.

Sophie climbed to her feet—her knees were shaking, and tears were running down her face—and pressed her hand over Dracy's wound, slowing the flow of blood.

"How did you know?" Lais said.

"How did I *know?*" she repeated. Her ears were ringing. "Was that the only one?"

He looked into the case. "All that's left in here is the scrip. What in the name of *Temperance* was that thing?"

*This is what it takes to make you people curious about technology?* She found herself wondering if she could imitate the dunno, don't care shrug.

"Steel," Dracy said. "That was steel."

"Teeth!" Lais said.

A crewman was running up with bandages now, to patch up the captain.

"Seriously?" Sophie heard an angry edge—hysteria, almost—in her own voice. "You don't have grenades here?"

Blank expressions greeted her.

*I suppose it's only fair,* she thought, clutching the rail to steady herself. *I don't know magic, they don't know modern weaponry.*

"I think someone wants you dead, Lais."

## CHAPTER 6

"Horse racing must be pretty cutthroat if someone's willing to blow you up over a foal," Sophie observed a couple hours later.

She and Lais were topside, drinking a thin, yeasty ale and looking at the stars, familiar constellations that suggested that, missing continents or not, this was Earth.

He waved his glass. "My family's passion is racing, but I'm something of an oddity."

"I know how that feels."

"I've been trying to justify my peculiarities by expanding our business into other areas."

"Touchy areas?"

"You might say that." He looked at her speculatively, then said, "Come to my cabin."

She followed him below, to a cabin that was only slightly larger than hers. A big leather portfolio lay open on its bunk; tied into it were leather-bound books, an array of what looked like magnifying lenses, and a loom. He unlocked a small cupboard, the twin to the one in her quarters, and drew out a small wooden case. Within were strung strands of fine thread, each next to a pinned and labeled specimen of a spider.

"Mmm, sciencey." The case had wooden hinges and a wooden latch, she noticed: Iron was apparently scarce here. "So?"

"Spidersilk is a key component in shipbuilding scrips," Lais said, indicating the threads. "The best silk fetches an incredibly high price. People weave sheets of fabric for the magical texts."

"All of this magic is tongue of newt, eye of bat stuff? You write these things on specific substances, using inks brewed from rigidly set out recipes?"

"And using specialized tools, depending on the intention."

She remembered Bastien, scratching words into the conch shell with what looked like an ivory dentist's pick. "And when the text is destroyed, the magic goes too."

"I cannot understand how this is unknown to you."

"You've never seen a hand grenade."

"No end of wonders in this world," he said; from his tone it was something people said often. "I'd never have guessed there was a lady anywhere who knew nothing of inscription."

"I grew up in a land of gunpowder and cold steel. Tell me about your specimens. These look like they're all females?"

"You have a good eye." He touched one of the spiders. "These are lesser chindrella. Their silk's decent, but not top of the line. I've been working to raise one that produces better thread."

"How's that going?"

"I'm getting close."

"You've moved from horse breeding to spider breeding. You're a genetic engineer." No wonder she got along with him: Sophie and scientists, her mother was fond of saying, like a house afire. "Would anyone kill you for building a better spider?"

"They might," he said seriously. "But their method was peculiar. If you'd never seen a . . . grenade?"

"Definitely a grenade. And just so you know, I'm hoping to *never* see one close-up again."

"Dracy and I would have let it burst at our feet." He leaned past her, closing the case and sliding it back into the cupboard. The move put him within inches of her. She felt a sudden urge to run her hand through those golden locks of his. *Seriously, this guy belongs in a Hercules costume.*

"I owe you two debts now, Kir," Lais said.

"Give the Stele Islanders whatever food you can scare up."

"My family will repay the debt to our business, of course. But I can't repay Stele for my life."

"I'm just passing through," she said. "There's nothing you can do for me."

"No?" His hand eased around the small of her back. Pressure, but not a pull.

"You know," she said, letting him draw her closer, "Dracy seems to think you're an incredible cad."

"They take their sacred matrimony seriously where she's from," he said. His hand was tracing a circle around the base of her spine. "What about you? What does the land of cold steel say about such things?"

"It says if I'm being packed off home, I might as well have some fun beforehand."

With that, she kissed him, tasting apricots and just a hint of the ale, running her fingers up the nape of his neck as his arms closed around her.

Sophie had had a couple of shipboard romances over the years—one with a Canadian grad student on a narwal-filming jaunt to the Arctic, another with a German who was the world's foremost expert on forest carbon budgets as well as a fanatic about meditation. She tended to enjoy the affairs in the moment and overthink them afterward, but it worked all right as long as she knew she wouldn't see the guy again.

With Lais, she was something of a mess. The first night, after sex, the weird anger she'd felt over the grenade resurfaced. She'd burst into hysterical tears, ranting: *How could you not know what a grenade was and where the hell am I and what kind of people are you all anyway?*

He hadn't been put off; to her surprise, he all but cried along. Nearly getting blown up had shaken him deeply, and he wasn't too macho to admit it.

They'd spent a couple freaked out hours churning through it: the ransom demand, the grenade, the blast itself. Her mind kept latching onto the idea of it blowing up in her hand, of her fingers being blown off.

She wasn't even sure when they segued from processing their trauma to resuming the lovemaking.

To spare Captain Dracy's sensibilities, she and Lais tried to keep the fact that they were sleeping together under wraps. By day, they spent their time on deck, acting chaste and talking about spidersilk, about magic, weapons, and science.

Lais was a treasure trove of information about Stormwrack, patiently answering question after question. His own bafflement about her ignorance never seemed to resurface. A week was seven days, he told her, a month was five weeks plus a day, a year ten months. He knew some

English words: called them Anglay and had an atrocious accent, but he understood "table" and "clock" and, most important, "faster."

He'd never heard of Earth; even after she'd explained, he seemed to believe she was an overly sheltered person from some very remote island.

Lais was able to put names to the various species of sea life she'd collected, to tell her a bit about the local ecosystem. There were things he didn't know. His home, and thus his area of expertise, was farther south. But he understood the basics of wildlife management.

It made sense. Stormers would be keen to preserve animal and plant species—even if an organism had no magical use that they knew of, there was always a chance they'd discover an inscription that made use of it.

She asked questions, took notes, told him tall tales about San Francisco. At night, they had whispery, athletic, enthusiastic hammock sex.

On the second evening aboard they were all sitting out on deck when Dracy raised her head, squinting. "Wakelight," she said, pointing to a faint glimmer, barely visible against the fading light of sunset.

As they neared the glimmer, it brightened to a candle flicker. It was a floating balloon, about the size of a bathtub; it had the texture of a jellyfish body, and within was an intricate, crystalline blossom, pinkish in color—a wild rose, Sophie thought. The flower glowed within its protein float, as if there was a flame within it, as it rose and fell on the waves.

"Apprentice spellscribes practice making them," Lais said, behind her. "Look, there's another."

The other was tiny, barely a mote . . . and they were making more or less straight for it.

Sophie scooped up a pail that had been tucked under a bench near the rail, then tied and threw a knotted rope overboard.

"What are you doing?"

"I need a better look at that."

She let herself down the rope, enjoying the feel of the wind rushing through her hair. Winding the rope around one wrist so that she was secure, she reached out with the pail, skimming the surface of the water. *Only one shot at this . . .*

It was all she needed. The little flicker splashed into the bucket, right on target, and she tucked the rope handle of the bucket into her elbow and hauled herself back up to *Estrel*, passing the pail to Lais before pulling herself up and over the rail.

This one wasn't a rose: Growing within the pouch of protein was a woman's face, a flat profile much like a cameo.

She lifted it out of the brine. The clear skin holding the crystal had the gelatinous solidity of a sea jelly. At its base was a round skirt of ruffled cellulose, the color of seaweed and the shape of a paper muffin cup, on which the spellscrip letters had been inked in gritty, crystalline ink. "You say the spellscribes make these?"

"It's part of their training. They form all manner of pretty things out of sea salt, and leave them to grow in the Fleet's wake. The lights mark their passage. We're getting close."

"Wow." Sophie eased the light back into the bucket before she could damage the lettering on its base. The tiny cameo glinted, like candlelight, undulating with the movement of the ship.

Next morning, halloos from the sailors brought them out of Lais's cabin.

On the horizon they could see a forest of masts and sails, more ships than Sophie had ever seen in one place, a massive expanse of seacraft. The masts bristled upward, some dwarfed by ships as colossal as aircraft carriers, others just toothpicks on beads that zipped along the water between the giants. Wheeling, man-made objects circled in the air above them: hang gliders? Further above were birds, flocks of the opportunistic gulls that followed any convoy.

"The Fleet," Dracy said, radiating disapproval—not at the ships, but at the sight of the two of them.

*Guess we shouldn't have expected to fool you, huh?*

"It's so big!" Sophie had been so interested in the flora and fauna that she hadn't gotten around to asking much about society, civilization. She had gathered there were different island nations, about two hundred fifty of them, and that the Fleet was some kind of shared defense force, a seagoing cross between NATO and the UN. But this wasn't some convoy. It was practically a city. "I never imagined anything on this scale. How many ships are there? When will we catch up?"

"We're not to approach," Dracy said. "Your people are coming to us."

"Says who?"

The captain pointed out a small yacht that was making for them against the wind. "Messenger ship, Verdanii flag."

"Could I override that order, too?"

"From a Convenor?" Dracy shook her head. "Pack your things, Kir."

Dejected, she returned to her cabin. "Dammit!"

"I am sorry, Sophie." That was Lais, leaning on the hatch to her cabin. One of his smaller leather valises dangled from his fingertips.

"I have to go back to San Francisco, I do. But to go without knowing when I can return . . . when there's so much here."

"You're a true explorer," he said. "It's a crime to banish you to the outlands. The people of the Fleet could use someone with your spirit of inquiry."

"I don't know why the landmasses are the way they are. I was so intrigued by the magic and the spiders I didn't ask about government and politics. Now I'll never know." Stupid, to be crying . . .

"Here," he said, handing her the valise. "I can get another."

"Thanks." She opened it, tossing her notes in the bottom, along with the world chart and her gathered shells and bits.

"Have a care for your Fleetspeak scrip." He tapped the locked cabinet. "You want my spiders?"

"Can you spare them?"

"I'm breeding them, remember?" He handed her the frame. "What did you call that? Renewable resource."

"As good-bye gifts go, it's a little weird."

"There's this, too." He pulled her close, giving her a long kiss.

"You'll be careful, Lais? Someone did try to kill you."

He shuddered. "You know I haven't forgotten."

She felt a little flash back to that sensation, the grenade in her hand, and swallowed. "Watch yourself."

He rubbed his chin—three days of spun gold stubble—over hers. "I'll go straight home and bury myself in a haystack."

"Kir Sophie," someone called. "Your transport's here."

Feeling more than usually like an orphan from a Dickens novel, she climbed to the deck and exchanged stiff good-byes with Dracy, then shouldered her camera case and clambered down to the waiting yacht.

She barely had her feet on the deck when a uniformed boy was leading her below, to a windowless cabin.

The woman waiting within was tall, curvy, and copper-skinned. She bore herself like a queen. She said nothing until the messenger had closed them in the room together. Then she said, "You're Beatrice's daughter, all right. I see it in the eyes."

"Who are you?" She was getting mad now; it felt better than weepy.

"A cousin," the older woman said. "Annela Gracechild, of Verdanii."

"Do you know if Gale is okay?"

The older woman waved a sheet of yellow paper. "She's alive, apparently thanks to you. Captain Parrish sends that he's taking her to Erinth. She will recover."

She had promised herself she wouldn't beg, but . . . "Listen, I know Gale wants me gone, and Beatrice thought nothing of me, but do I have to go? I've barely scratched the surface of what's here. I want to have a look around, and I won't make trouble, and I don't even have to say I know them, Gale and those guys. You can call me Jane Doe or something. If I saved her life—doesn't that get me a tour of the Fleet, at least?"

Annela held up a hand. "Bringing you so close was enough of a risk. I'm sorry, but—"

"Why? Nobody will tell me what I've done. I'm *not* useless. Why does everyone . . ." She made herself finish. "My entire birth family seems to hate me. What is the deal?"

"You've done nothing, child. It's difficult, I know, unfair. But you must return to your adopted kin on Erstwhile and keep silence. Forget about Stormwrack, Sophie."

"And if I can't?" It was a bluff. What had Gale said? She'd bring down ruin on them all.

"You have little choice," Annela said kindly. "If you won't seek your peace, we'll scrip you forgetful."

"You'd . . . give me amnesia?"

"It's not what I want. We are kinswomen. But you seem possessed of a truly all-devouring curiosity—"

"That's not a disease!" The words came out sounding braver than she felt. If they could teach her Fleetspeak in a matter of hours, they could certainly wipe her memories.

"Those who question find the ill in everything," Annela said, in a tone that hinted it was a common saying.

The wrongheadedness of that took Sophie's breath away. She sank onto a chair. "When are you going to pack me off?"

Satisfied, Annela handed her an official-looking bundle of onionskin papers. "This is a travel visa for the time you've spent here already. It authorizes one visit, one week, here and back. I need you to sign it."

"Closing the barn after the horse escaped, aren't you?"

"Legalities must be observed."

She scrawled her name across it, deliberately misspelling Hansa, just to be peevish. "Now what?"

"Bettona?" Annela summoned an aide, who pulled out a small pocket watch, gold in color, scratched with magical, glowing letters. She lay a hand on Sophie's arm.

*Gale had a watch when we came here.* Sophie half jumped to her feet. "I'm going now? Wait—"

It was too late. The watch *tick-tick-tick*ed and the sheaf of paper fell out of her lap, in slow-mo, to the deck of the cabin and then, as it landed, she heard one last ringing, hollow *tock!* With that, Sophie found herself on her butt in an alley, about a block and a half from where she'd left her car.

## CHAPTER 7

Bram was waiting by the time she got back to their parents' place.

The car had been towed, of course, with her wallet and BART pass and all her stakeout stuff inside. She had to walk more than twenty blocks before she found a cabbie willing to take her home.

As they pulled up in front of her parents' postwar bungalow, her brother was pacing on the front porch with a phone to his ear. He snapped it shut and darted across the lawn. "Sofe. What's happened?"

"You didn't call Mom and Dad, did you?"

"Not yet. Until an hour ago I thought you'd gone diving with one of your hairball friends."

The cab driver honked.

"He needs money." Sophie sighed.

"Sit, before you fall," Bram ordered, pointing at the porch swing and reaching for his wallet.

Her brother was usually turned out as neatly as a pin, with preppy over-tones: pressed slacks, nice shirts, sweaters over top. Today he'd thrown on a pair of jeans and an Invader Zim T-shirt, and he hadn't put his contacts in, either. He had a terrible fear of looking like a nerd; on a normal day you wouldn't catch him in anything so casual. His chestnut hair was fluffed every which way—he must have rushed over to the house in an all-fired hurry.

*What got his wind up?*

Sophie took his advice and collapsed on the porch steps, setting down Lais's valise and the camera case and letting her emotions crash in on her in waves: great swells of dejection, rejection, humiliation, sprays of fury. A mother who didn't want her, all the tantalizing biodiversity of that other world, and magic, too. A huge sandbox she wasn't allowed to play in. By the time her brother had gotten rid of the cabbie and come up to sit beside her, she was bawling.

Bram put an arm around her and waited it out, giving a passing neighbor the stink-eye when she paused to stare.

"You smell like a week at sea," he said eventually.

"I'll avail myself of the all-holy hot running water soon," she said, sniffing.

"Better not say you missed the amenities more than me."

"You were the only thing I did miss."

"Chill, Ducks, or I will call the parents."

"No! It's better that they're gone. And don't call me—" A hiccup broke up her words. "Ducks."

"Sofe, you're scaring me a little."

"Sorry, Bramble." She pulled herself up, feeling heavy-limbed, and hauled her stuff into the house. She pulled out her camera, popped her battery into a charger and the chip into the laptop computer that lived by the kitchen island. Then she opened the fridge. The yogurt was green and the only thing that looked edible was an apple.

*Haven't had fresh fruit in a week,* she thought. *Yet what I want is pizza.*

"Sofe."

"I know, I know." With a sigh, she pointed at a snowdrift of papers, bank statements from their mother's office. "I went through the parents' files."

"I figured as much. Looking for your birth family again?"

"I found them."

"What?"

"There was a receipt for a safe deposit box, not the usual bank. I had to dig around for the key, then went in and forged Mom's signature."

"Jesus, Sophie. That's serious fraud."

"I know, but look." The computer had booted; Sophie clicked into her online documents and pulled up a file. "I found the adoption agreement."

"And photographed it, I see."

"Wouldn't you?"

Bram clicked through, speed-reading. "Private adoption. It doesn't look like they paid for you, just promised no contact with the birth family. Ever. No surprise there—we figured as much."

Sophie tapped the screen. "Here's her name. Beatrice Feliachild. It's

Vanko now: she's married. I traced her to Bernal." Sophie opened the folder for her camera chip and pulled up a shot of her birth mother. "She lives a twenty-minute drive from here."

Bram leaned in, fascinated, and began clicking through the images. "Bizarre . . . I see the resemblance. That curly hair of yours. At that length, it's rather pre-Raphaelite."

"The eyes—I have her eyes."

"Anime eyes," He nodded. "I can't believe you found her."

"Neither could she," Sophie said.

"She's been in San Francisco all this time?"

"Looks that way. She runs a center for sick kids and their families— kids having surgery."

"So she's a saint?"

"She's a wingnut."

"And is her husband your biodad?"

"I'm pretty sure not. Asking about my father was like setting off a bomb in her face." Bomb. Her mind wandered, briefly, to Lais, and the grenade. Someone was trying to kill him. Would he be okay?

"I take it the mother-daughter reunion was suboptimal?"

She found herself welling up again. "She called me a viper, Bram."

"I'm sorry, Sofe."

"Stupid. It was stupid even to try."

"I hate it when you say that. I don't think you're stupid."

"What do you know?"

"I know it all," he said, putting on an air of serenity. "I am supergenius."

"You are superdork."

"I know you've looked at the fridge three times since you got home. Hungry?"

She nodded. Crying exhausted her, and she'd been wound pretty tight even before Annela Gracechild had zapped her off home without so much as a thanks for flying, buh-bye.

"Go have a shower. I'll burn your clothes and call the Thai place. They'll bring food, you can tell me everything and then we'll swing by impound and pick up your car."

"You know about the car?"

"Told you, I know everything."

"Don't be a jerk, Bramble."

He held up an envelope. "City mailed out a notice."

"Don't burn the shirt," she said. "It's a sample."

"Of what, the power of reek? If I'd been driving that cab, you'd still be on the hoof home."

Like most of Bram's ideas, the shower was an inspiration. She soaped up, luxuriating in the feel of a week's mung coming off, of working real shampoo through her curls. She turned up the water until it was as hot as she could endure and cried some more. She came out scalded pink, feeling scraped and empty.

By the time she'd put on a clean pair of jeans, a tank top, and her favorite chenille sweater, the smell of red curry and coconut milk was drifting upstairs.

*No more fish broth, anyway.*

Bram had opened a bottle of pinot noir and cleared the table, stacking their parents' documents tidily on the counter. He had opened up the cartons and laid out two plates, cloth napkins, and some lacquered chopsticks Mom had brought back from a dig in Vietnam.

"This is going to sound wild," she said. "Keep an open mind, okay?"

He nodded.

Okay. Take the plunge. Glossing over her three days of stalking Beatrice, she began by telling him about seeing Gale being attacked by the two men in the weird scrubs. Then—before he could whip out his phone and call his therapist for some kind of emergency trauma session—she jumped right into the impossible stuff. Ending up in an ocean, in Stormwrack.

"I can document this," she told him. "Some of it, anyway."

Bram was trying mightily not to look worried. "You can document lost time and teleportation?"

She reached for the laptop, accessing her e-mail account. Gale's phone had dutifully forwarded the pictures Sophie had been taking. She selected a message at random, opening it. The image was of Lais, on the deck of *Estrel*.

"That's not magic, Sophie, that's Conan the Barbarian."

"They grow the men cute there," she said, her mind's eye offering up the memory of the gorgeous man in the rowboat, the one they'd said was captain of Gale's ship. What had his name been? She opened the next e-mail attachment: the sea mount with its improvised flag. Nothing special there. A third, and there it was: the wide shot of the ships and masts and sails, the city at sea.

Bram kept his tone neutral. "Kind of blurry, but it looks like a tall ship convention."

"It's the Fleet," she said. "Stormwrack's capital seems to be this big convoy of—oh! And the Fleet has its own language, which I learned overnight, by magic. If need be I'll find a linguist—they can tell you it's a real language."

"Ohhh kaaaaay."

"I'm not delusional, Bram. You know I'm not delusional."

He produced his own phone, reading: "Losing my mind. Send doctors with Haldol. Sofe."

"What?" Oh—the texts she'd composed on Gale's phone. "Come on, I was kidding."

"How about this? Bram: Sank a fishing boat and 3ppl drowned. Turns out bad weather is my fault."

"It's what Gale said. Someone was trying to do her in and the storm . . . oh."

"What now?"

"Just . . . it's strange. The only two people I got to know there were both attacked. That's an odd coincidence, don't you think?"

"It would be," Bram said carefully. "If it wasn't something that—"

"That what? Was all in my mind?"

"Bramble: just used a skull with glow-in-the-dark teeth as a dive lamp."

"I *did* use a skull—"

He set the borrowed cell phone aside. "There's a lot of death and guilt and creepiness in these messages. I'm thinking that finding your birth family, defying Mom and Dad, breaking their contract with your birth mother . . ."

"I feel guilty and it's made me all morbid and delusional?"

"Do you feel guilty?"

"No! Whatever agreement they all made, I never signed on."

"Sofe, you don't seriously expect me to buy into parallel worlds and magic scrolls on the basis of a few pictures from a crummy cell phone."

"The pouch!" she said suddenly. "It's magic. I can show you right now."

"Pouch?"

She opened her camera case. "I ended up with . . . well, I guess I stole this purse thing from Gale. Accidentally. I'll get it back to Beatrice; it's got an Amex in it."

"Sofe, maybe we should just go get the car."

"I'm not lying. I have charts, pictures, a magic pouch and spider samples and shells. And I found Gale's watch in the alley near Beatrice's—she dropped it in the fight. Both times I traveled, there and back, there was a timepiece."

"Okay, but—"

"Okay nothing. You are gonna believe me."

"Sofe, you've clearly had a rough few days."

"Shut up, Superdork." She pulled out Gale's pouch, laying it flat on the table. "Take a good look. Nothing up my sleeve, right?"

"Sofe."

"Just run your finger along the zipper, Bram."

Lips pressed together, he obeyed.

Nothing happened.

"Dammit." That was how these things went in movies, right? You pulled out your proof with a big "Haha, now I'll show you!" and whatever it was—talking frog, the One Ring, whatever, it just sat there and refused to perform.

"Let's just go to impound, Sofe. You can chill, we'll call Doctor Brown and—"

It wouldn't matter. He wouldn't be able to ignore the photos, or the Fleetspeak. *You are gonna take me seriously.*

But—just for a breath—she wondered. Pictures didn't prove anything, and she didn't know for a fact that any of the samples she'd brought home from Stormwrack came from species Earth didn't have. Proving a negative was fiendishly hard. It wasn't as though she could afford to have someone run the DNA on all those bits of shell.

Did magic even work here? "I swear, Bram, it worked, it did—"

"It's an inanimate object."

"No!" She touched the zipper herself, as she had all those other times. "Maybe magic doesn't work on Earth. That might make sense, right—"

"Listen to what you're saying, please."

The pouch unzipped itself, flapping open with a sound like a sigh.

"Nyah nah, so there," Sophie said, as her brother stared at it, openmouthed.

*Showed you, Mister Brain,* she thought, feeling strangely pleased. *You three, with your advanced degrees and academic honors and me just a pretty face with some swim medals and a biologist fetish, I can't possibly—*

Bram pulled up his chair, fully absorbed with the pouch. He imitated Sophie's gesture. Nothing happened.

"Like this," she said, and the pouch laced itself.

He tried again, failed again. "It's just you."

"Huh!" She pulled up next to him. "I didn't feel any wires, and there's no room inside for—you know, for robotics. The fabric's waterproof, and it's lined, but—"

"Open it again?"

She did, and he pulled out the contents of the pouch carefully, repeating the examination she'd done days before, feeling for something, anything that might explain.

"Maybe it's gene-locked," he murmured.

"Or magic," she said.

"We'll need to get it scanned," he said. "Run it through an X-ray, check for ferrous metal."

"You believe me now?"

He looked askance at her. "I see why you thought . . ."

"Oh, don't you dare," she said, punching his arm.

". . . why you thought you might need psych drugs, I was gonna say."

"That's not what you were gonna say. And I have more, remember?"

"I apologize six ways to Sunday for impugning your sanity," he said. He was still palpating the pouch. "What else have you got?"

Hammering on the door made them both jump. "Zophie Hansa, are you there? Face me, you thieving bitch!"

"Who's that?" Bram said.

"I'm not sure," Sophie said, "But she's got a wisp of a Fleetspeak accent."

## CHAPTER 8

The woman at the door was in her late teens and had Beatrice's fox chin and dark, wide-spaced eyes. Her hair was paler—*like Gale's*, Sophie thought. If it had any curl to it, you couldn't tell: It was drawn back in a ponytail so tight it made her eyes pop. She had the body of a marathon runner, clad in a pair of jeans and a Berkelium Genius T-shirt. Her fists were clenched, so hard her knuckles were white.

When she saw Sophie, her furious expression congealed into sick surprise. "It's true? You're who they say?"

"I'm Sophie." This was obviously another female relation. They were coming to *her* now; maybe it wasn't all over.

*She can help me convince Bram!*

"You're the girl from Gale's photograph," Sophie said.

"You're a sister?" the girl demanded.

"If Beatrice Vanko is your mom. Gale said I had a sister, so—"

"Thieving, secretive, conniving sister—and elder? You're elder?"

"Hello? Thieving?"

"How old are you?"

"Twenty-four. You want to come in?"

"No." Bram startled them both. "If she can't calm down, she can't come in."

"Bram . . ."

The girl looked past her. "Who are you?"

"A brother," he said. "Younger. Do you have a name?"

Sophie heard her teeth grind.

"Verena," she said at last. "Feliachild."

"Here's the thing, Verena," he said. "Sophie's a lovely, obliging person and as far as I can tell, she's taken nothing but abuse from you people."

"Nobody asked her to come looking for us!"

"We're full up here on bellowing." With that, he closed the door in her face.

"Bram!" Sophie protested.

"Shh. She'll knock again when she chills."

"I want her to come in. She can fill in the gaps about all this stuff." She waved at her collection of souvenirs from Stormwrack.

"Sofe, you can't let these people walk all over you."

"These people? Bram, are you having trouble handling this? Me having . . ."

"Having what? Family?" His voice could have shaved steel.

"Bramble—"

"Promise me, Sofe. You'll show some spine here."

"Okay. Sure, yes. Anything you want."

"What'd I tell you?" he muttered. "Sweet and obliging."

A brisk little *tap-tap* at the door.

*I should've thought about this being hard for him,* Sophie thought. "Just a second!"

She enfolded her brother in a hug before he could fend her off, and said, in an exaggerated, little-kid voice: "Make ya a trade."

"Trade what?" His face was still closed.

"Grouchy sis is here to take me back to Stormwrack, I know it."

"So?"

She couldn't help bouncing. "Come with me! Please, Bram, please?"

"Sofe . . ."

"Seriously, Bram, why'd I send you fifty raving text messages? I needed you out there!"

"She's not taking you back," he said. "There's nowhere to take back to."

"You promise to come, I promise to have a backbone."

"Doom will befall the whole Feliawhatever clan if you go back, remember?"

"You don't believe in fate. Anyway, if we aren't going, promising costs you nothing."

He rolled his eyes. "Fine. Let me go."

Sophie scrambled to the door, throwing it wide.

Verena was waiting, stiffly, almost at attention. "Kir Zophie, would you kindly admit me to your home?" She said it in Fleetspeak, with only a trace of sarcasm.

Sophie tried not to beam. "Come on in."

She stepped inside awkwardly, taking in the Thai food boxes, the comfortable furnishings, the framed family portraits. Her eye fell on the table: the chart, Lais's spider case, the shells, and bits of sample. At the sight of the magic pouch, her teeth scritched together.

"How's Gale doing?" Sophie asked.

"They took her to Erinth. She'll recover."

"If she doesn't, will they use magic?"

"No. She's been scripped a fair number of times already."

Sophie shot Bram a triumphant look. "That's right—there's a maximum, right?"

"A limit." Verena was still glowering at the pouch.

"On magic? A limit on magic?"

"Of course on magic," she snapped.

"See?" Sophie stuck her tongue out at Bram. "Mmmmmmmmagic."

He was rising above. "Why don't you tell us what brought you here, Verena?"

Verena took the pouch from the table. She peered inside, seeming to inventory the items, the coins, the flower, the badge—

"I used most of the battery charge on her phone," Sophie said, apologetically. "I was gonna get everything back to Beatrice."

"Sure you were."

"You don't know me," Sophie said. She'd promised Bram, after all. "Stop accusing me of theft."

"It's not an accusation to say you told the Stele Islanders you were holding Gale's pouch," Verena tried to zip the bag, sighing when nothing happened.

Sophie racked her memories. "I was literally holding it at the time—"

"I know you told some salvage captain you could order her to Zunbrit Passage."

"I wouldn't say it exactly played out like that—"

"You negotiated services for that Tiladene gambler so he'd buy food for the people on Stele."

"He's a biologist, actually, and I'm so not apologizing for helping get food to those people. Gale said the storm was our fault."

"And, finally, you bore the pouch from Stormwrack to Erstwhile—to here."

"What's the problem? You can take the pouch back right now."

"The problem is I'm meant to hold Gale's position, not you. But now you've usurped it. The idiotic thing thinks you're her heir." Verena poked the flaccid lips of the pouch, then hurled it. Sophie caught it left-handed and it promptly zipped itself shut.

"The ugly purse has opinions?" Bram asked. "It . . . imprints?"

"This is a bad joke," Sophie said. "My birth mother can't stand the sight of me, the aunt says I'm a danger to everyone, little sis is all "you're a thief" and ragging on me about an inheritance—"

"But hey, the handbag likes you." Bram leaned against the back of the couch. His eyes crinkled.

*Oh, no,* she thought, *We're going to have a laughing fit and this poor kid's going to explode on us.*

She looked at the pictures on the mantel, Mom and Dad, steadying herself by thinking about how much this would upset them. Imagining Dad's face, cinching tight, hurt, had its usual steadying effect.

*Say anything.* "When did you find out about me?"

Verena's eyes flicked in the direction of the clock. "I had no clue until . . . about two hours ago."

"And what did Beatrice say? Do we have the same father?"

Verena shook her head. "Mom said you were a half sister. From an earlier relationship."

"With?"

"Not with my dad, is all. That's everything I got out of her, okay? Having you just turn up, and then Gale's attacked . . . she's freaking out."

"Yeah. Listen, I see why she's upset, and why you are."

"Upset?" Verena's voice rose. "You haven't begun to see upset."

Bram's expression clouded, but Sophie shot him a warning glance, before he could get overprotective again. *She's a kid,* Sophie thought. *A teenager whose world has been flipped upside down. Cut her a break, Bramble.*

Instead of lecturing her about her manners, he said: "Why don't you help yourself to some curry?"

"Yeah," added Sophie. "We'll eat, and you can tell us how I can go about putting this inheritance mess right."

Verena shifted sideways, a movement that reminded Sophie of a cat with an angry, lashing tail. With a huff, she took the offered seat.

"I'm not sure," she said. "Either Gale or Mom, or maybe both, will probably have to disinherit you."

"As opposed to just throwing me away?"

"If that's not enough, the Allmother, on Verdanii, might have to repudiate you. Or you her."

"Verdanii?" asked Bram.

"One of the bigger islands, right?" Sophie said. She pulled the kiddie map across the table and nudged it over to Verena. After a second, her sister tapped the biggest of the landmasses, drawn smack in the middle of the map's northern hemisphere.

Bram took up a pen and promptly wrote the island's name on the map. "I don't know, Sofe. Should you be agreeing to get excommunicated from a whole country?"

"She asked what she might have to do," Verena said. "Does she want to make this right or not?"

"Listen! I don't want Gale's—you're talking about wealth, right? Money, material stuff?"

"And position," Verena said.

"I don't care about stuff or position. I just wanted to meet my . . ." Her gaze slid to Bram. ". . . my genetic relations. I didn't set out to usurp anything. Magic, paperwork, whatever the process is, we can do that."

"We'll have to ask Gale about the inheritance laws."

"Not your—our—Beatrice?"

A dismissive head shake. "She's still hysterical."

"So," Sophie said, trying to hide triumph. "We go to . . . Erinth? It was Erinth that they took Gale to?"

Verena tapped another island, well west of Verdanii, closer to the equator, one of a chain of islands that bounded a circular-looking sea. "Yes."

"Hold on, Sofe." Bram wrote "Erinth" on the smaller island. "Verena, Gale told Sophie it would cause problems if she didn't stay away from Stormwrack."

"Ha! You believe me now?"

"I believe the part about you causing trouble."

"She's already caused a ton of trouble," Verena said. "My mom has been drinking since last night. She didn't tell Dad about you, either, and . . . it didn't go down well. And this issue with the courier pouch may seem trivial to you, but I've been working toward filling Gale's shoes my whole life. You can't just stumble in off Nob Hill and become a Fleet courier."

"I don't want to, I promise. I just wanted to know you guys. Didn't Beatrice tell you anything about my birth father?"

"Mom won't talk about that." Verena reached back, finding the base of her ponytail and cinching it even tighter, her jaw working. "Look, Verdanii women are meant to be tough and talented. The expectations are high. From what Gale's told me, my . . . our . . . mom could never quite measure up to being a Feliachild. She had some meltdown twenty-five years ago."

"Twenty-five," Bram said.

*And I'm twenty-four. Great, I've already caused a nervous breakdown and a fisher-killing storm.*

"Mom came here—had Sophie, I guess—and vested her courier post in Gale."

Bram smoothed out the map. "She ran to San Francisco?"

"Mom hates Stormwrack. She's been here ever since. But on paper, the courier position passes to her first daughter."

"So she loaned the job to Gale and it's supposed to go back to you."

Verena glowered. "I'm the second daughter now."

"If worst comes to worst, can't I just 'vest' it back to you?" Sophie asked.

"Oh, gee, that's generous."

"Focus, guys," Bram interrupted. "Verena, if we're going to go to some Oldee Englishee island and strip Sophie of rights she didn't even know she had—"

"Because she *doesn't.*"

"Your aunt said it would mean trouble, or danger. For all of you, not just Sophie. Isn't it in your interest to consider the faint chance that Gale knows what she's talking about?"

"Bram's right," Sophie said. *Big surprise there,* she thought. "You gotta at least check that I'm not gonna cause a hurricane or a plague."

"A plague? Really?"

"Gale said there'd be trouble."

"Why does it fall to me to check? Sophie's the one who's created the problem."

"And you're the one who wants it solved, aren't you?" Bram said.

Sophie asked, "Do you even know what she meant? Couldn't the problem she referred to be this whole inheritance thing?"

"Probably." Verena said. "Supposedly there are prophecies, about Gale—"

"Prophecies?" Bram couldn't help it, he laughed. "Suddenly I see why you're not worried."

"You don't believe in predestination, do you?" Sophie asked.

"If anyone could predict the future, it's the Verdanii."

"That's not an answer," Bram said.

Verena shrugged. "I want to believe we choose what happens to us. Otherwise, we're . . ."

"Fate's sock puppets?" Sophie suggested.

"Yeah."

"But you still don't know why they packed Sophie off," Bram said. "Not for sure."

Verena shook her head.

"Could you just go see what you can find out? We need time to pack anyway," Sophie said. She could see her brother stifling a groan.

*So much for playing it cool,* she thought, but for Bram's sake she tried not to grin.

## CHAPTER 9

After Verena left, Sophie and Bram went to retrieve her car. She spent the next four hours dragging Bram around electronics and camera stores, acquiring equipment she could use for data collection, all geared for exploring a world with no Internet or electricity.

"Small stuff," she told him. "Portable items with little batteries."

"You're keeping the receipts, right?"

"Just check the user reviews."

She found a decent solar battery charger and a new video camera. It was consumer-grade, not pro, but it had a good lens, memory to burn, and the salesman had thrown in the waterproof housing.

She topped off the spree by getting an upgraded phone that was nearly as powerful as her laptop. It would sync with both cameras on Bluetooth, providing a backup for everything she shot.

Once she had the tech organized and tested, she dropped their parents an e-mail saying the two of them were going sailing.

Verena returned the next morning. She was clad in a silky-looking tunic and calfskin pants, and she had two pages, in an unfamiliar language, that she said were invitations—travel visas—to visit Erinth.

"These came from Annela?" Sophie said. They were short, compared to the pages she'd been given before.

"No, the Erinthian travel office," Verena said. "I'm covering my backside a little."

"Did you learn anything?"

"Gale's big issues seem to be the inheritance, which is already messed up, and Mom freaking out, which has already happened."

"You spoke to her?"

"She's still unconscious. I talked to some people she's close to in the Erinthian court."

"And the prophecy thing?" Sophie said.

"What do we care?" Verena said. "We all agreed we don't believe in foretelling."

"No. But if Gale does, it explains why I got the boot."

"Gale's house has the prophecy—well, a transcript." Verena shook her head. "You're not mentioned."

"What *does* it say?"

"It's secret."

"Doesn't matter." Bram shrugged dismissively.

"He's right," Sophie said. "We're back to sorting out how to make you Gale's . . . apprentice?"

Verena nodded.

"So let's go already!" In addition to the cameras, Sophie had a trunk full of diving equipment and a duffel bursting with clothes, antibiotics, a first aid kit, and instant food: protein bars, instant soup, dark chocolate, banana chips, and a pound of trail mix. If she ended up among starve- lings again, everyone was getting a big calorie fix.

"Stand by me," Verena said. She produced a heavy, lead-colored clock, laying it flat on her palm like a metallic pancake or a tiny serving tray.

"Gale had that pocket watch," Sophie murmured to Bram. "She fum- bled it when those guys attacked her and *splash*, we were in the ocean. The woman who sent me back used a watch, too."

It was bait, of sorts, and he couldn't resist. "Timepieces. Does that imply Stormwrack's another time?"

"Oh!" she said. "They call this place Erstwhile."

"Implying our world is a past Earth?"

"But how could the landmasses be so different? Even millions of years—"

Verena interrupted them. "I'm trying to concentrate here."

The clock ticked, metallic clinks that tapped on Sophie's consciousness like icy raindrops against warm flesh. Her vision blurred, as if her eyes were suddenly swimming in tears. Blackness roiled in, but without faintness.

When the murk cleared, they were standing in a dim, round chamber walled in black bricks and lit by torches. High above them, something was beating out seconds in sync with Verena's clock. Weights, big ones, hung above, strung on massive chains whose links appeared to be carved from wood.

"This is the grand clock tower on Erinth, behind the palazzo," Verena said.

*Made it, made it back . . .* Sophie thought gleefully. She put out a hand to her brother and another to her luggage, reassuring herself that both Bram and her equipment had come through.

"Teleportation," Bram breathed. "I don't believe it."

"Teleportation or time travel. Magic. Told ya."

"I am going to find physics that explains this. Somewhere within M-theory is—"

That scritching-teeth sound, from Verena. "Do you guys ever stop?"

"Come on," Sophie protested. "I know this is old news to you, but even so, you must see that it's incredible."

If Verena agreed, it didn't show on her face.

Bram, however, was practically crackling. "Can we go out? Can we see?"

"We're not staying here. You can leave the bags."

Bram had brought a single midsized backpack, about a fifth as large as Sophie's duffel. It probably contained two outfits and a bunch of tools. It was dark leather and brown canvas, high-end, masculine but not macho. He was out of the nerdwear today, dressed for a hike: boots, light water-resistant jacket, fisherman's sweater over his shirt, and dark pants.

He shouldered the pack, declining to ditch it, as they filed up a spiral staircase, through a heavy wooden door and out into a wide, manicured garden that ornamented the courtyard of a grand villa made of black stone. Below the villa, a city spread down a coastal hillside, overlooking a big port filled with sailing ships at anchor.

Sophie pointed out a sail: "Bram. That's Gale's ship."

"The one with the tasty captain?"

Verena shot her a startled look. "Pardon?"

"It's just I forgot his name," Sophie explained, blushing. *Spectacularly tasty,* she thought.

"It's Parrish," Verena said. She flagged down a boy in plain blue livery, speaking a few quick sentences. The cadence of her speech had a familiar rhythm, but the words—

"What's she saying?" Bram murmured.

"Dunno," Sophie said. "They taught me the Fleet language, but the islands seem to have their own dialects."

"Latinate—sounds like a romance language," he said.

"*Passegiare*," she agreed, repeating the one word she'd caught. "That means walk, I think . . . in Italian?"

The kid ran off. Verena said: "The servants will deliver your baggage to Gale's apartment."

"Thanks." Sophie had spotted a red froglike creature about as big as her thumbnail, waddling across the base of a marble fountain. It had an elongated tail that tapered to a curling, hairlike wisp. Crouching close, she pulled out her video camera and zoomed in. The amphibian froze in place. "Bram! I'm positive this is a new species."

"Holy crap," Bram said.

"I know, right?" she said. "Everywhere you look, there's something new. So what do you think? Past Earth or—"

He pulled her upright, turned her so she was facing uphill. "You need to stop and smell the terrain. *That* is an active volcano."

The mountain rumbled, as if it were pleased to have been noticed. It had the perfect cone shape of a volcano picture drawn by a child—the sloping sides, the cut-off point of its tip. *Like Vesuvius*, Sophie thought. Could it be Vesuvius? A flag of smoke stretched from its caldera, marking the direction of the wind.

"Cool!" She took a 360-degree shot, starting with the volcano, catching the city.

Verena said: "It's perfectly safe, Bram."

"Active," he repeated. "Volcano."

"The Erinthians sank a massive intention into the top of the mountain—Muerdia flows slow and steady."

"Intention—that's another term for magical spell?"

"Yeah. It blew a few centuries ago and wiped out half the city, so—"

"If you're trying to reassure me, Verena, you're doing a lousy job."

Sophie had panned down from the volcano to the palace. The heaviness of its stone walls gave it a solid look, and the doors were big and heavy, too. Overall, though, the structure didn't look as though its primary purpose was military. There were no turrets and parapets, no slits for boiling oil or archers. It rose five stories high, with large windows on the upper levels and abundant flower gardens at its base. The windows on the upper three levels opened onto large balconies, and royal blue silk was wound into their railings, adding a band of color to the otherwise sober-looking structure.

Lemon and lime trees planted in a keyhole formation around the palace formed a promenade that led to a gate downhill from the palace itself. Guards stood watch at the gate; about a hundred feet below them, an outdoor market was at full boil, vendors and customers gesturing and shouting as they argued, presumably over prices for fish, vegetables, and whatever else they were trading.

Sophie finished her circle, coming back to the wall and the red and black amphibian there. "Are the frogs toxic, Verena?"

"Why don't you eat it and find out?"

She met her half sister's gaze, holding it until Verena blinked.

"Sorry," she said. "Come on. There are about a zillion of the things on the path to Gale's, if you want to catch one."

Sophie looked at Bram, who shrugged, as if to say: *What else are we gonna do?*

They followed Verena around the side of the palazzo, passing more servants, all of them dressed, to Sophie's eye, like extras from a Renaissance costume drama—the women in long skirts, the men in balloon pants, hose, and puffy-sleeved coats. A uniformed guard let them out through a gatehouse on the side wall. It led to a secluded path walled on either side by lava gateposts and tall glass lanterns. The posts were covered in a creeping vine, not unlike ivy, with unlobed chordate leaves and bell-shaped orange flowers. A stream ran alongside the path, and more of the red amphibians rested on damp ground cover near the water.

Sophie plucked one flower and a sprig of the vine and packed them in a plastic sandwich bag before hurrying to catch up.

Bram was still getting his geology geek on: "How do you tame a volcano, Verena?"

"You can go up to the caldera to see the inscription if you want," she told him. "It's safe, and the path's—"

"I'm not leaving my sister."

Sophie threw an arm around him. "Isn't this cool? Aren't you glad you came?"

He elbowed her. "It's not enough to go looking for a few biological relatives, you mad overachiever? You have to find a whole birth planet."

"I'm the mad overachiever. Who's got two and a half advanced degrees?"

"Who'd have one herself if she didn't keep chickening out on defending her thesis?"

"Jerky jerk," she said, but she felt her face heating. *Thanks for telling little sis I'm an intellectual lightweight.*

Change the subject. "So, Verena, does courier mean what it sounds like? You do deliveries between here and home?"

"Yes and no. There are a few Stormers in the know about Earth, and a few who actually live there, mostly in San Francisco—"

"Why San Francisco?" Bram asked.

"It's easiest to get through there," she said. "Gale does carry messages, from their families and such. She gives the letters to Mom; Mom sends them out. There's also a couple spellscribes who make sure Stormwrack remains undiscovered."

"Because . . . ?"

"The Convene—that's the government—believes that establishing contact would hurt both societies."

"Gale brings the mail back and forth? That's her job?"

Verena nodded. "It's a minor government post."

Sophie frowned. "I thought she was way more important."

"She is. The courier badge gives her freedom to travel and nose around. She spends most of her time here, doing favors for the government. Meddling in politics."

"Like a spy?" Bram said.

Sophie thought of the attack in San Francisco, the one that had brought her here. "So there's lots of people who would have had a reason to attack her?"

"Unfortunately, yes."

"Does she know who stabbed her?"

"If she does, she hasn't said."

The walled path wound downhill, taking them maybe three hundred meters from the palazzo before forking deep into a residential district. There was nobody else on it; it had the feel of a private walkway. Verena led them through a vine-draped gate, through the back courtyard of a four-story building that looked like an apartment block, and past two guards with swords. A barefoot servant scrambled to open the door, leading the way, huffing, up three stuffy flights of stairs, to a landing with two more guards.

"This is Gale's place." Verena raised her hand, but before she could knock, the door swung wide.

*Hello, Mister Tasty!* Close up, Captain Parrish's good looks remained Bollywood-perfect. He looked to be about thirty, with coloring that, at home, she'd have said made him South Asian—Indian, perhaps, or Bangladeshi. His skin glowed like hand-polished walnut, and his black, lamb's-wool curls all but begged to have someone's fingers plunged into them. And his mouth—Jane Austen probably would have called those lips "full" or "generous." Sophie, on the other hand, would have gone with "edible." Everything about that mouth suggested sweet, ripe fruit.

She shot a sidelong glance at her brother and was gratified to see that he looked a little stunned.

*Poor guy—people must stare at him all the time. I wonder if someone did this for him . . . or to him? With magic?*

"Hi," she managed. It came out a little breathy.

Parrish cleared his throat, looking inexplicably stricken. "Verena, Gale has been asking for you."

"How is she?"

"Improving." He stood aside to let them in. "Who are your friends?"

"Sophie Hansa, Bramwell Hansa, this is Captain Garland Parrish of the sailing vessel *Nightjar*," Verena said. "Give me the pouch."

Sophie blinked . . . this last had been to her. "Open or closed?"

"Closed," Verena said, scandalized.

She handed it over and her half sister stomped off, vanishing down the hall.

Bram drifted past them, across the polished floor of dark rock and out to a balcony at the far end of the wide parlor. There was a guard out there, a uniformed shape visible through gauzy orange curtains, but Bram was oblivious to him. He gazed out at the mountains, groping in his pack for his laser range finder. He wore the sort of absorbed expression that meant he'd be tuning out everyone around him for hours, possibly days. His lips moved ever so slightly—math was happening.

Leaving Sophie, for all intents and purposes, alone with Captain Gorgeous.

"Um . . . don't mind Bram," she said.

"No, of course," Parrish said. His voice was a resonant baritone. He was examining her closely. "You are Gale's niece?"

"Not if she has anything to say about it." She spied a shelf of books— books!

"I thought you'd been sent home."

"Verena fetched us back." She pulled down one of the books, trying to avoid thinking about his gaze, heavy as the weight of a hand, on her back. *Silly,* she told herself. *There's a whole world to explore here; you can ogle pretty men back home.* "Did Gale tell you how we met?"

"An attack in . . . your home city."

"I think you all call it Erstwhile. Hey, is that the term for the whole world? All of Earth, I mean, or just San Francisco?"

He seemed to be considering his response. "Kir Hansa . . ."

"Sophie, please."

"The fact that Erstwhile exists—that it isn't a myth, or a remote island in the East—is a government secret."

"Seriously? Classified info? And me with no security clearance."

He didn't return her smile. "You'll have to be circumspect."

"Why? You're in the know, obviously, and Verena grew up there—"

He put up a hand, and—as if on cue—a teenaged girl came into the room, carrying a tray of anise-scented cookies and four black glasses filled with steaming fluid.

"Discretion is important," he said, looking from the servant to the guard on the balcony.

Sophie opened the book. It was typeset in curlicued Roman lettering—another argument that this was Earth, in some sense. The words were Fleetspeak.

Oh, this was interesting! It turned out the spell that had taught her the language had made her fluent, but not precisely literate. She had to sound out each word, like a first grader, before it made sense: "Blossoms Majesta of Redcap Island are daughters and sisters of the reigning king; they run the government, and one should never visit the island without first finding out which princess is currently in charge of foreign affairs." Diplomatic protocol. Boring.

Parrish coughed, probably hoping for some kind of acknowledgment that he'd told her to be secretive.

She closed the book. "I'm no good at fibbing, Captain."

"Discretion is a skill you would need, were you to remain here."

*He's so sure I'm going. Why are the cute ones always so arrogant?* "Okay, then. Have you been to . . . our home city?"

"Yes."

"Really?"

"Once or twice. Kir, what are you doing?"

"Call me Sophie." She had opened a second book, a massive tome full of diagrams of family trees, and shut it just as fast. "I have until Verena disinherits me, right? I'm picking up what I can."

The next book was called *Writs of Exception,* and read like law. Small print, and dry, wordy statutes.

"So, Captain, you've been you-know-where? Have you met my mother?"

"Of course."

It wasn't the answer she'd expected. "Wow. You know Beatrice? What's she like when she's not freaking out?"

"Freaking . . . I couldn't say."

*Arrogant, maybe, but he is adorable when he's rattled.*

"Kir—"

"Sophie."

"If you explained what it is you're seeking among Gale's books . . ."

"Answers. Anything useful," she said, and he stiffened, cooling so fast she might as well have slapped him.

*Damn! What've I said now?*

"Inheritance law?" Parrish said, voice thin.

"What? No! If Gale and Verena can't sort out the heir thing by themselves, what possible chance would there be that I could help? I was hoping more for a field guide. Plants and insects?"

The faint hint of a smile formed. It was a nice smile . . . she nearly dropped the book. "You're *curious.*"

*That's right,* she remembered, *these people seem to think curiosity is a disease or something.* But Parrish didn't look offended. She said: "What about some geology? The continents on this—"

Parrish's eyes flicked to the guard on the balcony.

*Right, the big secret.* "I'm interested in how the landmasses formed."

"Mythology?" Now he looked baffled.

"Hang on . . ." She'd just absorbed what he had said. "Inheritance law? You think I'm looking up how to hang onto all this?" She waved an arm, indicating the apartment.

"Gale is a wealthy and important woman."

She laughed. "Unless she owns a natural history museum, I'm not that interested."

"No? Not in her fortune? Her position among the Nine Families of Verdanii? Unlimited right of passage to your home city, and a Fleet Courier badge?"

"I didn't set out to have the damned pouch imprint on me," she said. "It's a purse, not a gosling. Nobody in their right mind would expect— and, really, why does it do that anyway?"

He frowned, apparently processing.

"Okay. Sure, I'm human. If someone handed me a billion dollars on a silver platter, I'd take it. Anyone would. But this isn't real. It's not mine. What do you think I am?"

"Who were the men who attacked Gale?" Parrish said. "How is it you were present just when she needed aid?"

"You're the one who's her friend. How is it you weren't present?" she snapped, and that hit him—she could see it. "Are you saying I set her up?"

"Did you?"

"Sofe?" Bram had broken out of his math fugue. "Everything okay?"

"Accusations of duplicity aside, we're dandy." They had been arguing in Fleet, but now she switched to English, glaring at Parrish.

*Unlimited right of travel to and from Stormwrack does sound kinda nice,* a traitorous inner voice murmured.

*Shut up,* she thought at it, and she knew, *knew* that guilt had flickered across her face, and Parrish had seen it.

"Your pardon, Kir," Parrish said. "But finding out who attacked Gale is—"

Verena interrupted them by bursting out of the bedroom, at full stomp. Gale shuffled behind her, leaning on a cane, her complexion pasty. "You're *not* to duel your sister—"

"Duel?"

Gale saw Sophie. Typically, she looked horrified. "Oh, Verena. What have you done?"

"I had to bring her!" Verena said. "She's seduced your pouch. As for dueling, it's the fastest way to clear this up. A ritual exchange of blows—"

"I'm *so* not fighting anyone," Sophie said.

"Fake fighting," Verena explained, between clenched teeth.

Gale, if anything, looked more upset. "Neither of you is to go anywhere near the Dueling Deck. I forbid it. I absolutely—" She sputtered, then gave in to a coughing fit.

"Could everyone please speak English?" Bram's plea startled them all. Everyone turned to stare and he amended. "Assuming you can."

Gale drew a long whistling breath and switched. "Sophie is penniless, Verena, and arguably without country. She would qualify for a court-appointed dueling proxy." Her accent, to Sophie's ear, sounded faintly Germanic.

"Gale, please." Parrish maneuvered the older woman toward a couch. She perched with an air of reluctance, glaring from one girl to the other.

"You promised you'd wait at home until I came for you, Sophie," she said. "And who've you brought into this now?"

"My brother, Bram. Bram, this is my birth mother's sister, Gale Fe—"

"You told him everything?"

"I don't *know* everything," she said. "I hardly know anything. Maybe if you'd just explained what the big hairy problem was, I wouldn't be blundering about offending every single person I meet and causing trouble. But I've got you saying I need to go and Verena saying I need to come back, and seers, apparently, saying 'Que Sera Sera.' Captain Tasty here's all but accused me of having gotten you attacked to get my grubby paws on your earthly goods, which seem to consist of a law library and a gene-locked semi-sentient purse—"

"Sofe, pause for breath," Bram said.

"She's right, Gale," Verena said. "If you and Mom had been honest with me, this could never have happened."

Sophie turned to her sister. "Oh, good. The person on my side is the one who wants to duel me."

"Dueling?" Bram said. "We're dueling now?"

"Fake dueling. Right? Right, Verena?"

"Whatever it takes," Verena said icily.

"Silence, all of you!" Gale rose, pacing to the balcony, seeming to stare through the uniformed guard and out over the city.

"Why did Mom hide her away?" Verena demanded. "A first daughter of Verdanii—anyone would have been happy to raise her."

Gale shook her head. "There were contractual issues—"

"You're tiring yourself." Parrish led her away from the balcony, but she balked after two steps.

"Hush, Garland. This isn't like you—why are you fussing?"

"You're weak."

"Sudden death, remember?" Something passed between them; he let his arm drop.

"Verena, Sophie, I promise to talk to your mother. I'll beg Beatrice to tell you everything. I'll compel her somehow, my word on it. But right now, the important thing is to get Sophie disinherited and home, before anyone discovers—"

A cry from the street interrupted her. She turned to the balcony again, separating the sheer curtains with a thrust of her cane.

Parrish was already moving, but it was too late. Two hairy blurs the size of German shepherds dropped onto the balcony. One flung the soldier up and over the balcony rail.

The other launched itself right at Gale, bowling her to the marble floor, as, outside, they heard the crack of the guard's body striking the cobblestone street.

## CHAPTER 10

The thing—the *monster*—attacking Gale had the lithe build of a ten-year-old and an oily-looking salt-and-pepper pelt. Its grizzled face was squashed flat, like a bulldog's. Its eyes were rheumy; bits of sand, hair, and other detritus were stuck on the whites and in the wet brown slicks running down its cheeks.

It bore Gale to the floor, wrapped long, thick-knuckled, hairy fingers around her throat, and squeezed.

There was something clumsy and mashed-together about it, as if it had been built from parts of several different animals.

Another one dropped to the balcony.

"Mezmers!" Parrish had already tackled the creature that had seized Gale. He had his face turned upward, to the ceiling, as he grabbed for the creature's fingers.

Verena produced a long knife—or maybe it was an actual shortsword—from within her coat.

*Dueling,* Sophie thought, as Verena advanced on the creatures, swinging wildly, shading her eyes.

The monsters were fast. One sidestepped the blade, bounding aside and into the path of the maid who had brought in their tea. The girl froze, dropping her dust rag: Sophie grabbed her arm, whirling her out of reach as the thing snatched at her. The maid collapsed, dead weight in Sophie's grip.

"Wait!" Sophie yelled, hoping to startle or delay it. "Stop, stop, stop!"

It gathered itself to pounce.

The laser range finder bounced off the creature's face. A second later, a heavy stone vase struck its chest. Bram had resorted to throwing things.

Sophie dragged the limp servant toward the big double doors of the apartment. *Lock her out in the hall,* she thought, *out of danger, and let those guards in . . .*

Her brother had the same idea. He yanked the door open for her—and then stiffened as he came nose to nose with a fourth mezmer out in the hall. It stood, naked, its bloodied hands raised as if it were making an offering. Scattered around it were Sophie's clothes and the shreds of her duffel. Two bleeding guards and a uniformed porter lay on the floor.

Sophie let her reflexes take over: She let the maid fall, shoved her brother aside, and pushed the double doors shut. She wasn't quite fast enough; she caught the creature's head between the edges of the doors. It shrieked in pain and fury, and pushed against her.

"A little help here, Bram! Bram, what's wrong?"

"He must have—looked—into its eyes," Parrish panted.

*No eye contact.* Sophie turned her face from the monster, which was mewling and skittering, its feet sliding on the blood-slicked marble floor of the hall as it tried to force the doors open and thereby free itself to maul her. She put all her weight into heaving against it, keeping it pinned.

Its breath, hot on her chest, smelled of onions and raw meat.

"Will Bram be okay?"

"It wears off—" Verena yelped in pain.

"Soon? Wears off soon?"

"Not soon enough—ow, damn!"

Bracing her weight against the door, Sophie risked a look back into the parlor. Verena had fatally skewered one monster: her sword had run through its mouth. She and Parrish were wrestling to break the other's grip on Gale. It wasn't going well—Verena's hand had been poked full of spines and was dripping blood. The group of them heaved to and fro. Gale's eyes were bulging; she was clawing ineffectually at the hand around her neck.

The monster at hand gave a mighty shove at the door.

Sophie pushed back.

*Observe, dammit!* The dead mezmer was splayed on its back in a spreading pool of normal-looking red blood. It too was unclothed; its genitals lolled, moist, dirt-encrusted, and obscene.

Naked . . . Sophie checked her balance against the double doors, and then hefted one boot straight up between them.

It worked: She caught soft flesh and the thing howled, pulling back involuntarily. Sophie let it slip out from between the trap of the two doors and then slammed them shut, throwing the bolt. Then, making for the dead monster on the floor, she seized the sword Verena had left in it. She pulled so hard that when it came free easily, she almost flung herself to the floor.

A gritty crack.

Parrish had the surviving creature pinned. It still had one hand wrapped around Gale's neck. Gale herself had lost consciousness, or . . .

*No, she looks dead, no, that snapping noise, no, no . . .*

Parrish twisted, trying to cover the mezmer's eyes without getting his hand bitten. "Cut it off her," he panted.

Sophie raised the blade, forcing herself to take a second, to steady herself. She brought it down in a chop, cutting at the elbow, thinking about golf swings, tennis, follow-through. *If I hurt it enough, maybe it'll let go . . .*

But either the mezmers were delicate or the sword was impossibly sharp, because it cut through with only a sticky whisper of resistance, as if both flesh and bone were as soft as the flesh of a ripe pear. The severed arm fell, releasing Gale's throat. The creature stiffened in Parrish's arms and began to wail.

Verena pulled Gale flat, laying her head on her chest, listening for a heartbeat before fumbling to start CPR with her uninjured hand. Her eyes were dry and incredibly wide, almost bulging.

Parrish got to his feet, holding out his hand for the blade. Sophie handed it over mutely, expecting him to kill the thing. Instead, he cut a curtain into strips, binding the monster's stump before it could bleed to death and then wrapping another around its disturbing, filth-encrusted eyes. He shoved it into a heavy chair and tied it quickly.

Then he knelt beside Gale, laying a hand on her face. "Stop, Verena. Her neck's broken."

Her half sister's expression, fury and bewilderment, refusal to believe, shock, reminded Sophie that she didn't belong here.

*Give them some space,* she thought. She picked her way over the scattered furniture to Bram. The maid was stirring, shaking as if with deep cold, her teeth bared. "It's okay," Sophie said to her softly. "You're okay."

She took Bram's hand and sat beside him on the floor, leaning him up against her. Her pulse was hammering; she could still feel the sword slicing through the thing's arm, see the gout of blood.

*Blood's everywhere.* A footstep-smeared slick of it lay between her and Gale.

Verena was still trying to force life back into their aunt's body.

Parrish murmured: "Stop, Verena, stop. It's over, let it be. It was always going to happen, you know that."

He reached for her awkwardly but Verena wormed out of the attempted embrace, her expression proud, hurt, and angry.

"I shouldn't have brought you," Sophie whispered to Bram.

Bram shivered delicately.

Pounding at the doors and shouts in not-actually-Italian interrupted her. Parrish stumbled to the door. The two dead guards and the porter were still there, lying among Sophie's stuff. One last man—the one who'd been at the back gate—was there, sword bloodied. At his feet, the gutted remains of the monster were soaking into Sophie's second-best jeans.

"Kir Feliachild's been murdered," Parrish told him, tone level. He stepped aside to let the guard in, then vanished down the hallway.

"Where's he going?"

"To report to the palazzo, probably," Verena said. "The Conto will want to hear it from him."

"Sofe?" Bram opened his eyes. He seemed perfectly alert. It was how he used to wake up as a baby, too—fast asleep one minute and apparently ready to do vector calculus the next. "Are you hurt?"

"Not a scratch on me," she said, fighting tears. What right did she have to cry? Verena, Parrish—they knew Gale. Who was she but an upstart, troublemaking, interloping clod?

"I felt its thoughts," Bram said. "They're . . . telepathic?"

"Hush," she said.

"I'm fine, Sofe." He sat upright. "Optimal. Can prove it, if you want. Ask me anything."

"Don't want proof."

"They were on the roof, waiting for their chance. Waiting for days," he said. "This isn't about you. It's probably tied to that other attack on Gale, in San Francisco."

"We're supposed to be coy about San Francisco."

"Sofe, this isn't your fault."

The surviving guard took a position beside the tied-up monster. Verena was still kneeling by Gale's body. After the flurry of the fight, now there was nothing to do but sit and wait for . . . who? Cops?

*No point in being completely useless.* She went out into the hall, stepping over the bodies with a little moan, and popped the lock on her trunk. She flung it open, dug until she found the first aid kit, then returned to the . . .

*The crime scene*, she thought, and her stomach heaved once.

"Show me that hand."

Verena held it out without arguing. Sophie took a look. Then she bent, making herself examine the monster arm she'd severed. The quills were shorter than a porcupine's, small tapering pins that bristled with little barbs. Yanking them would make the injury worse.

"Can anyone help, Kir?" The guard's tone was sharp; he seemed to want the maid to get moving.

"Um . . . I could use a basin of clean water."

"Just pull them," Verena said.

"Is this your dominant hand?"

A slow nod. She was in shock, probably. Why shouldn't she be? They were two feet from the murdered body of her aunt.

"Let's not turn you to hamburger, okay?"

"Don't treat me like I'm a kid," Verena said, but there was no heat in the words.

"I'll help her." Bram got the maid to her feet and urged her toward the kitchen. He was trying to repeat the phrase Sophie had just used: "Warm water, clean with?" His pronunciation was off, but the girl seemed to know what he wanted.

"He'll know as much Fleetspeak as me by the end of the week," Sophie grumbled. "Verena, what are these things? Parrish called them mezmers?"

"Oddities," she said. "They've been scripped for this."

"Scripped."

"Magically altered."

"Animals . . . changed into killers?"

Verena shook her head. "Not animals."

The sourness rose in her belly. "They were human?"

"Assassination requires judgment," Verena said dully. "Strategy. Target recognition."

"Patience and teamwork," the guard agreed.

*I cut off his hand. It's a person and I maimed him . . .*

Bram returned with a steaming bowl; Sophie put Verena's injured hand into it. Red billowed from the punctures, tinting the water in cloudy, sea-jelly swirls. She set her watch. "Soak for ten minutes, okay?"

"You can't trust an animal intellect," Verena said. "So you transform a person. They do the job and they can't speak, they can't tell anyone on you."

Sophie switched to English, for Bram. "Verena says they're people."

He nodded. "I wondered. When it scrambled my mind, I heard . . . gabble. Words, in this Flitspake language of yours."

"Fleetspeak," Verena murmured, correcting his pronunciation. "Where is Parrish?"

"You said he went to tell the palazzo."

"This is gonna kill him," she said. "He and Gale have been sailing together since he was eighteen."

Time crawled. Sophie picked twenty quills out of Verena's hand, making a fairly neat job of it, before slathering the cuts with an antiseptic gel she'd brought from home.

In time, Parrish returned with an impossibly large number of people, most in uniform: guards, officers, clerks with slates and chalk. There were two white-clad women and two white-clad men, all four of them stunning beauties, all four of them moving as if they were strangely weak. This quartet seemed to be there just to stand over the body while holding lit candles, quivering with the effort of staying on their feet as they wept over Gale.

It was both grim and massively boring. There was nothing to do but watch and wait. The guards had brought a big wooden crate with them, and they dumped the monster bodies and the severed arm in it like so much trash, bearing them away. They took the surviving mezmer, the one Sophie had maimed, into custody.

"Will they autopsy the mezmers?"

"Why would they?" Parrish said. Having brought the cavalry, he'd lowered himself to the floor at Gale's head, and now was sitting cross-legged between the mourners.

"Clues? Evidence?"

"It's up to the Conto," Verena said.

"Who?"

"The ruler of Erinth—Conto means Count."

"I doubt they'll do any evidence-gathering as you'd consider it," Parrish said. "They'll check the mezmers for brands, but we witnessed Gale's death. There's no question as to how she died."

"What about corroborating evidence?" Sophie said.

He stared at her, or through her. "Our word is enough."

A crew of workers appeared, dressed in dove gray and wielding mops and buckets. They attacked the clutter and the blood with equal fervor, setting the room to rights. They gathered the scattered contents of Sophie's duffel, separating out the bloodied things before bringing everything else inside from the hallway.

Sophie followed her stuff as they carried it into a rose-pink bedroom.

"You don't travel light, do you?" Verena was right behind her.

She bit back a retort: Verena probably needed a distraction just as badly as she did. "It's just equipment."

Verena turned over one of the flippers. "You're a diver?"

"Videographer."

"What is all this?"

"Wet suit. Dry suit. Mask. Rebreather. Dive computer. Tanks, with about five hours of air in them. My camera—"

"There's a camera around your wrist."

"Video, yeah. This bigger rig is my good one. Digital SLR, you know? For stills?" She opened the case, revealing the camera body, five lenses, and a waterproof housing. The tripod was strapped beneath, next to a plastic jug of alcohol—for DNA samples—and a small crate of corkable plastic tubes.

"And a first aid kit."

"Diving's got its hazards. The rest is clothes: thermal socks, undies, swimsuits, jeans, shorts, sweats, skirt. Sandals, boots, running shoes. Soap."

Verena stirred the bits and pieces, peering into one of the boxes. Sophie hadn't unwrapped the solar battery charger; it was still nestled in its original box, lovingly crated among pillows of plastic and small Styrofoam peas. Finally, she said: "Lotta baggage."

"Cheap shot," Sophie returned.

To her surprise, her half sister gave her a weak grin.

"Count yourself lucky." Bram had trailed after them. "If she'd had another day there'd be an entire film crew packed in here."

"Look who's talking!" Sophie bent, pulling out a heavy surveyor's transit. "I didn't bring this."

"It wouldn't fit in my backpack," Bram said.

*He had that scope, too.* A thread of happiness wound its way through all the other emotions. He brought equipment. Maybe he hadn't entirely believed her, but he'd given her the benefit of the doubt.

Verena looked over the kit again, her expression sober. "I don't want to rain on your parade, guys, but the chances of Annela letting you leave here with footage of Stormwrack—she'll confiscate it all."

"Guess we'd better stay out of Annela's way, then," Sophie said. Bram grinned.

The volume of the sobs coming from the other room rose, drawing them back to the parlor.

Five gray-robed soldiers had brought in a long sheet of the glassy stone that seemed so ubiquitous here, an ornate panel swirled with bright colors and perforated with handholds.

Parrish knelt, sliding his arms under Gale. His handsome face was absolutely still as he lifted the body onto the bier, arranging her arms at her sides. One of the mourners handed him a small pillow. He placed it under her head.

*He looks devastated.*

Sophie had started to cry again. Bram took her hand, squeezing it hard.

"What of her throat, Kir?" asked a soldier. Gale's neck was marked with scratchy red weals. The knife wound in her chest had bled, too.

"We—" There were twenty or so people in the room now, and they all waited in silence for Parrish to swallow his emotions and answer, waited so long Sophie began to think they might sit there forever, waiting for the body to rot.

"The Conto gave her a shawl at his elevation. It's probably . . ." He gestured at a wardrobe.

Verena opened doors, digging around, coming out with a coffee-colored sheet of silk covered in small pearls.

"That's not it," Parrish said, but he took it anyway, draping it over her neck and bloody upper body, letting the edges hang. Verena turned back to the wardrobe and produced a frock coat, black in color with silver trim, and offered it to him.

Parrish put it on, moving with the care of someone who was trying to hide the fact that he was drunk.

By now, some of the courtiers had sprinkled a path of flower petals and small beads on the floor, making a path to the door and down the front staircase.

The gabble of murmuring voices, outside the balcony, had been rising. They were obviously going to take the body out the front way and go in a procession to . . . the palazzo?

"There really won't be any police?" Sophie asked again.

Parrish had taken a place at the head of the glass panel. "Pardon?"

"Police. Forensic investigation. Isn't anyone going to try to figure out who did this?"

"Gale's Verdanii and a Fleet courier. The Conto will look into whether any Erinthians had a hand in this. If it's an international matter, the investigation will extend beyond his . . ." Parrish foundered.

"Jurisdiction?" offered Bram.

"Yes, I think that's the Anglay word."

Verena said: "It falls to Gale's heir to sort out the matter of her death and report the truth to Fleet and family."

Sophie was shocked: "They expect you to do it? You just lost her. You're in mourning."

"Ah, you've forgotten," Verena said, with a glimmer of bitterness. "Gale didn't get a chance to disinherit you. This disaster is your problem, Sophie Hansa, and it'll serve you right if I go back to the outlands and let you choke on it."

## CHAPTER 11

Verena's words hung in the air like a bad smell on Sophie's shoe, ugly and inescapable.

She opened her mouth to answer—*I can't investigate a murder,* she was going to say, or *We'll get the stupid estate fixed, so just chill.* Maybe she would have just pointed out that if their mother could make Gale her proxy, then she could make Verena hers.

But the tiniest wince from Bram brought her back to the here and now: the body on the bier of heavy volcanic glass. "What does Gale need from us now?"

"She's ready to go to the palazzo," Parrish said, face as expressionless as if it were carved. "Bring her pouch."

She and Verena reached for it simultaneously.

Sophie drew back. "You do it."

Her sister shoved it across the table. "Put it on."

The mourners arranged themselves around the obsidian bier, Sophie and Verena behind Gale and the pallbearers, Bram a step behind. Parrish buttoned up the frock coat Verena had given him. Its buttons appeared to be made of curled seed cones. His eyes met hers; they gave back nothing but blackness.

He fitted a gloved hand to a lower corner of the bier, raising Gale to his shoulder, in perfect sync with the five soldiers. The fragile mourners in their gray robes led the way out the front door.

It was slow going on a hot evening. The crowd had swelled, but it parted as they emerged. People were sobbing, and Sophie heard whispers spreading: *Justo!* And *En Haggio!* Instead of asking for a translation, she kept her head down and her lips zipped as the group inched through the piazza.

Her thoughts were anything but slow. *Investigating a murder. That's probably not impossible, as long as I can get Verena to pitch in. Parrish, too. Gotta sort out this inheritance thing . . . will there even be a will? Do they do wills here or is it just a done deal? At least if it takes awhile, I'll get a good look around Stormwrack. Oh, I'm awful, what an opportunist, stop it, Sophie, she's dead, murdered, and this isn't a research expedition anymore.*

Parrish's head came up once, his gaze seeking the harbor. Gale's cutter had replaced its sails with loose black drapes. They flapped uselessly from its yards, giving the ship a forlorn, mournful appearance.

*The crew knows, then. But how?* She added the question to the list of things she'd ask when they could all speak again.

They walked directly up to the palazzo, no discreet back path this time. The solemn parade seemed to go on forever. They passed a bird that resembled a lark but sounded more like a shrike, passed a strange assembly of frail, lovely, oddly similar-looking young women dressed in umber togas and leaning on walkers. Old people in plain smocks approached the bier and laid various objects on Gale's body: flowers, small bound sheaves of wheat, and little wooden tools.

A flyaway bit of one sheaf blew away and stuck to Sophie's shirt. She tucked it into her pocket, unable to repress the urge to keep it as a sample.

*Verena said they won't let me bring anything back.*

*We'll see about that.*

She thought briefly of Gale's pocket watch; she'd found it behind a Dumpster in the alley where she'd been attacked. Even now it was sitting in their parents' house, next to their desktop computer.

Inside the courtyard, Parrish and the others approached a set of posts that had been erected, like tall table legs, in front of an ornate fountain. A man in a gold-colored topcoat awaited them.

She had an inappropriate humor moment: *He looks like that actor from* Robin Hood. *No, damn, I'm going to laugh.*

The man—the Conto, she assumed—was holding a wreath woven of leaves and small citrusy fruits, red in hue and about as big as Ping-Pong balls. As Parrish and the others lowered the bier onto the six posts, he laid the wreath on Gale's chest, taking the time to whisper something in her ear and then leave a kiss on her lips. The crowd loved it. A scandalized murmur spilled out from the plaza.

A finely dressed woman paid court to Gale next, miming an odd gesture—scratching at her eyes? She was followed by a teenaged boy and then a girl who merely air-kissed Gale's cheek.

Finally, the gold-robed man gestured to Verena and retreated into the palazzo.

"Come on," Verena whispered. They left Parrish at the head of the bier, following the man and his entourage indoors, into a slightly overheated parlor that overlooked the plaza and the sea. The crowd was filing past the body.

The Conto said something in the Italian dialect, as Sophie had dubbed it, breaking the silence.

"My sister speaks only Fleet," Verena said.

Sophie glanced at Bram.

"Translate what you can," he murmured.

"I said the day has finally come," said the Conto. "After a lifetime of courting death, Sturma has been murdered. Verena, my deepest sympathies. My guard is at your disposal."

"Finally, someone's talking cops!" she said to Bram.

A table had been laid out with an array of white foods—little rounds of bread; anemic, roasted potatoes; slices of a pale meat.

"Mourning fare—very bland stuff, I'm afraid." The Conto was broad-shouldered and barrel-chested, with huge, ring-encrusted hands. It was just him, now—the woman and kids and all the courtiers had left. "I can have some spices smuggled in."

"Not hungry." Verena leaned against the thick red curtains of the window overlooking the courtyard, staring at the body, or perhaps at the figure of Parrish, standing immobile beside Gale.

The Conto turned his gaze on Sophie. "You are the wayward child who came to her aid at her sister's, aren't you?"

His speech was so stiff she found herself wanting to answer formally, too. Instead she said: "I smashed a guy in the face with a plastic box. Gale did the real fighting. I'm no warrior." Grief or perhaps regret, surged within her. "If I was, maybe she'd still be alive."

"I wouldn't have seen her again, if she'd met her fate that day," he said. "Nor been able to honor her wishes now. You've done us all a kindness."

"You spoke to Gale after she got stabbed? Did she tell you anything about who attacked her?"

"We talked of the past, of our families. She asked if anyone here might be paid to claim an adult daughter—as illegitimate, I mean."

"Why?"

"She thought to establish a place for you, here on Erinth."

"A place—fake parentage, a paper trail?"

He nodded.

Sophie couldn't help but smile: Gale had liked her at least a little, then. "You didn't set that up, did you?"

He shook his head. "No time."

"Could you still?"

"No," Verena said, without moving. "You hold Gale's pouch now. Besides, if the Conto buys you a fake ID, people will assume you're his illegitimate daughter. It would cause problems."

"And we have plenty of those already," she said. "Didn't you say we have to go on a big hunt for the killers?"

Verena sighed, addressing the Conto. "It couldn't have anything to do with local politics, could it, Kir? You and Gale were allies. Your elder brother's oldest son . . . she mentioned he'd been trouble."

"Terzo has been grasping for my throne." The Conto's lip curled ever so slightly. "But if your aunt believed she'd been set on by my enemies, she would have told me immediately."

Verena slumped a little. "That's true. She wouldn't leave you hanging."

"Still, Terzo does have a wide circle of questionable friends; he's close with a Sylvanner boy."

"Sylvanna," Sophie said to Bram. "That's the country that does a lot of magical research and development. The Stele Islanders were suspicious of them, too."

"Sylvanners wouldn't use mezmers. It's not subtle," Verena said.

"It's a good excuse for me to examine my nephew's friendships," the Conto said, "But I suspect your answers will lie elsewhere, girls."

"Where elsewhere?" Sophie said. "I gather Gale had a lot of enemies."

"Did she ever," Verena said.

"I'll have my ports minister copy you a list of visiting ships here in Cindria."

He and Verena fell silent—brooding, maybe, or just letting the grief sink in. Sophie took the opportunity to quickly fill in Bram, who was having a good look at the obsidian panes in one of the smaller windows, at the construction of the casement itself. A few stars were visible in the darkening sky . . . he had an eye on those too, as he listened.

"You got international politics flying thick and fast here," he said, when Sophie was done. "But the murder must be tied to the earlier attack on Gale, right?"

She nodded. "Conto, the men who stabbed Gale, before, they said something about Tempranza—Temperance."

"That was probably just an oath," Conto said.

"*Temperance* is the flagship of the Fleet," Verena explained. "People say things: By the fury of *Temperance*, *Temperance*'s teeth, in the name of *Temperance*."

"Damn, I thought I was onto something. So now what?"

"Gale's wish was to pour her bones into the Erinthian fire. We'll process up to the caldera at dawn tomorrow."

"So soon?" Hours spent watching crime dramas on TV kicked in—she found herself wanting to demand that they do an autopsy. But what would they find? They probably didn't have a crime lab here, or anything like it. And Gale was killed in front of five witnesses. As Parrish said, there was no doubt as to how she'd died.

"Yes. Ceremonies must be complete before the Allmother of Verdanii can send someone for the body."

The Conto's words seemed to hit Verena hard; she paled, and turned back to the window.

"I must return to my family," the Conto said. "You'll stay here, of course, as my guests. I'll put a clerk and two guardsmen in your service."

"Thank you," Sophie said. "Um, if I should bow or salute, if there's some formal thing I should do here, I don't know it."

"No need, Kir." He nodded and vanished.

"They're just chucking her in the volcano at dawn?" Bram said.

"If the Verdanii show up they'll haul her home and do full burial with honors, for weeks," Verena said, switching to English. She'd dried her eyes and her voice was steady. "Gale hated that kind of fuss. Besides, she always said she was more at home with fire than with earth."

*She looks so forlorn,* Sophie thought.

Aranging a few of the bready things on a plate with a slice of the meat and a fruit that looked like peeled lychee, she took it to the window. "You should have something."

"Stay away," Verena said, voice sharp like their mother's had been, all those days ago when Sophie had first approached her.

*Fine, I tried.* She ate the fruit herself—it *was* lychee—and sat beside Bram.

"Fleetspeak," he said. His pronunciation was better this time. Then, in English: "My name is Bram Hansa—I am learning your language."

Sophie translated the phrase, and he repeated it a couple times. Her brother's memory was remarkable—not truly eidetic, but he had constructed himself an array of weird mental shortcuts. He could remember most anything. If Bram knew one thing, it was how to learn.

"Please excuse me; I'm not familiar with your customs."

She taught him the phrase.

"Could you write it out?"

"I don't know that I can spell everything right. You wouldn't believe it—what they did to me was only verbal—"

"Right. Speaking and writing aren't quite the same. Wow—that is *so* interesting."

"I can sound out words, and once I do I recognize them, it's fine, but—"

"Get the clerk to write whatever you need," Verena said.

"Won't we need him to write letters? Notices to people, saying Gale's died?"

"Gossip will already be out," she said. "There was a spell on her. It broke when she died—it must have."

"How do you know?"

"Her ship's flying black rags." She beckoned the clerk. "Please write down everything Kir Hansa says to her brother."

"Of course, Kir."

Verena gestured at the darkening courtyard. "I'm going out to stand with him."

"Him?" Bram said, after she'd gone.

"Parrish, I guess." Sophie looked downhill, toward the bier.

Though day was nearly over, people continued to file past the body. As the sun set they melted into shadows, becoming a river of candles, glimmering down the piazza. Torches stood at the corners of the bier, sending twisting pillars of orange motes up to the waning moon.

"I'm new here; I don't know your customs," Bram said, in English.

Sophie repeated the phrase.

## CHAPTER 12

By dawn, Bram had drawn a phrase book and a long list of vocabulary out of Sophie and the clerk, and was working on understanding basic grammar. It was an education for Sophie, too—since she had never studied Fleet, she didn't consciously know the rules. She just knew what sounded right. The clerk, fortunately, was happy to spell out the basics for them both.

"This word Kir you've been using," Bram said at one point.

"It's the honorific. Mister, Miss, or Missus."

"Gender neutral?" he said.

"Seems that way," Sophie said, and the clerk nodded.

By then she was reassembling the various flower arrangements in their suite.

Translating for Bram wasn't quite enough to occupy her mind—she kept flashing back to Gale, dead on the floor and the sense memory of cutting off the mezmer's arm. So, as she'd taught him Fleetspeak, she'd also pulled apart the bouquets, taking pictures of each plant, noting the ones she knew and the ones she didn't recognize.

When that was done, she took the video camera out to the balcony, panning slowly across the courtyard, gathering grainy, ill-lit footage of Gale's body, of Parrish and Verena standing vigil over her.

"You could go, too." She repeated the words before she realized Bram had actually spoken to her. "Sorry, what?"

He had sent the clerk away, and was paging through twenty or so sheets of notes on Fleetspeak, watching her with a concerned expression. "You could go stand by the body too, if you wanted."

She sat beside him, leaning in. "It'd be wrong to go play sad niece for the crowd. Gale didn't know me."

"Nobody who knows you would ever believe you were pretending to be sad."

His words triggered a massive upwelling of feeling: grief, the urge to cry yet again, and a bit of that mad feeling she'd had aboard *Estrel*. "She was unconscious for most of the time I knew her. It hurts, but it's . . . selfishness, you know? I'm sad for me. I didn't get to know her."

"You think that makes you a bad person?"

She put up both hands. "Bramble, this is no time for your amateur therapist routine."

Before Bram could answer, the Conto swept through the door, leading a small crowd. Sophie recognized the same well-dressed boy and girl who'd been with him at the bier that night. His kids, she assumed. Trailing them were a half dozen of the plainly dressed servants, laden with long, dove gray robes.

"Did you sleep, Kirs?"

She shook her head. "Time to go?"

"It's only been a few hours," Bram objected. "It's dark."

"The walk up takes an hour when one is burdened." The servants cloaked them both, covering Sophie's day-old clothes. The Conto glanced around the room. His eye lingered on the flower arrangements Sophie had disturbed.

*You don't miss much, do you?*

The cloak was plain, soft, and heavy. The fabric felt expensive, and smelled of sourness and old dust.

"Come, this way."

They trooped downstairs, arriving to find the soldiers shooing the working- and middle-class mourners from the courtyard. It was a quiet, orderly process that left Verena and Parrish all but alone at Gale's head and feet. The servants had a cloak for Verena, too.

A half dozen men and women, dressed in black frock coats that matched the one worn by Parrish, stood in two rows a few meters from the bier. One, a man of perhaps twenty, handed Parrish a bicorne hat, black in color, with a long, blue-black plume. It matched his black and silver coat. A dress uniform? Parrish put it on, giving it a brisk push to compress his curls, which were so dense they looked like they'd spring it off, given half a chance. The hat was aligned fore-and-aft, not wide, not Napoleon-style. It made him a foot taller.

Parrish took a second to clasp the younger man's arm. He bowed formally to the other five, who responded by stiffening to attention. Then, marching half-time, they encircled the bier.

"They must be from *Nightjar*," Bram whispered. "Gale's crew."

Sophie nodded.

The sailors raised the body off the bier and the procession began to move, circling the piazza once before taking a narrow side road up between the tall black buildings. People lined the route, but there were no more offerings. The air was oppressively humid and with the sun only just rising, it was cold.

*I could be knitting under this cloak and nobody would know the difference,* Sophie thought. She took the opportunity to fumble out her video camera.

She had long ago taught herself the trick of shooting from the hip, of holding a camera at her side, angling it to catch the faces of passing individuals in crowds and on the street, people who might freeze up if they knew they were being photographed. It was panning for gold: nine out of every ten seconds of footage were useless, but occasionally you caught something brilliant.

She slid her camera hand out of the cloak and aimed at the crowd to her right. Filming made a decent distraction from the building fatigue and the crushing weight of sadness, the woeful and bereft faces, the soft sobs and the reverent whispers that filled the air.

There was plenty to record on the hike to the caldera. They left the city behind soon enough, and with the first glimmers of sun came a symphony of birdsong, blended warbles and whistles, half of them familiar, half not. There was almost no vegetation on these slopes: tufted grasses, a few forbs. It was entirely different from the lush path behind the palazzo, with its amphibians and ferns.

As they climbed up from sea level, the air seemed drier. A baked smell was rising, it seemed, from the soil itself.

Twenty feet away, a lizard stirred on a ledge. In the dim light, it looked like a gecko. A dead beetle on the ground tempted her; she wanted, badly, to just scoop it up, collect it. But Verena trod on it unknowingly before Sophie could give in to the socially inappropriate urge.

A familiar face among the watchers made her breath hitch.

The man caught her eye and recognition jolted between them. His lips skinned back from his teeth.

*Just shoot,* Sophie thought. She angled the camera, pointing right at him. He saw the movement but didn't turn away or try to hide.

Leaving him behind, they moved on, around a rise and into the glow of molten stone, into firelight and heat. The procession gathered behind them, forming an audience on a large outcropping of porous volcanic stone.

The caldera of the volcano had a symmetrical, impossibly man-made appearance. It was almost perfectly circular, with broad skirts of igneous rock that rose fifty or so feet above the level of the lava. A notch dug into the coastal side of the mountain formed a spillway, reminiscent of the low side of a dripping candle. Super-heated stone escaped downhill from this lip, a slow-motion lava fall that terminated in a fiery pool a hundred feet below. This, in turn, flowed into the rolling hills.

A footbridge of glazed black bricks arched over the fall. The uniformed pallbearers made for it, laying the bier with Gale's body across its rails and then, but for Parrish, clearing off.

Directly across the caldera from the bridge stood an enormous marble figure of a woman, milk-white and as tall as a three-story building. She stood on the lip of the caldera, hands out in a soothing gesture, the unmistakable hush-hush pose of a mother calming a fussing child in its cradle. Blue letters in the magical alphabet—someone had called it spellscrip, hadn't they?—ran from her elbows to her fingertips. The red light of the lava reflected and shifted on her stone skin.

A distant ululating shriek reached them from the harbor, a chorus of voices raised in lament, impossibly loud.

Verena seized Sophie's arm before she could turn. "Don't look at them."

"Why? What happens now?"

Another wail.

"You and Parrish have to give Gale to the caldera."

"No speeches, no eulogy?" She'd persisted in thinking of the Erinthians as Italian in their sensibility; she had allowed for a full morning of religious ritual. Deep down, she'd been expecting the pope, or someone like him, to march over the horizon with ten cardinals and a cloud of incense to make a six-hour ceremony of it.

"That shrieking sound is a Verdanii ship. It'll be flying flags demanding we stop."

From his place beside the bier, Parrish was looking at the two of them.

"You should do this, Verena," Sophie whispered. "It's your job. Me standing here is a mistake, you know that."

"Do it, Sophie, please."

"I don't know if I can."

Verena shook her slightly. "As long as the heir—you—fulfills Gale's wishes, there's no diplomatic incident. Otherwise, the Conto is defying Verdanii."

Another high-pitched shriek.

"Please. Don't leave Parrish out there holding the bag."

*You're all about Parrish, aren't you?*

Sophie stepped out onto the bridge, facing Parrish across the body of poor Aunt Gale. She had a sudden remembrance of her, buried in that bed of rag blankets in that terrible, patched-together hut on Stele Island. Then the gritty snap—was that really just yesterday?—as the mezmer broke her neck.

*Here lies Gale, slain by monsters.* Somehow it seemed surreal and un-utterably tiring.

"Kir Hansa," Parrish said. "We must hurry."

Reluctantly she grasped the handle of the bier, mirroring his motion as he raised the head of the obsidian pane, up, up. The little offerings began to drop into the fall of lava, the miniature wheat sheaves immolat-ing in bursts of firelight. Finally, when Sophie had her arm practically levered straight up from her head, Gale's body slid off the bier, falling soundlessly into the pyroclastic flow.

She set her teeth against what sounded like a crackle.

"Return the glass, too," Parrish said, opening his hands. She did, let-ting the sheet fall, end over end, into the flow.

"Now what?"

"Walk on," he said, offering his arm. "This might be our best chance to talk before the others catch up."

"Talk about what?" Not sleeping had made her snappish.

"I wish to suggest a course of action."

"Let me guess," Sophie said. "I go home, button my lip, leave the birth family alone and never think of Stormwrack again."

"It's too late for that."

She waited.

"Erinth is, as you see, a remarkable place. There's plenty here to examine: the terrain, I mean, and the wildlife. The Conto would happily provide you with guides. If you charged me and Verena with certain responsibilities, you and Bram might explore the flora and fauna of the island at your leisure."

"Responsibilities? You mean I should turn over the investigation of Gale's death to you."

"Yes. We would also consult a lawyer about the estate and the Fleet courier commission."

She was outraged. "You think I'll get in your way."

"Lower your voice."

"You are so not the boss of me, Parrish."

"If you truly came here to examine the wildlife, why not exploit the opportunity?"

"You think I'll screw things up!"

He didn't back down. "You don't understand the culture here. You don't know Gale's history, or anything of the Fleet. Your brother doesn't speak the language—"

"Oh, Bram? Give him a week."

"You didn't care for Gale," he said, and there was more force in his voice now. "You'd just met, and she wanted nothing to do with you. Please, Kir, I'm not trying to be unkind—"

"Funny. You're doing a stunner of a job." She wasn't even sure why she was so mad. "You've known me a day and you already think I can't handle . . . You're trying to pack me off where I can't do any damage . . ."

"Yes. Step aside, study the island, feed your curiosity and let me—me and Verena, that is—"

"Will it improve Verena's legal position if I do? Will she magically get the estate back?"

His plummy lips tightened. "No, Kir."

"Then screw that. Unlike you, I actually have a clue or two. The guys who attacked Gale said *Temperance* . . ."

"An oath, I'm sure."

"I know what cursing sounds like," she said. She'd had time to think it over. "They weren't just blowing each other off. Besides, it came up several times. Tempranza, Yacoura Tempranza. It's why I retained it."

They rounded a switchback along the trail, and she saw the other mourners were indeed starting to catch up.

"And your other clue?"

She pulled her arm free. "I'm not saying."

"Excuse me?"

*Ha. Made you angry.* "Not until you agree to drop this idea of ditching me, and let me participate in the investigation."

He was practically standing at attention. "That's not up to me, Kir."

"No? Whose call is it? The Conto doesn't seem to care as long as the job gets done. Verena?"

He winced exquisitely. "No."

"Wait," she said. "You're not saying—you're saying me?"

"You. You're our employer now, Sophie." Parrish pulled in a slow, ragged breath, but when he spoke, his voice was steady. "The crew of *Nightjar* answers to you. We are bound to do whatever you say."

CHAPTER 13

The procession continued downhill, along the path of the lava, which flowed with unnatural sedateness through a plain occupied by glass-blowers and workers with kilns, all of whom took off their caps as they passed. Sophie caught a snatch of barely comprehensible Erinthian, naming the canal, referring to it as Fiumofoco . . . river of fire?

They followed it all the way to the sea, where it disappeared into the water, forming an extended curtain of rising steam that crawled out to sea, flagging the direction of the prevailing wind. They walked up the beach to the wharf, circling the eastern edge of the capital, Cindria. She estimated they'd gone about ten kilometers.

The exercise helped her unwind; she felt the fatigue less as a sharp, tense pain—jabs and edges of knives, scraping the skin—and more as an overall ache.

Formality leached out of the procession as they continued back to sea level. A few tottering children were whisked away discreetly by their parents, the families disappearing down thin alleys lined by black lava buildings. All the buildings here were made of the same porous stone, Sophie noticed, and none of them had windows looking up at the volcano. It was as if the whole of Erinth had turned its back on the looming danger on its edge.

Up and down the procession, conversations broke out. Verena and Bram caught up with her, while Parrish strode on ahead.

*All too eager to get away,* Sophie thought, watching him go.

"Why don't I go alone to explain to the Mothers that Gale's remains are gone?" Verena pointed at a tethered ship with a thoroughly bizarre shape: bulletlike, like a submarine, but with masts and sails. It seemed to have a baleen on its bow, and its sails resembled living trees—cedars, perhaps, from the look of them—clad in gossamer sail fabric.

Despite Sophie's fatigue, her curiosity stirred. She lifted her camera, and took a few seconds to capture the craft. "Would it be better to go by yourself?"

"Yeah. You don't want a bunch of furious Verdanii in your face, believe me."

Sophie imagined having to justify herself to a bunch of angry grieving women, each as impressive as the mighty Annela Gracechild . . . or as hostile as Beatrice. The thought was just about nauseating. "Can you see about untangling the inheritance thing too, with them?"

Verena looked a bit surprised. "I meant to try, yeah."

"You can be open about it, you know. I don't want it, any of Gale's . . . her stuff, her life, her job. Do whatever you have to to sort out the paperwork."

"Right, of course," she said. "Thank you, Sophie."

"I'll get the wheels rolling on investigating her death, if I can," Sophie added.

If Verena had any doubts about this, she didn't show it. "Captain, you'll take care of them?"

Parrish looked back and inclined his head gravely.

*Oh, and the seventeen-year-old reminds us both that I need a babysitter*, Sophie thought. She decided she was too tired to fight about it. There'd been a second there where she and Verena had almost been getting along.

They staggered back up to the palazzo, she and Bram, amid a dwindling crowd of courtiers. By the time they got there, they were almost leaning on each other.

"It's almost noon," he said. "I gotta pass out for a while."

"Me too." She looked at Parrish. "Nobody seems too freaked out about my camera. Why is that?"

"It's not our way to show interest in mummer objects—mechanicals," he said. "They're expensive to build, unreliable, and generally less effective than magic."

"That can't be true," Bram said.

Parrish shrugged. "It's what people believe."

*People*, Sophie thought. *Not you*. Well, Parrish had been to San Francisco; he had a better sense than most of how far technology could take a society. "Will it explode any state secrets if I show a servant a couple images?"

"Just don't say where it's from." He shook his head. "If they ask, say it's outland mummery."

"Outland mummery," she repeated, yawning.

They went back to the suite and she sent for the scribe. "Can you sketch? Or are you just a text guy?"

"I can make drawings, Kir."

She flipped on her view screen, playing through the footage of the procession, and found the image she wanted, freezing it on the screen. He watched politely. As Parrish predicted, he showed no interest in the camera itself.

"See this guy?" The scribe nodded, bending close.

"Can you make a picture of the outfit he's wearing? And another of his face?"

"Of course."

"I'm gonna lie down for an hour," she said. "Do the best you can."

She stumbled through the doors leading out of the parlor and found a private suite, swathed in silk and red velvet, as luxuriously appointed as any five-star hotel. The same plate of the bland food—mourning fare, the Conto had called it—was waiting on a low table in an alcove near the balcony. She caught a whiff of humidity and perfume, and followed her nose to a steaming bath. The servant who'd wrapped her in the long gray cloak before the burial was standing ready to remove it.

*It's as if she's been here the whole time, just waiting.* The young woman shook out the cloak, folding it with deft expertise, then reached for Sophie's shirt, seeming intent on stripping her bare.

"I'll take it from here," Sophie said.

The girl looked at her, uncomprehending.

"Done. Go 'way. *Basta? Finisco?*" So much for the language being just like Italian. She finally made a shooing motion that convinced the young woman to leave.

She eased herself into the tub, letting the hot water leach away tension, bit by bit, until she caught herself dozing off. Clean and relaxed, she stepped out and wrapped herself in a towel woven from plant fibers she couldn't identify.

The bedroom, next door, overlooked the courtyard gardens and the fountain. It had a bona-fide princess bed: four posts, heavy red drapes and curtains of a gauzy silk that made Sophie wonder, suddenly, if she and Bram ought to be worried about malaria. Were they mosquito curtains, or just decor?

A low teak table near the French doors was piled with two stacks of clothes. One stack was familiar: It was some of the stuff that had gotten scattered and bloodstained in the fight with the mezmers. Apparently someone had been able to patch them back together and clean them.

The rest looked like it was locally made. A stiff handwritten card sat atop the stack: "Replacements for your lost garments," it said, in Fleet. "Conto Secondo en Erinthia."

*This must be what being Queen of England is like,* she thought, fingering a dress that hung beside the pile, a formal gown ornate enough to be a wedding dress, and white to boot. *All your logistics handled for you, without you even asking.*

The bed was turned down. All that was missing was a chocolate on the pillow. She climbed in wearily. It was soft and just the right degree of cool. *How do they do that? More magic?*

She wondered if the annoying Captain Parrish was wallowing in similar opulence or if he'd insisted on lying in the stable, or on a bed of nails.

*Gorgeous and arrogant. So many of the people here on Erinth are gorgeous, must be magic too, he's magically prettified. It's all so odd, the sailors' uniforms like something from the Napoleonic Wars, was it Admiral Nelson or Wellington, no, Wellington was the land guy, but it's that same silly hat and the Erinthians do use some Italian words. Can't be Italian unless this is Earth, right? I wish I knew more languages . . . Bram probably does . . .*

The babble in her head continued, but the words were increasingly hard to make out, as if her own voice belonged to someone who was moving away from her, something about froglets with tails, and then she was dreaming about one, about chasing it, extending her hand to catch the froglets and finding ducklings under a leaf, ordinary ducklings from home. She reached, trying to catch soft gold feathers as it scrabbled and fled, and somebody sliced her wrist, cut off her hand and no, that was her, she was holding a severed hand. Gale's hairy, severed hand? There was so much blood and all the choking noises and that final snap, the neck breaking . . .

She woke to darkness, her mind hooked on an image that was half dream, half memory: a mezmer, with its long fingers wrapped around Parrish's throat. Its wrist was scarred, as if at some point in its life it had worn a shackle. She was momentarily convinced she could smell one of the things.

She lay still, breathing the now-stuffy air, listening until she was sure she was alone.

She got out of bed, tangled in the bed curtains as she groped for the lanterns, and ended up having to use the LED screen from her smartphone to find the matches and get the thing lit.

Still braving monsters, she circled the room, daring imaginary critters to grab her, fluffing the curtains, opening and closing the wardrobes.

Finally she drew a deep breath—in case she needed to scream—and jerked open her balcony doors.

Nothing there either. Peach light blazed over the horizon. Dawn was breaking; she'd slept the day and night through. Guards patrolled the courtyard; people bustled to and fro, carrying everything from mops to laundry to food. Sophie supposed the servants were always up well before daybreak, polishing everything and putting on breakfast.

She was staying in the palace of a Renaissance—well, Renaissance-y—royal court. A thrill of excitement went through her. "Practically time traveled," she murmured.

Leaving the balcony open, she found a space on the enormous floor and stretched, working out the kinks in her muscles left by the previous day's hike and the odd exertions of Gale's funeral. Big muscles first, slow and easy, bend and pull, contract and extend, and as her body warmed she worked her way to smaller areas: neck, ankles, hands, and feet. As she stretched, she worked on quieting her mind, focusing solely on the movements and the sensations in her body. By the time the hum of nervous energy, residue of the nightmare, had faded, she was sheened in sweat.

Maybe Bram would want a run later. Would the Erinthians mind if they jogged up the volcano trail?

*What I could really use is a swim*, she thought. *Or maybe another round with someone like Lais the promiscuous spider breeder. I wonder how he's doing?*

She took a pair of clean, pressed jeans off the table, examining them for bloodstains and finding none. Her blouses had fared worse, apparently— she'd been left with almost no shirts. There was no question of putting on the over-the-top princess gown, so she tried matching her pants with a little jacket from the Erinthians' contributions. It was crimson, with slightly puffy half-sleeves, less casual than her few surviving T-shirts but comfortable and, she hoped, not entirely ridiculous.

The sitting room was empty but for the unmistakable signs of Bram at work. He had gathered up a bunch of maps and what looked like a history of the Erinthian court, texts with familiar-looking words, Romance-language spelling. They were open and arranged in an order that would make sense to her brother; she had seen piles like this before.

Separate from the main mass of pages and books, sitting under her camera, was the pair of sketches she'd asked for—a rendering of the weird outfit, reminiscent of medical scrubs, and that face from the crowd.

What had Verena begun to say the other day? Something about the chances Annela would confiscate all her footage.

"And that's why we make backups, right?" She pulled out her smartphone, setting it to sync with the video camera's files. "That's why we maxed the credit cards."

Leaving the gadgetry to synchronize, she snagged one of the bready cakes from the food tray, along with a delicate flower that smelled like apple, carved from a fruit. She bit into the fruit, tasting carefully for any hint of bitterness, and swallowed one bite to see how it would settle.

She nibbled at the cake, expecting the dryness of day-old baked goods, sans preservatives, heck, maybe a weevil or two to add to the old-timey allure of it all. Instead, her tongue found steam, fresh-from-the-oven heat.

Frowning, she pushed the mourning fare to the edge of the tray, lifted the cloth napkin it lay on to reveal a polished hardwood tray below. Its handles were wrapped tight with a treated cord of black leather.

Inscribed to keep food fresh? But there was no spellscrip anywhere on the tray, unless it was under the cord. She tried nudging it aside and saw a glimmer of green text.

After helping herself to another of the cakes, she slipped out into the corridor of the palazzo, and turned her back on the stairway leading out to the courtyard. Framed oil paintings, most of them portraits of expensively dressed men, lined the plaster walls; wall-mounted lanterns ensured she could admire them at her leisure.

She prowled to the corner, found another window overlooking the water, and turned up a wide, circular staircase. She had just started climbing when the *click-tick* of claws on stone startled her. Whirling, she pressed her back to the wall, bringing up her hands, drawing breath to shriek—

A lapdog came bounding after her, a long-snouted smile on its tiny face. It skidded to a stop about a yard behind her and snagged a crumb she must have dropped, without knowing it, from the cake.

*Whew.*

"It's mourning fare," she told it, for no reason. It hopped up onto its hind legs and did a quick begging dance before churning past her, up the staircase. Its trunk was shorter than that of a dachshund, its coat cream-colored and silky.

The dog barked once, looking back at her with shining, shoe-button eyes.

Sophie followed it to the top of the staircase, which led, it turned out, to a rooftop garden framed by trees in pots and abundant flowers. In the middle was an elaborately carved fountain: a ship, canted upward at the bow, caught forever in the act of breaking a marble wave. Real water sprayed out over the stone, drops glistening in the dawn light.

Someone had left an overturned bucket at the edge of the fountain. The dog hopped up, raised itself to the lip of the fountain, and dropped its face into the water, drinking, tail wagging.

"I bet you think you're king of this place," Sophie told it. The dog blinked, expression serene.

The fountain was at the center of an arrangement of cane tables and chairs. Sophie sat in one and the dog was in her lap a second later.

"Murder investigations aren't that different from any other kind of science," she told it. "Gather evidence, form theories, test them. Right?"

She sat, letting the sun warm her, petting the dog and watching as songbirds darted in and out of the garden, lit in the trees, and chirped with lusty verve for the beginning of a new day.

After awhile longer, she went back downstairs to their rooms. The dog elected to abandon her almost exactly where it had picked her up, bolting down another endless corridor as fast as its short legs would carry it.

The light on her phone was blinking, indicating that it had synced successfully with the video camera. She scanned the books, finding the same protocol book they had seen at Gale's, the one with entries on Stormwrack's various nations. Bram must have set it out for her.

*Mind reader*, she thought fondly, grabbing some milky white sausages for protein before sitting down with the tome.

*Cool! The countries are arranged alphabetically, and the alphabet runs from A to . . . yep, A to Z, just as it does at home. We can add that to the list of evidence that the two worlds are connected.*

Most of the entries were illustrated, but only a few had what she was looking for: sketches of people in traditional costume. Others had ships, flags, animals, or maps of the nations' territory. She tried flipping, forcing herself to stay on task. Each page held some tantalizing fact or another; details about terrain, things about history, and a surprising amount about the animals and plants native to each island . . .

*Just look for the clothes, Sophie. Ignore the animals and all these notes on wildlife . . . oh! The natural resource base in each microclimate affects the spells they can do . . .*

The realization had a weight to it, a sense of significance. She remembered the kid from Stele Island, telling her Sylvanners liked to develop spells using other islands' resources. Then there'd been Lais, with his spidersilk—

She wondered what it would take to get a copy of this book for herself.

A tap at the door broke her train of thought. A servant appeared. "Do you need anything, Kir?"

"I think I'm okay." He moved through the room soundlessly, lighting more lanterns and then pausing as he noticed she had pulled the food off the tray.

"Perhaps some coffee, Kir, or tea? His Grace says your nation's customs don't require that you fast after a loss . . ."

"We'd love some coffee," she said, for Bram's sake. "Listen—what's your name?"

"Steward will do, Kir."

"Uh, okay. So, Steward, the outfit in this picture. Do you know it?"

He raised the scribe's sketch to the light. "It might be a worker from Isle of Gold. The clothes would be considered nondescript, for clerical work or messenger tasks perhaps. The Golden are strangely modest at times, for all that they're so wealthy."

"Are you sure?"

"No, Kir." He shrugged delicately. "There are so many nations. Ask a launderer, or the Contessa's seamstress."

"Okay. Thanks."

"I'll bring the coffee," he said, whisking away the magic food tray.

"Isle of Gold," Sophie murmured, paging through the protocol book. There were about two dozen "Illo," "Isle of," "Issle," and "Islandia" entries.

Bram emerged from his room, looking rumpled and wholly alert. "Someone mentioned my favorite alkaloid."

"Your caffeine delivery system's coming. And the steward thinks the guy who attacked Gale might be from a place called Isle of Gold."

"What are you wearing?"

"Conto gave me some stuff. It's probably polite to wear it, right?"

"It's optimal if you're hoping to look like casual Friday in *Alice in Wonderland*."

"If I wanted a lecture from Fashion Cop, I'd have brought Fashion Cop."

"I'm a first-rate multitasker."

They fell silent as the steward slipped in, bearing a silver tray that smelled of French roast.

Sophie bounded to her feet, giving her brother a hug. "Admit it—aren't you glad you came?"

"Glad you're not delusional, anyway."

"Don't be a jerk, Bramble or I'll stick my tongue in your coffee."

"You're not the boss of me, Ducks."

"Don't call me Ducks." In the normal course of things she'd flounce over to a couch now, feigning offense, and bury her nose back in the protocol book. Unfortunately, the thing weighed about as much as a desktop computer. She sat gingerly, balanced it on her knees, and resumed paging through.

"Here we go," she said. "Isle of Gold."

"What's it say?" Bram asked. He had picked up her video camera and was using it to shoot all the opened books he'd set out.

She translated: "Isle of Gold is one of five nations formerly known as the Piracy—"

"Of course. They would have pirates here."

"—A barren rock unfit for agriculture and without much of a fishery, its difficult-to-navigate coastal waters and dense military fortifications led to its becoming the treasury of a shifting alliance of thieves, smugglers, and raiders during the decades of warfare that plagued the seas. Okay, from the looks of it, a bunch of countries put together a fleet—"

"*The* Fleet, presumably."

"Yeah. Which battered the pirates into submission. Now the former bad guys have gone legit, just barely."

"So what are they doing now?"

"Since the days of the Fleet Compact, Isle of Gold has specialized in trading rare goods, spell ingredients, and . . . oh, holy crap!"

"What?" Bram paused with his cup halfway to his mouth.

"Slaves." She was scanning ahead.

"Slaves?"

"It's just dropped in there, oh by the way we have slaves, la di dah. We own people. People for sale!"

"Sofe. Don't go on a rant. It's early, and you don't know who might overhear."

"I don't give a bleeding cowflop if the Conto himself kicks us into the harbor with a steel-toed boot. Slaves, Bram!"

Oh. He had that so-very-annoying *Sophie-is-overreacting* face on, the one that filled her with the urge to slap him. "Okay, yes, it's suboptimal."

"By which you mean gross and horrifying?"

"Did you think there'd be nothing about this place that would upset you?"

"You think you can minimize this? Bram, if you're telling me you're not—"

"Of course I'm appalled, but—"

"Really? That's appalled? Because you're giving me Spock face. What if that scribe we've been bossing around is a slave?"

"He's not." That was Parrish, standing at the door with a bunch of rolled-up papers and a wicked case of hat hair. "Erinth is one of the free nations."

There was an awkward pause. Finally, Parrish added, in an oddly cautious tone: "Which of the bonded countries are you studying?"

"Sophie thinks one of the guys who attacked Gale in San Francisco might be from Isle of Gold," said Bram. He was only too happy to change the subject.

*Of course he is. Wouldn't want me to go on a rant, would we?*

There was that anger again. She was starting to recognize it: as fallout from all the fights and murder attempts.

*Breathe.* She looked over at an arrangement of dried flowers, making herself take in their physical details.

Parrish unfurled one of the sheets of paper. "The men who attacked Gale, Kir. You're sure you heard them say Yacoura *Temperanza*?"

"Repeatedly," she said, knowing her tone was frosty, knowing too she couldn't help it. "And it's Sophie, I told you."

"Isle of Gold would make sense," Parrish said: "The Piracy has a century-old honor grudge against *Temperance*."

"Why would anyone have a grudge against a ship?"

"*Temperance* has been the flagship of the Fleet since the Fleet was a half dozen ships hunting pirates in the Stringent Sea," he said. "Her master can sink any vessel simply by speaking her name. There are a few decades of history and warfare involved in the tale, but essentially it was *Temperance* who broke the Piracy. The threat she continues to represent, to anyone who—"

"Gets out of line?" Sophie snapped.

From behind Parrish's line of sight, Bram pulled a face that meant "Don't be offensive."

"If you like," Parrish said, untroubled. "*Temperance* is considered an essential component of the Cessation."

"A deterrent," Bram said. "Anyone gets combative, they can still be sunk. Anytime, any place."

"Precisely."

"So the Fleet's not all one big happy family?"

"As with your homeland," Parrish said, his diction clipped, "There is a certain amount of factionalism and squabbling."

*Oh, that's kind of sweet! He gets all formal when he's on the defensive.* Sophie shook that thought away. He wasn't sweet. He was aggravating. "You sink a ship by saying its name, and you ensorcel someone by writing their name. Names mean a lot here."

"Yes," he agreed.

She added this to her long mental list of questions about magic and things to learn about the culture. *Right on the list under OMG, why do you have slaves, what kind of people are you?*

She wrenched herself back on task. "So the pirates want to take *Temperance* out?"

"They've tried before. The last time they failed was some years ago. Gale was involved." He unfurled another of the pages he was holding, looked for a bare surface to lay it on, and ran up against Bram's mounds of open books, the scattered pages of his homegrown Fleetspeak-Anglay dictionary and a long series of notes that looked mathematical. Finally he held the page up against a wall so they could see it.

The sheet was a tight little grid of information about ships: names, nations, specifications, cargo. "There is an Isle of Gold ship here in port. *Barabash.*"

Sophie set the protocol book aside. "Why don't we go see if any of her crew's in the market?"

"That sounds suboptimal," Bram objected.

"Pardon?" Parrish said.

"Don't mind him—he talks like a computer when he's tired."

"I meant dangerous," Bram said.

"The mercato's safe enough," Parrish said. "We can take the guard the Conto offered us."

"I'm supposed to investigate Gale's murder, Bram. I can't do it all here from the penthouse suite. There's no Internet, in case you haven't noticed. I can't just hit a search engine and type in 'mezmer-making homicidal jerks currently on Erinth.'"

"Has anyone mentioned, Sofe, you're not a cop?"

"Come on, we're basically talking about going out and chatting up a couple of sailors. I'm good at that—"

"They're not sailors, they're pirates."

"Ex-pirates," she said. "From what the book said, they're semi-legit."

Bram looked at Parrish, probably wanting more reassurance that it'd be safe for her to leave the heavily guarded palace.

*Like it's up to him!* "Stay if you want," she said. "I'm going."

"Sofe . . ."

"It can't be any riskier than cave diving."

She could see Bram rolling that around in his head, hating the simple truth of it: Her entire family had been forced, years ago, to come to grips with the fact that she did risky things all the time. "Fine, go, you're right. I'm gonna keep on with . . ." He waved a hand at the books, meaning the twin quest to learn to speak Fleet and figure out where they were.

"Wasn't asking your permission," she said, barely managing to keep her voice light.

The guards more or less appeared, trailing behind her, as she made her way down to the palazzo gates, Parrish at her side.

"I don't see what geography has to do with the problem at hand," Parrish said.

"What?"

"Your brother. The atlases and sea charts."

"Bram's taken over wondering about the continental . . . irregularities, between here and home. Anyway, he's not on the hook to solve Gale's murder—I am."

"Were it my sister 'on the hook,' I would feel compelled to help."

"Him hoovering up every shiny bit of knowledge that comes our way will help, sooner or later. Besides, he's not gonna be much use until he's learned more of the language. Listen, Parrish, we're neither of us any good at denying our intellectual curiosity."

"I've noticed."

"Our parents are very big on the idea that if you have a question, you should go find the answer. I'm getting that that's uncool here, but—"

For just a moment she could see the pain of loss on his face. All he said was: "Gale was like that, too."

"Anyway, I'm glad Bram's not stuck looking into sordid, monster-making assassins."

His answering nod seemed halfhearted. She remembered that he'd offered to buy her off with a grand tour of the island, tried to convince her to go off touristing while he chased Gale's killers.

The memory made her feel self-conscious. Was she whining? "Of course," she went on, "everything here is interesting."

She was trying to be gracious after the fact, but the statement was true enough. Their route had taken them down to the market, a round piazza encircled by wooden stalls where vendors were hawking bread and meat, cloth and glass. Little kids worked the crowds, trying to interest pass-ersby in the products being sold by, she assumed, their elder relations. Others sat in the shadow of the carts, working lessons on slates while watching, apparently, for shoplifters.

A fair number of people seemed to recognize Parrish, and more than one handed him a black ribbon as he passed.

A young sailor—she thought it might have been one of the other pall-bearers, from yesterday—approached. He was a little taller than Parrish, and *Nightjar*'s uniform fit him so precisely it must have been tailored. His expression was warm and he seemed to know everyone in the market. He had bloodshot eyes and his own handful of black ribbons. "You look terrible, Garland. Haven't you slept?"

"Antonio Capodoccio, this is Kir Hansa," Parrish said gravely. "Our employer."

"Only temporarily. And call me Sophie," she corrected.

"Tonio is *Nightjar*'s first mate."

He bowed. "I am at your service, Kir Sophie."

"I'm so sorry about Gale," Sophie said.

"Grazie, Kir."

*Grazie,* she thought. That *was* Italian. "You a hometown boy, Tonio—you're from here?"

"Yes." He pointed up the hill, at one of the black buildings. "My family lives near the Cortile Beata."

"Beata . . . is that a religious reference?" Erinth didn't seem to have much in the way of churches, just the volcano and its guardian statue.

"It means Court of the Beautified," Parrish translated, absently. "It's the cosmetic inscription quarter."

*Is that where your looks came from?* she wondered, but did not ask. It didn't matter, and it wasn't any of her business. It was way off point. Even so, her mind niggled at it: He was bossy, but didn't seem vain. But he had to be vain to have had his face made for him, didn't he?

*Is there any point in thinking about Captain Tasty? Come on, Sofe, ex-plore the mercato.* The men dropped a few paces behind her as she fell into observation mode, once again shooting video from her hip. The gabble of voices, most speaking languages she didn't know, formed a wall of white noise: Her thoughts clarified as she looked around.

*Court of the Beautified*, she thought. All these conspicuously beautiful people here. And many of them seemed sick; they had coughs and canes, or moved as if they hurt. She saw one such beauty, raven-haired, with glossy skin and bright flashing eyes, scolding a man twice her age. He was nodding and bearing it, as if she was his employer or, no, maybe . . .

*His mom*, she guessed. *The cosmetic magic makes them seem younger than they are, but it doesn't make them young. She could be his grand-mother.*

It seemed a testable theory: closing her eyes, she primed her ears for sounds like Ma, Mamma, Nonna.

She was listening to the gabble of the market so intently she didn't notice, for a second, when someone spoke to her.

". . . Kir Feliachild's heir?"

Sophie opened her eyes. One of the men who had attacked Gale, back in San Francisco—the one she'd filmed yesterday on the funeral procession, was standing beside her.

*Okay*, she thought, as her heart went into overdrive. *It's all perfectly okay.* Parrish and Tonio were steps away, the Conto's guards were discreetly browsing nearby and she could see the man's hands. *You just told Bram you do risky things all the time.*

*Yeah, Sofe*, his voice seemed to reply. *You understand those risks. Drowning, hypoxia, hypothermia, falling—*

The concept was the same. Clear your mind, focus on what's happening now, think before you act. Diving mode. She turned slightly, putting the corner of the merchant booth—a table laden with shells, corals, and sponges—between herself and the stranger.

"Who are you?"

"I have the honor to be called John Coine," he said. "And you, Kir?"

"Sophie Hansa. What do you want?" she said.

"The same thing we wanted from your aunt," he said. "Yacoura *Tempranza.*"

"The Heart of *Temperance*?" She tipped her camera up—her hand was sweating—but if he saw her do it, or cared, he didn't react. Why would he? He didn't know what it was.

"That's right, the lost Heart."

"Kir Coine," she said, since that seemed to be the catch-all polite address here. "I can probably get you arrested right here and now for attacking Gale."

"You can prove I sent mezmers after Kir Feliachild?"

"I saw you attack her at home, remember?" she said.

"Ah, so you're the unarmed, screaming fury who set on us in the outlands." He looked her up and down, assessing.

*I was screaming?*

"That's pretty much an admission of guilt right there." Could it be this easy? All she needed now was a cop.

He seemed amused. "You might make a go of an accusation, I suppose."

"More of a go than you'll make out of bullying me for something I don't have."

"I'm sure if you exert yourself, you'll discover how your aunt mislaid the heart, all those years ago. You have the same bright eyes as she."

"My shiny eyes aside, what makes you think I'd share anything I learned?"

His lips were a dead pink gray, like earthworms, and when he smiled there was nothing of warmth in the expression. "Kir Feliachild was a dry, determined rope of a woman, knotted tight around the Fleet Compact and with nothing else to care for. Your grip's not as tight, is it?"

She felt an absurd sting of hurt—even this creep of a pirate thought she was some kind of powderpuff, a pushover. "What does that even mean? I'm not rope?"

"Sponge, rather." He picked one off the cart, contemplating it. "You can always wring something out of a sponge, if you squeeze."

"You couldn't squeeze me for the way to the bathroom if you had to puke," she said. "I'm not helping you with anything. I can't even believe I'm sitting here chatting with you about—look, you and your stupid games and intrigues, I don't care. You're a murderer."

She began to move, thinking to summon Parrish and the guards, even as she kept one eye on the man and her camera between them.

"Opal," Coine said. "Your middle name is Opal, is it not?"

"So?" But her flesh crawled, just a bit. *They need the whole name to scrip you. Does that mean they can magic me up any which way they want?*

"I expect whoever created those mezmers used slaves, or convicts," he said, affecting carelessness. "But perhaps not."

"What you did to those people was sick." Saying it brought back the memory of the blade, of herself slicing through the monster's shackle-scarred wrist.

"My people believe room remains in this supposedly tame world for wilder things. For blood debts and vengeance," the man said.

"And grenades?"

"I admit nothing, but you should consider: Perhaps those mezmers angered whoever inscribed them. There's a fate to be feared, wouldn't you agree?"

She glared at him. "Where did you get my name?"

"The sea offers up many forms of bounty."

*Lais Dariach knew my middle name*, she thought. *And some of the people from the salvage ship, the* Estrel. *Captain Dracy. They saw the shell.*

"If you've hurt someone else—"

He interrupted: "As you're from the outlands, girl, perhaps you haven't realized how many terrible intentions I might lay upon you. Do you want to find out?"

He tore the sponge in half, threw the vendor a coin, and sauntered away into the crowd. Sophie pushed after him, keeping him in sight, tracking him with the camera. He seemed unaware of her pursuit, or indifferent to it. She caught a shot of him at the edge of the market, and then . . .

*That guy!* Coine was moving toward his partner in crime, the guy whose face she'd smashed with the camera case, all those days ago in Beatrice's San Francisco neighborhood. His nose still bore the remains of a bruise.

Coine's eyes met those of the other man, and he shook his head slightly. They veered from each other, taking different directions into the crowd.

*Interesting*, she thought, zooming in on the second man. *They don't want me to see them together.*

"Sophie?" Parrish, suddenly, was right beside her.

"What's wrong with you? Didn't you see me chatting with the pirate? And look, his friend there? The one slipping off into the crowd? The two of them are the pirates, Goldens, whatever you call them, who stabbed Gale in San Francisco."

"Are you certain?"

"Oh! I am going to start pulling your hair every time you ask me that. Look at his nose—I did that."

"The gentleman slinking off toward the docks?" Tonio said. "He's not from Isle of Gold."

"No?" Parrish asked, surprised.

"No, Kirs. He's with the Ualtar Diplomatic Mission."

CHAPTER 14

"What's Ualtar?" Sophie said. Parrish, at the same moment, asked Tonio, "Are you sure?"

"Of course." Tonio chose to answer his captain. "He was trailing the Low Priest of the Embassy like a kicked dog just yesterday, both of them wearing that put-upon look they get in free nations, when they have to carry their own possessions and wipe their own asses. I remember the bruise on his face. Your work, Kir Hansa? Good for you!"

"Call me Sophie," she said. "I hit him with a shockproof, waterproof camera case."

He broke out a dazzling smile. "I wish I'd seen that. Sophie."

Tonio hadn't struck her as the bloodthirsty type. She was about to ask about Ualtar again when shouts rose around a beribboned ring at the heart of the mercato.

"Speaking of fisticuffs . . ." Parrish turned.

"Is it Verena?" Tonio said, shading his eyes against the sun.

Was it? Sophie squinted into the whirl of activity. "Holy—she's fighting?"

Parrish, to her surprise, brightened. It was the first time he'd looked anything but miserable or offended since Gale died. "Come on."

They pushed closer, sidestepping through an increasingly dense crowd of onlookers.

As soon as they arrived it became apparent the . . . fight? . . . duel? . . . was a friendly one. Verena's teeth were set in a fierce half smile. The sword she was wielding—against a wiry, unarmed man who had spellscrip lettering branded into both of his arms—was made of wood.

"The usual wager?" Tonio said, and Parrish shook his hand. Neither man looked away from the ring.

Sophie steadied her back against a heavy-looking light sconce, centering the ring in the video camera's frame.

She was just in time: The whippy guy brought his hands together and suddenly he was covered in a flowing coat of sparks.

The mezmers who killed Gale had been a mishmash of bestial traits in scabby, thistle-barbed rags. *Dirty,* Sophie thought, remembering the slime, grit, and unclean gunk in their eyes. They'd seemed foul, wrong. This man had no such aura. He was an ordinary-looking fellow, clad in fiery motes that emerged from those spellscrip brands on his arms. Crackling and popping, the motes launched themselves at Verena, who parried them with the wooden sword. One got past her guard and she dodged, stomping it as it hit the mat. Another she simply blew out.

She wheeled past the corner of the ring, snatching up a dripping rag hung on its corner post.

"They're old rivals," Parrish explained. "Many nations run a dueling league—for sport, primarily, though the best of them sometimes go to the law. It's something of a practice for visiting fighters to spar with the local champion. Verena's been trying to defeat Incindio since she was thirteen."

"Unsuccessfully," Tonio put in.

"It's only a matter of time," Parrish said.

"You say," Tonio said, "but tonight you're buying my wine, Garland."

"Hands off my purse; she hasn't lost yet."

Verena feinted with her toy sword and then brought the rag around with a slap; there was a hiss of steam and the sparks along the duelist's right forearm and hand were snuffed out. The crowd roared its approval as the rag burst into flame.

Shaking the burning shreds aside, Incindio tucked the right arm behind his back and continued circling.

"Point for Verena," said Parrish.

"She has been practicing," Tonio conceded.

"She's grown a little, too. Longer reach."

"What is she now, seventeen?"

*She wanted to duel me,* Sophie thought uneasily. There was no chance she'd last more than seconds in a ring like this. *Would I get to pick the weapon? Shockproof camera cases at fifty paces?*

Dueling, slaves. Stormwrack's landscapes were so vibrant, she thought.

She could lose herself in them, just sink into finding and filming the flora and fauna forever. But there was something about the people . . . Would one call them uncivilized?

The judgment sat uncomfortably; it was culture shock and ethnocentrism, she knew, that sense that always came to a traveler at some point, the idea that home was better. There was plenty wrong in the good old U.S. of A., she reminded herself, lots of violence, plenty of people making bad money for hard work. Shootouts and meth labs and all the modern ills. A couple people with swords and magical sparks could only hurt each other; contrast that with someone letting loose with a machine gun in a crowd.

*Don't get on your high horse, Sofe.* That was what Bram would probably say.

Okay, fair enough. She would do her best to observe and not judge.

With another shower of sparks, Incindio leapt to the upper rope of the fighting ring, flipping up and out of range of the sword, bouncing on the rope as if it were a trampoline, and cartwheeling in midair. Verena took the opportunity to lunge after another wet rag, but she misguessed her opponent's direction; he came down behind her, kicking her ankle out from under her.

There was a *whoosh* as flames ran up Verena's leg. She rolled out of Incindio's reach, apparently unburned, coming up on the other leg. Hopping, clutching the rag, she swept her sword out defensively before he could follow up his advantage.

"She's not hurt?"

"In a fight like this, if you're tagged you must approximate the injury. It's an honor system."

"Care to double?" Tonio said, with extravagantly pantomimed carelessness. Parrish laughed, a gleeful, boyish trill, infectious and surprising from someone so sober, and nodded.

The two combatants seemed more in earnest now. Incindio lashed out with the left arm; Verena, still hopping, managed to parry. She had the wet rag balled like a softball, ready to fly. A fierce, concentrated expression, like happiness, like Bram on the hunt for the answer to a puzzle, suffused her face.

"Look, Kir! She's drawn out the Conto's nephew," Tonio murmured. "He loves a good fight."

Leaving her camera fixed on the ring, Sophie followed his gaze. The boy watching the mock duel from across the piazza was maybe eighteen, with curly auburn hair and a face right out of a Dante Gabriel Rosetti painting—big eyes, expressive mouth, skin smooth as soap. He was surrounded by a bevy of expensively dressed teens who were chattering and exchanging coins—bets, Sophie guessed—but he was rapt, entirely absorbed in the blow-by-blow between Verena and the flaming man.

"A true sports fan," she mumbled, taking a second to pan the group, getting everyone in the entourage.

"What is that object, Kir?" Tonio asked as she returned her attention to the fight. Verena seemed to be tiring.

Before Sophie could frame a reply Parrish interrupted. "Erstwhile mummery."

"Ah, like Kir Gale's phono?" His curiosity vanished.

She found herself nettled by the exchange, as if Parrish had said, "Quaint garbage from the Nation of Stupid."

Verena ducked under a blow, dropping to her knees and then doing an odd martial-arts pivot from that position, to escape another. She slashed her sword across Incindio's face and, as he recoiled, threw the rag at his heart—and the cluster of sparks gathered there—as hard as she could.

It seemed an impossible move to counter, but the flame man threw himself back against the ropes, catching the rag left-handed. As his arm smoked and guttered out, he blew a stream of flames at Verena. She couldn't bring her sword back around in time to keep them from enveloping her head.

Bowing, Verena threw the wooden sword straight upward. The sparks followed, bursting into full-blown flames and immolating it as it whirled in midair. The crowd bellowed and cheered.

"Well fought!" Tonio bellowed, applauding madly. "Brava, brava!"

"She did lose, right?" Sophie said.

"Barely," Parrish said. "She's catching up with Incindio."

If Verena was disappointed by this result, it didn't show. The sparks on her leg and around her head winked out, but for a crown of winking motes in her hair. Her opponent, an ordinary-looking man again, drenched in sweat and soot, offered her a hand up and then pulled her into a hug.

"That was amazing," Sophie said, as her half sister joined them.

Verena acknowledged this with a nod, but she was waiting for Parrish's reaction.

"It was close," he said, voice warm. "I'd say you're about evenly matched now."

She colored, seeming pleased. "'Cindio said that too, but he's such a flatterer."

"How'd it go with the Verdanii?" Sophie asked.

"Sorting the inheritance is on hold until we find out something about Gale's death. And, you know, I've been asking around and I'm not sure I think the Conto's nephew was involved, anymore. I wasn't expecting the whole island to go into mourning . . ."

"Kir Gale was beloved here," Tonio said.

"Yeah. So I'm thinking . . ." She dropped a short bow in the direction of the pre-Raphaelite prince, who acknowledged it with a mere flutter of his long lashes. "Terzo's too canny to risk being vilified for getting rid of her. It's bad politics."

"We may have another line of inquiry," Parrish said, turning to Sophie. "You are sure . . . I apologize. What I meant to say was—you say the Ualtarite we saw was involved in the attack against Gale?"

"I'm good with faces," Sophie said. "Especially the only one I've ever bashed in. Anyway, his pirate friend, John Coine, said they wanted the item we talked about before . . . Heart of *Temperance*? Yacoura?"

"The Heart is lost," said Verena and Tonio, almost at once, almost in the same tone.

Parrish seemed to ignore this. "Was Convenor Gracechild on the ship from Verdanii, Verena?"

Verena shook her head. "They knew the Conto would give Gale to the Fiumofoco. I'd say Annela sent a small, slow ship on purpose. The family saved face by showing up, but managed to let Gale have what she wanted. I have a formal protest to deliver. It's kind of perfunctory."

"Then they don't mind that the Conto cremated her," Parrish said, with obvious relief.

"Tell me about it. All we need is Erinth and the Allmother at each other's throats."

*She's feeling a little better,* Sophie thought.

"You're saying the men who attacked Gale near Mom's were from Ualtar?" Verena said.

"Tonio says the guy I recognized is from their embassy," Sophie said.

"That makes no sense," Verena said. "What would the Temple of Ualtar want with defanging *Temperance*?"

"Can we go and find out?" Sophie asked.

"Go where? To the embassy?"

"Well . . . or to Ualtar, I guess."

"We could do that, if you wished," Parrish said.

He was obeying her, because she was the boss. "I'm asking if it's a good idea."

"I can't help thinking we may have learned all we can here," Parrish said. He was, tacitly, addressing Verena. "The Conto will assess whether there is, in fact, any connection between his nephew and the murder. It's in his best interest."

"And he loved Gale," Tonio put in.

"Yes. We can rely on him to send us a message if he learns of any link."

"I bet there isn't anything to learn. Terzo conniving with a bunch of clerics . . . doesn't seem right," said Verena.

"No. Then again, the Isle of Gold, working with Ualtarites . . ." That uneasiness Sophie had noticed before seemed to surface. "It's almost fantastical."

"John Coine didn't want me to see them together," Sophie said. "And he all but bragged about attacking Gale back home. I have video you can look at."

"This hints at a bigger plot."

"You'll have to explain the politics to me and Bram. If we did leave, how long would it take us to get to . . . Ualtar?"

"Six days if winds are fair," Parrish said. "They're quite a closemouthed culture—they don't like outsiders. It will be hard to learn anything from them."

"Especially if we're there on official business," Tonio put in.

"Are they good neighbors?" Sophie asked.

"Pardon?"

"Is there anyone nearby who might know what they're up to? Someone who might gossip?"

The captain looked at her with more respect. "We could visit a few of the nearby islands, I suppose."

"Sumpter," Tonio said. "Or Tiladene."

"I know a guy from Tiladene," Sophie said. The memory of Lais, their brief affair on *Estrel*, and his spider-breeding project, brought a smile to her face.

"Lucky you," said Tonio.

He sounded sincere; she grinned, even more certain that she liked him.

Restlessness caught her, like wind lifting a kite. The prospect of going, rather than sitting, awakened a hunger within her. "Bram should be in on this discussion," she said. "Let's go up, deliver Verena's protest from the Verdanii, and tighten up the plan. How soon could we sail out, hypothetically?"

Parrish looked to Tonio. "We've restocked?"

"Job's half done. The rest of the provisions are loading this afternoon."

"Then we'll go after sunset." Parrish looked to Tonio. "Ready the ship, but be discreet. Leave up the mourning sails until the last minute; there's no sense in announcing our departure."

"Done, Kir. Don't forget to send my mother that cask of wine." With one of those tight Erinthian bows, Tonio strode off.

Verena blushed. "You've got to stop betting on me, Parrish," she said, but she seemed pleased.

They hiked up through the market, Verena accepting shouted, good-natured congratulations on her honorable loss to Incindio, Parrish apparently deep in thought. Sophie paused at one stall in the market; the vendor was selling plated, fused shells, much like tortoiseshell but with a deeper arch to them; their shape was almost as curvy as Parrish's bicorne captain's hat.

*Hump-backed turtles*, she thought, imagining the creature they must have come from. The shells had been converted to baskets and filled with an arrangement of dried flowers and beetle carapaces, a macabre display of dried biological samples.

"Get it," Parrish advised. "The price is reasonable, and buying things earns you goodwill with the people."

"She won't be needing goodwill," Verena said, her own evaporating. "Her position here is temporary, remember?"

"I don't have any money," Sophie said, attempting to defuse the sudden spark of resentment.

"*Nightjar* does." Parrish gestured and the vendor handed some over.

That put paid to any conversation until they were up in their rooms again.

*Dear Miss Manners,* Sophie thought. *The obnoxious but cute boy my half sister likes just bought me a tortoiseshell full of dead flowers. Now she's all hosed at me. What do I do?*

Their suite at the palazzo was crammed to bursting with open books. Bram had opened a library's worth on the floors of every room, and was scrawling notes on the terrain, maps, histories, and a few carved reliefs. He was going over it all with the exhausted scribe, the two communicating in a mishmash of romance language words and broken Fleetspeak.

"Bram," Sophie said. "Let the guy catch some sleep, okay? We need to talk."

He peered up at her, as if from a distance.

"Come on, come back to the here and now," she said, briskly, clearing the books from the couches.

"That's just it," he said. "We don't really know where here and now are."

"I know—cool, huh? Make any progress?"

"Grigo found me an ancient, end-of-the-world myth that reads a bit like Noah's ark." He unfolded himself from the floor, where he'd been sitting cross-legged among the papers. "Here, let me. It'll make it easier when I pick this up later. How about you? Catch your murderer, by any chance?"

"On video, no less," she said.

"Seriously?"

By now they'd made a hole big enough for them all to cram together on the couch. She pulled up a small table, propped up the video camera atop the stack of books so that its little screen was resting dead center, and sat in front of it, working its controls. Bram plopped down on her left. Verena perched on the armrest, near Bram. After a moment, Parrish took the only remaining spot, next to Sophie.

"Okay, look." She brought up the video of her conversation with the pirate, John Coine, and cranked up the audio. She'd forgotten about the threat he'd made, until the little tinny speaker played his words again: "Your name is Sophie Opal Hansa, is it not?"

Both Parrish and Verena straightened in their seats at that.

Bram hit PAUSE. "What's the deal?"

"They can enchant her, if they want," Verena said.

"They'll turn her into one of those things?" Bram demanded. "Mezmers?"

"Unlikely. He obviously wants Sophie to find the Heart," Parrish said. "Coine is trying to frighten her."

Sophie started the file playing again. "How can he be so upfront about it?"

"Golden tradition. You show yourself to your enemies before you clash, if you can."

*Enemies.* She didn't like the sound of that. "He's practically bragging about killing Gale."

"He didn't know you had captured his words. But if it came to a trial, his defense would probably be justification. Isle of Gold has always claimed the right to pursue the Heart," Parrish said. "It's the involvement of the other gentleman that concerns me."

"Other guy?" Bram said.

"Just watch," Sophie said. On the little screen, Coine was sauntering away. He spotted the broken-nosed Ualtarite heading his way, and waved him off. The man peered in Sophie's direction, seeming not to recognize her as she zoomed in, bringing his face closer.

"Could Tonio be wrong about his being Ualtarite?" Verena asked.

"Doubtful. Tonio's feelings about Ualtar are . . ." Parrish ran aground there. "I don't know the Anglay word."

"Tonio really dislikes Ualtarites," Sophie said. "That much was screamingly apparent."

"How could Coine have learned your middle name? Who knew it?" Verena asked. "Here on Stormwrack, I mean."

"Just the guy who did the inscription that taught me Fleetspeak, and a few people from the crew of that salvage ship, *Estrel.* Lais from Tiladene saw the conch shell, too."

Verena and Parrish exchanged a look.

"Yes, I was careless," said Sophie. "How was I to know it mattered?"

"It's obviously a big deal, Sofe," Bram said.

"And believe me, I have added it to the long list of things to be freaked out over. So, Parrish, if we were gonna ship out of here tonight and check out Ualtar, what would we need to do to get going?"

"The palazzo staff have most of the actual packing in hand." Parrish looked at one of the guards who'd been quietly attending them all day, and switched back to Fleetspeak. "Would you ask the Conto to make inquiries after Lais Dariach and after the salvage ship *Estrel*, Captain name of . . . Sophie?"

"Her name's Dracy," Sophie said. "Do you think something's happened to them?"

"I couldn't speculate." He looked at the guard.

"It will be done, Kir, of course."

"The Conto can send whatever he learns to us."

"You do! You think someone on *Estrel* told them my name."

He nodded.

She swallowed, fighting a rush of emotion: anxiety, guilt, and fear.

"If we're going, I better deliver that protest," Verena said, springing up so suddenly the servant had to rush to open the door for her.

"Hand me that protocol book again," Sophie said. Bram opened it across both their laps, and she paged to the end, looking for Ualtar, reading aloud. "The brotherhood of Ualtar believes in a doctrine it calls Perfectibility of Man: believes everyone must rise to an ever-increasing state of grace, and that those who fail to strive are inferior. I bet that means they mistreat their livestock and keep slaves."

"Yes." Parrish bent close to her, and she caught a whiff of soap and something like cloves. He ran his finger down, past the text to a column of statistics: land area, the name of the ship that represented them within the Fleet, and finally down to an entry marked "Economy." It was followed by a "(B)."

"B for bonded," he explained. "The free nations are indicated with an F."

"F for free. Very discreet. F or B, no discussion?"

"It is a sensitive subject," he said. "The people who compiled this particular volume wished it to be complete. For that they required cooperation from all the nations. I can find you any number of treatises that discuss and condemn the practice of bondage, and an equal number that praise it to the skies."

"How many countries of each side?" Bram's grammar was off, his accent was terrible, but he had followed the conversation—they'd slipped into Fleetspeak when she was reading it off the page—and replied in kind. Parrish looked frankly amazed.

*Ah, yes, behold the wunderkid,* Sophie thought.

"Over half of the nations are free," he said. "Ualtar is unique among the bonded nations in that their perfectibility doctrine allows for the possibility that a person may not only rise from bondage to freedom but that, if one performs the correct rites, they may become a full citizen."

"So that makes them odd one out among the slaveholders?"

"To some extent, yes. They are regarded as unpredictable, or unreliable, perhaps. Ualtar has always done exactly as it pleased," Parrish said. "They have never—there have been attempts, during the past century, to break the Charter and return the nations to a state of war. The Temple has never been involved, so far as I know. They have an unnecessarily large navy, but even so they're considered a lesser nation."

"Did you get that?" Sophie asked.

"About half," Bram said.

She repeated the main points, dragging the conversation back into English. Then she returned her attention to the book. "Didn't Gale have a copy of this back at her apartment?"

"She did," Parrish said. "I can have it sent to *Nightjar* if you like."

"It'd help." *Maybe we can scan the whole thing,* she thought. "So . . . in the meantime, all this inheritance mess sort of happened because I blundered around helping people on Stele Island and *Estrel.* What can I do to not make it worse?"

He gave her a small, approving smile. "It would be better if Verena was seen to be in charge aboard *Nightjar.* If she had Gale's cabin, for example, and you and Bram were guests."

"Of course I'm not taking the master bedroom!"

"That said, we are honor-bound to take orders from you."

"I'll keep my bossiness discreet."

"Ha," Bram said.

She gave his ankle a halfhearted kick, looking down at the book again: "Ualtar lies in the southwest equatorial region, and some of its economy rests on exports of sugarcane and banana. The island also enjoys a monopoly on the silk strands used in inscriptions for ship rigging."

"This would be why they can do as they please. The spidersilk monopoly—" Parrish was interrupted by Verena's return.

"Okay, protest's delivered, Conto's briefed, the servants will be sent after dark to pack us up. He asked about the stuff at Gale's apartment, Parrish—what should happen there?"

"I think perhaps *all* of Gale's books should be sent to *Nightjar,*" he said, looking at the progress Bram had made through the royal library. "As for the rest . . . perhaps it could go to the glaziers' widows and widowers? Gale wanted you to have her Dotty Aunt coat, and the jewelry, so that's aboard ship already."

Verena's cheeks blotched suddenly. Redzone, Bram called it—the mottling of the face that meant tears were close. *Poor kid,* Sophie thought, and amazement bloomed within her. This was her sister: They were related, they had the same DNA. She herself went redzone, just like this.

They looked at each other for a second, Parrish and Verena, practically radiating grief.

"Okay," was all Verena said.

Waiting to go and not having anything to do to help with the preparations was going to make her restless. Sophie made herself run through one of her meditation exercises again, and then, when she felt calmer, sat down with one of the natural history books and started flipping.

## CHAPTER 15

By nightfall they were packed up and gathered on the dock, waiting to meet the rowboat that would take them to the ship. Some of the men and women at the oars looked familiar to Sophie; after a moment, she realized two of them had been pallbearers for Gale.

They rowed out across the acrid-smelling water of the Erinthian bay to *Nightjar.*

She was a small cutter, maybe seventy feet long, built for speed and maneuverability—to run, Sophie thought, but not so much to fight. Her crew complement was twenty-five. Sophie was half expecting them to pipe Parrish aboard, but this wasn't the Royal Navy, despite all the Age of Sail flourishes. Instead, Tonio met them on deck with a friendly "Welcome!" in Fleetspeak. The crew was packing away the black bunting and untying the sails.

"I've put Verena's things in Gale's cabin," Parrish said. "You and Bram are aft, with the books."

"Thanks," she said. "The point here is to find out enough to get a report on Gale's murder off to—off to the Fleet?"

"The Fleet Watch, yes, and Convenor Gracechild of Verdanii."

"And then to get Verena officially made boss of you all so the magic purse can change hands?"

"Yes."

"None of which is going to happen until we get somewhere where we can play detective, am I right?"

"It should be about a six-day sail."

"Perfect." That would give her time to catch her breath, and just look around while Bram learned more of the language and sifted through books.

She pulled out the camera and took a last look at the Erinthian capital.

The outlines of its black stone buildings were barely visible against the bulk of the mountain, but their windows glowed with faint lamplight, as did the lights marking out the mercato. The palazzo itself was the brightest object in the cityscape, but even it seemed a dim mote compared to the firelight coming from the mountain above, the red glow of the volcano and the stitch of red-hot lava, the fiery canal crisscrossing its way down to the sea in a series of regular, man-made switchbacks.

"Can we see our route?" she asked, once she'd taken the shot.

With a nod, Parrish took her to view the charts.

"We'll sail southwest across the Sea of Bounty," he said, drawing a line down across one of the unfamiliar clusters of islands. "Ualtar and Tiladene are in the southern hemisphere, here and here. It's a bit of a haul, but the winds should be favorable."

The next three days were as close as it got to Heaven.

Erinth had seemed so very Mediterranean that Sophie couldn't shake the idea that this was, somehow, a bearing for Africa. Despite the charts showing vast, un-Mediterranean distances and not the slightest hint of Crete—let alone Turkey or the North African coast—she kept expecting something along those lines to heave up, olive groves and all, shining like a mirage on the horizon.

At sea, they might as well have been on Earth; everything might be normal.

Normal, that was, you looked across the deck and saw miles of rope, sand-brown twists the width of a baby's arm, neatly bound to spars and hooks, coiled on the deck, old-fashioned sinews that held the ship upright against the wind. Normal, until they encountered a pod, thousands strong, of what she dubbed warm-water narwal—slender, pinkish, unicorn-horned mammals, with long fanning rear flukes that earned them their Fleet name: fairyfen. The ship slid past a minor island nation, Bristlemere, where men and women in longish black kilts were said to live as a tribe in a single city dug under the ground. The surface had been given over almost entirely to the ordinary-looking black sheep who grazed its slopes.

Sophie saw a dozen birds she recognized, another ten who yielded up their identities to the reference books she'd loaded into her smartphone before she left, and ten possible new species. Of the ten, she got six on video.

She hung out on deck by day, watching, photographing everything she could, examining her dried bouquet of plants and bugs, and helping Bram with his Fleetspeak. She managed to unpack her new solar battery charger without scattering too many polystyrene packing peas around her cabin—it would be criminal to leave litter in this apparently pristine ecosystem—and juiced up all of their rechargeable hardware. She backed up the videos she'd shot so far to the phone, setting up a folder that would automatically sync with her online data storage accounts whenever she made it home.

"Data loss happens," Bram said one afternoon as she configured the folders, quoting something he and his friends liked to call Robson's Law.

"Not if we can help it," she murmured, keeping her voice low.

She left the gadgets in their cabin, transferring images, and led him up to the foredeck. Verena was there, drilling with her sword. She practiced daily, alone or with Parrish, sometimes for hours.

"I wonder if there's one in every port," Bram said.

"One what?"

"Some fighter she has a thing with. A duelist."

Verena chose that moment to stab a target dummy with especial ferocity.

"She's trying to impress Captain Tasty," Sophie said, keeping her voice careless. She didn't want Bram to think too deeply about Verena and her swordplay.

"Yes, she's got it bad." He'd brought Gale's index of nations with him; he was combing for new vocabulary, finding words he didn't know and asking for translations. "Poor kid; I don't think he's into her, do you?"

"No?" Sophie shrugged and waited for the conversation to move on. She had a page before her too—it was crammed with questions, mysteries about Stormwrack and ideas for investigating them.

"Too young for him, maybe. She's, what . . . seven years younger than you? And Parrish has probably known her since the cradle."

"You're probably right."

She didn't stir from Bram's side for over an hour, sat there patiently translating and helping him look through the atlases for anything that might serve as a landmark—Mount Everest, Baffin Island, what have you—until there was no chance he'd follow that thought about Verena back to the same place she had. Then she sought out Parrish.

He'd put away the dress uniform as soon as they'd set sail, packing the silly bicorne hat and silver-trimmed frock coat, changing to a pair of brown breeches and a plain white shirt. None of the crew wore insignia or any sign of rank; a few, Tonio included, had pinned black rags to their belts—but Parrish wore no such overt signs of mourning. The loss was nevertheless palpable. There was no concrete sign Sophie could point to, but grief blanketed him like freshly fallen snow.

"I'm wondering something," she said.

He waited.

"Just before Gale was killed, Verena said she wanted to duel me."

"I remember," he said.

"Gale said no. She said I was broke and that someone would give me a . . . dueling proxy?"

"That was the gist," Parrish agreed. His demeanor was, suddenly, extremely cautious. *Walking on eggshells,* Sophie thought. *No, talking on eggshells.*

"Who would do that? Give me a proxy, I mean?"

"The Fleet's various nations . . . they squabble, quite a bit," he said, "It's the price of the Cessation, or so Gale liked to say."

"Yeah, and?"

"Our court system is therefore overburdened. Trials are a cumbersome process. If Verena were to have to sue you for her inheritance—"

"Which she won't."

"—it might take a decade, even more, for the two of you to come to resolution."

"Effectively leaving me in possession of everything," she said.

"Yes. And so, for anyone wishing to expedite the settlement of a dispute, there is the Dueling Court. Either party to a case may challenge the other. If the other refuses—"

"The case is lost?"

"Conceded." A sound in the sails, burr of wind changing direction, caused him to raise his head and examine the rigging minutely. "This is unfair, obviously, if the opponents are grossly unmatched. So when a challenge is issued, the Adjudicator's office evaluates whether it is appropriate to appoint a proxy."

"So then it's a fair fight?"

"No. It's very rare for anyone to beat an Adjudicator."

"Appointing a proxy, or deciding not to appoint one, is basically picking the winner?"

He nodded.

"So the whole thing's another deterrent? Like threatening to sink pirate ships with *Temperance*?"

"That's right. One doesn't issue a challenge unless they are very much in earnest."

"A court system based on threat and bluff, and who blinks first," she said. "Very theatrical."

"I've come to think much of what we call government is a form of performance." He examined the surface of the sea with an intensity that reminded her of a cat. The wind had gotten brisker: It was stirring up jagged little waves, dark blue in color, and the air was cooler.

Sophie scanned the horizon: What was he looking for? There—a flash of paper-bag brown. "Is that a person?"

"Where?"

She pointed as it appeared again, an enormous arm, rising and falling in a swimming motion, a front crawl. As she squinted, she could make out more: the back of a neck, a head, a churn of something kicking, far back where feet should be.

"I don't believe it." Parrish lit up. "You've spotted the ginger giant."

He snapped out his spyglass, took a look, and handed it over. "It can be tricky to focus it—"

She looked. Brought closer, the figure did have a ginger-root exterior: it was a human-shaped collection of lumps, as crude as a child's clay construct. Its eyes were black spots set into gouges, its mouth a mere seam. The knobs of its fingers budded from the potato-shaped expanses of its hands. It was swimming northward, crawling through the sea at a steady pace. White dots—seabirds?—rode its shoulders and head.

She handed the glass back so he could look again. They were standing right beside each other; she felt a thrill of something primal, at the nearness of him.

*Forget your hormones—you're looking at a giant!* "That is so cool. Any idea how big it is?"

"Tall as ten adults, if the stories are true," Parrish said.

"Could something like that evolve?"

"No, he's scripped."

"A made thing, like the mezmers and that duelist, Incindio?"

"Yes. It's supposed to be good luck to spot him," Parrish added.

The ginger giant paused in midstroke, turning in the water, treading. It turned to face *Nightjar,* seeming to look straight into the spyglass. The huge mouth opened, revealing a nest of fibrous golden strands. It gulped air and then sank below the waves, sending its escort of white birds shooting skyward.

"Stories also have it that he's shy," Parrish said.

"Big ol' giant, just swimming the high seas." She found herself bouncing, and he was beaming, just as delighted as she. Despite wanting to hug him, she made herself take a step back. "Help, we got giants! This damn ocean is lousy with giants!"

Parrish let out a peal of laughter. "Remember that heron-giant?" He'd half turned, speaking as if to someone standing just at his right. "Was it—"

Then he checked himself; the smile vanished and he aimed his spyglass astern.

*He forgot for a second, about Gale.* Wind ruffled Sophie's hair, a gust cold enough to take the heat off the sunshine, and she shivered. Her sense of delight froze into sorrow. An aunt she'd only just found. And then, to lose her . . .

*Right, this is depressing. Back to business.* "If Verena challenges me and I'm not competent to fight, the Dueling Court gives me a proxy and she dies?"

It took him a few breaths to answer. "Few duels are to the death. One can surrender."

"And you can't kill someone once they've bowed out?"

"An Adjudicator can't, nor any Officer of the Fleet," he said. "For civilians, the standards are more lax. Accidents happen. But it is something of a disgrace, to run someone through when they've surrendered."

"So if Verena fought a proxy she'd be defeated, but she wouldn't die."

*Gale said I'd ruin the whole family if I came back here. Is this what she meant?* Sophie chewed this over. "I'm not broke now, though, am I? There's the ship, and you said there was money."

"And the estate on Verdanii, with all the Feliachild privileges, plus your Fleet courier stipend."

"I'm on a payroll? That's nuts."

"They should have worked harder to properly vest your sister," he said, sounding thoughtful.

"Tell me this, Parrish. I'm rich now, so I can't have a proxy. And I'm no fighter. Obviously I can't beat Verena—I'd have to concede. A challenge would be a slam-dunk for her, right?"

He nodded.

"So why's she up there carving strips off the practice dummy?"

"They might declare you incompetent and give you a proxy anyway."

"Is that likely?"

A complicated series of expressions worked across his face. What he came out with was: "No, not really."

"Then that's exactly what we'll do! Verena can challenge me, I'll cave, and the deed's done. Everything mine is hers."

"Gale said you were to avoid the Dueling Deck."

"But why?"

"I . . . couldn't say. I'm sorry."

"That means you totally could say, but you won't."

That infuriating arrogance again. "Yes, I'm afraid it does."

"Aren't I technically the boss of you? Don't you *have* to tell me stuff?"

"Honor doesn't permit, in this case," Parrish said.

"You're keeping a secret for someone."

"I swore."

"It's important!"

"A person who cannot keep their word has no place in this society."

"Whose secrets? Gale's secrets?"

He turned on his heel, making his way to the stern.

She hurried to match his pace. "So—if I wanted to be legally competent, enough to make it impossible for some Adjudicator to stick me with a proxy, what would I have to do? I can't just take up swordfighting."

Again, that expression of unhappiness. "Fulfilling the obligation to investigate Gale's murder should be argument enough that you're a competent adult."

He was scanning the skies now. For three days, they had been crystal clear, bright sun and a fresh wind from the east, but now a layer of haze was rising off the horizon, frosted by little scallops of gray and white cloud.

"Tonio," he called. "Change course: Make for Tallon at full sail."

"Those clouds are miles off and in the rearview," Sophie objected.

"Stele Island moths migrate on calm nights, remember?"

"Oh." She took a second look at the clouds, feeling cotton-mouthed. They didn't look like anything special to her. "Magic?"

"I'm afraid so."

"Did I just hear you talking moths?" Bram had joined them.

Sophie swallowed and spoke in English. "The storm, that first night with Gale. They said it was created by magic." *All those fishers died. And it was my fault.* She'd managed to fold that particular guilt to the back of her mind, but now it rose up, fresh and smothering.

Around them, sailors leapt to unfurl *Nightjar*'s sails. There was a creak as the ship heeled starboard, taking a new course, due north.

Verena strode up, whisking her shortsword into its sheath. "We're under attack?"

Parrish didn't equivocate. "Yes."

"They're after Sophie?"

"We can hope that they merely wish to alarm us. There seems little point in sinking us if they want her to find the Heart."

Bram glowered.

"Hey," Sophie said. "It's not my fault."

*Isn't it? Gale said I shouldn't come back. Now Gale's dead. If we sink, that's Verena too.*

*Poor Beatrice, back in San Francisco, I wonder if she even knows her sister's died and now to lose a daughter, both daughters, in fact . . . oh!*

"Beatrice!"

Parrish microflinched.

*Ha, Captain—I'm not the only one with a terrible poker face.* "All this 'Stay away from the Dueling Deck' stuff is to do with Beatrice's secrets, isn't it?"

"I couldn't say, Kir."

"Excuse me—dueling?" Bram said.

"What about Mom?" Verena said in the same instant.

"I think you should all get below," Parrish said.

*Changing the subject. Got it in one, this all has something to do with me and the past and Beatrice. I wonder if it goes far back enough that she was still with my biological father?*

"We only just saw that fog bank." But the mist was closer, rising in little ribbons off the water around them, and the clouds she could barely see a minute ago had grown to thunderheads.

"Come on, Sofe," Bram said.

Sophie balked. "Look, Parrish, I've sailed. A lot. I've been in storms. I can help."

"Sailed," he said. "In mummer ships."

"Sorry?"

"Petroleum-fueled vessels from Erstwhile."

"Okay, yes, they weren't all rigs and sails and belay the afterburners, but—"

"I can't have an unrated sailor on deck," he said, in that clipped tone. "I'll check you, once we've survived this."

"More hands make lighter work—"

"No."

"I thought I was in charge here."

He drew himself up. "Go below now, Kirs, with all due respect, or I'll have Sweet haul you down and guard you."

With a scowl, Sophie followed Bram down the narrow staircase.

Verena seemed to consider arguing too, but then she brought up the rear.

*Nightjar* was, by now, riding swells big enough to make walking an exercise in lurching from one side of the corridor to the other.

"He is *so* infuriating! Verena, how do you stand him?"

Verena ignored this outburst, instead speaking to Bram. "Don't worry. She's a good ship, and he's a brilliant sailor."

"I'm not afraid," he said. "I'm deciding whether it'll save time if I throw up now."

"You are a little green," Sophie said.

"There's no magic spell for preventing seasickness, is there?"

"Of course," Verena said. "But we don't have a scribe on *Nightjar.* Anyway, none of the crew's prone to the heaves."

"Worth asking, right?" Bram led the way to the cabin he and Sophie had been assigned. It held a pair of bunks and a tiny dressing table between them. Their things were lashed below the bunks. Bram perched on one. Then he started as a blue streak, furred and long, darted out from under the blankets.

It was a ferret, Sophie saw, or something like it. It had the basic weasel shape, the length, but running through the thin fur of its coat was an intermittent glow, a glimmer like blue light. Its tail was long and reptilian and terminated in a snake's head. It darted to the middle of the meager floor space, looking from one of them to the other, and then clawed its way up Sophie's jeans, curling against her belly.

"It's harmless," Verena said. "Parrish has a thing for rescuing animals who've been experimented on. The snake isn't venomous."

"Looks like a mud snake." Sophie ran a finger through the fur. The glimmer was spellscrip, magical lettering that had somehow been imprinted on its flesh. The join, at the tail, between mammalian skin and scales was gradual, a speckling pattern that might have been freckles, that grew and roughened into small and eventually bigger scales.

Bram didn't spare the animal more than a glance; the flash and shimmer of lightning, coming through the volcanic glass of the portal, had drawn his attention. "Do we need to board up the window?"

"No," Verena said. "*Nightjar*'s seals are sound."

*Magical experiments,* Sophie thought, *spellscrip on flesh.* "Was Parrish ever experimented on?"

"Parrish just likes animals," Verena said. "He can't be enchanted."

"Can't be enchanted?" Bram was breathing in and out with forced regularity—in through the nose, out through the lips. "How's that work?"

"One of his names is lost," Verena said.

"I'd figured him for having had one of those Erinthian beauty spells, at least," Sophie said.

"Born that way," Verena said, her tone wistful. "Gale used to call him monstrous. Overly blessed by nature."

They were heaving up and down, ever more briskly. As the bunk lurched beneath them Sophie was reminded of the time she'd tried bull-riding.

Shouts and running feet rumbled above. It was easy to imagine the crew running to and fro, tying off rigging and hauling sails as the fabric rent, to imagine people being washed overboard, drowning, and wouldn't that be her fault too?

There was a groan—beams straining.

"Sitting this out seems so wrong," Sophie said.

"Parrish can't know you won't get blown off deck," Verena said.

"I suppose not." *Arrogant bastard,* she thought.

"He should know I would be fine," her sister added.

"Guys," Bram said. "How is bitching about it helping?"

He was right, of course, but sitting around like little kids, waiting to drown, or hopefully not . . .

"Sent to our room." She sighed again.

"Ducks here would offer to fly the plane if we were on a bumpy flight overseas," Bram said to Verena.

"Don't call me Ducks. You're just trying to start a scrap to distract yourself from the nausea," she said.

"I wouldn't have to distract myself if you'd pitch in," he said. "Make yourself useful."

"Useful how?" she echoed. "We can't solve the murder from here. Not enough info."

"We don't have enough to sort out the Earth–not-Earth thing, either," he said.

She unfolded her page of questions, passing it across the bunk to him.

"You Hansa kids have a dull idea of fun," Verena said.

"This is *interesting*," they replied simultaneously, and she laughed.

"Tell us about you," Sophie said.

Verena's smile vanished; she was, suddenly, as alert and wary as the mutated ferret clinging to Sophie's lap. "Me?"

"Yeah. Were you born in San Francisco? Or, you know, here?"

"Why?"

"We're sisters. Do I need a better reason to ask?"

She sucked at her teeth, considering. "I was born in San Francisco. But, on paper, here too. Mom took me to her childhood home when I was young and presented me to the Allmother. Officially, that makes me a true child of Verdanii."

"Like Gale and our mother and Annela Gracechild?" Sophie asked.

Verena nodded.

"Allmother," Bram said. "Women run the show on Verdanii? It's matriarchal?"

"A person's status there is largely dependent on their genetic relationship to the Allmother."

"Who is what? The Queen?"

"Basically. She's head of the Consensus of Mothers—the national government."

"So," Sophie said. "Do they own slaves?"

"Actually—" A little tartness now. "Verdanii is considered the voice of the Free faction. They—we—are against bondage."

"Peace, love, and motherhood, then," Sophie said.

"Don't oversimplify. We're not saints," Verena said.

"And what about men?" Bram asked.

"Guys have been allowed to sit in the Consensus for a couple generations. I think there's maybe four out of the ninety-nine."

*We've drifted off the topic of Verena herself,* Sophie thought. *She dangled cultural bait and we took it.*

"What about you?" she said. "You had that Berkelium shirt. Are you in college already?"

"I'm graduating high school in the spring," she said. Sure enough, they were back to the short answers as soon as they started talking about her. "I had applied for early admission to Berkeley, but—"

"To study what?"

"Economics and international development."

"But what?" Bram's words came out a yelp: There had been another blast of thunder, near enough to send a shock of impact through the air. Sophie's ears rang.

"What?" Verena said.

The ship was lurching now, up and down, side to side. They were hanging onto the bunks to stay in place. The ferret's little claws were dug into Sophie's jeans.

"You were applying to Berkeley, but . . ." Bram managed.

"I'll have to give that up," she said. "To take Gale's position."

"Just like that—your life in San Francisco's over? You're here in the Age of Sail forever?" Bram looked aghast. Maybe it was just the nausea.

Verena shrugged. "It was always the plan."

"Oh crap," Bram groaned. "This needs to stop."

Sophie swapped bunks—the ferret clung to her jeans like dead weight—and wrapped her arms around him; he wouldn't need her to tell him the storm might go on for days. "It's okay," she said. "We'll be all right, promise. Solid ship, good sailors."

She peered out through the portal at the monstrous black swells. The clouds, above, rolled like great crushing boulders, illuminated by a steady fusillade of electrical flashes.

The electricity seemed to pool where her vision had settled, becoming ever more dense, and then a bolt of lightning poured down from the sky, connecting with the ocean like a whickering, jittering cable. Instead of flashing out, it thickened and maintained, sweeping closer, its color changing from electrical white to the pale rose of grapefruit flesh. The ship rolled, rising at the bow and throwing Sophie against the portal. She steadied herself by slapping her palm against the obsidian window . . . and as they peaked, high on the crest of an enormous wave, she thought she saw the silhouette of a ship, far off, the shape of a hull and a weird, splayed mast, shaped like a Y with lightning flickering within.

As her skin made contact with the volcanic glass, the whip of ropy lightning out on the water sought out Sophie's hand.

She recoiled. The power followed her through the bulkhead, flickering coolly against her palm.

She felt her hair shifting and moving as static electricity raised it.

"There's a pull, like a kite string," she said, marveling at the bright jolts. Lightning, in the palm of her hand . . .

"Sofe—" Bram said. The starched white curtain had burst into flame, and the bulkhead, where the cord of power cut through it, was smoking.

She had to get up on deck before the whole ship caught fire.

"Ferret!" She turned halfway so Verena could pry the panicked animal free, then made for the upper decks at a run. The bolt of power came along with her, like a string dangling from the sky. It spread down her hand to her wrist, a jagged, flickering sleeve. The skin of her arm tingled, heating up. The muscles of her forearm prickled, as though they'd been asleep.

*Find us* Temperance, *Outlander,* a voice crisped into her ear. *We'll give thee thy heart's desire.*

"Shut up!" She made it to the upper hatch without cutting the ship in half. As she reached for the handle of the hatch, there was a surge of white sparks; the boards blew to splinters.

She burst onto the deck into a torrent of chilly rain. The sleeve of electrical energy jolted on her skin, fizzing against the raindrops. The power snaked down to her elbow, stretching up beyond her fingertips into the sky. It reminded her, again, of a kite string. One of the ship's booms passed through the bolt and it sliced the ropes and sails as neatly as a saw, leaving a burn mark on the spar itself.

Sophie ducked as the boom swung. The ship heaved violently and the sail flapped, untethered, slack and useless, its bottom edge crisping and sparking before rain doused it. Her electrified hand set the water on the deck rail to steaming.

Despite the chaos of the storm, she heard shouts of dismay from the crew. Above that, Parrish shouted orders.

She hurled herself at the port rail, holding her arm up, trying to keep the lightning clear of the rigging.

The greatest boom yet of thunder accompanied a strobe-burst of electrical activity from above. Spots swam in front of her, coalescing into a shape: an octopus?

*Okay,* she thought, *what are my options?* She couldn't work her way aft without cutting more ropes, more sails. What if this unnatural bolt of energy hit a crew member?

*Heart for a heart,* the voice said again. It was John Coine's voice, she was sure of it. *Are we agreed?*

"I'll throw myself overboard!" She hurled the words into the wind, teeth bared in a feral grin. "Where will you be then?"

A gust bowled her to the deck; she writhed, bracing herself and trying to keep the cord of lightning from doing more damage to the ship.

*Metal.* The handle of the hatch had been made of iron. It had looked manufactured—Parrish or Gale must have imported it from home. And hadn't she seen . . . ?

The ship tilted, climbing another wave, and she took the opportunity to skirt the rail, contorting in a weird limbo to try to keep the bolt of lightning over the edge, working her way toward the cutter's stern. She heard someone—Tonio?—calling her name, but she kept going, finally hurling herself in a baseball slide, hands out, reaching for the only piece of metal she could find . . .

. . . the anchor chain.

Electrical power poured through her, into the anchor mechanism. Now she felt it, waves of current, roiling, *thrum, thrum* and then with a last thrash the connection broke, fizzling. The cord of lightning lashed upward and then slurped back up into the angry sky.

"Burned my hand," she said, falling to the deck. The anchor steamed.

The deck beneath her heaved as a swell pushed her to starboard. Sophie slid, stunned, coughing, as water sluiced over her.

*Is it coming back?*

It would be better to go into the drink than to become a tool for slicing the ship to bits. Bram, Verena, the ship's crew . . . if Coine was after her, he could have her.

She gathered herself to spring.

Someone caught her by the scruff of her jacket when she was halfway to the rail.

Parrish, of course.

Instead of going out in a glorious dive, her feet slipped out from beneath her and she landed on her butt.

He knelt beside her. "All right?"

Sophie sputtered like a drowned kitten, trying to draw breath to tell him to let her go. *I'm trying to do the noble thing here and I'm about to lose my nerve . . .*

"It's all right," he said, as if she'd voiced the thought after all. "It's over."

It was true. With one final mumble of thunder, the clouds split, revealing a perfect circle of blue sky that spread like oil across the gray plate of clouds.

"The storm—"

"Going as fast as it came," he said. "Magic, remember?"

She blinked. She was still seeing spots. Or, rather, that cephalopod shape again, bullet body and tentacles.

"When you put yourself at risk, the weather lightened. They don't want you dead."

"Bluff and deterrents," she sputtered.

"Someone's trying to scare you," he said.

"Goody. I can't wait to see what happens if they ever get truly homicidal," she said, extracting herself from his grip and making a vain attempt to brush herself off. Her jeans were lacquered against her legs, pulling on her skin, wrenching her knees and ankles.

"Indeed," Parrish agreed. The seas were calming. He gave her one last, assessing glance and went to help the crew secure the runaway boom.

## CHAPTER 16

She went below, peeled out of her wet clothes and dried off as quickly as she could before opening her trunk. Setting aside the ridiculous white ball gown the Conto had given her, she dug for something dry and practical from among the Erinthian contributions to her wardrobe. She came up with a set of black breeches and a pale green blouse. Bram had to help her with the buttons on the blouse—the burns on her hand were superficial, but the lightning strike had left her feeling oddly stiff.

"Where'd Verena go?" she asked as he smeared some of her first aid gel on her palms.

He shrugged. "Sofe. I've been thinking. You need to bail on all this before things get worse."

"You want to just run home?"

He tucked the tube of gel back into her first aid kit, repacking it within the pile of equipment of her trunk, his expression neutral.

"What about Gale's murder? The whole inheritance mess?"

"What about people chasing you with frigging typhoons?"

"Us. Chasing us." She sat on her bunk and let him see her considering it, being reasonable, weighing the options. It was a trick she'd adopted to placate their father: make a show of thinking it through, so he couldn't accuse her of grasping for an easy or shallow answer. She counted to twenty, and then said: "It's only my responsibility if I take it on, is that what you're thinking?"

"Exactly," he said. "They can't make you do Gale's old job, and there has to be some way for Verena to win over the magic purse without you putting your neck on the line. As for all this intrigue—who's running the court of Erinth, whether anyone can sink or find or destroy this Heart of *Temperance* . . . how is that our concern?"

"It is a little like we're playing with someone else's international politics."

He chuckled. "Breaking the Prime Directive."

"Who am I to do that, right?"

"That's not what I'm saying. If anyone was going to poke her nose in, Sofe, it should be you."

"Right."

"Don't start with the 'I'm stupid' stuff. You're quick, and when you take the time to look at them, you understand people really well. You're not corrupt."

"Yet you're telling me to just cut and run."

"Yeah! 'Cause think: What'll it do to Mom and Dad if we just vanish?"

It should have been a powerful argument, but she had struggled with this for ages, ever since she'd begged for permission to go skydiving for her sixteenth birthday, and seen her father fighting to smother his anxiety as he put her on the plane. They never said a word, Mom and Dad; they encouraged her to do exactly what she wanted. There was guilt, sure, but she lived with it.

Of course, she'd always been able to rationalize that they had Bram, safe and brainy at home with his laptop and his incomprehensible math.

"Also, you're not a cop," Bram put in.

"These people could use a few real cops."

"Which you aren't, no offense."

She couldn't help feeling insulted. "Running wouldn't solve anything. That Ualtarite or whatever followed Gale to San Francisco. If they attacked us at home, what could we do?"

"But—"

"And he has my name, remember: They might not even have to follow me home to . . . I dunno." She gestured at the ferret chimera, with its snake's tail.

Bram closed the trunk. "You're rationalizing. You *want* to be here."

"What if I do?"

"Is it worth dying for?"

"They didn't sink us, okay? They could have, but they didn't. It was just a scare tactic."

"And you don't have the sense to be scared?"

"See, you are calling me stupid."

"I'm not—"

"I'm staying," she said, feeling mulish now.

"What could make it worth the risk?"

"I think this whole 'stay-away-from-the-Dueling Court' thing has something to do with my birth parents. I think Gale knew if I went there, I'd find out . . ."

"What?"

"I don't know. I got into this to find out about my . . ." She stumbled, unwilling to say "family" or "real family." ". . . my background, okay? And I know, I *know* that Gale and Parrish are hiding something. And it's to do with Beatrice and dueling."

"You know."

"You just said I'm good at people. When we get to the Fleet, I'm gonna find out more about my past."

"Like what? How?"

"They're lawsuit-happy. Maybe I'm named in some other case, or Beatrice is. Or it has something to do with this slavery stuff. Beatrice is Verdanii, and you heard Verena—they're supposedly the head of the antislavery faction. Maybe the shameful thing she's so upset about is she helped someone escape, or had an affair with a slave."

"That's not a theory, Sofe; it's something out of a fairy tale."

"Hello, there's magic here."

"That doesn't make this *Gone with the Wind* romantic. Magic aside, if we assess the situation, apply a little scientific rigor—"

"That's not my strong suit, what with being the intellectual lightweight of the family and all—"

"I'm not saying that."

And he wasn't, but she was mad now.

So was he: "You sure you don't just like this feeling of being . . ."

"What?"

"Chosen."

She laughed. "Princess dresses and magic purses? What am I, Cinderella? One day my real parents will come and whisk me off to a palace?"

He folded his arms. "Well?"

"It doesn't make any difference, Bram. In the end, they still aren't gonna want me."

He shut one of the toppled books, looked her in the eye, and said, "Then why bother?"

"I have to know. I wish I didn't. I don't want to hurt you or Mom and Dad, or even Verena and Beatrice but—"

"You're curious, it's natural, but—"

"It's *not* curiosity," she said, and now her voice was rising. "It's not brain stuff at all. It's a hole, a hunger, or . . . I can't explain it and I feel terrible about wanting it. The way Mom and Dad looked all heart-punched on my eleventh birthday when I asked about my birth family, or the time I made that crack about my real parents . . ."

"You were little."

"I might as well have kicked Mom in the teeth. You think I don't remember exactly how hurt she looked? It's right here, high res." She tapped her forehead. "It's ungrateful and wrong and it feels *mean* that I can't just walk away from this and accept my wonderful, wonderful luck. But you know what? It also hurts that I had to wait for Mom and Dad to take off for Sicily to go rooting through their stuff for the truth. Something's missing, and it's not about me liking Verena better than you—"

"You know I'm not that insecure."

"—or preferring Beatrice to the parents. I need to do this, Bram."

"Mom and Dad deserve better than to have the two of us disappear without a trace."

"Get Verena to take you back," she said. "I'm not going home until I get some answers or they kick me the hell out."

She stomped back out on deck. The storm clouds had broken into low cumulous clusters, gull gray, dotting a shockingly blue sky. The crew was working to replace the ropes that had been cut by the strand of lightning. The wind was from the south and they were skimming along, still northbound, at a good clip.

Verena and Parrish were about twenty feet up the rigging on the mainmast, untangling a singed rope.

"Are we very far off course?" Sophie asked.

Parrish pointed at a faint scrim of land on the horizon. "They've driven us closer to Tallon. By design, I suspect."

"Design?"

"*Temperance*—the ship that Isle of Gold is fixated on—is Tallon's representative to the Fleet. The Tall are a nation of shipbuilders. And the last time anyone saw Yacoura—"

"The Heart is lost," Verena said, as though she was explaining, but she'd said that last time, too.

Part of a spell, maybe?

"It was last seen there," Parrish said.

"They don't want us getting too far from the Heart."

"Which suggests they're in a hurry." Parrish climbed down to the deck, raising her wrist so he could look at the electrical burn on her palm, which was tingling as the ointment soaked in.

"It's not serious," she told him.

He nodded but didn't let go. "We cannot give them what they want."

"No negotiating with terrorists?"

"Yes. Nicely put."

"We could let Coine *think* we're looking, couldn't we? If we had a legitimate reason to go to Tallon; if there was some point?"

A gleam of something . . . was that approval? "Such as?"

"Well . . . we need to repair, right?"

"No, damage to *Nightjar* is minimal."

"But Tallon . . . they're shipbuilders? Lots of international trade? Lots of people passing through? Lots of gossip?"

"Totally," Verena said. There was a chilly edge in her voice: Sophie extricated her arm from Parrish's grip.

"We were looking for someone who'd tell us what was up with the Ualtarites. A busy port . . ." She faltered. Why did all of her ideas sound so much better before she gave them voice?

*You're not a cop,* Bram had said.

"Sorry," she said. "Is this stupid?"

"It's quite sound," Parrish said. "Let them think we're concerned enough to consider seeking the Heart."

"We are concerned," Bram said, coming up on deck. "We're super concerned."

Sophie pretended she hadn't heard. "Okay. We'll play-act at looking for the Heart and snoop around trying to figure out why the Ualtarites are helping John Coine."

Where Erinth had the air of a Tuscan city in the midst of the Renaissance, Tallon was more of a navy town. Its wharf was long and businesslike; the locals were almost all in uniform. As foreigners, in civilian garb, they would be conspicuous.

The shore had weathered the same storm that blew *Nightjar* into Tallon's waters, but if anything had been blown out of place it had already been lashed back down, and possibly scrubbed for good measure. The place was all whitewash and chalky stone.

From the look of the harbor, *Nightjar* wasn't the only ship making for land in the wake of the storm: A number of sailing vessels, most of them small and many looking the worse for wear, were arriving. Sophie had a good look up and down the wharf, looking for the Isle of Gold ship, *Barabash,* that had been anchored in the Erinthian port. No sign of it. She looked up the Isle of Gold flag in Gale's protocol book—it was a gold triangle on a bloodred background—and searched again. Nothing.

A large vessel with a peculiar, Y-shaped mast caught her eye instead.

"Gale had friends here," Parrish said, interrupting her. "Now we're in port, I'll go tell them about her death in person."

"Do I have to come?" Sophie asked.

He shook his head. "I'll see if we can get a meeting with the intelligence office, in case the Tall know what's going on."

"Will they tell us?"

"Gale hid Yacoura for them, remember?"

*Calling in a dead woman's favors,* Sophie thought uneasily. It felt like spending money that belonged to her sister. "How will they feel about us looking for the Heart?"

"They'll understand that we're making a pretense of it. In the meantime, I'm not sure there's much for you to do." He seemed to weigh his next words. "Bram, the cartography office on the Hilltop Academy is one of the finest on Stormwrack. If you are still trying to understand our geological history—" He waved at the sea charts, the rings of islands.

"Thanks."

He turned to Sophie. "The academy also possesses a natural history collection."

"Where?"

He pointed straight up one of the tidy little streets to a stone building with immaculately groomed parade grounds. "Perhaps Tonio can take you?"

Instead of agreeing, she turned to Verena. "What about you? Another duel?"

Verena shook her head.

"She should go with you, Parrish," Sophie said. "You're meeting up with important spy types who knew Gale, right? Verena should get to know them, for when she gets the pouch imprinted."

Parrish inclined his head, assenting.

They broke into parties, Parrish and Verena making for the residential district, Tonio leading them up the hill toward the academy, a brick building whose pilasters and cornices made it seem faintly Georgian. It was a short walk, but an awkward one—Bram was silent—still angry, Sophie thought. It was a relief when Tonio introduced him to a cartographer and the pair of them vanished up one of the academy's staircases.

"Aren't you going along to translate?"

"Kir Bram can make do in Fleet," Tonio said. "He's picked up a lot of the language—and they're just looking at maps, after all."

"He's a supergenius."

"Garland—the captain, that is—ordered me to stay with you. I believe the natural history laboratory is this way."

"We're not going."

"No?"

"I'd be glad to, normally, but I have other things on my mind."

Tonio looked uneasy. "Such as?"

She grinned. "Playing cop."

"Captain said—"

"Captain Parrish isn't in charge, is he?" She led him back to the wharf, past a small squad of teens in red dress uniforms, kids from a rainbow of ethnic backgrounds, and then through a small park where old men and women were playing some variant on croquet.

"Garland should be in charge," Tonio said. "Until certain matters are smoothed out."

"Tonio, you seem like a smart guy."

Good manners obliged him to answer. "Thank you."

"So tell me. That storm, it could've drowned us all, right? We could have drowned. You, me, Parrish, both my siblings?"

"That's life on the Watch, Kir."

"I don't know what that means."

"*Nightjar*'s crew is often at hazard. We keep our heads down as we can, but Kir Gale was in a dangerous business."

"Until I offload all this onto Verena, my life's at hazard too."

"That's true."

"So we're already living dangerously. Why waste time?"

"Captain Parrish would take it amiss to lose two employers in a single week," Tonio protested.

"Give me a break. He'd barely notice I was gone."

He stopped dead, gaping at her. "Kir—"

"Sophie."

"Surely you've noticed . . ."

"Okay, never mind, I'm sorry. That was unfair. He'd notice, obviously. I'm not saying he's heartless."

"Heartless," he repeated.

"He just lost his best friend, right? Or his partner in crime? He's in mourning. It's obvious he's shattered. I'm not on his radar."

"I don't know radar, Kir—I mean Sophie, your pardon—"

She could feel her face turning red. "Why are we even talking about this? How Garland feels about me doesn't matter."

The words seemed to open a little hollow in her gut, though. *How I feel about him doesn't matter either,* she told it. *It's all a big side issue. A distraction.*

"That's not—" Tonio swallowed, seeming to consider his words. "All right. Consider this: If you get killed, it might make the situation, with the Verdanii succession, worse."

"Now that *is* a fair point." They had reached a boardwalk that fronted the wharf, a stretch of restaurants and supply houses, orderly people conducting business in an orderly way. "What are the chances we can find a lawyer type?"

"Lawyer?"

"If I wanted to make a will, leaving all my alleged stuff on Stormwrack to Verena and everything else to Bram, would that be binding? Would the magic purse care?"

"You should be able to make a Fleet-valid will here," Tonio said, brightening at the prospect of a safe bureaucratic errand.

"Genius!" she said. She had something else in mind, but there was a little time to kill. "Can you do that thing where you say 'Charge it to *Nightjar*' and they go for it?"

"I'm the first mate." This apparently meant yes: He found her a small law office and authorized the payment. It didn't take long to spell out what she wanted.

"Come back in a few hours to sign the documents," the clerk said.

A couple hours.

Sophie felt an itch of pure cultural displacement; if she'd been home, she would have texted Bram now to see how he was doing.

What the hell. She pulled out her phone, texting:

*I was a jerk. Sorry.*

It gave her the usual reply:

*Message will be sent when we return to service area.*

"What are you doing?"

"It's a custom . . . like . . ." She twitched the ragged black scarf hanging at his hip, a memento for Gale. "I'm trying to make myself feel better about something."

"Ah. You know, Kir, that taxidermy museum has a fine collection. Your Erstwhile recording device . . ."

"No! No, no, no." She dragged the reluctant Tonio down the wharf, toward the ship she'd seen earlier. It had, as she'd hoped, come into port while she was pushing legal paper. "See that ship? *Ascension?* There's the flag of Ualtar."

He looked at it with obvious distaste. "I'm surprised you recognized it."

"I looked it up," she said. "So . . . they don't seem damaged. They didn't come here because the storm hit them."

"They could be bringing spidersilk to the Tall," Tonio said. "The silk is used in inscriptions for shipbuilding."

"It doesn't look like a freighter." It was a massive ship, one that must have been put together with some kind of magic, because it didn't look remotely seaworthy. Its single mainmast towered above the deck, disproportionately tall, and it split into two arms, forming a Y. The rigging of its sails was segmented in a way that seemed familiar.

"Kir—Sophie, why are we—"

"Ualtarites do church," she said. "I read it in Gale's protocol book. Every day, church at high noon, everybody welcome. They're the 'anyone can perfect themselves' people, remember?"

He was aghast. "You can't mean to board her?"

"You bet I mean to," she said. "I've had a genetic family for all of a week. And then these people killed the one relative who'd give me the time of day."

"I won't allow it."

"Ha. I'm in charge, remember? Come or don't; I know they're not your favorite people ever. I'm going." Setting her camera to record, she paused at the gangplank, accepting a long veil from a surprised-looking girl before marching aboard.

A brief struggle played itself out on Tonio's face before he followed.

The Ualtarites were already gathered, kneeling on the foredeck in neat rows. Sophie took a spot at the back, shadowed by Tonio—who shot her a surprisingly angry glance as he folded himself into position.

A tall woman in a silvery cloak stepped out in front of the gathering, commencing the service. She spoke a language Sophie not only didn't know but didn't find familiar at all.

She propped her camera between her knees and imitated the listening pose of the true believers arrayed before her.

*Observations,* she told herself. The Ualtarites were Caucasian, mostly, like the Tall. They were fair-skinned, but a few had epicanthic folds on their eyes . . . which was noteworthy, but probably irrelevant. Those congregants whose arms were bare had scars—patterned scars, so the injuries were made deliberately. Ritual scarring, maybe, to do with the faith?

The ship was clean, very white, nothing out of place. And there was a recurring design motif . . . spiders. All their bolts and buttons had stylized spiders on them. The pattern on the priest's vest was a web.

*Come to think of it, that's what the rigging in that Y-shaped mast looks like: a loose spiderweb.*

Sophie had seen a shape like this during the storm, had glimpsed a ship out in all that blackness and thunder, a hull with an electrified branching Y reaching skyward.

She turned her wrist, filming the deck, pausing to record the unusual design of the ship against the background of the busy wharf. The Y-shaped mainmast, with the rigging between its arms. Its mainsail was woven in as a spider might weave a web into a break in the branches of a tree. There was a looseness to the cords; when the wind blew, she imagined, the sails would bell out extravagantly, more like a hot air balloon than a traditional rig.

She remembered the Verdanii ship they'd seen on Erinth, the one that seemed to have live trees as masts. It, like this split-mast ship, probably couldn't be sailed safely at home. No, the strain on the arms of the Y would be too much, and how could they navigate? Could it tack?

As the service droned on, she considered: What did magic mean, exactly? The ability to defy the laws of physics? To create little pockets of something—space, time, both?—where they didn't apply? Or to access other universal rules that twenty-first-century science, at home, just hadn't touched yet?

The spiderweb sail ruffled in the breeze, gaily defying common sense and physics.

*I wonder what Bram will say about this?* She shouldn't have let herself get drawn into arguing with him; it always made her miserable. But the larger question of what magic *was* would intrigue him. And it tied into the problem with the landmasses. If this was Earth, whatever had happened to the continents almost certainly had been . . . unnatural.

Despite everything, she'd gathered a fair pile of observations about Stormwrack. It was random data, a clutter of facts, not enough yet to form a pattern. *Krill in a net,* she thought. Meanwhile Bram had focused on the geography question. That was always the way; she flitted around looking at whatever was shiniest, while he got down to work.

*Well, he hasn't solved anything yet either,* she told herself. *And I can focus, I can. I'm supposed to be snooping around, for Gale's sake.*

The sail caught her eye again. Spider ships, spider people. She would have bet there was some kind of spider tie-in to the religious ceremony she was sitting through.

*Anansi's a spider god. Anansi's a trickster, though.* This service seemed overall too stodgy to be trickster worship. No whoopee cushions. She'd always imagined Anansi with a high-pitched giggle and a ready bag of practical jokes.

She flashed on Parrish, giggling as he traded bets with Tonio. And he hadn't been magicked into being good-looking, either. What had Verena said Gale called him? Monstrous. Overblessed by nature. Something like that. *Cute, fit, honorable,* she thought.

*Stuffy, bossy, infuriating.*

The priest had wound one of the worshippers 'round in what almost looked like mummy wrappings, and moved on to what appeared to be a sermon, speaking charismatically—still incomprehensibly, in Ualtara—to the congregation. Everyone listened, heads bowed, patiently on their knees. A few had white cords in hand, and were knotting and unknotting them as they listened. Tonio had a glazed expression, the face of a man waiting out something incredibly unpleasant.

Okay, what did she know?

First: Gale was killed—John Coine had said as much—because of this Heart of *Temperance* thing. They'd decided Gale would never give it up, so they got her out of the way.

So . . . *Temperance.* A deterrent. The ship that sank pirates, back in the day, which was why the Isle of Gold guys were after it.

But these Ualtarites weren't pirates. What did they want with the Heart?

The Ualtarites weren't upfront and in anyone's face about cooperating with John Coine. They were letting him do all the talking, take all the credit. They couldn't have known that Sophie would see their embassy guy. They'd whipped up a storm when *Nightjar* headed south, toward their homeland, and had instead driven them north.

What was it Parrish had said? *Temperance* was a key part of their century of peace—Cessation, they called it.

A ship that could sink anyone—freighter, pleasure craft . . .

*Don't be silly. It's the government—they wouldn't sink yachts for the hell of it. Pirates, yes.*

*Or . . . warships.*

What if the Ualtarites were helping the Isle of Gold because they wanted to go to war?

*Okay,* she thought, *but I saw that Fleet. It was huge. It's not as though* Temperance *is their only fighting vessel. It's just Bad Cop. They could probably enforce their Cessation without it.*

Spiders, something about spiders . . .

Her attention snapped back to the service as the congregation rose to its feet, reciting something in an overlapping choral drone, the men singing the two lower notes, women higher. The raised voices had a repressed energy, a sort of "nuh-nuh-nuh" that reminded her, briefly, of that feeling of the lightning moving through her during the storm, waves of power. It filled the available space around it, reverent and exotic. Faith and passion. She found herself beaming at Tonio, who'd offered her an unnecessary hand up.

The sound built, receded, built again and then broke all at once into one long collective, resonant "Ahhh!"

Like that, spider church was over. The priest sang something that seemed like a benediction and the sailors headed back to their stations without so much as a pause for chat.

Tonio let out a long breath and stretched his legs. "Can we leave now, Sophie?"

"Let's see what happens if we just wander the decks."

"Teeth!"

"The big protocol book says Ualtar is scrupulously gentle with anyone who comes aboard for church. Come aboard, attend the service, safe passage off again."

"There might be an exception for people who take the opportunity to spy."

"We can say I have to pee."

"You'd be better off flashing Gale's—I mean your—I mean *Verena's* badge if you're challenged."

"Maybe they won't challenge us," she said, setting off. "Sometimes if you look like you belong, you can get away with—"

"We don't look like we belong." There was that edge of anger again.

"Nobody's tried to stop us so far." She peered over the bulwark to the lower decks. Down on the docks, the crew was unloading big spools of glistening rope, heavy cords used in rigging. Nearer to hand, she saw a collection of cases of thread, little sewing spools of lumpy or beaded strands.

"Glue," Tonio said. "Little bubbles of it. They string them into frames and spellscribes write with them—stitch them, I think—into fishers' spells and to scrip up sailors."

"Scrip them for what?"

"Ropemonkeys tie their knots true, always. Rope never slips from their grasp, and they can climb rigging like monkeys. Sweet, the bosun's helper on *Nightjar*, she's a knotter. Her parents saved for three years to buy the inscription for her."

She rolled that around in her mind again: What was magic, exactly? "That's a skill a person could just learn."

"It's good to have someone around with real talent. Nice to be that person, too. Kir Gale used to say that was the true power of magic, that gifts weren't arbitrary province of Nature. She said it was good that people who truly yearned to be set apart could simply do so—chart a course for themselves and sail it. She seemed to find it a particular shame when a person wasn't fitted to their position."

"Like being just average smart among a family of geniuses," Sophie said.

"I assumed she was thinking of her sister, Beatrice."

"Did you agree with her?"

"Kir Gale was a wise woman," he said, "She knew more than I ever will."

"That means no, right?"

Tonio had the grace to look sheepish. "Amia madre says a person should seek their gifts within before running off to the magic shop."

"Your mom sees magic as a shortcut. The lazy way?"

"It's an old argument," Tonio said. "There's a saying: If you purchase perfection, how will you know if you could have achieved it yourself?"

"I can see how it would be a matter of ongoing debate. So, Tonio, what's your gift?"

"Look!" He almost sounded cheerful to have a change of subject. "They've sent security after us."

"Security" meant a seven-foot giant, wearing a bandolier of carved stone orbs. Cannonballs? Blond, broad-chested and clad in a simple blue tunic, the man had a longish beard that had been separated into plaits—eight of them, naturally—and hung with milky white beads.

He was, to Sophie's surprise, beaming: "Were you enlightened by the ceremony, Kirs?"

*Why did I think this was smart?* Sophie managed to keep herself from grabbing for Gale's purse, from brandishing the badge within. Instead, she groped for a suitable response. "Your people are clearly very spiritual," she hazarded.

Bigger smile.

"Unfortunately, we don't speak your language."

"If we knew you were coming, we'd have got you translators," he said, "For you and your serveling here. But our priestess wrote up short accounts in Fleetspeak and 'Rinthian for you."

She accepted the proffered scroll. It had a somewhat lurid illustration of birds pecking out the eyes of the damned below the text, and a spidery rendering of the sun above, reaching out its eight arms to the virtuously bright and beautiful. "Thank you."

"*Grazie,*" Tonio echoed her, his tone distant.

He nodded indulgently, as though he'd handed them lumps of gold or at least something as good as a doughnut. "Is there aught else, Kirs?"

"Yes," she said, pushing the word out before Tonio could defer and get them escorted off the ship. "I'm here on business, as a matter of fact. Right, Tonio?"

"Fleet business," he affirmed weakly.

"That so?"

"Yes. I'm . . . acting on behalf of a . . ."

"A Fleet courier," Tonio said. "Verena Feliachild of Verdanii."

The giant stroked the beads entangled in his beard, seeming baffled.

"We're looking into her death. Not Verena's, I mean. Her predecessor's." There she ran out of steam. "I have a badge."

"Waaaaahl. Ain't that unusual?" the big man said. "I'll take you to our exec officer then, shall I?"

"Thank you," Sophie said.

"This way."

They followed him belowdecks, Tonio looking ever more grave. "We only have your word that the gentleman we saw on Erinth was one of the two who attacked Kir Gale," he whispered. "These people aren't like the Golden; they'll take a prickly view of having their honor challenged."

*He's right, what am I doing?* "What's that smell? Fabric dye?"

He took a big huff. "Ship stinks of magic."

*Okay, relax. Go at this sensibly. It's a process of inquiry, same as science.* She glanced at her camera . . . yes, it was still recording. Their enormous escort ignored it, just as everyone else had.

She had wondered if they would end up having an audience with the priest who'd conducted the ceremony, but the executive officer was perhaps fifty, motherly in appearance, and seemed unsurprised to see them.

*Of course*, Sophie thought—*she probably sent the Friendly Giant up to get us.*

She had a milky lens of glass strapped over her left eye and her white-gold hair, which fell to shoulder-length, was plaited into eight strands and bound with thin silver wires. Her office was a disaster: clutter everywhere, bits and pieces of equipment and paper strewn on every surface, floor too. It was the sort of mess one rarely saw aboard a sailing vessel— the constant rock of the ship would jumble things further. As she looked, Sophie spied a few shards of broken glass on the deck, a testament to items that had dropped off the desks and shelves and shattered.

"Tanta Maray," the woman said, interrupting Sophie's inspection by introducing herself. "Of this great Missionary Vessel *Ascension*, and privileged to sail her."

"Sophie Hansa. I'm on a private cutter, *Nightjar*. This is the . . . my . . . our first mate, Antonio Capodoccio—"

He didn't tell Maray to call him Tonio. Instead, with a not-very-deep bow: "We have been honored by your hospitality, Tanta."

"We throw out threads to any who might strive for perfection," she said. This last phrase, delivered in a neutral tone, somehow made it clear she thought they were unlikely candidates. "What can I do for you?"

Sophie circled the cluttered office, filming the desk with its scraps of paper, all covered in writing in what she assumed was an Ualtarite language, a scattering of pens, an ordinary-looking box of paper clips, an astrolabe, and a framed scrap of leather, written in spellscrip, that was half hidden by the paperwork. A shell, a tarantula carapace, and—

*Oh.* she thought. *Oh, no.*

"Kir Hansa?"

She had to take a second to reach for calm. "I—we—sorry. We met a man from the Isle of Gold, John Coine. He was on Erinth about a week ago. We think he's involved with the murder of a Fleet courier, Gale Feliachild."

"The Fleet oversees us all, like a stern and overbearing parent," Maray said. "Little wonder that now and then her children rebel, even violently."

"Are you saying Gale Feliachild deserved to die?"

She could almost hear the click as Tonio's nerves ratcheted up another notch.

Maray shook her head. "The murder of any individual, believer or no, is a tragedy. I was merely observing that, in the abstract, the occasional loss to the greater body of the Fleet is to be expected. It is a living organism, like any other, and sometimes its parts—"

"Die off?" *She's amused. She thinks this is funny. It's a game and she thinks she can outplay me,* Sophie thought. "That's pretty heartless, but we'll let it pass. The thing is, this particular . . . can I call John Coine a pirate, Tonio?"

"Not to his face, Kir. Golder or Goldman."

"This particular Goldman seemed like he might know a guy from your embassy on Erinth."

"Embassy staffers, by virtue of their position, must be friendly with everyone," Tanta Maray said. "In any case, it is the Ualtar way to reach out to everyone we can, however depraved."

And that was a bit of a dig, and not at Sophie. Interesting. "Right, very nice. Save our souls and all that."

"Whenever possible."

*What would a cop say?* "What if this member of the Ualtarite diplomatic mission had been seen, by a . . . by a witness? If he'd been involved in an earlier attempt on the courier's life?"

"I'd say the witness was mistaken." Maray's eyes narrowed, and suddenly the air she'd had, of a cat batting at a small mouse, was gone. "Has this diplomat been questioned?"

"The Erinthians are looking into that end of it," Sophie said. "Since it's all political, and on their turf."

Tanta Maray nodded, acknowledging this. "Kir Hansa, I assure you there will be no tie found, on Erinth or elsewhere, between the Ualtar theocracy and the murder you're investigating. We are innocent. It would be unwise to suggest otherwise. It sounds as though your evidentiary thread—"

"Wow. All of a sudden you sound like a lawyer."

"I have many talents. It hardly takes a legal expert to point out that if all you have in terms of evidence is a single sighting of a Ualtarite citizen—"

"Government officer."

"—with this John Coine—"

"They weren't discussing the weather or trade negotiations or whatever international business you guys might have with each other. The guys had knives out, stabbing my aunt!"

"So you are the witness?" Maray looked at Sophie more closely, seeming to weigh her. Her air of concern vanished. "Well, people make mistakes."

Dismissed again. Sophie mastered her feelings enough to look Maray in the eye. "I saw him."

"Kir, I can only protest Ualtar's innocence," Her tone was casual, but she had stiffened. "I suggest you pursue some other avenue of investigation."

Anger made her reckless. "Okay, another avenue it is. This ship's purpose is religious? It's a missionary vessel, you said?"

"Yes."

"Why's it delivering cobwebs?"

Tonio coughed—no doubt trying to shut her up.

"Practicality and spirituality need not be mutually exclusive," Tanta Maray said. "Common sense and conservation of resources are aspects of perfection, too."

"And there's a magical . . . factory? Workshop? Aboard?"

"We do many things."

"Would you be able to create mezmers here?"

"I know little about the inscription. But we aren't making mezmers here, Kir Hansa; it's a vulgar spell, one that sinks its victims and its perpetrators further from the ideal. You have my word that this ship hasn't been near Erinth in six months. We can copy our ship's logs to the Watch, if you like."

"Yes," she said. "That would be great."

Maray's lips thinned.

*Oh*, Sophie thought. *Didn't you expect me to say yes?*

"I'll have to lodge a protest, of course, at your refusal to accept our word."

"Thank you for your—" Tonio began, but Sophie interrupted.

"Lodge away. But just so you know, I do believe you when you say you weren't near Erinth. I'm thinking . . . maybe you were sailing the Zunbrit Passage?"

Maray's face revealed nothing, but the tension within the cluttered room intensified.

"There was a little salvage vessel called *Estrel*," Sophie said. "Small crew . . . nice people. Captain name of Dracy. Perhaps you know her?"

She could see the woman considering her response. "I do know that ship."

"I figured you had," she said, looking directly for the first time at the lantern, the one holding Dracy's father's glowing skull.

"We did not, alas, reach out to the *Estrel* for spiritual reasons. That ship sank in a storm. It was a rescue attempt."

"Bet it was a sudden storm," she said. "And maybe a bit localized?"

"Quite sudden, yes." Maray's teeth clicked. "By the time we arrived, all we could do was pick up the pieces."

"Survivors?"

"Regrettably, there are none."

"There wouldn't be, would there?"

Now Tonio put his hand on her arm. "You've been most helpful, Kir Tanta."

"Tanta's my title, boy," she said. "Maray's my name."

"We should go," he said. "Sophie? The Tanta is a busy woman."

She shook off his arm. "Were there bodies? The *Estrel* crew, did you recover any bodies?"

"Taken by the sea, Kir, like the ship itself."

"Sophie . . ."

"It's okay, Tonio," she said. "The people who killed . . ."

Tanta Maray raised an eyebrow. "Careful, Kir."

". . . who killed Gale Feliachild," she said. "They're keen to get their hands on this Heart of *Temperance* thing. Yacoura."

"The Heart is lost," Tonio and the Ualtarite officer said, in virtually the same tone of voice.

She thought again: *Gotta be some kind of spell doing that.*

"The Golders don't care if I know they killed Gale, Tonio. And Maray probably doesn't care that I think she ran down the *Estrel* and got one of the crew to give up my name, or witched up the storm that blew us to Tallon."

"Believing something and making others credit it are two different things." Tanta Maray smiled and removed the lens over her eye, revealing a web-clouded socket beneath, a nested hole of silk in which small white spiderlings bundled and writhed.

*Oh, yuck.* Sophie liked spiders as much as the next biologist, but that didn't keep her from taking a healthy step back.

"I think you may be entirely unfit for Fleet work, child. You have no gift for artifice."

"You mean lying?"

"Discretion, rather."

The murderers might think it's better if I know what they're up to, if they think it'll get me looking for the Heart."

"Among the imperfected, fear can be a powerful call to action." A spider wobbled over the edge of her eye socket, dangling by a leg.

"So's being angry," Sophie said. "Captain Dracy and her crew weren't involved in any of this."

"The innocent come to grief all the time. Is there anything else?"

"No. Thanks for your time," Sophie said. "Should we see ourselves out?"

"Of course. Thank you for attending our religious service. And you, Kir Hansa—" This was said pointedly, to exclude Tonio. "May return anytime."

The giant was waiting to escort them off the ship.

"Oh no," she said, as soon as they were back on the docks. "The *Estrel* crew. Poor Captain Dracy."

"It wasn't your fault," Tonio said. "Kir Sophie, don't cry."

"Tell me you have jail here, Tonio. If we prove anything on these guys, will there be consequences for them?"

"It will go to the courts and be there forever, Kir, but in the meantime the guilty parties will probably be confined to the Fleet brig aboard *Docket*." They had reached the boardwalk, and as he stepped out of *Ascension*'s shadow, he made for a bench and collapsed onto it. "Garland is going to have me horsewhipped."

"Seriously?" She wiped her cheeks. "He doesn't actually do the evil navy discipline, does he?"

"He may take it up when he hears about this. You mustn't get yourself killed, Sophie—"

"Oh come on, we got away with it. And the thing is, it was worthwhile. I think I get everything, Tonio."

He smiled weakly. "Then we can go back to *Nightjar*?"

"We have to pick up my shiny new will, remember?" She sat down beside him. "Buck up. I'll buy you a sandwich. There's a vendor coming this way."

That got her a nervous laugh. "Scare a man to death and then feed him. You've more in common with Kir Gale than you know."

Was it strange that his words pleased her? She gave him a friendly elbow in the ribs, relaxing on the bench beside him, feeling the satisfaction of a good day's work: hazard survived, progress made.

The vendor was a young woman in a starched outfit and cap that reminded Sophie of old-fashioned nursing uniforms. She was rolling a blue-and-white cart filled with turkey sandwiches: whole grain bread, white meat, hot yellow mustard, and a layer of dill pickles. They were wrapped in flimsy squares of fabric that did double duty as napkins.

They got one and split it, watching the girl as she continued down the cobbled wharfside path, trying her luck with the various ships tied up along the beach. Here at the waterfront, the sails and masts were a forest that all but blocked out the sea. The sound of carpentry—hand saws and hammering—rolled off their decks. Riggers swarmed the masts, sorting ropes and hanging sails. Back the way they'd come, loaders and stevedores moved goods on and off ships like *Ascension*.

Everyone was hard at work: The hum of industry seemed to rise from the stones underfoot. She turned, taking in the town, the shopping district that ran along the waterfront and the square blocks of little white houses beyond. Was loafing just not allowed here? She spotted a playground. Half a dozen parents were supervising little kids at play. A lone guy with a missing leg was sitting on a bench playing a small instrument that looked like a squeezebox and feeding scraps to a dog.

Instead of asking Tonio about the Tallon economy, she said: "There's something I'm wondering about. How is it you're the one who's not welcome back on that Ualtarite ship? You were polite."

"Whereas you practically accused them of murder."

"Can I help it if she left Dracy's lantern sitting out on her junk like a smoking gun? What did you do to offend them?"

"I'm especially imperfect," he said, dabbing the corners of his mouth and then unfurling the scroll the giant had given him, showing her the illustration of the damned.

The pile of bodies, as Sophie looked at it, shimmered a little. "The images are meant to show depravity?"

"Indeed."

"So there's a dancing girl, representing the concept of slutty woman-hood. Typical—they would be prudish sexists, wouldn't they? And the guy bound up in cobwebs who's clutching a purse . . . that'd be greed."

"This," Tonio said, exasperated. He tapped a picture of two men bound up together, oblivious to their doom, kissing. "They gave it to me, be-cause . . . the word your brother uses is . . . delightful?"

"Gay," she said. "You're gay?"

He nodded, rising to his feet. "The law office will close soon, Kir. Sophie, I mean. Are you going to go in and sign that will?"

*Changing the subject,* she thought, *deflecting.* It was another thing she hadn't considered about this place . . . even if some of the three hundred or so nations of Stormwrack were outright liberal, there would be places where the attitudes were medieval.

She said: "So they're murderers, slavers, and homophobes. Cheer up, Tonio. Getting them in trouble with the Fleet will be so very awesome."

He looked a little wrung out, but he smiled.

"I'm sorry I made you take in their church service. If I'd known, I'd . . . well, I'd have apologized first. Or brought someone else." *Like who? Bram?*

"You have a good heart, Sophie," he said.

She went in and signed her will, then arranged to have a copy sent to Annela Gracechild. When she came out, Tonio was staring at *Ascension.*

"Isle of Gold means to carry all the blame for Gale's death," he said. "It's why John Coine approached you openly."

"That's what I think too. The Ualtarites didn't think anyone would find out they were involved."

"They know now—that you know. You told them it was you who saw the Ualtarite. You accused Maray of sinking your salvager friends."

"I should've played it cool, right?"

"Yes."

"I'm lousy at mind games."

"Why would the Ualtarites involve themselves? What possible reason could they have?"

"I've got one whopper of a theory about that," she said. "Let's hook up with the others and see if there's some way we can test it."

## CHAPTER 17

*Nightjar*'s galley was a utilitarian space, home to a plain wooden table with benches long enough to seat six on either side and two chairs at either end. With Parrish at one end of the table and Verena at the other, Bram and Sophie ended up across from each other.

Bram was avoiding her gaze, which meant he was still mad. Tonio was the odd fellow out, and he emanated a faint air of misery. Sophie figured he was unhappy that his captain was about to find out he'd "let" Sophie go aboard *Ascension*.

"If Parrish has a proper perspective, he'll be mad at me for taking you among the rabid homophobes," she had told him on the way back.

"He's perfectly capable of being upset with us both."

"Maybe we can gloss over that part of our outing," she said, and that got a weak chuckle. "Besides, how much more uptight could Parrish possibly get?"

The ship's cook had gone for takeout, hitting up the locals for a thick lamb stew and a hearty pull-apart loaf of a bread she would have called challah. Parrish had come back from his visit to Gale's unnamed friends with a basket of produce: fresh carrots with a hint of gold color in them, crisp spinach leaves, and a turnip that had been diced fine and soaked in vinegar as a sort of relish for the rest.

It looked like he'd picked them himself; muddy smudges marked the knees of his breeches. "Verena and I checked with Tallon security but they had nothing useful to share," he said as they sat. "Our investigation seems stalled."

"Tonio and I—" Everyone's eyes were on her—everyone's but Bram's. She found her words had dried up.

Oh, this was ridiculous. She knew what was going on, she did; all she had to do was tell them. What was this, stage fright?

The old sense that her idea would fall apart when she explained it, that they'd poke holes in her theory and tell her she'd been silly, guilty of shallow thinking, of not really examining her hypothesis—

*Come on,* she thought, even as she felt her face flood with heat. *It's just Bram and Verena, and Tonio already knows. And Parrish.*

She could almost hear him: *That's an interesting chain of associations, Kir, but what you're proposing is impossible, and you scared Tonio badly in the process.*

She looked to Bram for help.

"Come on, Ducks, don't choke now," he said. "Have you cracked the case or what?"

*Don't call me Ducks.* The thread of annoyance helped.

"When I was aboard *Estrel*," Sophie made herself say, using Fleetspeak but choosing simple words for Bram's sake. "There was a Tiladene man named Lais Dariach. Someone was blackmailing his family horse farm with an inscription; he'd paid a ransom."

"We know this," Verena said. "You diverted the ship to help him. It's part of the issue with the inheritance."

"I'm not bringing it up to rub your nose in it," Sophie said. "The thing is, so much has happened that I forgot to tell you something. The ransomers tried to kill Lais at the drop-off. The whole thing with the stud horse was pretty much intended to draw him out."

At least nobody laughed.

"A murder attempt?" Verena said.

"They used a grenade."

Parrish frowned. "I don't see the significance—"

Sophie's heart sank.

"She's right," Bram interrupted. "You don't make grenades here, do you? From what I've seen and read, your industrial base isn't much for heavy metals or mining. That anchor chain Sophie fried, you imported it from our world, didn't you?"

"And painted it so people wouldn't go 'Eww, Iron!,'" Sophie added.

Bram said, "And what gunpowder you have is rationed, right?"

"The Ualtarites attacked Gale in San Francisco," Sophie said. "And whoever attacked Lais used what you call mummer technology. We know John Coine and the Ualtarite guy traveled to Erstwhile to get Gale. I'm thinking they bought military hardware while they were there. Both murder attempts are tied to home. Unless I'm wrong . . ." There she faltered, but nobody seemed to notice. ". . . wrong about how hard it is to get from one world to the other . . ."

"You're not wrong," Verena said. "Almost nobody knows about Erstwhile in the first place, and travel's extremely restricted."

"The grenade connects the attempt to kill Lais to the attack on Gale in San Francisco," Sophie said. "Come on, Parrish, doesn't that have to be significant?"

"It's definitely a link," Verena said. "Two separate sets of killers making sneak trips to Erstwhile . . . the odds on that are tiny."

With obvious reluctance, Parrish nodded.

"What would Ualtar want with some polyamorous horse breeder? It makes less sense than them wanting Yacoura," Tonio objected.

"Ualtar has always had considerable friction with Tiladene," Parrish said. "They're sexually conservative, and Tiladene's disavowal of marriage and monogamy—"

"It's not about sex," Sophie said. "Lais is a biologist. He's been breeding chindrella . . . building a better spider."

Silence fell around the table.

"Holy seas," Verena said. "The guy's trying to break the Ualtarite cobweb monopoly?"

"Yes! Exactly!" Sophie felt a wave of relief. "The two islands are physically close to each other, aren't they? Similar microclimates? Maybe Lais lifted some samples, or a few Ualtar chindrella ended up on Tiladene. Either way, he's trying to produce the higher-quality silk."

Sophie's eyes stuttered off Bram's closed face, and finally she looked at Parrish. "Tell me I'm wrong. Is there a motive in there for killing Gale?"

"It's very nearly a reason to go to war," Parrish said softly.

"Which kinda brings us back to Yacoura, right?"

He nodded. "It does."

"Tell us the rest, Sofe," Bram said.

She did, the words coming more easily now. She showed them her footage of Maray's rathole of an office, complete with the shot of Captain Dracy's precious lantern, and concluding with: "We need to find out if Lais is safe. If so, we need to warn him. Do you guys use homing pigeons, or smoke signals, or what?"

"Mostly or what," Verena said.

"Meaning magic?"

"Of course."

"The Tall have an excellent clarionhouse," Parrish said. "Tonio, go ashore and express the query about the Tiladene, Lais. Inquire after him and indicate concern for his safety."

"Aye, Cap'n."

"We have to tell the Fleet about the conspiracy," Verena said.

"Agreed," Parrish said, "But we must compose that message with care . . . We can't openly accuse the Ualtarites without more evidence. We'll have to confine ourselves to knowns."

"A fact sheet," Verena said. "Of course."

"In the meantime, we don't want to wait to warn the young Tiladene when he's in danger."

"I'll go now," Tonio said.

"It's up toward the college, isn't it?" Bram said, pushing up from the table.

"Where are you going?" Parrish asked.

"The cartographer's office turned me on to a bunch of old stories about a time before the current era. Noah's ark type stuff . . . floods, mass extinctions. There's an old woman who's apparently an expert and I'm having tea with her tonight."

"What about the murder?" Parrish said.

"Sofe's got that in hand," Bram said. "And the three of you are pitching in. You don't need my help."

Sophie gave Parrish a sharp glance. "Do we?"

He threw up his hands.

"Come on, I'll walk you to the deck," she said.

"Suit yourself," Bram said, a little coolly, leading the way upward. "Who asked his opinion?"

"I'm guessing he thinks you're a bad brother," she said, switching to English.

"Captain Tasty?"

"Captain full of himself."

"You'd say if you wanted help. In fact, I assume you'd rather not have it."

"Yeah. Sorry to be petty, but I'd rather play at being Holmes than plod along twenty steps behind as your Watson."

"Don't do that, Sofe. You just put together a decent theory of the crime. There's no reason to think I'd have done any better."

"Except for your having the giant brain, none at all." But she felt a rush of relief; they were back on familiar ground. He was going to let go of being mad.

"Seriously, cut it out. You're heading up an official investigation and you're making progress despite having no experience whatsoever."

"I've had it easy. I've bashed around gathering information from people who—up to now, anyway—seemed all too happy to basically wave their guilt in my face. Maray's a slob. She left that lantern lying out. Not exactly a feat of deductive brilliance."

"Seeing the diplomat on Erinth, finding the lantern—that was luck. You saw the pattern," he said. "It's more progress than I'm making on the landmass stuff and where we are. If it turns out the answer's just magic—"

"Pretty profoundly unsatisfying, that?"

"The stars prove we're located where Earth is. You figured that out your first day here without any help."

"You're trying to make me feel better."

"What bad brother would do that?"

"You're the bestest brother," she said, and gave him an impulsive hug. "Look, I'll make up this fact sheet or whatever and you find out your creation myths. We'll give Verena her toys back, figure out what's up with the Dueling Court and get our asses home before the parents report us missing to the FBI."

"You're done seeking your roots?"

"It's cool here," she said. "I kind of love it. But homophobic religious fanatics and slavery are taking the shine off it all. And I'm in Internet withdrawal. I actually texted you this afternoon."

"You gotta stop doing that," he said.

"I know, right?"

"Listen, about what you said earlier, about needing to know your birth family. I didn't mean to be insensitive."

She hugged him again. "You're my family. You."

He pinched a little hank of her hair and tugged it, an old and familiar gesture that meant they were okay again.

"Kirs?" Tonio had been waiting, out of earshot, beside the gangplank. Bram hitched his pack and joined him.

A bell clanged twice, the sound ringing up and down the wharf, and all the rhythms of human bustle changed. Aboard the half-built ships, workers stowed their tools and prepared to make for home. Aproned clerks in the pasty shops began setting steaming, labeled parcels and pails on their counters—meals, Sophie guessed, for people with standing dinner orders. Pubs opened their doors. A few patrol officers took up posts here and there, watching the flow of people with an attitude of amiable goodwill.

Within five minutes it seemed like all of Tallon was walking home, an orderly parade of workers, clumps of uniformed men and women coalescing, chatting, breaking apart to form in other configurations.

As they passed through the crowd, Bram and Tonio stood out. They were obviously not part of the pattern.

Were there island nations where a stranger didn't stick out? Sophie thought of the cities of home, the way you could get lost in them, disappear into anonymity.

"Blackberries," she murmured.

"Pardon?"

Parrish's voice made her startle; she hadn't realized he was there.

"Invasive species," she said. "Himalayan blackberries. They took root in the Pacific Northwest, even though it's not their original niche. They've crowded out plants that evolved there over centuries."

"Like bullfrogs," he said, and when she looked at him, surprised, he said, "I've been to Erstwhile, remember?"

She was, oddly, pleased that he knew this bit of trivia about home. "Once they're established, you don't even see them. They're part of the landscape. But there must have been a time when they stuck out, when they were exotic."

"You are extremely different from any woman I've—" As their eyes met, he coughed a little and seemed to lose track of his thought. "You were saying? About the blackberries?"

"Just noticing that Tonio and Bram are conspicuously not . . . was it Tallmen?"

Her brother and the first mate had climbed up the hilly main street, about two blocks, and the two of them were shaking hands and separating. Tonio was making for a smart brick building to the east.

"No, they're not Tallmen," Parrish agreed, but he was elsewhere suddenly, his attention drawn to her brother and then—

"What is it?" The entire city had thrown a switch, out of work mode, into relaxation. The hillside, the cheery, tired people greeting each other in the street, lanterns going on in the residential districts in a spreading circle from the wharf as people made it home with their pails of dinner . . .

But Bram wasn't the only bullfrog. A gray-dressed shadow was following her brother.

"Verena," Parrish called, voice sharp. He was on his way down the gangplank, moving at a flat-out run.

*Three blocks, he's only three blocks ahead,* Sophie thought, hard on his heels. *Parrish is fast, and I could sprint that distance, even with the hill. If not for the crowd . . .*

Now they were on the ground instead of up on deck, they'd lost sight of Bram.

"What is it?" Verena was catching up as they pelted toward town. Her hand was on her sword but she hadn't drawn it.

"Someone's following them."

The Tall were a helpful people—everyone who saw Parrish coming drew aside, minimizing the jostling as he, Sophie, and Verena tried to cut their way through to the uphill artery. The light was going, and the hill was steep.

Bram had reached its crest. For a second Sophie could see him clearly, as he stood tall in a shaft of sunset, his leather backpack and his glasses and around him all the uniformed Tall. He looked like an advertisement for something. It would make a decent portrait.

Sophie flashed on Gale's words. *If you stay in Stormwrack, Sophie, you may bring down worse, and onto your closest kin . . .*

*Look back,* she thought fiercely. But the sun would be in his eyes.

"Bram!" she screamed.

Parrish was a hundred yards ahead, closing on the shadow. It would be okay.

"Bram!"

Her brother turned his back on the view of the setting sun and the wharf, vanishing from view.

Parrish hurled himself at the fellow in gray, catching him by his shoulders.

He let go just as fast.

Sophie had just enough time to see that it was John Coine, from Isle of

Gold, before the guy . . . he blurred. There was a hum and Coine was gone, just a lump or a cloud or something, airborne, surging toward and over the hill. Parrish had resumed the chase, running in the direction Bram had taken. He too was shouting: "Bramwell! Bram!"

He had his hand tucked against his chest.

"He's hurt," Verena said. "Seas, they've hurt Garland."

The cloud reappeared, rising over the crest of the hill.

It was bigger, and it had something—

—*man-sized something, a Bram-sized something, no, no!*—

—at its heart. His leather backpack dangled from the aerial clot for a second before dropping to the street.

A hum came from the shape, and as it continued to rise into the air, Sophie realized she knew what it was. It was wasps, or bees, some kind of flying colony insect. Each of them had a little thread of silk caught in its jaws, a string bound into the bigger knot at the center and they were rising out of reach now and all the homeward-bound Tall were pointing, openmouthed, as the hum of flying insects overrode their conversations.

Parrish was right behind it. He'd leapt to a six-foot-high fence, sprinted along its length and from there bounded to the rooftop of one of the tidy bungalows. He bolted up and over its shingled peak as the cloud of insects flew past. From there, he flung himself to a window ledge on a two-story building.

He launched himself into the air, arms extended, and seemed to catch something solid inside the cloud. The whole shape wobbled, drawn down by his weight, and then he was dangling in midair, from an ankle wrapped in the silky threads.

Bram's ankle.

Sophie pelted after them as the swarm buzzed and struggled, losing altitude, dragged down by the combined weight of the two men. She snatched at Parrish's legs once, missed, leapt again and caught him by both boots, pulling him down. For one instant they all three drifted, as if aloft in a hot air balloon. Something stung the back of her hand and she held on tighter. Then her feet touched down on the cobbles.

"Pull!" she said.

"No," Parrish said. His voice was tight—the sound of angry wasps was intense here. "Get hold of—I can't . . ."

She swung her other arm upward, catching his coat, but as their center of gravity shifted, Parrish's grip broke. He fell more or less right onto Sophie.

Verena made one last attempt to catch Bram's dangling foot, but the loss of drag had given the cloud upward momentum when they snapped apart; it rose to an altitude of fifty feet, clearing the highest roofs.

"A net!" Parrish shouted. He had Bram's shoe. "Does anyone have a net?"

"Too late, Kir," shouted someone. "'E falls from that height . . ."

"Can't use flame neither," someone put in.

Now the swarm was a hundred feet up, and moving fast, making for the wharf. Sophie tried to follow the cloud with her eyes, but the setting sun blinded her; she blinked hard, and when she looked again the cloud had vanished.

Parrish rolled off her. There were about twenty dead wasps on his hands, their stingers embedded in the swollen flesh. Angry welts ran from his fingertips to his forearm, crisscrossed by strands of broken silk. "I'm sorry," he said. "I'm sorry, Sophie."

She began to sob.

CHAPTER 18

Sophie had never understood why people thought it was better or somehow more grown up to bite your lips and daub your eyes and apologize for being upset. Stiff upper lips were for the emotionally constipated, as far as she was concerned.

"That's not quite true," Bram had pointed out once. "You don't blow like an oil well if you're on a climb or a dive and something goes wrong, do you? You chill right out and act to ensure your survival."

Which was different—she wasn't dangerous! But there was no risk to anyone now, so she proceeded to melt down like a four-year-old with a skinned knee. She sat on the wooden sidewalk clutching Bram's leather backpack, and sobbed so hard her ribs felt like they were cracking.

After a second, Parrish sat beside her, holding his badly stung arm out from his body and struggling for breath . . . He'd run all the way up the hill and then, in pursuit of Bram, halfway back to the beach, jumping from rooftop to rooftop as he did.

"He's alive," he managed. "Sophie, they won't kill him."

"It's a snatch," Verena agreed. "Kidnap and ransom."

Through a scrim of tears, she could see Verena standing off to one side, dancing from foot to foot, apparently unsure as to what she should do, giving little embarrassed smiles to the Tallmen toiling up the hill after their day's work.

"I've screwed everything." Sophie heaved out the words. "Up."

"The situation is suboptimal," Parrish said, having picked up the term from Bram, and she cried even harder.

"Sophie, come on," Verena said. "We'll get him back."

She ignored this.

"Garland, you should see a doctor."

Parrish nodded, absently, as if this was a great idea, something he should definitely get to in the near future.

Verena was right about that.

"Get up!" Sophie wiped her face messily. There was something in her hand—she'd torn one of the buttons off his frock coat. Tucking it into her waistband, she hitched a hand under his arm, pulling upward like a mule. "Up, up. Get up!"

After a few tugs he relented.

"Where's the nearest doctor?" Verena addressed a patrol officer who'd planted himself a little distance away, with the apparent goal of being helpful. The patrolman jerked his head—follow me, he meant—and they trooped off, single file and moving against the throng, which parted politely. People looked at them, but didn't rubberneck. They respected authority here, Sophie thought, filing away the observation and feeling absurdly guilty that she was still observing things now, with Bram gone.

*Not gone, grabbed. By pirates and religious zealots. Homophobic, slave-holding religious zealots. What have I done?*

They arrived at a little white house that couldn't have looked more like an old-timey military infirmary if it had been built by a Hollywood set designer: light green counters, silver instruments, smell of soap. All that was missing was a big caduceus on the wall. There was nothing electronic to be seen anywhere.

A medical clerk ushered them into a back room, where an old man clucked over Parrish's stings and mixed up a tub of chalky fluid that foamed like beer. "Soak those bites in this," he said.

Parrish slid out of his coat and began to struggle with the buttons on his cuffs.

"Let me," said Verena, rolling up his sleeves for him.

"You too," the doctor said, plunging Sophie's left hand into the bath—she'd gotten a couple stings. After taking a second glance at her, he wadded a clean handkerchief into her right hand.

She soaked the one hand, wiped her face with the other, and spent ten more minutes crying herself out.

"Better?" Parrish asked when she stopped, not in an obnoxious *are-you-done-yet?* way, just asking.

"*Not* better." She pulled in a long breath. "We'll have to go after the Heart of *Temperance* now. You see that, don't you?"

"The Heart's lost," Verena and the doctor both murmured.

"Why does someone always say that?"

"It's the spell," Parrish said.

"I figured that much, but what's the deal?"

"It's easier to demonstrate," he said. "Verena, what do you know about the Heart of *Temperance?*"

Her brow furrowed. "Gale told me it lay in a sea cave on the boundary between the land of the living and the land of the dead. No. She'd never say something so fanciful. It must've been someone else."

"Someone else is wrong, then," the doctor said. "Yacoura beats within the chest of a lady woven of grass, who wanders the far foggy isles of the Outlands."

"Please, Kirs." Tonio had pushed his way into the treatment area, over the protests of the doctor's clerk. "It was swallowed by a giant bird. She laid it within a ruby egg in a nest atop a mountain where nothing but flamingos live."

"The type of inscription involved is called a Legend." Parrish's hand brushed Sophie's, within the tank of bubbling remedy.

Sophie stepped back automatically, but the doctor caught her, pushing her wrist back down with a stern "Tsk!" Her fingers tangled with Parrish's within the bath. He had a dead wasp caught in his hair, his knees were muddy and his collar was open. The skin under his eyes was darkened, almost purple. His skin, even through the foaming water, was noticeably hot—heated by his immune response to the venom, probably.

Sophie curled her fingers into a loose fist, claiming a little space.

"Come to think of it," Verena said, "I remember hearing the Heart was hidden in a chamber within the anchor of some ship *Temperance* sank. *Lucre?*"

"You see how the inscription works?" Parrish said.

For once, Sophie was almost grateful for his aplomb. "Everyone has their own story?"

"It's remarkable if you ask the question in a crowded tavern," Parrish said. "There are a thousand stories about the Heart."

"But you're not affected—why? Oh! Because you helped lose it."

"Sophie, it may be better if it stays lost."

"Not up for debate," she said. "They have Bram, they want the thing and you, apparently, are honor-bound to do what I say." Her voice had risen, and though he didn't quite come to attention, something in him snapped to, stiffening into a more formal stance. "Isn't that right?"

"You're in charge on paper—" Verena protested.

"Until my brother's not kidnapped, I am totally in charge."

"Very convenient," muttered Verena. "Parrish, you're not going along with this?"

He met her gaze squarely. "Until Sophie can relinquish Gale's estate, *Nightjar* answers to her. As do I."

"You could resign," Verena said. "If you cared—"

*Oh, this is hitting the edge of nasty.* "Bram," Sophie said. "The point is Bram, Bram, Bram. Now, I'm not telling weird tales about Yacoura. Is that because I'm an outsider? Or does the spell have something to do with me?"

"Seas! The world revolves around you, doesn't it?"

"Either it's about the magic purse and Gale's job, Verena, or it's about Beatrice."

Verena's scowl dissolved into surprise. "Mom's not involved in this. She's nothing to do with Stormwrack anymore."

Parrish wheezed, rippling the roiling, blood-tinged foam of the medical bath. Perspiration sheened his face.

"Are you okay?" Sophie said.

"A little feverish, perhaps."

"Doctor?" she called. "How much venom would have been in those bites?"

He looked at them both carefully, peering into Parrish's eyes, and went digging through his cupboards for a flask. "Drink," he told Parrish, holding it to his lips, slapping his arm back into the tub when he reached for the glass himself.

"Why not hide it with Beatrice?" Sophie said to Verena. "She's out of the picture; nobody can find her. If she could disappear a whole baby, she could certainly tuck an inscription or two in her attic."

"Garland?"

He was starting to droop.

The doctor lifted Sophie's hand out of the bath, wrapping it in a towel. "Captain Parrish needs to rest."

"No," Parrish protested. "We're in a hurry."

"Young fellow," the doctor said.

"Will he be all right?" *Bram grabbed, Bram grabbed by the Ualtarites, raging homophobic zealots, Bram in danger and it's my fault, all my fault, and now if Parrish isn't okay, what will we do?*

"He'll recover, don't worry. You, young man, help me—" Tonio caught Parrish by the arm as he staggered; he and the doctor muscled him over to a starched white cot.

"Just a few minutes," he mumbled.

"Parrish? Am I right?" Sophie said.

He looked drowsy and thoroughly unhappy. "Yes. The key to finding that certain inscription lies with your mother. Verena will have to fetch her from your homeland."

"Go," the doctor said, shooing everyone out into his waiting room. "Come back a' morning. He'll be fine."

"Don't go far," Parrish said. "I'll join you—"

The doctor shut the door in their faces, leaving the three of them gaping at each other.

Finally Sophie said, "I shouldn't have pulled rank like that. I just—"

"He's your brother," Verena said stiffly. "I get it."

"Thank you."

Verena stared out through the doctor's front window, at a square where some of the Tall were seated in groups of two or three on painted white benches that had been set up around a bandstand; they were munching the things in their dinner pails and chitchatting. "We're going to need to fetch Mom and sail out of here before the Watch shows up. They'd order us to find some other way, to leave Yacoura alone."

"We might have more time than you think," Tonio said. "Someone's damaged all the blotting paper at the clarionhouse. I couldn't express a warning to the Tiladene, and we're not going to be able to contact the Fleet."

"Excuse me?" Sophie said. "They don't have more paper?"

"It's magical . . . it has to be prepared," he said. "And you won't catch the Tall restocking until they've thoroughly assessed the security breach. They're very bureaucratic here. I had a scribe copy me six versions of the dispatch on ordinary pages. We can post them on outgoing ships."

Verena frowned. "We're going to have to split up, then."

"Why?"

"Someone *has* to tell Annela what's going on," she said. "Whatever's happening, it affects the Cessation. And Bram's kidnappers are without honor."

"Of course they're without honor!"

"No, it's—look, Sophie, it's so serious here to break your word; you can't guess how much of a taboo it is. Even kidnappers and blackmailers generally stick to their agreements, especially in cases like this, where their motives are political. Because they're acting for their island, see?"

"To be labeled a people without honor would be a devastating blow for any nation," Tonio agreed. "At the very least, there'd be a move to stop trading with them. The risk they're taking is immense."

"I'm not following you. They're kidnappers," Sophie said. The stings on the back of her hand were throbbing.

Verena said: "What happened with the Tiladene fellow and the racehorse, the people booby-trapping that inscription to blow up . . . what was the guy's name?"

"Lais Dariach," Sophie said.

"It's unusual. Generally speaking, if someone gets blackmailed and they pay the ransom, everything comes out okay."

"Verena's right," Tonio said. "Under normal circumstances I'd say that if we got . . . that certain inscription, we could swap it for Bram without much fear. But if the same people involved in this are the ones who tried to kill your Kir Dariach—"

"It's all connected," Sophie said dully. She was more certain than ever. "All part of the same conspiracy."

"We can't trust them to make the switch honorably."

It was stupid to be upset about this, Sophie knew. She'd been watching cop shows since she was a kid, and at home you could *never* trust kidnappers. If they hadn't said anything, she'd probably have assumed the people who'd snatched Bram couldn't be relied upon to let him go. Now, finding out that they should play fair but simply wouldn't—

Verena gave Tonio a look that probably meant: *Don't get her crying again.* What she said was: "One of us has to go home, and the other has a duty to go report to Annela."

"They'll never believe me," Sophie said automatically.

"Annela will believe Garland. Besides, you convincing Mom . . ."

"Oh, good point." She thought back to the total disaster that was her last conversation with Beatrice, and then imagined having to tell her that first, Gale was dead and second, she needed a favor.

Verena was right. It would be easier to go with Parrish and try to sell Annela Gracechild on a big political conspiracy.

"It'll be quick for me to go home," Verena said. "I can transit by myself, and I have an open travel permit. If you went back to Erstwhile, you might not be allowed to return."

"Screw that. I'm not leaving here without Bram."

"I should never have brought you guys." Verena rubbed her face. "I've made a complete mess of everything."

"It's my fault," Sophie said. "I stole your purse."

"And now you're going off to the Fleet to report in," she said. "Sorry. I don't mean to be self-centered. Of course your brother is the priority— but it's going to cement your hold on my position."

"Please, forget what I said before. We'll get the you-know-what, rescue Bram, and then you can challenge me. I'll forfeit and if the purse doesn't like it, we'll tell Annela to go at its zipper with a scalpel."

That got her a tired chuckle.

"Seriously. Challenge away, any time you want."

"I believe you." Verena nudged her ankle with one booted foot.

She nudged her back. "All I want is to take my brother and go home."

"We'll get him back," Tonio said.

Verena was looking at the two welts on the back of Sophie's hand. They had begun to ooze a thin, gold-orange fluid. Wasp venom, presumably. She had nothing to sample it with. "Do they hurt?"

"Everything hurts," Sophie said, but then she realized it wasn't true . . . it just felt that way because of Bram. "No. They tingle a little, like licking a battery. Or . . . there's a noodle house near Berkeley that makes a hot mapo tofu that sort of has this electrical burn . . ."

"Shalin?"

"Yeah."

Verena handed her a strip of cloth, seeming to expect Sophie to dab at the venom.

"We can ask the doctor how sick the venom will make Parrish," she said. "If you're worried."

"He just needs to sleep it off, as *Dottore* said," Tonio said.

She felt a pang, a sense of let-down. She'd suggested it for Verena's sake, but now she wanted to know, too. She touched her fingertips again, remembering the unnatural heat of his skin in the foaming bath. Remembered him running over the rooftops, graceful as a cheetah, bent on saving Bram.

Tonio broke her chain of thought by adding: "Anyway, it'll do Garland good if it's a bit painful."

"Excuse me?" Verena gaped at him.

"Flailers, you know. If it hurts enough, maybe he'll stop beating himself for losing Gale."

"Sorry . . . flailers?" Sophie said.

"Garland was raised by monks." Tonio made a swinging motion with his right arm, as if he were lashing himself with an invisible cat-o'-nine-tails. There was an undertone of bravado to his words; he was probably worried too. "The people of Issle Morta have worked self-blame up to one of the great crafts."

"You're speaking out of turn, sailor." The door to the treatment room opened and Parrish appeared, still looking feverish. Though he'd chastened Tonio, he didn't seem angry. His arm was in a sling; what skin she could see was covered in bites and marked with the same seeping orange streaks as Sophie's hand. His fingers and wrist were puffy. "It's all right," he said, mostly to Verena. "I can sail. *Nightjar* will make for the Fleet."

"*Dottore* said you should sleep."

"I've convinced him I can rest when we're underway. Tonio, ready the ship."

Tonio hopped up and made for the door without any further objection.

"You sure you're good to go?" Sophie said.

"Tonio's opinion to the contrary, I'm not self-destructive. Bram's safety is our chief concern."

She felt tears threaten again.

"You don't mind if I ask the doctor if you're at death's door, do you?" Verena said stiffly.

He made a clumsy "suit yourself" gesture and she stomped off into the back room.

Sophie let out a long breath. "They won't kill Bram outright just for being queer, will they? The Ualtarites?"

"How will they know?"

She shrugged. "They knew about Tonio."

"They would have researched the *Nightjar* crew when they targeted Gale. In any case, I think the Golden will hang onto Bram. That was John Coine we saw, wasn't it?"

"Yes. So that's better? If Isle of Gold has him?"

He had been leaning, ever so slightly, on the door frame, but now he straightened, standing on his own. "They don't share the Ualtarites' prejudices."

"But?"

"We should make for the ship."

"Don't hold out on me. What are you worried about?"

"Bram's mind is remarkable. He's practically an object of value in his own right. An intellect that sharp, hungry for knowledge, honed further by magic, could be turned to a thousand mischievous uses."

"Figures. If only I could text him. Hey, bro, act like a stupid." As she said the words, she felt the tickle of an idea. It was followed by a surge of guilt.

Verena returned with the doctor, clearly satisfied, or as close as she got to it. "Okay, let's ship out."

"We need Sophie's badge," Parrish said, and Verena looked stricken.

"Gale's badge," Sophie corrected. The protest rang false somehow; hadn't she just told them all she'd cling to the job like a burr if it meant saving Bram? She pulled it out. "Why?"

"I've asked the doctor's clerk to prepare a bill for our treatment," he said, pointing with a sausagey finger at a page. "Sophie, impress the badge into the softer paper here, and sign below."

"We haven't had to do this before. Are we broke or something?"

"I'll explain later," he said. "Thank you, Doctor."

"Straight to bed. And salt bathing," he said. "You too, young lady, if you don't want those stings to scar."

"Okay, thanks."

As they made their way to the wharf, walking slowly, she could hear Parrish's breath whistling a little.

*Nightjar*'s crew was readying her to weigh anchor as they arrived.

"Okay," Sophie said. "You, to bed."

"Soon," Parrish said.

"What was that business with the badge?" Verena asked.

Parrish said: "Official invoices signed and stamped to Fleet Accounts are expressed out via the clarionhouse, on a priority. Once the Tall replace their sabotaged paper stores, the doctor's fee will be one of the first things sent out. The invoice will show up on *Constitution*—that's the ship that administers the government, Sophie. *Nightjar*'s official purchases are flagged."

"So?"

"I included a short piece of code as a note, under the amount. It asks the Watch to dispatch a ship to Tallon. Verena and I told Gale's friends here in town how things stood. They'll pass the story along if . . . if we're unable."

"If we get sunk, you mean? These friends won't know to tell the Watch about the bad guys grabbing Bram."

"Sophie, half the town saw them take Bram. It will be reported."

"Yeah," Verena said. "It was a pretty brazen grab."

"Audacious," Parrish agreed. "Even by the Piracy's standards, that was extraordinary."

"They're trying to draw attention away from the Ualtarites," Sophie said.

"Pardon?"

"We aren't meant to know they're in this together, remember? They don't want us to know the whole point is them killing Lais and invading Tiladene," she said, thinking: *Doesn't this follow? Maybe I'm wrong. What do I really know about this place?*

*Besides that it's a terrible, stupid, crazy, savage, awful place? I should never have come.*

But Parrish nodded. "Perhaps. Though I can't see why Ualtarites would consider reclaiming the Heart an advantage."

"Isn't it obvious?" Sophie said.

They looked at her as though she were half crazed.

"They . . . well, I mean, what I was thinking is they aren't actually gonna let the Golden smash the Heart of *Temperance*. What would that get them?"

"A pissed-off Fleet, unified and fully capable of flattening them when they launch their wannabe war with Tiladene," Verena said.

"Yeah. It's not like they'd be sinking *Temperance*, right? Just making it impossible for her to remote-sink their warships. And the Fleet must have other combat vessels."

"What, then?" Parrish said.

"Don't you think it's possible—I mean, maybe I'm wrong, oh, I guess perhaps this is stupid. I just thought they'd hold it hostage instead. It's a big symbol. If they threaten to bust it, get everyone all up in arms about whether to call their bluff or not—"

Parrish blinked. "A deterrent?"

"It just seems that it's what you all do here. I thought I could imagine that Tanta Maray woman saying 'Hey, Fleet? You ignore our little raid on the slutty spider-breeding heathens, or we'll squash your big-time symbol of the super truce.'"

"Cessation," Parrish corrected.

"Wow," Verena said. "*Wow*. If it worked, if the government backed down, Ualtar and Isle of Gold could pretty much do whatever they pleased until someone got up the nerve to steal it back."

Relief—at being on the right track after all—flooded through Sophie. "Or calls their bluff."

"It would be nearly impossible to get the Convene to agree to sacrifice *Temperance*, especially if the crisis develops quickly," Parrish said. "You're right, Sophie. That's why they sabotaged the clarionhouse—to buy themselves enough time to get positioned. They don't have Yacoura yet."

"We have to get moving," Verena said. It was as though Sophie's words had dialed up some inner tension in all three of them—Tonio and Parrish, too.

*Because it's war,* she guessed. *A hundred years of peace and now someone's trying to throw it in the furnace.*

"I'll head home at dawn to talk to Mom. Garland, you promised that doctor you'd sleep, and Sophie . . ."

"What?"

"I dunno. You got wasp-bit, too, didn't you?"

"Resting would be wise. Who knows when the next crisis will arise? Kirs, good night," Parrish said, offering them a bow. He went forward, conferred briefly with Tonio, then vanished into his cabin.

Sophie stayed where she was, standing against the rail, letting the cool night air glide over her arms, a silky, comforting caress. The stings on her hand twanged faintly with every shift of the breeze; it felt as though there were little pins embedded in her skin.

*Parrish must've been bitten fifty times.*

He had certainly done everything he could to save Bram.

She thought of what Tonio had said, about him being a flailer. Was he in his cabin right now feeling guilty about having failed?

There was plenty of guilt to go around, wasn't there?

The crew moved around her, quietly putting out sail under Tonio's direction. The ship was running fast; the breeze was light, but they were making the most of it.

Yet it would take days to get anywhere. She'd always thought of herself as someone who wasn't wired right into the Internet, but like everyone else she fired e-mails around the world in mere blinks, hearing back within the hour. Now there was nothing she could do, not one person she could contact. They were in this terrible all-fired rush, Bram was in danger, and if they screwed up or got delayed, a war might break out.

Even sailing at the best speed they could make, they might not reach the Fleet for a week.

She couldn't help herself: She groped through her things for her phone and texted her brother:

*Sorry. I'm so sorry. Don't get hurt. Don't let them know how smart you are. Don't tell them your middle name.*

*Message will be sent when we return to the service area.*

A splash, fifty feet off the bow. Sophie tensed, bracing for another magical assault, or perhaps something worse: a submarine attack, flying monkeys with swords, who knew? But it was a bottle-nosed dolphin, skimming along the same course as *Nightjar*, zooming along the ocean and it wasn't alone. Suddenly they were at the center of a pod of at least two hundred striped dolphins, *stenella coeruleoalba*, in the moonlight, chasing along the ship for the fun of it, chattering and squeaking a bit as they did. The whole ocean stretching endlessly to the sky, the familiar stars above, and despite everything, despite Bram being in danger and all this complicated incomprehensible legal stupidity, despite Gale being dead and Parrish having his arm all ballooned up and Bram being gone . . . how could she think of anything but Bram being gone?

All these smart dolphins, frisking at sea, chasing them for the fun of it, and her the only one with leisure to watch and marvel. Sophie caressed her camera but didn't try: it was too dark—she didn't have the right equipment. You had to know when to take your shot and when to just stop and drink in the beauty.

She stayed out on deck, watching them, until she was chilled to shivering and the pod had moved on.

## CHAPTER 19

She woke to a predawn tap of a sailor on her cabin door. "It's Sweet, Kir Sophie. Breakfast in thirty minutes."

"Thanks."

She got up, stretched, and made herself meditate, once again forcing her mind to stillness before she contemplated her hodgepodge of outfits from home and Erinth.

*Brother kidnapped, a war to stop, and I have absolutely nothing to wear.*

The formal dress was hanging, inside out, from a corner of the hammock, an impractical frippery. She fingered its petticoats, examining the cushy, quilted material, the weight and construction of them. "Little pockets," she murmured, tearing a line in the fabric and teasing out the quilting of one, which turned out to be a soft, precisely cut rectangle of sponge, the color of coffee with cream.

"You can always squeeze something out of a sponge," she murmured, taking a bit of shell—one of her samples—and sliding it into the hole she'd made in the petticoat. It disappeared neatly. She scooped up her filthy jeans next, scraping two crushed wasps off of the blue cotton, dropping them into one of her plastic test tubes. She filled these with alcohol, corked them, and hid them in the petticoat, too.

She still had the button she'd pulled off Parrish's dress coat. She looked from it to the petticoat, but instead of concealing it in her skirt, she hung onto it as she turned her attention to the real task at hand—not saving her bits and pieces of Stormwrack samples, but getting dressed for the day.

*I wonder if Parrish will actually soak that arm of his?*

The Conto had given her a long-sleeved white shirt. She put it on, drawing the cuff over the bites on her own hand. They had mutated into pinkish boils with little crisped-looking curls of dead skin at their peaks.

When she flexed her fingers, stretching the skin, she felt a tightness that wasn't quite pain.

She put on the white shirt with a belt—it was long enough to pass for a dress—and a pair of spandex leggings beneath.

"It's not like Fashion Cop's here to complain," she said to the snake-tailed ferret as she tucked Parrish's coat button into her waistband. The ferret made a sort of chirruping noise, rubbing at her hand affectionately and apparently hoping to get picked up.

"Are you adopting me?" She set it on her dressing table so it could lap a bit of her water. In the morning dimness, the spellscrip branded onto its skin glowed, the letters clear though their meaning was incomprehensible. It wound and unwound itself on the dressing table. The snake head lashed back and forth, blinking.

*If you'd sit still, I could take a shot of that text on your flanks.*

Instead, she pulled out all the tech in her travel chest, synchronizing the phone and the digital video camera again, cramming the smartphone's memory with video files.

*That's what I bought you for,* she thought. *That's why I charged up the credit card.*

She'd spent every cent she could scrape together when Verena said she'd take them to Stormwrack. *Buying toys and urging Bram to come keep me company. And even now, with Bram in danger, what am I doing? Preserving data when I'll probably never be able to explain where I got it?*

*It's his data too,* she rationalized.

Another tap: Verena, poking her head in. "What are you doing?"

"Keeping busy so I don't go insane with worry."

Verena edged inside. The ferret nosed at her hand.

*Maybe it's not fond of me at all,* Sophie thought. *Maybe it's just breakfast time.*

"I've been thinking," Verena said. "Bram's never been scripped before. When you get to the Fleet, you can get Annela to load some pretty decent protection onto him—a luck charm, toughness, whatever. She'll know what to suggest."

"Bram wouldn't have to be present?"

"It's all in his name. The Fleet has the best scribes in the world and this is a matter of—well, national security, basically. They'll help you."

"What if they hurt him before then?"

To her credit, Verena didn't lie—she just shrugged.

"It's better than nothing, I guess."

"When are you heading back to San Francisco?"

"I'm waiting on the angle of the sun—forty minutes or so."

"How does that work?"

"It's complicated," Verena said.

"There's clocks involved. Gale had that watch, and Annela's assistant or whatever—"

"Her name's Bettona," Verena said. "Explaining how I go back and forth to Erstwhile would take more than forty minutes even if *you* didn't end up asking me five hundred questions about astrophysics and black holes and time travel and who knows what else?"

"And I bet you're not allowed to say in any case."

"You're starting to catch on. Listen, is there anything you need from home?" She waved at the pile of clothes and gadgetry.

"Take my phone back to the Internet, will you? I've written some reassuring e-mails for our parents—they won't have missed us yet, and this'll buy us some more time."

"They're queued up?"

"Good to go, as soon as the phone finds a connection." She opened Gale's magic purse, closed the phone inside, and handed it over. "Here. Maybe if you carry the pouch to and from Earth, it'll warm up to you."

"Fat chance of that."

"Worth a try, right?"

"Nothing else you need? I'll probably be back before you reach the Fleet, but even so I'll be in San Francisco for at least a day."

"Sure, why not? Bring me . . . let's see. Good wishes from your mother, a trank gun and taser—since I can't duel—a squad of fanatically loyal ninja marines, a document scanner, Bram's therapist, a dirigible, a glider, the UCSF evolutionary bio department, and maybe an order of mapo tofu from Shalin."

The faintest hint of a smile. "Medium spicy?"

"Extra hot."

"Which reminds me. Parrish said breakfast's on."

"How's his arm?" Sophie made for the hatch. The ferret pawed at her elbow and she let it climb her and settle its negligible weight on her shoulders.

"Looks better to me. He's lost that feverish look."

She wondered if she should say something about Captain Arrogant. But what? So, sis, the cute boy . . . how much do you like him? The answer to that was obvious in any case. She fingered the button from his jacket.

*How much do I like him?*

She shook the thought away and said, "He's a good guy."

Verena grunted. "Sea smart, land dumb."

Parrish cut off any chance of bonding, over his cuteness or other qualities, by choosing that moment to show up.

"Good morning," he said, his tone brisk, all business. His arm was speckled with the same weals as Sophie's, fifty or sixty of them. On his walnut skin, the redness was less apparent, but the dry peaks of the bites looked worse.

At least the arm looked like an arm now, and not a balloon.

"I've been thinking of ways to improve upon our tactical situation once we get to the Fleet," he said. "It's occurred to me that Bram's never been scripped—"

"So we can cast a protection on him or something?" Sophie said. "Verena suggested that."

"Of course she did." He smiled approvingly.

*There's affection there for sure,* Sophie thought, looking from one to the other, *but is it sexual, or more . . . cousinly? Do they have chemistry?*

Breakfast turned out to be a peculiar stew that reminded her of a Newfoundland delicacy, fish and brewis. It was a combination of bread pudding and lightly salted orange fish, served with a side of pale, rose-colored slices of a tangy preserved fruit. There was strong coffee. Bram's favorite alkaloid. Sophie picked at the food, letting the ferret high-grade out the best pieces of meat.

Verena checked her watch. "Twenty minute warning."

Parrish gave her a bulging envelope, closed with a big red seal. "I'm not sure if this will help persuade Beatrice to help us. She didn't much care for me even before Gale—"

"Don't start," Verena said. "You and Gale sailed together forever. It's not like you fumbled her the first time out. Her finally getting killed, it's not your fault."

His expression was unreadable. "Let's hope Beatrice sees it that way."

"Oh, you know my mom. She'll ladle out blame in equal portions. Some for me, some for you, some for Sophie . . ."

"Fish for breakfast," Sophie said. "Guilt for lunch."

"Your mother may be high-strung but she's not unfair, Verena," Parrish said.

*That wasn't chemistry, that was definitely cousinly.*

*Okay, Sofe, stop! What do you care about Verena's unrequited crush?*

She wrestled her thoughts back on point. "If Beatrice does this for us, for me and Bram, I'll leave you all alone," Sophie said. "Tell her. I'll back off. I just want Bram returned—"

Whatever Verena might have said was interrupted by a cry from above: "Sail!"

"Crap." Was it the *Ascension,* come to sink them after all?

Moving with both speed and precision—he was stunningly graceful, Sophie thought, and she remembered touching his fingers in that medicinal, foaming bath—Parrish finished his coffee, fumbled to shove his ridiculous bicorne hat down over his curls and made for the hatch, swinging his coat off its hook as he went. By the time Verena and Sophie had made it up to the main deck, he was every bit the official figure, complete with spyglass, ramrod straight and scanning the horizon.

Fog had risen in the night, leaving the sea half shrouded. Sophie thumbed on her camera, scanning in the same direction he was looking.

There. A trim-looking . . . would you call that a caravel? Three-masted, square-rigged . . . it was barely visible, an outline etched on rolling fog.

Beside her, she felt rather than saw the motion of Parrish clicking his spyglass shut and turning on his heel. "Nothing there."

"It's two points west of our bow," she said. "I don't recognize the flag, though."

"Sophie," he said. "Please, don't—"

"Don't what?" She'd recorded a few seconds of the ship; now, as it vanished behind a cornice of mist, she flipped the camera screen to display mode to show him what she'd caught. "Am I good or what?"

"That's a Fleet flag," Verena said, her head pressing against Sophie's as they peered at the screen. "They've sent someone to find us. To escort us! This is good!"

But it wasn't. That was obvious from Parrish's expression.

"You were gonna pretend you hadn't seen her," Sophie accused. "You were going to boot it in the opposite direction and vanish into the fog. What the hell?"

"I assure you, I had not seen the flags this ship was flying . . . until now."

"Meaning what? You got half a glimpse and were gonna run away before you were sure, so you could say truthfully that we didn't know who they were? Parrish?"

"Yes." One word, bitten off so short it was almost prissy.

"But why? Don't we want the Fleet? Haven't we been trying to get—"

He pressed his lips together. "It's done now."

"What's the problem?" Verena was still examining the image. "That's . . . that's a Judicial flag, isn't it? It is—that's a serious Judicial array. Who the hell is on that ship?"

"The ship is flying the official colors of the Duelist-Adjudicator," Parrish said. "It's his private sailing vessel."

"They're ordering us to match course."

"Indeed."

"Why would the Duelist—" Verena began.

Sophie said: "Could we sort out the inheritance, then? Could Verena challenge me?"

Her sister brightened. "I think we'd have to go to the actual Dueling Deck. But maybe the Adjudicator could file the paperwork, or at least advise us."

"Great!"

Verena's watch beeped again. "I'm supposed to leave in ten."

"You'll have to wait," Parrish said. "Now we've seen them, we're honor-bound to obey."

Sophie's nerves, already strained, snapped entirely. "What's the big deal? You like honor and obey. You're practically made of honor and obey, as far as I can tell."

Verena said, "We've been trying to connect with someone official for days. Why not them?"

"It's because they're Duelists, isn't it?" Sophie said.

That got them a nod.

"What is the problem here with the Dueling thing, Parrish? Why was Gale all stay away, stay away? Did someone challenge me in utero?"

He avoided her gaze.

"The truth's sailing toward us at fifteen knots or better, isn't it? You think they're gonna keep her big secret?"

"She wouldn't have wanted this." Parrish leaned on the rail, just for a moment, as if trying to will the larger ship away. Sophie saw fatigue there, and a lingering pain from the wasp bites in the way he shifted his weight off the arm. Beneath that, she sensed, was something bigger, a great depth of feeling. *He sailed with Gale all those years, and I keep forgetting that he's sad, he's grieving. They must have been so close. I wonder if he has anyone else at all . . .*

She thought of her family. *I had it so good, and now maybe I've lost Bram. What'll I say to Mom and Dad?*

She'd have to give up diving, get a nice safe job in town and devote herself to being boring and taking care of them.

*I've destroyed two families, all in one cruise.*

"She's right, Garland. At this point either you tell us or they do," Verena said.

"Of course," Parrish said. "If the ship's here, it's all come out anyway. Sophie, Verena . . ."

"Yes?"

"Aboard that ship. I mean, the Duelist-Adjudicator himself . . ."

"Yes?"

"He's rather an imposing individual. His name is Clydon Banning, and he's from—"

"Now you're stalling!" Sophie said.

"Come on, Garland, it'll be okay," Verena said. "Choke it out."

He rubbed his jaw, as if checking for a beard, and squared off, just a little, like a soldier in trouble. "Clydon Banning is your mother's ex-husband, Verena. Nobody's ever said anything to me directly, but the Duelist-Adjudicator is . . . it's almost certain he's Sophie's father."

## CHAPTER 20

Father.

The women gaped at Parrish.

Finally, Sophie said: "Are you going to tell us anything more?"

He colored. "I should leave that for His Honor."

"That figures." She was so mad she was shaking.

Instead of pummeling him, or even bellowing about his being the latest in the long string of people trying to hold her at arm's length from the truth, Sophie turned on her heel and marched to her cabin.

As soon as she had slammed the door and thrown the bolt, she regretted it. She had a zillion questions.

Pride kept her from running back up to demand the answers.

"He wouldn't give them anyway," she told Blue, the ferret. "Who does he think he is?"

She paced the cabin in a stew over Captain Tasty . . . okay yes, he'd busted a gut to rescue Bram, and Verena was incredibly crushed out on him, or resenting his reticence and unswerving loyalty to a dead woman—which, okay, pretty admirable in its way except that it was making all this harder. And anyway, at the end of all this she was going home . . . It wasn't as though they were embarking on a beautiful, lifelong friendship. Rather than chew over all that she pressed her face to the portal and stared at the Duelist-Adjudicator's flag. The ship seemed much closer now, as if it had leapfrogged five or so of the miles between them. Perhaps the window glass had a curve to it.

*Birth father. Gonna finally meet the birth father.*

*What if he's just come all this way to tell me to stay the hell out of his life?*

"He could've sent a note for that. He's coming toward, not running away. That's got to mean something, doesn't it?" Blue whined at her.

*Beatrice was horrified by the mere mention of him.*

*He's her ex-husband. You're allowed to hate your ex. And everyone—well, Verena and Gale—they both basically said that Beatrice was a high-strung drama queen.*

*I could ask Parrish if that's true.*

*OMG, forget Parrish!*

The ship, she noted, was making astoundingly good time.

She reached for her phone, thinking to send Bram another comfort text: *Found my father, eek, what if he's Darth Vader or something?*

. . . and remembered she had given it to Verena.

She went into a frenzy of looking at all Gale's books for information on the structure of the Fleet's court system. What exactly was a Duelist-Adjudicator?

Nothing.

"It's a pretty self-explanatory title, isn't it?"

Blue batted at the square of sponge she'd liberated from the princess dress.

Well, that at least would keep her busy. She fished out the rest of her small samples—seeds and shells and snips of leaf, insects in alcohol—concealing them at even intervals within the petticoat until, up on deck, the sailors began to bring the two ships alongside each other.

"I could've spent all that time and energy changing my clothes," she said suddenly. "Damn!"

*Changing into what? What did you wear to meet a . . . oh, she was so overthinking this!*

She fought back a flood of tears, reaching for reason. Her father could reject her in a peasant shirt and spandex tights as easily as anything else.

"Want to come?" she asked the ferret. "Moral support?"

Blue unwound itself, sniffed, and then settled by her pillow, the snake's head of its tail stretching out into a thin ray of sunshine coming through the dark glass.

Sophie went back up on deck.

The two ships were perhaps fifty feet apart now, easing ever closer. *FJV Sawtooth* was painted on the caravel's prow. As it came between them and the sun, its shadow fell like a blanket, chilling *Nightjar*'s decks.

Her crew was dressed in trim black uniforms with little pillbox hats and an insignia—a sword and a fist, crossed—embroidered in gold on their shoulder. They were neat and efficient as they brought the ships alongside, matching speed and course with *Nightjar*.

A tall, lean man in a black half-cloak leaned on the rail—over it, almost—scanning the ship, alert as a tracking dog on the scent. As his gaze lit on Sophie, he broke into a wide, bright-eyed, thoroughly delighted grin. "*Perza vrai? Il Feliasdottar?*"

Sophie waved mightily. "Hello! Hello!" To the others she whispered, "He doesn't speak Fleet? He has to speak Fleet to be a judge, doesn't he?"

"He's attempting Verdanii," Verena said. "His accent's trash. It's polite of him, though."

"Hello!" Sophie called again.

"Sophie—" Parrish murmured. "You mustn't tell him anything about Erstwhile."

"State secret, right?" she said coldly. "I remember."

"It's more than that. Your mother's peace of mind, her sense of having found refuge—"

She rounded on him. "What'd he do?"

"It's—I wouldn't say exactly that he—now isn't the time."

"Fine. I won't tell him about San Francisco."

He drew away with a tight bow. *That's right. Bug off, Mister Secret-Keeping Captain of Secrecy.*

"He doesn't look like the incarnation of evil," she whispered to Verena. Her half sister laughed.

"Hello," Sophie called again. "Kir . . . Banning? Hi!"

The man—her father? really?—beamed. He all but glowed.

Clydon Banning was fiftyish from the look of him, an athletic fifty, with wavy chestnut hair and an unmistakably wolfish expression. He had strong-looking hands, straight, perfect teeth and wore a cutlass at his hip.

"It's true," he said. "A daughter. I see the Banning in you! You must be twenty-four, yes?"

She nodded.

"What's your name?"

"Sophie. Sophie Hansa."

By now the two ships were barely within reach of each other. He leapt up to the rail. "Captain?"

"You're welcome aboard, Your Honor," Parrish said. "Of course."

Banning's black-clad sailors laid a plank from rail to rail. It barely reached, but her father—her father!—leapt onto and across it, practically skipping, then hopping down.

"Might I?" He made as if to open his arms, but didn't grab.

A little dazed, Sophie nodded. Clydon Banning folded her into a hug. His cloak was heavy wool; it was like being enfolded in a blanket with hard buttons. For good measure, he kissed the top of her head.

*Great. I'm gonna cry again.*

"I can only imagine what you've been told, child, but I beg you, don't credit it until you know me," he said, ever so quietly, into her ear. Then he released her.

Then he addressed himself to Verena. "Kir . . ."

"Thorna Feliachild," Verena said. "Your Honor."

"Rumor of Gale Feliachild's murder has reached the Fleet. Is it true?"

She nodded.

"My condolences to all of you. She was a determined, resourceful woman, devoted to the Fleet Charter and the Cessation. We're all the poorer."

"Thank you, Kir."

"Please—we're family now. Cly will do." He had left a hand resting loosely on Sophie's shoulders, but addressed Verena. "You're Gale's child?"

"Her heir, yes," Parrish interrupted.

She could almost feel the chill pass between the two men. Their faces were untroubled, their voices calm, but the frost was nevertheless so palpable that Sophie half expected to see her breath fogging between them.

Cly seemed to reach a decision. "Sophie, will you come and see *Sawtooth?* We have much to discuss. I want to know everything."

"Yeah, sure. I mean, of course, I'd like to. But—"

A glint there. "But?"

"Well . . . we're sort of on a . . . mission. Solving Gale's murder. The people involved—Goldmen, and Ualtarites—they've grabbed my brother."

"Brother?" For a second Cly's jaw worked, and when he spoke his voice was breathless. "There is a son as well?"

"No," she said. *Would he have rather had a boy?* "I mean, not your son. Not Beatrice's, either."

"Ah." The emotion was gone. "You were fostered?"

"I want to get to know you," Sophie said. "I can't tell you how much I've gone through—how much I've put others through—for this. But Bram's in danger, and there are all these political ties to the crime. We were going off to the Fleet to report . . ." She watched Parrish, looking for any hint she might be heading into troublesome territory.

"The Golden may be involved in a conspiracy to break the Cessation," Parrish said.

"War?" Cly was visibly jolted; his lip curled in something that might have been a snarl. "What are you doing about it?"

"Verena has to contact Beatrice. She has information we need."

"She lives?" The smile on her father's face held, but his eyes were unreadable.

"She does," Parrish said, with obvious reluctance.

"You're not bound for Verdanii."

"I prefer not to comment on our course, Your Honor."

The crinkle again. "As it happens, I too have messages for Beatrice. Perhaps, Kir Thorna, if you're going anyway . . ." He snapped out an order to a flunky who'd made it across to *Nightjar* before *Sawtooth* had pulled back its makeshift gangplank. With a bow, the younger man produced an official-looking, sealed and beribboned envelope.

"If you'll be good enough to deliver this?"

Verena accepted it warily. "What is it?"

"Court business," Cly said.

"I imagine it's a summons," Parrish said.

"Whatever family matters Gale may have divulged to you, Captain, I hardly think it's your role to speculate or gossip."

*If only he had gossiped,* Sophie thought. "Summons?"

"Child," Cly said. "Forgive me. This is difficult, and the captain means to do his duty as he sees it, I'm sure. I will explain, you have my word."

She felt a slight impulse to defend Parrish. Then again, he'd had his chance to tell her the story, ten times over, and he'd flat-out refused.

"Verena?" she said.

"I have to talk to . . . to Beatrice, if we're going to rescue Bram," she said. "And this . . . is official. We're duty-bound to deliver it."

"Do that," Cly said. "Sophie can tell me what we need to do to throttle this rebellion in its cradle—"

"Can I do that?"

"Within the limits I mentioned earlier," Parrish said.

Meaning she couldn't tell him about San Francisco. "Right."

"We can trust the Duelist-Adjudicator to act in the best interests of the Fleet."

"If you can't, the Charter and a century of peace are just about sunk," Cly said drily. "Captain, we'll amend your instructions as necessary once I understand the situation. Sophie, please, let me show you *Sawtooth*." He swept out his cape. She saw a blade—the sword—and for a second she imagined he was going to go all Errol Flynn on her: grab a rope and swing them both across to the other vessel. Instead, he was gesturing at his crew, who were once again maneuvering the ships so they could lower a make-shift bridge.

She turned to Parrish, who gave her the faintest thread of a nod. She scrambled across, up to the deck of the larger ship. Two uniformed sailors were waiting to hand her down from the rail to the deck.

"You were pretty short with Parrish just now," she said, as Cly bounded down.

"Mmm? I do apologize. Since I learned there was a child—a daughter—you! I've been in a bit of a state. You've been kept from me all this time, and I've no doubt that fellow was in on it." His eye roamed back to *Nightjar,* and his lips pulled back from his teeth. "I'm a patient man, Sophie, extremely patient, but some things strain the temper."

"Parrish makes me crazy, too," she said.

"I also talk too much when I'm excited."

She laughed. "So do I."

"Tell me all about yourself! You were fostered, you say? Where? Beatrice didn't raise you?"

"Oh no," she said. "I've been waiting for answers a lot longer than you have. If anyone's going to spill, it's you." She turned, taking in the ship. Yes, *Sawtooth* was what she would have called a caravel: square-rigged, with a look that said old-fashioned even by the standards of all these sailing ships. Its crew, compared to *Nightjar*'s, would be huge, at least a hundred sailors, probably more like two.

The ship's fighting deck was literally a fighting deck: It had three rings for practicing swordfighting, two for boxing or wrestling, and a row of practice dummies much like Verena's, except that they looked hardier, more expensive.

"Young duelists in training," Cly said, as she looked over the various combatants clashing in the rings.

"Lawyers who kill," she said. "You're all lawyers?"

"Of course," he said. "Do you fight?"

"No," she said. "Very definitely no."

"Well. If you ever wish to learn . . . or perhaps you don't believe in it?"

"You're fishing for info on me again," she said. "You were going to tell me about you."

"Guilty as charged—you're very sharp, Sophie." That bright hunter's smile again. Despite herself, she felt a glow of gratification.

"Where shall I start?" He offered her his arm, then led her along the fighting deck, offering an airy gesture to two combatants. The men, who'd been standing ready and apparently waiting to command his attention, were wrestlers. At Cly's motion, they began to circle each other. "I joined the Fleet when I was younger than you are, and I've been its creature for almost as long as your aunt Gale was."

"Why?"

"Pardon?"

"Why'd you join?"

"I had an aptitude for both personal combat and for book learning, so I was asked to, by—excuse me. Hold! Andre, you're favoring the left leg. Is it still injured, or not?"

One of the wrestlers flushed. "Merely the habit of recovery, Your Honor."

"I'd better not catch you feigning weakness in court, Counsellor. Continue."

The wrestlers resumed circling.

"Sorry, Sophie, where was I? Ah, yes, I'd written my examinations and been made a Clerk-Adjudicator, a sorry scrap like all of these, when I met Beatrice Feliachild.

"What can I say about your mother at twenty? She was beautiful, of course. I imagine she still is? But where most Verdanii are so self-sufficient, so entirely . . . oh, cloaked, I suppose, armored in their own sense of moral rightness . . ." He paused, seeming to consider his words.

In the ring, the two wrestlers had begun the head-slapping dance for position, reaching for each other by turns, twisting free, circling faster. Now the allegedly injured one, Andre, lunged in and snagged his opponent by the ankle, flipping him—but failing to pounce and pin him before he escaped.

"Beatrice needed someone," Cly said. "She wasn't at home among her people, which is always a tragedy."

Sophie thought briefly of her parents and Bram. Was that her problem? She didn't fit?

"I've never been so drawn to a woman," Cly said. "I courted her, or she me, to her family's considerable and vocal disapproval. Eventually I asked my father to approach the Allmother to beg a marriage contract."

"So you loved each other?"

He frowned. "We both believed so."

"What the hell went wrong, then?" The wrestlers came together in a clinch, their upper bodies quivering with strain as each tried to muscle the other over. "You were young and stupid and temperamentally incompatible?"

"Is that what your mother says?"

She remembered the look on Beatrice's face. Horror. It was horror. Cly seemed nice, all things considered, but— "I'm asking *you*."

"Some of it was our youth, yes," he said. "My position was also a source of strain. An adjudicator survives within Fleet society by maintaining an impartial face to all comers. You have only two choices. One is to withdraw from society—see few, befriend nobody. The other is to throw yourself into every engagement. Accept every invitation."

"See everyone? And befriend—"

"Befriend nobody."

"It sounds lonely either way," she said.

"Yes."

"And you picked which path?"

"I am a social animal, Sophie." The smaller of the two wrestlers finally threw the other, flinging him a good three feet beyond the marked boundary of the ring, where he landed with a thud that vibrated through the deck. "I chose company and conversation, however shallow, over a life of solitude in service."

*I'd probably do the same,* Sophie thought. And then: *Does he have any other family?*

"That was stunningly adequate," Cly called to the younger judges, who both wilted. "Rematch after lunch. Come, Sophie." They strolled on to one of the fencing rings, where a man and woman were going at sword-play with a speed that made Verena's duel with Incindio, back on Erinth, seem pokey in comparison.

*I couldn't win against the least of these guys,* Sophie thought. *If they appointed a proxy for me, I'd get the whole estate: the job, the houses, the magic purse. And Cly's my father. Would it be up to him?*

Cly continued to reminisce: "The need to mingle socially, night after night, wore on your mother. She is emphatically not a sociable creature, as you may have observed. I wasn't understanding. I had a vocation; she had yet to chart a course for her own life. It seemed obvious to me that if she couldn't choose, she might at least contribute to my success."

"Nice," Sophie said.

"I was spoiled as a child, and somewhat hard-hearted. Beatrice was spoiled too, of course, but more tender in spirit. In that we were—how did you put it?—temperamentally incompatible."

"Was it violent?"

She had his full attention, suddenly—it was like falling under the spotlight of a police chopper. "I beg your pardon?"

*Tactful, Sofe. That was the height of rudeness.* Bram's voice, and she felt a pang. All this was just time spent not rescuing him. Worse, it was chasing this that had got him abducted.

But there was no getting out of it now. "How unsympathetic were you? Did you hurt her? Did you threaten her? You're pretty much a fighting machine, aren't you? I bet lots of people find you pretty . . ."

"Yes?"

*Could you have gone out on more of a limb?* "Pretty terrifying."

*Oh, and there are probably at least three people who overheard us.*

Parrish was probably watching from *Nightjar.* If Cly tossed her overboard . . .

*Stop obsessing about Parrish already!*

"Have I been made out this much of a monster?" Cly asked, reaching for her hand. "Child—"

"I'm not a child." She jerked back. "Answer my question."

"No!" He pulled himself up, almost to rigid, military attention, the way they all seemed to do here when things got argumentative. "I'll swear any oath you care to name. I never struck, cut, or made physical threat upon your mother. I've never dealt violence to anyone, for that matter, without just legal cause and the full power of the Charter behind me."

"Okay, look, I'm sorry."

"I am a well-born, well-raised, honorable gentleman of—"

"Really, I'm sorry! I had to ask."

"This is what's been said to you? Am I slandered to such a degree, to my own flesh and blood . . ."

*Oh, and they say Beatrice is a drama queen?*

"Cly," Sophie said. "It wasn't anything they told me—they told me nothing. I just assumed—"

"You assumed?"

From bad to worse. What could she say now? She could feel everyone eavesdropping: the crew, the junior judges. "Everyone's made such a big deal of keeping this secret. Stay away from the Dueling Court, they said. Stay away from Storm . . . from the Fleet. Go home, never come back. I'm sorry I assumed the worst, I am.

"But come on! There's something rotten at the heart of this. There has to be something they're afraid of. If it's not you, what is it?"

Like that, the tension was gone.

"Ah, of course," Cly said. "The obvious inference was that the rot lay with me."

"It doesn't?"

"I'd have reached the same conclusion." He shook out his hand. "The Feliachilds, that cur Parrish and the Allmother herself have conspired to hide my child from me."

"Cur?"

"I cannot know their side of the argument, and I'm sure their actions seemed reasonable at the time. But from my perspective it seems apparent their reason was petty, self-serving . . . sordid."

"What reason? Why'd they hide me?" *What'd I do? What's wrong with me?*

"Beatrice and I come from very different nations. A Verdanii woman can set aside a man if he displeases her, but my people frown on divorce.

Our marriage negotiations were complex. Time passed, and Beatrice wanted to leave me. I can understand her wishing to be free of our marriage. It had gone wrong, terribly wrong. She was desperately unhappy. We did have terrible arguments. But on paper, in the binding document we both signed—"

"Yes?"

"The possibility of divorce had been conceded, reluctantly, by my father," Cly said. "But only until such time as the union produced children."

"Seriously?"

He lay a hand on hers, peering into her eyes. "Are you all right?"

She nodded, though in truth she felt a little stunned. "Me being alive meant no breakup?"

"She couldn't have divorced me if it were known she was pregnant. Could never have divorced me once you'd been born. And by turning up now . . . your very existence makes you evidence of breach of contract. You've invalidated my divorce and branded Beatrice Feliachild a fraud. A bigamist too, if she's remarried."

*Which she has, and you're fishing again.* Instead of calling him on it, Sophie asked: "So that letter you gave Verena, for Beatrice. Captain Parrish said it was a summons?"

"It is," Cly said, and there was no mistaking the satisfaction in his tone. "An arrest warrant."

## CHAPTER 21

*If you stay in Stormwrack, you'll bring trouble to your closest kin.* So Gale hadn't been referring to some big D destiny thing at all. It wasn't prophecies or soothsaying or fate she was afraid of.

*Just a lawsuit,* Sophie thought. *What a relief!*

Whatever she might have said next was interrupted by a shout from the crow's nest: "Spell! Two points north—"

The seas were boiling.

"What now?" she groaned.

Cly cast an eye on the water. "You said it was the Golden who had your brother? This might be their ransom demand."

"I already know what they want."

"There's a formal show of threat—their traditions are grandiose."

Something white blue was rising from the froth, a solid form . . . an iceberg, Sophie realized, a gigantic jagged crag made of ice, with a face carved into it. A hundred feet high, dripping and glassy, its eyes were whitened by what looked like hammer blows that cracked and crazed the frozen water's surface, so that it resembled a shattered windshield.

"Holy crap," she muttered.

"Have you never heard of a kalassi?" Cly asked.

She shook her head.

"In the days after the Fleet took to sinking their ships, the Piracy resorted to other means of raiding. This was one of their more effective spells."

The iceman had continued to rise and grow until it towered above both ships, until it bobbed on the water, the form of a man, bare-chested, submerged below the ribs. It wore the face of John Coine.

He cast a disapproving eye over *Sawtooth.* "You've involved others in our business, Sophie Opal Hansa."

Before she could answer, Cly put his hands on her shoulders. "This woman is my daughter, Kir. If anyone has involved me, it is you."

"How's Bram?" Sophie said. "If you've hurt him . . ."

"The boy breathes."

She felt a rush of relief, so strong her knees buckled. She grabbed for the rail, steadying herself. *He's alive.*

"Will you exchange our heart's desire for him?"

Her voice wobbled, but she got the words out. "I've figured out a way to maybe get your stupid inscription. But after that stunt you pulled on Lais, with the grenade . . . if you're not gonna exchange him fair and square, why should I trade with you?"

"This is why you've run to Father?"

In a movie, the iceberg's voice would be cranked up to timber-shattering volume. But this one wasn't even amplified. Somehow that made it scarier.

Cly looked from the iceman back to Sophie. "If you have no honor, Kir, she cannot transact with you."

There was a boom as a second berg shot up out of the water, this one shaped like a hand, massive, fingers splayed, with long nails. Huge mussel shells were embedded on its fingers, like diamonds on rings. It stretched delicately, taking a grip on *Nightjar's* forward hull, curving like talons.

"Easy, child—it's all bluster," Cly purred in her ear, before she could scream. "Affect a bored aspect, if you can."

"Why does everyone here expect me to be some kind of actress?" she said.

"The art of the bluff—"

"Come on. It's all just willy-waving."

"Now you're being coarse."

The hand pushed up, up, lifting *Nightjar's* bow out of the water, a meter, then two, then five. Gale's crew grabbed for rails and rope. The cutter looked suddenly small, frail. She felt a real surge of fear, for the people aboard and for the ship, too.

As she watched, Tonio lost his balance, falling toward the stern. The bosun's assistant, Sweet, caught him—lassoed him, practically—with a loop from one of the buntlines.

The ice face looked at them, inquiringly. "Shall I go on?"

"Sophie," Cly said, "can you recover the inscription without your aunt's ship?"

"No. Of course I need *Nightjar*. It's got—"

"Shh, never mind what's aboard. Enough that something is. Are you prepared to give them what they want? No matter the cost? You cannot fail."

"Bram's my baby brother," she said. "I'd give them my eyes."

"Understood." Raising his voice, Cly said: "Bandit, I didn't much care for the former owner of that vessel, and truth be told I have a legitimate grudge against her captain."

"What's that to me? Raise up blade to him! There's plenty in Fleet would thank you for skewering the incorrigible Garland Parrish."

Cly tsked, sounding regretful. "Because of my position . . . it would look ill if I challenged him."

"T'would be murder, I suppose, but what care I?"

"If you can shake the flailer off *Nightjar*, you can have him and welcome. My concern begins and ends with my family. If the boy Bram were further harmed and my daughter's heart broken . . ."

He'd very neatly implied that Bram was his son, Sophie noticed, without saying so.

"A vendetta would damage your almighty position," Coine said.

"I am old enough to retire, young enough to pursue you, and rich enough to make a good chase of it." Cly leaned forward, smiling, looking like the prospect of such a hunt would be a delight, a lark. "I have influence, Kir. I've spent a lifetime accumulating favors without collecting. You, your family, your treasure hoard, your health, your happiness— they are all at risk if you anger me. I'm reckoned by some an ill-tempered and vengeful fellow."

"A vengeful judge?"

"Ask my wife if you doubt it."

Coine laughed.

"Kir, I've been reining in the swampside of my spirit for thirty years. I beg you, give me a reason to run wild."

Sophie shivered. *Is he bluffing?* If he was, she couldn't tell: Just then Cly looked as though he'd happily slice all comers in half, just to make sure every single one of them bled red.

John Coine's enormous, icy face twitched a grin. "You'd make a good bandit, Banning."

"Be glad my position fetters me."

"We ain't gonna kill your son, if she delivers."

"You're accused of word breaking. We require an intermediary for the exchange, someone of impeccable reputation," he said. "And put down *Nightjar*, Kir—cheap theater is worse than none at all."

The ice hand broke into shards, allowing the smaller ship to fall back to the surface of the ocean with a slap and a splash that made Sophie wince. *Sawtooth*'s deck rose, riding the wave of displaced water.

"The boy shall be taken to the Fleet and put aboard *Sackcloth*," Coine said, and to Sophie's relief he sounded disgruntled, as though he were truly giving up something he hadn't wanted to. "He will remain until Kir Hansa delivers the ransom. You trust the flailers, don't you?"

"Who doesn't?"

"It will be done immediately."

"He'd be safe enough with the monks," Cly murmured to Sophie. "Will you agree to it?"

She nodded, relieved.

"On what surety, Coine?"

The ice figure rumbled, seeming to ponder. "Shall I give you my middle name?"

"Done," Cly said.

"It's Raille," he said, and spelled it. "Of course, if Kir Hansa doesn't pay, the boy will remain in the custody of Issle Morta."

Issle Morta was Parrish's home nation, Sophie thought. "For how long?"

"Unto death, child."

"Hey—" Sophie began, but Cly put a hand on her arm.

"It's agreed." He turned to Sophie. "We can't leave him with the Golden. It's already been a day."

"What does that mean?"

"How will Kir Hansa pay you?" Cly asked the talking iceberg.

A rowboat, also limned in ice, rose from the depths of the sea. It had a long rope coiled over its bow, and a skeleton laying across its seats. "Give Yacoura to Whitey here," Coine said.

With that, he broke into a half dozen smaller chunks of ice. One fell to the deck of *Sawtooth*; the rest bobbed on the surface, a peculiar threat.

"I think we came out ahead there," Cly said, his tone as mild as if he'd been trying to cadge a dinner reservation at an impossibly popular restaurant. "Would you like to continue your tour?"

"No!" she said. "I have to go back. Your ship's great, Cly, and we'll make time later, but I have to get back on task. I need to check in with Verena and Parrish."

"I understand." He gestured, and the sailors began signaling to each other across the water, converging so they could lay a plank between the ships again.

As she made to leave, he caught her hand.

"Sophie," he said, "when I learned I was a father, my greatest fear was you would have been reared to reject and hate me. What Beatrice has done in hiding you; I can't forgive it. But that she fostered you—that she left you free to make your own judgments about us both—I am grateful for that."

"Grateful enough to not prosecute her?" She watched him closely, expecting him to waffle or make excuses: to say it was complicated, or up to the courts.

Instead, he gave her a trace of that hunter's grin. "Not that grateful, no."

"I guess it's what you both do next that's gonna matter."

He nodded. "Your brother first. The rest of this domestic tangle can wait."

She returned to *Nightjar*.

"Is the ship damaged?" she asked.

"No. How are you?" Parrish said.

*Emotionally exhausted*, she thought. "My brother's kidnapped and I'm apparently evidence of fraud. And you knew."

He nodded.

"Cly seems nice enough, for a combat lawyer."

"I believe otherwise."

"Did I ask?"

He didn't reply, but of course she had.

"Did you tell him about your home nation?"

"I said I wouldn't."

He held out a sheet of curled paper. "I've tried drafting a fact sheet about the investigation into Gale's death, one that doesn't refer to Erstwhile or anything we can't prove. I believe we might convince His Honor to rush it to the Fleet. That would leave us free to go directly after Yacoura."

She looked over the series of bullet points. "On fourteen Maia, Gale Feliachild was set upon outside her sister's home by two dagger-wielding men. The attack was interrupted by her niece, Sophie Hansa. On sixteen Maia, Lais Dariach of Tiladene survived a murder attempt which was prevented by Sophie Hansa." She looked up. "This makes me sound . . ."

He raised his eyebrows, waiting.

"I'm no action hero, Parrish."

"The facts are what they are," he said.

"You skipped everything about Stele Island and the storm and jumped straight to the salvage ship, *Estrel*?"

"We believe the storm was magical; we cannot prove it."

She read on. "The weapon used in the attempt to murder Lais Dariach originated from the resident nation of Beatrice Feliachild, as attested by Sophie Hansa . . ."

"Is something else bothering you?"

"All this stuff that rests on my word," she said. "It's not like there's forensics."

"You saw Gale attacked, and you saw the grenade that almost killed Dariach. Your word as a witness is good."

"I saw the storm."

"You didn't see *Ascension*, or any inscription related to the weather."

"No."

"All that matters is that Annela can deduce a link between Kir Dariach's spider breeding, Ualtar, and the Golden's quest for Yacoura."

"Will this do it? It seems to me the Ualtarites have been successful in using Isle of Gold as a front . . . have they done anything that conclusively ties them to this? It's all John Coine, center stage. He even gave up his middle name, just now."

"That surprised me, too." Parrish's expression was grave. "The conspirators didn't expect you to get involved. The Ualtarite and Coine attacked Gale in San Francisco because they thought that there nobody would know them. The *Ascension* had the lantern from *Estrel*, which you recognized. That connects them to Coine because Coine knows your name."

"That's a pretty thin connection."

He nodded.

"I'd rather have a fingerprint from that woman, Maray, and a DNA test and some incriminating e-mails." As she said the words, the edge of an idea came to her. Evidence. A little backup. Insurance.

"Given your father's intervention, we now have no choice but to give Ualtar the Heart. Otherwise Bram will be on Issle Morta forever," Parrish said.

"Is it awful there?"

"Dull," he said. "I can't imagine someone with Bram's gifts being content. He'd have his life, but it might not hold much value."

"We could magic him home, right?"

"No." He didn't elaborate, but the word had a finality that brooked no argument.

"Well, his life's a start. Hang on, you said we had to give the Ualtarites the ransom? It's John Coine asking for it."

"I believe the Golden will hand Yacoura over to the Ualtarites. That way Coine can claim it's not in his possession. That's where they'll be vulnerable. If we can witness the handover, or prove it . . ."

"What makes you think Ualtar will take it?"

"The Piracy's goal for over a century has been to smash the inscription. Ualtar won't trust them to show restraint."

"Because they have a grudge against *Temperance*."

"Yes."

"Over all those ships of theirs it sank?"

"The raiders knew they were at hazard, I suppose," Parrish said. "But there's more. In the late days of the Piracy, when the Fleet consisted of twenty or thirty warships from Verdanii, Sylvanna, and Tallon and the other Founder nations, it had become less of a war and more of a mop-up operation. Spies would go out seeking the names of the Piracy's ships. The names would be sent back to the captain of *Temperance* . . ."

"Who sank them from afar. Hardly a fair fight."

"There was no sympathy for them," Parrish said. "They'd been sinking ships and killing people, taking slaves, stealing, torturing, maiming those aboard. Still, imagine being afloat, knowing that at any second a person across the world might destroy you with a breath . . ."

"Sure, terrifying. I get that," Sophie said.

"The Fleet wasn't unmerciful. The Piracy had been ordered to keep their ships in harbor. Anything tied up was left alone. But there was an

Isle of Gold ship that set sail, late one night, bound across the Nameless Deep through Harrow's Bay. It was on a course that would have crossed a major merchant's route, and though it had its name painted over and its figurehead wrapped in swaddling, there was nobody afloat, they say, who couldn't recognize *Lucre* on sight. The merchants spotted her, though she was trying to avoid their notice, and sent word to the Watch, who sent word to *Temperance*'s captain, Paola Fratti."

"And poof?"

"More of a smash, I imagine," Parrish said. His gaze was fixed on the horizon. "She was bound for the nation of Allium, with a skeleton crew of forty, most of them elderly sailors. The Piracy had by that time lost many of its younger seafolk to the war. The ship was crammed to the gunnels with wounded, the sick, with aged widows and widowers, and children. There were more than seventy orphans."

"Sick people and kids?" Sophie swallowed.

"The merchants were too far away to render assistance, or so they said. Accounts differ about whether they were not near enough to have helped, or simply chose not to. Sharks set upon everyone in the water. A single lifeboat with four survivors made it to the merchant fleet."

She made herself focus on his face. She didn't want to imagine it: the shrieks of the dying, the churn in the water. Blood. "Couldn't they have appealed to the Fleet for safe passage before they set out? Why didn't they tell someone they were sending out a medical ship?"

"They did," Parrish said. "They were flying a no-threat flag, and Captain Fratti received the application for safe passage a mere hour after sinking the ship. She resigned her commission; perhaps a year later, she hanged herself. The Piracy surrendered without condition and the Raiders' War petered out shortly thereafter."

"Basically, public opinion shifted when a bunch of dead orphans hit the news?"

He nodded. "It was felt at that point that the Piracy was broken. *Lucre* was the last casualty; when she went down, the Cessation began. The deaths softened feelings on both sides. Chroniclers generally agree that guilt over the massacre hastened the Pirate nations' being admitted to the Fleet."

A thrum ran through the ship, followed by a trio of little shocks, like the ticking of a clock.

"What's that?"

Parrish let his eye roam over *Sawtooth* before answering. All seemed quiet over there, or what passed for quiet; the clash of judicial weaponry seemed to go on ceaselessly. "Come on," he said, leading her below, descending to the very bottom of the hold.

Verena was there, holding her weird pewter pocket watch, looking put-upon—but then, when didn't she look put upon?—and accompanied by an obviously furious Beatrice.

Their mother was clad in a pair of jeans and a sea-green cable-knit sweater, and her hair was pulled back in a ponytail so tight that its few gray strands glinted like electrical wire. It enhanced her resemblance to Verena, while underlining for Sophie, once again, that her half sister was just a teen.

"Bodies are just piling up around you, aren't they?" Beatrice wore the washed-out, puffy-eyed look of someone who had been crying hard. "I gave you a perfectly good start in life, but you just *wouldn't* be satisfied."

"I—" Sophie again felt that slap of rejection, and a surge of anger, too. "I didn't mean to—"

"My sister's dead!" Beatrice shouted.

"Kir," Parrish said. "The Duelist-Adjudicator's personal sailing vessel is a hundred feet off our starboard side."

"Thank you for the warning, Parrish. I know you think my voice shrill, but it won't carry quite that far."

Verena said: "Do we have to turn Mom over to him?"

Beatrice had the opened warrant in her hand. "This rubbish document says I must present myself to the Fleet voluntarily at the first opportunity."

"Banning is the Fleet, in a sense. But if he doesn't know you're aboard . . . may I?" Parrish read through the warrant. "I'm no lawyer, but I believe if we keep you belowdecks . . . I'm hoping to convince him to hurry back to *Constitution* to report the situation so far."

*Loopholes*, Sophie thought again.

"What's a few days in the brig?" Beatrice looked around the hold. "I detest this horrid old tub."

"Did Verena tell you what we need?" Sophie said. "My brother, Yacoura, all that?"

She slapped a small black case into Verena's hand. "Tell your sister that what she needs is in here."

"Uh . . ." Verena passed the case to Sophie. Their mother favored them both with a scorching glare.

*Poor kid*, Sophie thought. *What a crummy position she's in.*

"So this is it, the Heart?" she said, making it a neutral comment, directed at anyone who wanted it. She realized she was a little surprised that her deduction had proved correct. The chain of logic she'd followed to the conclusion that Beatrice was hiding Yacoura had been solid enough, but part of her had been poised, as always, for some kind of smackdown: *Sloppy thinking, Sofe, shabby conclusion, failed result.*

Despite everything, she felt a quiet and unexpectedly deep sense of satisfaction at having successfully girl-sleuthed part of the answer. "How'd you end up getting tapped to hide it?"

"Tapped?" Beatrice snorted. "Strong-armed, more like. The people on Tallon were afraid Gale would get captured by the pirates and tortured until she gave it up. This one"—she meant Parrish—"bullied me into letting them work the Legend on me before I went back home to San Francisco with the flute."

Flute. Not the Heart itself then? Sophie opened her mouth to ask, but Beatrice rounded on Parrish. "This isn't some big, soppy family reunion, Captain. Get me out of her sight, or her out of mine." With that Beatrice swept past, clinging to Verena's arm and thereby dragging her along.

"Talk about a grudge," Sophie said. "She must have been in labor with me for four days."

"I couldn't say," Parrish said.

"I wasn't serious."

He smiled weakly.

"So . . . you bullied her?"

"If she says so." He shrugged. "She was the best candidate. The fact that her home was so remote . . . Gale's hidden a few things in Beatrice's basement, over the years. Are you in accord with keeping your mother hidden until she can turn herself in?"

"Of course. If it's playing fair and all, why wouldn't I?"

"I've reallocated the cabin you share with Bram to Beatrice, for discretion. I've moved your things to my cabin."

"Where are you gonna sleep?"

"With Tonio," he said. "Sophie?"

"Yes?"

"Nothing. It's out of turn."

"No, it's okay." She remembered she'd bitten his head off when he tried to tell her about Cly. "Frankly, any advice you have to offer would be welcome."

"Beatrice is flamboyant," he said. "She feels deeply, and she's unrestrained with her passions. It worked against her here; the Verdanii expect their matriarchs to present a serene face to the world, and Fleet society is very contained. It's something I think you've perhaps found frustrating. In our dealings, at least . . ."

"Contained? More like emotionally constipated. If I started tearing off my clothes here and now in the hold, you'd say something like 'I don't think this is the time, Kir—'"

*Oh my GOD why did I put that image in his head?*

"Ah—" He blinked, as though she'd smacked him. "Well, I—no, I. Ahem. My point is that being passionate or vocally emotional isn't, uh . . . it isn't necessarily a bad quality. It might even form the basis for some common ground between you, when Beatrice is in a better state of mind. She's a smart, generous, funny woman."

"Okay, yeah, I'm a little emo too. Message received, very delicately put. Go you, Parrish. But my state of mind is pretty much all *Hey, my brother's missing*! And Beatrice is freaking out all over me when she's the one who committed fraud. Divorce fraud, how stupid is that, that you even have such a thing here . . ."

"I believe His Honor has ensured that Bram won't be injured."

"Yeah. Daddy came through. Bram's safe-ish."

He looked at the black plastic case in her hand and didn't comment.

"Fine, yes, Mom's come through too. Why is this a flute and not the actual Heart of Temperance?" She opened the case—it was a plastic harmonica case, she realized—and inside was a little silver recorder, maybe six inches long, with a whistle-shaped mouthpiece and holes.

"Don't use it now," Parrish said. "It summons an octopus; the octopus hides the Heart."

"Why not now?"

"We must get *Sawtooth* off our bow."

"Okay." She took a long breath and with it came a prickling, hot feeling. Redzone—Bram gone, both birth parents here . . . she was drowning.

*Easy. Breathe. Ground yourself—look around.* A glow within the timbers caught her eye.

"What's this?" She followed the glint to a steamer trunk, a dull-looking case with wood-grained bands and a flimsy-looking padlock.

"It's our Watchbox," he said. "If we're sunk, it goes straight to the bottom of the ocean, along with its contents. Only an officer of the Fleet Watch can recover it."

"So what's in it now?"

"Not much. We aren't carrying any important secrets at the moment."

She opened it, finding a bottle of red wine and a flour sack drawn shut with a string.

Parrish looked at the bottle. "We got this for Tonio, Gale and me. His birthday's soon."

"You're using the official spy box to hide presents?"

"Tonio joined us when he was quite young. He used to be a bit of a snoop."

She looked in the flour bag. Inside were six skeins of light brown yarn, wool or alpaca, mixed with rougher stuff, twisted coarse strands.

"What's this?"

"It's Gale's hair."

She pulled her hand back and dropped the bag. "Ewww."

"Gale was scripped inconspicuous. People didn't remember her, didn't notice her, or take her seriously. And intentions are bound into every . . . cell, you'd say?"

"Cells, yeah. Of a subject's body?"

"Exactly."

She remembered Captain Dracy's lantern, made from her father's skull. "So you make magical objects from stuff taken off dead inscribed people?"

Parrish opened his mouth to reply, but there was a tromp of feet above deck, heavy feet, and a rush of others, scurrying about.

"What's that?"

Parrish closed his eyes. "I suppose it was folly to hope he wouldn't learn Beatrice was aboard."

They rushed back up to the main deck. Sure enough, Sophie's birth parents were there; Verena stood between them, her hand hovering near her sword. Cly had the big wrestler and two diminutive clerks behind him.

He looked entirely relaxed. Beatrice looked like she was building up to another screaming fit.

*Any of these fighters could slice Verena to ribbons, and Cly's the best of them.*

"Everyone chill," Sophie said, before the atmosphere could get uglier. "We can work this out."

Parrish had eased himself to Verena's side.

*I'm going to end up alone on the ship with a hostile crew and a bunch of chopped-up human remains.* She fought an edgy giggle. *And then I guess I can turn them into magic stuff.*

"There's nothing to negotiate, Sophie," Cly said. "Kir Beatrice will be taken into custody, and you can pursue your brother's ransom."

"*Nightjar* will convey Beatrice to the Fleet," Parrish said.

Again that little gleam of . . . happiness? "Dear boy," Cly said. "Would you disgrace yourself again by flouting the law so thoroughly? Consider your position. Gale's gone. Beatrice holds you in contempt. There is nobody but these two inexperienced girls to stand between you and . . ."

He paused, seeming to consider what he might say next, and behind Verena and Parrish, Beatrice shuddered. "Social oblivion," he concluded, his tone mild, and yet he might as well have said, "I will cut on you."

"Stop, stop all this!" Sophie said. "Cly—" She wormed her way into the bristling pack and made herself lay a hand on her father's sword arm, despite a sudden feeling that grabbing live electrical cable might be safer. "Where's the harm if we take Beatrice in? Really, can't we just do it?"

"Mmmm," he said. "If it's what you want . . ."

"Well, yeah."

"If you're *asking*—"

She felt a thread of wariness. Dracy had asked if she could redirect *Estrel*, all those weeks ago, and simply saying yes had been what bound her to the magic purse. Every utterance here could have meanings she hadn't anticipated.

"This is idiotic," Beatrice broke her train of thought. "I'll go."

"Kir—" Parrish said. "We needn't give you up. His Honor has a clear conflict of interest. He isn't going to set upon us, or forcibly arrest you. Unless I'm mistaken, he's just offered—"

"Ah yes, so magnanimous. Don't you see, Parrish, His Honor just wants the girl in his debt?"

"The girl? Is that how you refer to our flesh and blood? I suppose, having thrown her aside like a scrap—" Cly asked.

"Save your elocutions for Court," Beatrice said.

"I'm executing a legal warrant, and there are any number of Adjudicators aboard who can stand witness to my behavior and hospitality—"

"Which will no doubt be impeccable. You're smoother than you used to be, Clydon."

"You, my dove, seem entirely unchanged."

"Do I get any say in this?" Sophie said.

"You've done enough," Beatrice said.

Cly shrugged, as if to say, "I tried to do the right thing."

"If you're going, Mom, I'm coming too," Verena said. Cly's brows went up, at "Mom." *That's right*, Sophie thought. *Parrish tried to imply that Verena was Gale's.* "I'll take that report to Annela, Parrish."

Parrish looked from Beatrice—who was pale and tight-lipped—to Verena, and then back to Sophie.

Of course. She was, officially, still the one in charge of *Nightjar*.

"We need to stop messing around," she said. "Am I right? It's not just Bram who's in danger here, it's the Fleet or the Cessation or whatever you call it. Gale's murder was part of a political conspiracy. The longer we sit around playing dysfunctional family, the farther ahead of us the bad guys get. We need to get warnings to Lais and the Fleet, and we need to ransom Bram."

"*Sawtooth* can reach Tiladene within three days," Cly said, "if winds are fair."

Beatrice looked from Verena to Parrish, seemed to do a bit of complex reckoning, and then barked at Tonio. "Have my things transferred to *Sawtooth*'s brig."

"You needn't pretend I'll lock you up," Cly said. "The guest quarters will be at your disposal. Eugenia will be delighted to see you."

"Captain?" Tonio said. He was still holding the suitcase.

Parrish looked to her.

Sophie could feel her father taking it in, doing the math, confirming that it was she who was in charge. But . . . yes. If Beatrice was going to insist on going with Cly after all, who was she to fight it?

"I'm sorry about all this," she said to Beatrice.

"You're going to be. Sooner rather than later, if you let *him* draw you in." With a visible effort, Beatrice pulled herself together and stomped off. Verena, looking muddled and whiplashed, handed Sophie Gale's courier pouch. The weight of her smartphone, within, was strangely comforting.

"Do you have that fact sheet, Parrish?" Verena asked.

Within twenty minutes, they were loaded up and leaving. *Sawtooth* raised more sail, gliding away, carrying with it the sound of judges at practice, clashing swords and fists thudding against flesh, bodies hitting the deck.

"Any clue why Beatrice suddenly changed her mind like that?" Sophie asked.

"What she said," Parrish said, "was that she didn't want you beholden to His Honor so early in your relationship."

"Can he really be that untrustworthy? He's a judge."

"Untrustworthy?" He seemed to be considering it.

"Maybe once Beatrice saw him, she realized she'd made him out to be worse than she thought. People do that, right? Decide someone's a monster, inflate them over time?"

He didn't agree, she could tell, because he was silent.

She watched *Sawtooth* as it dwindled to a speck on the horizon, bearing away all her newfound biological relations: mother, father, and half sister. It was an odd feeling: not quite melancholy, not quite relief. The hollow she'd felt since she was about eleven, the *who am I?* itch, had gone. Instead there was a slow churn, an ache that reminded her of the residue of a caffeine buzz.

Cly certainly hadn't pushed her away. The memory of his arms around her returned: the crush and scratch of his wool cloak and the strong arms within, that peck on the top of the head.

"He wants me," she whispered. "Would have wanted me, way back then."

She could have grown up in this weird, half-primitive place. All it would have cost was the two of them, Beatrice and Cly, being contractually strapped into a marriage that made them both miserable.

*We had arguments, terrible arguments,* Cly had said. Sophie and Bram had friends who'd grown up like that, tucked into bed each night, wide awake, listening as their parents screamed at each other. She and her brother had congratulated themselves on that: Mom and Dad barely ever snapped. They'd yelled at her perhaps twice in her whole life.

"They've gone far enough," Parrish said, breaking into her thoughts. "Try the flute now."

She opened the case Beatrice had given her. The flute was tiny, made of silver, and its mouthpiece would have fit better between the lips of a doll. A single line of spellscrip, in magenta, was etched into it. "How was it safe or smart to put an animal in charge of hiding this super-valuable thing?"

"There's a long-standing tradition of using guard creatures to hide certain inscriptions," he said. "Animals have simpler lives; they can't be bribed or blackmailed. And the octopus was only one component of the Legend, remember?"

"Right. Everyone thought something different had happened to the Lady and her octo-pet." She pursed her lips around it and let out a little stream of air, thinking to warm it. What emanated from the flute was a long, peculiar warble, high-pitched and liquid, random and quavering. It made her lips tingle and tickle; the urge to stop and rub at them was overwhelming.

A splash from the port side.

She leaned over the rail. The mantle of a large octopus had surfaced; it was the color of blood, and it looked straight into her eyes. Sophie blew on the flute again—what the hell—and it stretched out tentacles on the surface, extending like a big red parasol, almost two meters in diameter. It seemed, somehow, to expect something of her.

"Now what?"

"I'm not sure," Parrish said. "I'd hoped it would just bring Yacoura."

"We are due an easy win," she said.

This opinion notwithstanding, the octopus collapsed, like a tent, head sinking first, limbs closing inward like a flower until it was below the surface, invisible. It popped up again, spitting.

"It wants us to follow it," Sophie groaned. "Is that right, Lassie? Has little Timmy fallen down a coal mine?"

The octopus dipped again, surfaced again.

"Lower a rowboat," she said. "I'll get my diving kit."

She trotted down to her cabin, where she was jolted, momentarily, to find it empty and tidied, the berths so stiffly made they seemed starched. Had someone come and taken her samples, her cameras? And—a piercing sense of hurt—where was Bram's stuff?

Then she remembered: Parrish had been planning to move everyone around, to hide Beatrice from Cly.

She went up to Parrish's cabin, tapping on the hatch before entering, even though she knew he was up on deck.

Parrish's cabin was small, smaller than the double room she had been sharing with her brother. The bunk, tucked into one corner, was covered in a blanket woven of coarse wool thread, with dyed green stripes. Bram's backpack sat on it, along with a sheaf of pages—his Fleetspeak-English dictionary and a huge sheet of measurements from the scientific instruments he'd brought with him. A big sheep's fleece was hooked to the wall above the bed. There was a desk on a hinge and chain, a swinging board that could be bolted against the bulkhead. A hardwood chest of drawers, six feet tall and with variously sized drawers, was affixed to the far end of the room, near a dressing table equipped with pitcher and basin, a straight razor and brush, and an orange plastic toothbrush from home.

The room smelled of . . . was it spice? Cloves, she decided, and a low, peculiarly pleasant whiff of something that made her think of buffalo.

A trio of meter-long cork shelves stood near the portal, covered with shells and pebbles, pieces of petrified wood, bits of coral, some bird skulls and other such treasures. Each of these items was carefully looped 'round with black thread and pinned to the shelf so that the ship's movement wouldn't send it all tumbling to the floor. Hanging in a small net was a light wooden sphere about the size of a volleyball, sandy in color, that had the islands of Stormwrack carved onto its surface. About a third of them had been painted with a green lacquer with the shine and texture of nail polish.

*Places Parrish has visited?* she wondered.

She looked at the chest of drawers, a potential treasure box if ever there was one. She was momentarily tempted to snoop.

Instead, she turned her attention to her own things, which were piled neatly on the floor beside the bunk.

She opened her trunk, setting aside the sack of polystyrene packing peas her solar charger had come in. The princess dress was next. Had anyone worked out what she was up to? It was inside out, but her little collection of samples remained hidden in its petticoats.

Relieved, she turned it right side out and repacked it before fishing out her diving equipment: swimsuit, wetsuit, mask, air tanks, rebreather, flippers. She tried to tell herself she wouldn't need the camera, but she couldn't do it; it would have been like leaving her leg behind.

She clamped it into its waterproof housing, checked the seals, and clipped it to the LED flashlight for good measure before she changed into her gear.

By the time she was back on deck, the rowboat was ready and Tonio was inside, waiting. She set her kit inside, one piece at a time, double-checking that nothing had been missed.

"You've hardly left room for anyone to row," Tonio objected.

"I'll help," she said, clambering into the boat. The octopus was nowhere to be seen. "Where's Lassie?"

"It will resurface if you blow the flute again," Parrish said.

"Okay."

"We're right here if you need us."

"Look, I'll follow it, you follow me. It's not gonna be a problem." She fervently hoped it was true.

"No," Tonio said, unshipping the oars. "This is all meant to be, don't you think?"

"I'll give you people a lot, but not predestination, not without serious evidence."

He looked away: "Let us hope you never find any, Kir Sophie. Knowing your future might be a terrible thing."

"Chasing my past hasn't exactly been an endless rain of lemon drops." She raised the flute to her mouth, and blew again. The octopus surfaced almost immediately, about fifty feet away, on a bearing north-northwest. Sophie wrangled the second set of oars into their locks and fell into a rhythm with Tonio.

They did that for about half a mile . . . the octopus surfacing to spit and wave, Sophie and Tonio following, *Nightjar* inching along behind. Then something seemed to bump them and the little boat picked up speed, racing after the octopus. Sophie peered over the side. There was something big and shadowy beneath the boat.

"Friend of yours?" Tonio inquired.

"I doubt it," she said. "I'm guessing he knows John Coine."

"Teeth! That can't be good."

The octopus kept pace beside them now as the rowboat raced along. Wind ruffled her hair.

She let a hand drop into the water, enjoying the caress of the sea and simultaneously assessing the temperature. The air and water both had a bite to them that reminded her of spring in the Atlantic. Still, the wetsuit would keep the chill off.

"Land!" Tonio pointed.

A hump of an island rose on the horizon, but their course took them east and south of it. Sophie trained her camera on it and zoomed in. It was volcanic: a pitted rock beach facing south. The rocks seemed to be moving; after a second, she realized they weren't rocks but iguana, black and leathery, indistinguishable at this distance from the infamous swimming variety associated with the Galapagos Islands.

"Kinda far from your home latitude, aren't we, guys?" she murmured.

When they were due east of the volcanic beach, the rowboat began to slow. The shadow below them vanished; the octopus surfaced, spat water all over her, and rolled the tips of its tentacles onto an oarlock, pulling itself up to peer at them.

"Good girl, Lassie," Sophie said for lack of a better idea. "If I had a fish, it'd be yours."

It dunked, resurfaced, dunked again.

She turned on the light, shining it under the boat, looking. No sign of the thing that had been towing them, no sign of the bottom.

Diving alone, in unknown waters. Stupid, stupid. Dive alone, die alone. And there was something down there. She looked at Tonio speculatively. But no—this was no time to be training anyone, and anyway she had only the one rig.

"You know," Tonio said. "The flailers would do what they could to make Bram welcome and comfortable."

"For his whole life." She laughed weakly. "Maybe we could jailbreak him from Issle Morta."

"They'd scrip him to death," Tonio said. "Their national honor—and their ability to protect future hostages—depends on their never letting anyone go."

*So much for that.* "Down I go, then."

"I'm sure Bram would prefer to—"

"Live out his life on an intellectually barren rock? He'd lose his mind from boredom." As she said it, she felt certainty descend. Cly might have the looks and charm of a TV dad, he might be a swashbuckling fighter judge from some exotic land. But that was all dream and vapor. Bram was her kid brother: That was real.

She made herself take her time. She checked every bit of equipment twice: rebreather, dive computer, mask, the light and camera and the tethers clipping them to her rig.

Half a click away, *Nightjar* was lowering its anchor.

There was something directly ahead of them, on the surface. She brought up the camera.

It was a sheet of wooden debris. A ship's deck? Yes, part of one, from the look of it—out on its edge, the boards fanned out, undulating in time with the waves, and as she took it in she saw joins—nails—and a scrap of sail.

Much of the raft's surface was obscured by growths of a trefoil plant not unlike the ivy that choked trees in the Pacific Northwest. Here, it had obvious adaptations to a marine environment; its leaves had a cupped shape, allowing them to catch rainwater, and where the vines met the ocean they were slicked with translucent slime.

"Algae probably," Sophie said. "I'm guessing it's a separate species in symbiosis with the ivy, protecting it from the salinity of the water."

"I couldn't tell you, Kir," Tonio said.

The raft had all the bustle of a spring meadow. Caterpillars gnawed at the leaves here and there, and were eaten in their turn by keen-eyed shorebirds whose shape and markings reminded her of curlews. The birds ate the caterpillars and then snapped the half-eaten leaves off at the stem, tossing them away. Near the middle of the raft, whose surface area could have held a small playground or a huge house, the surface was bowed down by weight of a dozen or so Bonaparte's gulls who were peaceably eating . . . what? Something plentiful, Sophie thought; had to be or they'd be fighting over it.

Fanning out from the edges of the raft were random bits of driftwood and other stuff, tangled in the ivy and a bit of fishing net. The entangled bits and pieces had attracted mussels, at least four species she could see, and barnacles. The density of the structure was too consistent to have been random accumulation.

They rowed to within ten feet of the raft's leading edge.

A triple not-quite-splash and three brown mammalian faces, hairy and heavily whiskered, surfaced aft of her. Otters. Their fur was blacker than any species Sophie was familiar with, and one had white patches on its throat. They regarded her with solemn curiosity as she found a spar, checked that it was really attached to the raft, and then tied up the rowboat. One of them tugged the rope, experimentally. Tonio splashed a little water at it.

"They'll make off with whatever they can get," he said.

She took video footage of the trio and then took a careful standing stance within the rowboat, raising herself up so she could examine and film the surface of the raft. The gulls in the middle had themselves a pond of sorts—a break in the floor of the raft where they were fishing up small invertebrates. They had a midden well clear of the water, a pile of lime and discarded carapaces that inhibited the growth of the vines around it. Insects whirled and crawled on their dung heap. They looked, from a distance, to be some species of cockroach.

A drag on her leg—the octopus had reached over the side and given her a tug.

"Just getting the lay of the land," she said to it, and it vanished, descending. To Tonio, she added: "Where'd all this come from?"

"The otters. We call 'em wreck farmers," he said. "They find a nice piece of floating garbage and build it out until—well, you see. In time it gets too big and breaks up, or there's a storm."

"In the meantime it's a temporary floating meadow," she said. "In three dimensions."

"If we left the rowboat here overnight, they'd tangle it up good."

"This is an amazing phenomenon," she said. "I could spend my whole life filming something like this. The relationships between the plants and the various resident species . . ."

"Your friend seems to think you're needed below," he said, frowning at the octopus.

"Right. Back to business." She checked the housing on her camera and all her diving equipment. "Any idea how deep it is here?"

"Bottomless, I should think, or good as."

Time to make what passed for a dive plan. "I've got three hours of air on this rebreather, Tonio, but I'm only going down for one," she said.

"An hour, Kir?" He looked doubtful. "You'd have to be a mermaid."

"I'll be okay," she said, as much to reassure herself as him. "If Lassie takes off for the bottom or beelines for anything hazardous, I'm coming back up to make a new plan. But for now it's down, forty-five minutes under, up. Keep it simple, right?"

"Simple," he repeated, in a tone that indicated neither agreement nor disagreement.

"Depending on how deep I go and how long I'm under, I may have to ease my way up to the surface. So if you see me sitting at depth doing nothing, don't try to rescue me."

"And if it's been an hour, and I don't see you?"

"I dunno. Worry?" There was no backup out here: If she didn't come up, there wasn't much he could do.

He nodded assent and then, with a glance back at *Nightjar*, offered her a dagger, black in color and about half the length of her forearm.

"I'm not sure I want that."

"Can it hurt to have it, Kir?"

"I guess not." On impulse, she hugged him. "Don't let them steal our ride home."

She checked her stance again and then went over the edge. The otters vanished, one rolling up to slap its tail, beaverlike, on the surface. Treading, she adjusted her mask, took a few breaths, looked at her dive computer and set it to mark time.

Then she went under, just three feet, looked up at Tonio and adjusted her buoyancy vest. She took the time to breathe, to show him she wouldn't drown. It wouldn't help anything if he came swimming after her in a panic.

After about thirty seconds he raised his hand: *Okay.*

She made a sign—"I'm going down," it meant—and dropped to ten feet, then fifteen. There was no sign of whatever had been towing the rowboat.

They were out in what should have been a sterile stretch of sea: clear water, bright light, decent visibility. The raft, though, was throwing off a lot of murk. If its surface had been a meadow, what had developed beneath it was something in the way of a city. Long streamers of seaweed stretched down from the surface, like the tentacles of a jellyfish, all alive with activity. The underside of the raft was encrusted with anemones; small fish hid within them, guarding clutches of eggs. Palm fronds dangled here and there; they, too, were encrusted with eggs. Three of the otters were worrying a loop of vine loose from the raft, working in tandem to shove another scavenged hunk of driftwood into its outer edge.

The seaweed growing from the floor of the raft had less spread than she would have expected—much of it was braided into itself, so that it tapered, exerting downward force on the center of the raft.

*Must be something heavy down there,* Sophie thought. The weight would serve as a keel, balancing the whole structure. She wondered how long a raft like this would last in good weather. The pieces would break apart in a storm, sending the fish and flotsam everywhere. Then, presumably, the otters would regroup.

She shone her light into the particulate stream. The octopus was returning from the depths.

She took her time descending. She had no diving partner, unless you counted Lassie. All she could do was be careful.

One of the otters paddled close, investigating. It put out a covetous paw to one of the cords clipped to her dive belt.

Suddenly the octopus was there, mantle spread in a threat, flashing red at it. The message was clear enough: *Get back, get back!*

Sophie saw one of its tentacles was truncated, a stump.

The otter retreated.

She imagined it responding in a squeaky cartoon voice: *Hey, relax, I was just having a look!*

Lassie led her farther down, closer to the braid of seaweed that hung like a curtain from the raft. Here and there fish had gotten entangled in the braid and been unable to work themselves free; they hung, staring dead-eyed, from the vegetation. She moved slowly, shining the light before her, watching for bits of net. As its beam took in the dark cord of vegetable matter she thought of the *Estrel*, and the lantern made of Captain Dracy's father's skull.

Sixty feet down, she found what was weighting down the braid of seaweed: a dense strand of matter she was tempted to call a root ball, dead and tangled. Invertebrates writhed within.

A heavy object, wrapped in sacking and six feet in length, was wound into the ball and affixed by the vines. Sea worms roiled in and out of it.

*A shroud,* Sophie thought, *some sailor's body.* She made herself breathe slowly and film it. Of course the otters would bind in any source of nutrients they could find.

The octopus snagged her again: *Come on.*

*Okay,* she thought. She was eighty feet down. *It better be close, Lassie.* Ninety.

A hundred feet.

A hundred and ten.

She'd been deeper, but not alone, not in unfamiliar waters.

Now the octopus stretched out again, rippling. Threat?

She turned a slow circle, shining her light in every direction. Nothing. Then she kicked, swimming closer to the root ball.

*Oh no.*

This corpse wasn't wrapped up. It wasn't exactly human, either.

The body was twenty feet long and combined human and reptilian characteristics. It had the upper body of a woman, but instead of legs her hips merged into a long, black, reptilian tail. It—she—reminded Sophie of the iguanas she'd just seen on the surface.

Another magically transformed person. And those were shackles on its wrists. Another slave?

*One of these may have been towing the rowboat,* she thought. It was about the right length, and what remained of its muscles looked bulky enough. A tail that long would make it a strong swimmer. She had no gills that Sophie could see.

It had been dead for a while.

Under the body's breasts hung a combination of purse and lockbox, a heavy container affixed with heavy, crisscrossing straps that buckled across her chest. Seaweed and vines were twisted around it; the otters were doing their best to make the body, and her bag, a permanent part of their makeshift keel.

Was the dead woman in cahoots with the octopus? Sophie tried to reckon whether Parrish would have told her if slaves were involved in hiding Yacoura. He'd only mentioned the octopus, who was currently sitting on the box, caressing it, probing the lock with its tentacles.

*Don't guess: observe.* She shone the light up and down, examining the dead woman.

The body was wearing a heavy tunic and a helmet, one shaped like those little skullcap motorcycle helmets. It had been pulled askew, its strap stretched somewhat over the face, whose eyes were already gone.

The distortion of the strap had tightened it around the dead woman's jaw . . . and there was something caught in her mouth.

Sophie let her camera drift on its tether for a second so she could switch the light to her left hand. Using the dagger Tonio had given her, she cut the helmet's strap, letting the helmet drift away. An otter darted in immediately, claiming it for the raft.

The body's mouth relaxed, saving Sophie the grim task of prying it open, and revealing enlarged, pointed teeth. As the lips gaped, the sea washed out the remnants of bloody foam and something else—a rotten, rubbery hunk of flesh with suckers—part of a tentacle.

*Ah ha!* Sophie thought. *So maybe you tried to take the Heart from Lassie here. You did take the Heart. And she fought back. Poor woman. I hope I'm wrong about you being a slave; I hope you had a choice.*

If one of these things had towed her rowboat to the raft, it wouldn't be far away.

*So stop fooling around.* She got to work on the entangling vines and then unbuckled the lockbox, taking it slow.

*No rush, don't rush, do it right the first time. Could the octopus really have killed something this big?*

She'd have to hope so. There was another out here, at least one.

*Probably not more than one, right? I mean, Lassie couldn't hold off twenty of them.*

Where was it? Why hadn't it come down here and got the lockbox while Lassie was fetching Sophie?

*Maybe Yacoura's not in here.* The chest strap came loose and she took the bag, turning her back on the body before tackling the assortment of smaller straps and locks. There was a velvet bag inside. She snuck a peek, and caught a quick glimpse of spellscrip. A sense of cold power roiled through her as she touched it, indifferent and deadly force—the power of earthquakes, avalanches, indifferent crushing deaths. The octopus unfurled, caressing it . . . and then let it go.

*Okay, Bram, you're just about saved.* Sophie wrapped the inscription, feeling more than a little relief as that feeling of sheer force abated. She forced the inscription into her wetsuit, tucking it between her breasts. It would, she hoped, be invisible.

As she pondered the question—why hadn't the other lizard-thing come for it?—she fiddled with the lockbox, rebuckling it, closing it up tight.

The corpse had no gills. Maybe the creatures couldn't function at this depth. Or maybe Lassie had done a good enough job of hiding the corpse that it didn't know where to look.

Either was plausible, as theories went.

*If it's the depth, it'll be waiting farther up.*

She clipped the lockbox to her dive belt, checking twice to make sure it wasn't interfering with her scuba gear. Then she checked her dive computer. She'd been down here for forty-two minutes, at a hundred and ten feet.

Not great. She'd need two stops.

She did the circle again, shining the light up, down, around, and took a second to think through her ascent. She wanted to come up clear of the raft, and she needed to stop twice. Once at twenty feet, for two minutes—no big deal. But she'd have to sit at ten feet for over twenty minutes.

There was nobody to help her if she got decompression sickness—

—or attacked by half-human monsters.

*Dive alone, die alone.* Bram's voice, in her head.

Well, she had Lassie, right? The octopus showed no sign of abandoning her.

Nothing for it—she couldn't just shoot up to the surface unless she wanted the bends. She would take it slow, photograph the root ball, shoot the diversity of life on the seaweed colony, maybe get a little otter footage too and keep her eyes peeled.

Right. Slow ascent to twenty feet. She kicked up, one two, leisurely rise. She checked the dive computer again, watched for monsters and nets.

She marveled at the root ball as she passed it. Its upper edge was at a depth of ninety feet, where the last streamers of seaweed were bound tightly into one another and there were bones and shells and even rocks stuck in the round structure of dead vegetation. The otters swam around tending it, poking runaway bits back into the holes in a sort of ongoing reverse game of pick-up sticks.

It was an elegant, beaverlike feat of engineering. The ivy got going above on a piece of floating wreckage, the weeds started growing below. They used the ivy runners to tie in more and more biomass.

*The more weeds it can support, the more life it attracts. The otters get shellfish, shelter, and all this stuff gets a nursery. The bones and heavy material wound in at the bottom provide minerals for the vegetation and weight to stabilize the raft. Anything that floats goes up top to keep it in the sun.*

She could spend her whole life examining this thing, she thought. Despite Bram's predicament, she felt a wave of something like love.

The diversity of fish species taking shelter in the raft's shadow was enormous—not quite as impressive as what she'd find on a well-established coral reef, but she saw many of the same species, mixed in with animals that looked similar: batfish for sure, and goby. There was no coral and thus no parrotfish, but she saw more anemones, growing on the scavenged spars and on long shreds of torn, scavenged sail. And at least a few cleaner fish stations, she saw—thirty feet above her a ray wafted in place, getting its parasites munched away.

She took another look around for monsters, saw nothing, and checked her watch.

She spent two blessedly uneventful minutes at twenty feet, filming.

She'd just kicked up, making for ten feet, when the iguana-man made its appearance.

He appeared out of the black, coming from around the far side of the kelp braid, and the only reason he didn't just grab her on the first try was that she'd been watching for him. She twisted in the water, holding the light out in front of her, hoping the brightness right in his eyes would do something, anything.

*Do you fight?* she remembered Cly asking.

*No,* she'd said, *not at all.*

The iguana-man seemed bigger than the dead woman below: He had the ballooning, overdeveloped upper body of a cartoon superhero, and his tail coiled and twisted powerfully, making him a streamlined and very fast swimmer. There was no chance Sophie could outpace him even if she didn't need to stay at this depth.

But the trick with the light worked, barely; she managed to dodge, and he was moving fast enough that he whirled past her with a rush of water and just the barest scrape of flesh against her foot.

Her fin went tumbling away—*there's a nonbiodegradable present for the otters,* she thought, and sure enough one of the little opportunists was already diving after it, indifferent to her predicament.

She had a death grip on Tonio's knife. It was probably ridiculous, but what else could she do?

*Not a fighter, not at all. Can't outrun it, can't break for the surface.* She mastered her breath, watching for opportunities, automatically stabilizing her depth at ten feet and noting the time.

Twenty-minute stop.

*Bram, think of Bram. Gotta do this for Bram.*

Her best chance was Lassie. The octopus had already killed one of them.

The iguana-man had got itself turned around and eased back toward her. And yes, by now the octopus was between them. It wasn't bothering to stretch or display this time, just waiting. It looked ridiculously small next to the bulk of the other creature.

But it must have killed the iguana-woman, and it had protected Yacoura once it got stuck there in the corpse's lockbox.

Sophie and the iguana-man stared at each other, connected by the beam of her LED spotlight, the octopus hanging between them.

*Stand-off.* Could they stay this way for twenty minutes?

The iguana gestured at the lockbox. *Gimme.*

*Good. He thinks it's still in there.* She shook her head, raising the camera again and taking footage of it: face, helmet, tunic, and the shackles on its wrists. At least there'd be a record of what had happened to her.

It gestured again.

*No.* Sophie shook her head again, more vehemently.

It feinted toward her and the octopus moved, liquidly, to just outside of grabbing range. Sophie blew bubbles, just to make a noise. She didn't especially want Lassie drowning lizard-man, or getting killed by it. She tried to sign this out, gesturing down at the corpse, pointing at the octopus, then waving at it in a "clear off" gesture.

He bared his teeth, letting out a little air of his own, and this time when he lunged at her

—*oh, he's so fast!*—

—it turned out that grabbing for her was the feint. He reached out with one arm as the octopus unfurled, catching it near its head. By squeezing and keeping his arm extended, he was able to hold Lassie at arm's length as it stretched and groped ineffectually for his neck with the tips of its tentacles, encircling but failing to get enough muscle around his throat to strangle him.

Smirking, the iguana-man coiled his tail, coming for Sophie one-handed.

*Guess you had a bit of time to think about how to deal with Lassie, after she killed your partner.*

Sophie shut off her light, kicking as hard as she could for the braid of seaweed, whipping herself around it by tugging on an outstretched ten-dril of vegetation and clutching Tonio's little dagger with her other hand.

As her eyes adjusted, she saw the bulk of the iguana body, black, mov-ing around the braid, his arm still outstretched. She edged around the braid again, keeping it between them, working to control her breathing. In, out, in, out, kick.

*Oh no, he totally sees me. What the hell am I going to do?*

A scaly hand closed around her ankle.

Sophie kicked for his face with her free leg. Her heel slid harmlessly off the biker helmet. The hand on her ankle tightened, squeezing. Pain shot through her ankle and shin. He was obviously strong enough to break the leg easily.

Instead, he twisted, trying to pull her close to his teeth—with his right hand occupied with holding Lassie at bay, he could hurt her but not ma-nipulate her.

Sophie took a firmer grip on the dagger Tonio had given her, bending like a hairpin.

*Move slow, move slow,* she told herself, *you've been injured before, don't screw this up, oww, he's going to snap my leg off!* She aimed the point of the dagger into the back of his shoulder. If she could just get him to un-lock his elbow . . .

Her first attempt glanced off his arm—she'd been tentative, and his skin was tough.

The second time she made herself concentrate, exhale, and thrust.

It worked; the iguana-man's arm bent, creating enough slack for the octopus to improve its grip on his neck. He let go of her ankle and grabbed for Lassie with the other hand, trying to stave off strangulation. The pair of them, locked in struggle, slipped downward into the murk.

*Ow, ow.* Pain sang up and down her leg. Sophie checked her depth—she'd sunk back down to fourteen.

They'd drifted closer to the raft as they struggled, bouncing through the tendrils and scraps of net at the heart of the underwater structure. She needed to remain at this depth, and she needed to get away from all these bits and pieces before her hoses got entangled. But if she swam clear of it, there would be nothing to hide her.

Even so, Sophie began swimming—clumsily, because she had no swim fins now, and her right leg was wrenched, hurting and uncooperative—for the clear water beyond the raft.

The struggle had attracted the otters' attention. They were swimming around, watching, clearly agitated by the threat to their structure.

She cleared the vines and other entanglements, turning in place, looking up, down, all around. There was no sign of the octopus or the iguana-man, her leg was throbbing, and—she realized, she was still clutching Tonio's knife.

She had never been so tempted to skip her safety stop.

*But that's silly,* she thought; *if the iguana kills the octopus, it can capsize our rowboat easily enough.*

Instead of making for the surface and risking the bends, she unhitched the lockbox from her dive belt, keeping an eye on the seas below as she gathered the bulk of its long strap, the one that had gone around the dead woman's chest, into a clump within her fist.

She waited, lockbox in one hand, dagger in the other, and an eye on her dive computer.

She had seven minutes left when the iguana swam past her, shreds of cephalopod in both fists and a thoroughly vicious expression on its face. It surfaced, presumably to breathe, and then undulated toward her. The knife wound was bleeding freely. The red stream it left behind it had attracted a half dozen sharks, the biggest of them no larger than Sophie's arm.

Sophie spread out, extending the hand with the dagger toward it, holding the lockbox behind her, letting the bunched length of its strap float free.

*Come on, come on.*

The iguana-man looked to be unimpressed by the threat posed by the dagger. He gestured with a shredded tentacle: *Gimme.*

Sophie gave the box a push, letting it go.

It was near neutral buoyancy—didn't sink, didn't pop surfaceward like a cork. It was behind her, and she had the little dagger, which iguana-man had to know was ridiculous, but all she wanted was for him to consider how to get past her for ten or twenty seconds.

*Come on,* she thought again. *Please.*

A swirl, behind her, and the iguana-man's expression changed. Surprise, anger, and then a sort of weariness played over his features. He put his head down and bulled forward in the water, charging, not at her but past.

The otter who'd grabbed the lockbox by its strap was determined, fast, and far more agile than either her or the iguana-man: it shot, bug-eyed, past Sophie, making for the heart of the raft.

Sophie watched them go, checked the time. She'd have until the monster caught the otter and realized the inscription wasn't inside the lockbox. Would it be long enough?

*Hope so—I'm all out of tricks.* She tried to feel out the injury to her right leg. Something in her thigh had definitely gotten pulled. The knee had gotten a good twist, but she could bend and straighten it. The resistance as she moved through the water made her ankle shriek with pain. She tried to feel the bones, but it hurt too much to manipulate the joint.

A wash of movement—the raft itself had swayed.

*Here's hoping it doesn't tear the whole otter farm apart,* Sophie thought, shutting off her light and swimming, slowly, for the rowboat. Tonio was there, ten feet up, as he'd been when she first hit the water.

She gave him a shaky two thumbs-up and checked the timer on her dive computer.

The final minutes of her stop passed with cruel slowness, but the massive lizard-man didn't come back.

She kicked once with her good leg and let herself rise to the surface.

"Monster dead?"

"Nope," she said. "He's chasing an otter—thinks it has the Heart."

"But you do?" Tonio asked.

"I sure hope so," she said wearily. Clawing open the velvet bag, she found an oak dowel about nine inches long, wrapped in wire and covered in blue spellscrip. That sense of power rolled off it again; it was like holding a storm cloud, or something like a missile.

"*Bene.* We'll throw it in that rowboat with the skeleton as soon as we get back to the ship."

"Not a chance," she said. "I have plans for this damned thing."

"Plans?"

"Presentation is everything," she said, as the raft heaved and the Bonaparte gulls leapt into the sky, shrieking in outrage.

Moving as one, she and Tonio grabbed for their oars.

CHAPTER 23

She stepped aboard *Nightjar* and promptly collapsed—the ankle wouldn't bear her weight. Parrish caught her, lowering her to the deck and feeling the joint.

"It's not broken," he said. "I'll have Richler—our medic—look at it."

"I need my stuff first," she said.

He picked her up, carrying her to his cabin.

"What happened?" he asked.

"Monsters," Rolling to her side on the bed, she pulled her trunk close and fumbled it open. "They had shackles. Does that make them slaves?"

"Yes."

"Poor bastards who didn't have a chance to say no. Lassie killed one, a while ago. The other killed Lassie, just now."

"And you?"

"And me what?"

"Did you kill it?"

"No! At least, I think he should be okay."

"Is there something I can help you find?" he asked. She was digging through the contents of her trunk, coming up with one of the glass test tubes she'd brought for sampling.

"Would you have a scrap of rabbit fur, something like that?"

He opened one of the smaller drawers in the great wooden chest, coming up with a handkerchief-sized pelt, with soft ginger hair and stripes reminiscent of a chipmunk.

"Thanks." She had found the packaging from her battery charger.

"What are you doing?" he asked.

"Wishing I'd brought a dye pack," she said, coming up with a pristine plastic bag, the kind that zipped shut, the kind they required on airplanes now for your toiletries.

"I don't understand."

"I'm packaging up the ransom." She carefully took a handful of the polystyrene packing peas and poured them into the test tube. A few stuck to her hand, a few fell into the bed, and a dozen bounced to the floor. They clung to the lip of the jar, inside and out. But she got a quarter cup where she wanted them and closed up the jar, dropping it on the bed beside her.

Parrish watched all this without comment.

"Don't look at me like that," she said. "We have to give it up, right? We can't leave Bram to rot on Issle Whatever it is—"

"Issle Morta," he said. "I didn't say we should."

"You hated it there, didn't you?" She slid Yacoura into the zipper bag, along with more of the little peas. Not as many as she could cram in—she didn't want it to be so pressurized it would pop at the first good squeeze—but enough to give the whole package the consistency of a bean bag. She zipped it shut, squeezed out the excess air, rolled it in her hand. Yes, that was about right. Then she took the scrap of fur and polished up the makeshift pillow until there wasn't a smudge on the exterior of the bag.

Finally she wrung out the wet velvet satchel the Heart had come in, sliding the zipped sandwich bag inside.

"The Ualtarites won't care how the Heart is presented to them."

"Do you know what static electricity is?" she asked.

He shook his head.

"When it's dry and your hair stands up, and crackles," she said. This whole idea suddenly seemed silly. Like so many things, it was clear in her head and sounded dumb when she articulated it. "Or you spark someone in the winter by touching them?"

"Of course," he said.

"What about Hansel and Gretel?" she asked. "Do you have that story? Two kids, lost in the woods, following a trail of bread crumbs home?"

"They tell it on Verdanii," he said. "The insidious stepfather makes the mother renounce her children, that one?"

"More or less," she said.

"I don't understand."

"Bread crumbs." She pinched a spoon's worth of the peas and flicked them at him. One caught in his curls; a few bounced to the floor and several of the rest stuck to his shirt, held there by static. "They're clingy, see?"

Parrish picked one out of the crook of his elbow, tried to set it aside. It clung to his fingertip until he blew it away. His gaze returned to the Heart of *Temperance* in its velvet bag.

"They'll open it," she said. "They'll want a look at their prize."

"And your crumbs will end up . . ."

"Everywhere." Sophie rolled up, trying to stand—and then half collapsed back onto the bed with a little groan.

"You should stay off that ankle."

"I'll take some ibuprofen. I bet you have a crutch on board somewhere," she said.

"I'll have it brought," he said.

"Here," she said, handing him the bag. "Don't pop it."

They went up on deck, her hopping, he seeming to restrain himself from the urge to steady her.

"Put it in the boat with the skeleton—carefully," she said.

Tonio slid down a rope, laying the velvet bag in the skeleton's upturned hand. The bones curved around it, gently, not squeezing. The rotten, algae-crusted rowboat filled with water, sinking from view.

"So that's it?" Sophie said. "Bram's got his get out jail free card?"

Parrish nodded. "Issle Morta will release him."

*He's okay, he'll be okay.* A wave of relief, and profound gratitude. *Thank you, Cly.*

"So, what now?" Sophie said.

"Now," Parrish said, "you see the medic while we set a course for the Fleet."

CHAPTER 24

Sometime over the four-day sail to the Fleet, Sophie realized she'd fallen in love with *Nightjar*.

The cutter was another Tallon ship, built sixty years earlier and initially purposed, Parrish told her, to carry mail in the Mirrorsea. The Fleet courier service had purchased her for Gale and she had bought it back from them over the years. She was seventy-two feet long, with hull timbers made from something called gasper spruce—Sophie scratched up a small splinter to take home as a sample. Her deck was pine, creamy wood polished to glowing.

A crew of twenty-five sailors, about a third of those women, kept the decks shining, cleaned the portals of Erinthian glass and devoted themselves in a host of ways to keeping her spotless and, more important, immaculately seaworthy.

They were all of them in a state Sophie would have described as unsettled. Little wonder, with Gale's having died. It seemed clear enough, though, that they trusted Parrish to see them through the transition to . . . well, to working for Verena, presumably.

Sophie had spent plenty of time on research ships over the past six years, almost as much as she had on land, and though she'd always been aboard to dive, she would have called herself a decent sailor. She had a strong stomach and a good sense of balance. She knew how to read a chart and had believed that she understood the rudiments of navigation, with or without the benefit of GPS.

But she had never been aboard a sailing ship that didn't also have a motor below and a ton of diesel fuel aboard; a ship with no radio, radar, or satellite uplink, no refrigerator, no antibiotics, not even a DVD player. The idea of being completely dependent on the resources aboard, from the fresh water in the hold to the books in the meager library, was both exhilarating and humbling.

She pestered Tonio to acquaint her with *Nightjar*'s masts, sails, and rigging, and with every lecture she realized how little she had truly understood.

Parrish hadn't been belittling her when he sent her below during the storm. He'd been right. She knew a boom from a jib, understood what it meant to reef a sail or to lower it entirely, but the knowledge had never sunk deeper than her skin. She had to think everything through before she came up with the right answer. Sometimes she'd hesitate for only a breath when Tonio quizzed her.

On a sailing ship, in bad weather, that second could spell disaster, just as it could in diving or mountain climbing or caving.

She limped around learning what she could, observing the crew, asking a thousand questions, and ignoring the small voice within that kept pointing out that she didn't need to know any of this, that she was eventually going home to the cushy technological safety nets of the twenty-first century. As for her growing sense of attachment to the ship—it was pointless. All she could do was consider trying to get one of her own, one day, at home.

Gale may have had money and houses, but if she had any treasure worth inheriting, Sophie thought, it was this—this trim, beautiful boat and the freedom to explore.

*Nightjar* was fast for her size, averaging, she judged, about 250 nautical miles a day, maybe more if pushed to her limits. She had been inscribed, as Gale had, to be a bit forgettable, just a hair beneath the notice of casual observers.

It was afternoon when they made first sighting of the Fleet, a forest of spars and sails, white and gray bristling on the horizon, with small dots wheeling above. Over the next few hours they clarified, becoming an orderly procession, a great flotilla, thousands of ships strong.

Sophie's previous glimpse, weeks before, hadn't prepared her to be in and among this incredible number of ships, for the spread of the Fleet—it was as impossible to hold it all in one's gaze as it would be to look at all of New York at once—or for the variety of ships. Most resembled, at least vaguely, old-time sailing ships, craft straight out one of C. S. Forester's

*Horatio Hornblower* novels, wood-hulled, stout machines built with the elegance and economy of the preindustrial age.

But the farther to the fore *Nightjar* sailed, making for what Sophie couldn't help thinking of as a downtown core, the more exceptions she saw. Most remarkable may have been a low-riding gray structure, as big as an aircraft carrier, at the head of the Fleet.

*Is that* Temperance? Sophie wondered. She was sailing into the pre-twilight sun; she couldn't get a good look at her.

They passed bigger, increasingly strange ships, craft that defied physics and common sense as the Ualtarite ship, *Ascension,* had, craft that had to have been worked with magic to make them seaworthy. One appeared to have a hull woven of wicker. Another had no sails, but appeared to be bound to the ocean, or drawn forward through it, by tens of thousands of blue, wire-thin threads. As *Nightjar* sailed past, Sophie saw one of the threads slacken momentarily. A long, eel-shaped creature broke the water. It was bound to the ship by the thread, which snapped it short like a dog who'd run out its leash.

One ship had a long, sinuous tail and redwood cedars for masts, and was trailing a series of barges, each of which had been planted with crops. Wheat shivered golden with the wind in its wake; a woman in a long wrap waved feathers at any opportunistic gulls who looked like they might be interested in landing on it.

"That's the Verdanii rep ship," Tonio said. "*Breadbasket.*"

"Rep?" Sophie asked.

"The Representative Ships are the core of the Fleet," Parrish said.

"Rep because each nation officially contributes one ship to the Fleet?"

"Exactly. See, they fly the Fleet flag highest, and then, below, their national colors."

*Symbolically putting the international community before the individual nation,* Sophie thought. "I recognize Tallon's flag, up there on *Temperance.*" She zoomed in at the great gray hulk leading them. Its hull was neither wood nor metal; from a distance, it seemed to have the color and texture of sharkskin. "But it's flying three flags, not two."

"The third flag designates purpose. The black cross flown by *Temperance* means it's military. The black circles on *Constitution*—" He pointed out a vessel decked out in red curtains and hundreds of flags, powered by an enormous and improbable-looking red-painted paddlewheel. "—symbolize writing. Governance."

"So not all of these are . . . Rep ships?"

"Only these flying the Fleet flag. In theory, the two hundred and fifty can sail together for a year or more without assistance or resupply."

"And in fact?"

"They've accumulated a host of support vessels and other followers over the past century." Parrish began to point out other flags, decoding their symbology: administration buildings, storage, living quarters, supply, fabrication—small seagoing factories, in other words—fishing, markets, meeting halls, schools. There were floating farms, saloons, workshops, and gambling dens.

Tonio said: "The farther to the rear you sail, the more marginal it gets. The tail of the Fleet's made up of scroungers and bumboats. They come and go, trading, making what they can."

"Getting around must be difficult."

"Key ships are connected by regular ferries, and there are taxis." He pointed out a quick-darting boat, a speck next to the big ship it was passing, and then pointed upward to a flight of swirling orange hang-glider contraptions, sweeping in an intricate dance above the ships.

"Flying rickshaws," Sophie said.

Parrish was counting sails. "I don't see *Sawtooth*."

"Nobody would dare sink Cly Banning," Tonio said quickly. "Don't worry, Sophie. Your family is safe enough."

*Family,* she thought. The word, applied to the trio of Beatrice, Verena, and Cly, had a chewy, indigestible feeling, like gristle. "Where's the ship they stuck Bram on? Where's *Sackcloth*?"

Parrish pointed out a dowdy-looking brigantine that looked as though its masts were overgrown by moss. Its designation flag was a red cross.

"Is it medical?"

"That is the ancient healer's flag, yes."

That was another little tie to Earth tradition, then.

"*Sackcloth* is the funeral ship. They burn, compost, or bury at sea, as dictated by the culture of the deceased."

"Service to the dead seems to be what the flailers do—sorry, is it okay to call them flailers?"

"Everyone does," Parrish said.

*Which doesn't mean yes,* she thought. "What I don't get is how hostage handovers fit in."

"Issle Morta has a special dispensation—it's called a Concession—to act as a sort of sanctuary for kidnap victims and refugees from justice."

"But we delivered. Bram's free to go. I want to see him."

"I'll arrange for Bram to meet us."

"Why? Where are we going?"

Parrish said, "We need to talk to Annela Gracechild on *Constitution* as soon as possible."

"What if they won't let him go?"

"You kept your part of the bargain," Parrish said. "The monks have no agenda beyond protecting the pawns in these exchanges from torture and homicide."

"Protecting? They'd have kept Bram forever, if I'd failed or cheated them."

"Yes. At last count, I believe there are three hostages to fortune resident on the island. One has been there more than forty years."

There was more weight in his voice than she would have thought this bit of trivia warranted.

"John Coine's pet monster tried to take Yacoura from me at the sea raft—they don't want Bram returned."

"Bram's out of his reach. Truly, Sophie, it's all right," Tonio said.

She felt a pang of homesickness. What mattered now was Bram. Getting Bram, getting this whole mess sorted and getting away, back to San Francisco, before their parents got home and found out the two of them had run off.

*Constitution*'s paddlewheel was grinding through the sea, tossing water in a cheery, rainbow-making spray off her stern. She was enormous, and Sophie couldn't help being reminded of the floating casino-hotels that plied the Mississippi. It was the rails and dowels and hardwood floors.

*And the flags and bunting. Plus the uniformed pages running everywhere. They have a bellhoppy look to them.*

When a small ferry pulled alongside *Nightjar*, Sophie, with Parrish's help, crutched aboard. She watched the little ship recede from view as they zipped to *Constitution*.

As the wicker ship came between them and *Nightjar*, blocking her view, she thought: *I might never see her again.* Her leg throbbed, the ache seeming to echo the knotty tangle of loss and regret.

At *Constitution*, the two of them transferred to a contraption that was essentially a seagoing elevator: a sealed car on pulleys that raised them from sea level to the main deck of the ship.

As the elevator snugged into place level with the main deck, Sophie saw Annela Gracechild. She had her arms crossed under her ample breasts and a bright but somehow unfriendly smile fixed on her face. "I could have you arrested," the woman murmured, as soon as she saw her. "You violated the terms of your transit visa and told someone about Stormwrack after explicitly promising not to."

"I'm sorry about Gale," Sophie said, instead of defending herself.

"It's an incalculable loss," Annela said, but the fixed, professional smile did not change. "Where is your sister?"

"Chaperoning Cly Banning and Beatrice Vanko," Parrish said.

"Teeth, Parrish! You let Banning take Beatrice?"

"Circumstances made it expedient. There's trouble brewing—serious trouble, if Sophie is correct."

"Don't I know it," Annela said. "Ualtar has recalled its entire missionary fleet and posted it in their local waters. Their neighbors are demanding we sail out to investigate. And I have Golden, of all people, making sly hints to the Convene that the Fleet ought to just stay out of this one."

"A blockade? *Sawtooth* went to Tiladene," Sophie said.

"The Piracy and Ualtar are in possession of the Heart of *Temperance*," Parrish said in the same breath.

Annela seemed to hear and absorb both statements, jumbled though they were.

"It's why Gale was murdered," Sophie added, through a tight throat, into the silence that followed.

Annela raised a hand for silence, scanned the deck, and then gestured for them to follow her below, to a suite of rooms that seemed to be equal parts office and parlor. She called for her assistant, and settled into a huge, overstuffed chair. Servants bustled in with tea and a plate of cheese and cookies, and then vanished again. One of them left Annela a bowl of orange globes, about three inches in diameter, and a paring knife.

Annela took up the knife and cut into one of the fruits. The orange exterior was a husk—as she stripped it off, it revealed a light-colored fruit that exuded coconut perfume.

"All right, tell me everything," Annela said, continuing to strip the fruit.

Sophie felt her throat tightening, just a little. She forced the words out: "I guess the first thing was that when Gale was attacked—the two guys, they were there, right? In San Francisco—"

"In the outlands," Annela said. "Always say outlands."

"Right, okay. Sorry." The sharp tone rattled her. "One of them, the two guys, is from Isle of Gold. His name's John Coine. The other is this Ualtarite—"

"You know this how?"

"What? Oh. Tonio recognized him on Erinth . . ."

"Tonio?"

"Antonio Capodoccio, *Nightjar*'s first mate," Parrish said.

"Your scamp of a shopkeeper's son? Is he reliable?"

"Of course."

Annela had extracted the fruit by now, setting aside the husk and rolling it in her palm before closing her hand around it and squeezing. "Go on."

Putting her conclusions into words made them sound flimsier than they were. And Annela had dropped her smiling public persona: Her fierce cross-examination made even the truth seem ludicrous. "Um. So, where was I?"

"A pirate and a Ualtarite. Sounds like the beginning of a bad joke."

"Heh. No. He's on Erinth . . ."

"Who?"

"The guy from Ualtar. Tonio said he was a diplomat."

"Parrish, why don't you lay out the facts?" The fruit yielded to Annela's squeezing, with a snap. She poured an ounce of what looked like coconut milk into a waiting cup.

He frowned. "Kir Hansa made most of the observations."

"It's okay," Sophie said, stung but also relieved. "Tell her everything."

Parrish looked as though he might object, but then, looking from one woman to the other, simply said, "As you wish."

He cleared his throat, but then there was a tap at the door.

A page trotted in, stiffening to attention. "Honors to the Fleet! Kirs! I have a Bramwell Hansa arriving on the taxi deck!"

Sophie leapt up, forgetting her leg, and pitched halfway into Parrish's lap. He caught her easily, setting her upright, and then handed her the crutch.

"Where are you going?" Annela said.

"You just ordered Parrish to lay out the facts, didn't you?" She hopped after the page as fast as she could. It was all she could do to make orderly progress up the steps of the great staircase with the long lines of bureaucrats and visitors. "Make way!" she wanted to shout. She imagined sweeping them out of the way with her crutch.

One of the taxi kites was landing atop the ship when she got there.

"Bram!"

He was wearing a monk's robe; he might have been a Franciscan friar, although his hair wasn't shaved or anything. Neither was his face, for that matter—

She hopped over and wrapped her arms around him. "I've never seen you with a beard," she said, into his shoulder.

"Mmmf mmm you too," he said. "What the hell, Sofe? Is that leg broken?"

"No, I'm fine. Are you fine? Did they hurt you?"

"Get off the pad, Kirs," said the kite driver.

"Bram—" She planted herself—they weren't gonna push her down the steps, not with an injured leg. "Did they?"

"I got a few wasp stings and the crap scared out of me," he said. "And this."

He held out his hand, palm down. There was a small black mark in the center of his thumbnail . . . under the nail?

"It's a very small pearl," he said. "Apparently they mark anything they take."

"They *mark?* Oh, Bram—"

"Don't go redzone on me, Ducks. It's been a crummy couple of days."

"Off the platform, Kirs, or I'll have ye carried," bawled the kite man.

"Don't call me Ducks." She welled up, fumbling for the rail.

Bram got her moving. "It's not infected, or—"

"Or booby-trapped?"

"Nope. The Issle Morta monks promised, no poison. If I want, I should be able to get a plastic surgeon to cut off the nail and fish it out when we get home."

"If you want? Unless you want to start painting your nails, people will ask about it."

He shrugged. "It's a badge of toughness. Taken by pirates, lived to tell the tale. You didn't lose my notes, did you? Where's Verena?"

"With my birth parents."

"Parents? Plural?"

"They're on their way," she said. "The monks took okay care of you?"

He nodded. "They have a Noah's ark legend, too, about the formation of the island nations. An ancient culture whose big sin appears to have been waste, wiped out by plagues of quakes, rain, floods—you didn't manage to pick up the story I was going to collect on Tallon, were you?"

"I was busy having the mother of all tantrums because my baby brother had gotten grabbed."

"Sofe, I'm fine."

"This had to hurt," she said, grabbing his hand and lifting it so she could see the pad of his thumb. There was a pink scab dead center. "They shoved it in with a needle or something?"

By way of answer, he gave her crutch a shake. "What happened to your leg?"

They had reached *Constitution*'s aft deck. She rebalanced with a hop, leaned against the rail, and tucked the sprained leg against the good one. They glared at each other.

Then Bram snorted. "Come on. Who you mad at? Me?"

"Oh, I'm real mad at someone," she said, but then she giggled.

"What happened to your leg?"

"It was a big reptilian sea monster, magicked out of a slave. Like the mezmers. It killed Beatrice's pet octopus."

"Better the cephalopod than you," he said.

"The leg's not broken. And my birth father found me, and the reason everyone's been freaking out and trying to send us home is basically that Beatrice having a baby violated her prenup, if you can believe it. Breach of contract, which is apparently more important here than keeping your flesh and blood."

He spent a second absorbing that. "So it's not some big fate thing after all? The trouble you were supposed to cause by coming back?"

"No. And hurrah to that."

"Free will triumphs," he said. "Details later?"

"As many as you want. Your turn."

He opened and closed the hand. "They wanted my middle name."

"You give it to them?"

He shook his head. "They don't ask, the first day. 'The first sting's for nothing,' is how Coine put it."

"Because they mark their property."

"They're all about tradition. So he did this, to the thumb. And yes, it did hurt, all the way up to the elbow. Couldn't use the hand all day, couldn't move the arm. 'We'll do the other thumb tomorrow,' said Coine, 'Less you give us your name.' They do one a day, under the nail, until you talk. It's like a game." He ran a hand through his hair and let out a shaky laugh. "Almost a religious ritual."

"I've decided we need to get our parents to adopt another kid." She fought to keep her tone light. "One with an interest in anthropology or sociology—"

"Well, Verena's into soft science," he said. "What's she studying? International relations? Sofe, stop crying, will you? I'm here; everything's trending back to optimal."

She wiped at her face. "I'm just relieved. But—your hand, Bram."

"Apparently, there's one person in all the world who resisted until the Golden had done all ten fingers—then he broke when they did the big toe. I was out of my mind scared, I won't pretend. Then all of a sudden morning came and instead of more . . ."

"Abuse? Torture?"

"Instead of *more*, they packed me up and sent me off to the penitent monks."

"That was my father," she said. "He made them—oh! There's his sail!"

"What?"

She pointed toward the horizon. "*Sawtooth*'s coming. And—damn, three points off her stern—I think that's *Ascension*."

She was right. Once she'd used her camera to bring it into focus, the Y-shaped mast with its spiderweb sail was as unmistakable as it was improbable.

"Come on," Bram said. "Let's get you off that leg and we can tell each other everything."

A bit of prowling revealed that *Constitution* had a mess aft, a fancy dining lounge. They ate toasted muffins and poached heron eggs off china, and watched from cushy chairs as Cly's sail got bigger and bigger. The ship had a flag out to signal for a ride—as soon as they were close, three of the little ferries started zooming toward them, racing one another for the fare.

Sophie said. "Let's see if Beatrice and Cly managed to sail to Tiladene and warn Lais Dariach without killing each other."

Using the telephoto on her camera, she could see her mother and Verena catching the ferry, making for *Constitution* at full sail. *Sawtooth* went on to take a position among an array of vessels all flying the Judiciary flag. *Ascension*, since she wasn't a Rep ship, sailed to a rendezvous farther back, midway through the Fleet.

Annela and Parrish turned up on the elevator platform at about the same time as Sophie and Bram. Beatrice spilled out first, more or less collapsing into Annela's arms with a wail.

"What kept you?" Annela said, over her shoulder, as she patted her . . . cousin? "Sophie said you set out for the Fleet days ago."

"Tiladene is under blockade," Verena said. "They wounded that friend of Sophie's."

"Lais?"

"We smuggled him aboard *Sawtooth* and then Cly bullied his way past a Ualtarite ship's captain who tried to stop us—"

"Is the Tiladene badly hurt?" Annela asked.

"Yeah. Cly has an amazing doctor aboard his yacht, because of the dueling. But he says it'll take magic to save him."

"Oh, dry your eyes, Beatrice—it's unseemly."

"You pack away the stiff upper lip bull, Annie," Beatrice said. "Or I will howl down this deck."

Annela sighed. "All of you, follow me."

She led them down to the lower decks, to a black-painted hallway and an unmarked door. Before opening it, she added, in a whisper to Sophie, "Don't babble at him, child. It'll confuse matters."

Sophie stared at her, rattled. "Babble? I don't think 'babble' is fair—"

"Answer yes or no if you're spoken to, and otherwise let me do the talking," she snapped.

"Let her be," Beatrice said. "You're not the Allmother yet."

Annela straightened to her full, regal height and swept into a room so simple that, after the dramatics in the corridor, it seemed a bit of a letdown. The room resembled a Puritan one-room schoolhouse, or maybe a prison lecture hall: hard wooden chairs facing a lectern, no ornamentation at all. A single individual sat at a long desk. He had Asian features, long black hair, a black robe, and a grim expression that seemed at one with the decor.

"What trouble have you brought the Watch now, Convenor Gracechild?" He droned the words.

Annela gestured at the hard chairs and, when everyone was seated, approached the lectern. "I bring the courier from Erstwhile and various members and servants of my family, Kir, to report on a situation that endangers the Cessation."

"What a relief," he said. "I thought you'd merely come to squabble beyond my door."

Sophie couldn't help it; she chortled. The man harpooned her with a look.

"Go ahead, Convenor."

Speaking quickly, Annela filled him in on everything, the attack on Gale, the storms, the threats on Erinth, the events on Tallon and after.

The black-garbed man made notes and didn't quite yawn, and when Annela finished he said, "Matters affecting the Cessation of Hostilities require a hearing before a section of the Convene. I shall prepare summons. Can anyone vouch for the honor of the two outlanders?"

Parrish rose. "Both of the Kirs Hansa can be trusted to tell the truth."

A snort. "A recommendation from you, Parrish, can hardly be acceptable. Does nobody know them better?"

Silence.

Bram elbowed Verena, but she looked away.

The man let out a wet, congested snort, as if this was a conspiracy, drummed up to add to the pile on his desk. "Do the outlanders at least comprehend that no mention of Erstwhile will be tolerated in Committee?"

Parrish looked at Sophie, who nodded. Bram followed her lead. "They do, Kir."

He fixed them with a hostile gaze. "If you are asked about any matter touching upon your homeland, your response is to be 'I cannot say.'"

"One other thing," Annela said.

"Yes, Convenor?"

"It's my understanding that the girl's full name is known to people of the nations so accused. And Kir Bramwell Hansa was in the hands of the Golden for a time."

"So you say."

"You better not say he's lying," Sophie said, grabbing Bram's hand and holding it up, to show off the pearl embedded under his thumb.

This earned another snort. "You're speaking out of turn, girl."

She opened her mouth to tell him how much she cared about that, but Annela thundered: "Sit down now, Sophie!"

Bram pulled his hand loose and gave her a tug. She wobbled back into her seat.

Annela continued: "I want a writ saying that should any contributing witness to these events suffer critical harm or be rendered speechless, their assertions will be read into the record as fact, unchallenged."

"Agreed. I'll inform the requisite parties when I make up the summons." His tone made it clear they were dismissed.

"Gee, thanks for sticking up for us," Bram said to Verena as the hatch slammed shut behind them.

"Couldn't," she said. "If he'd grilled me about how I knew I could trust Sophie, or how I got to know her at all, I'd have had to tell him about Gale's purse and the inheritance mess. It'd make her look worse—dishonorable, you know."

That damned purse. Sophie fought an urge to point out, again, that she hadn't known the thing would imprint on her like some kind of gosling. "So what happens now?"

"They'll summon a handful of Convenors," Annela said. "The group of you must convince them that there's a tie between the Golden and the Ualtarites, that the Ualtarites put this scheme together and are probably in possession of Yacoura."

"Won't that essentially accomplish what the Ualtarites want?" Sophie said. "They want the Fleet to know they've got the Heart—they want to threaten to break it, and *Temperance,* so they can roll over the Tiladenes."

"They need deniability," Annela said. "It's a tangle of law and honor, and I don't expect you to understand."

"Yeah. Complicated stuff like that is just beyond me." Having Bram back, knowing that Verena was safe, had made the threat of war seem vastly less important.

Annela ignored her remark. "Isle of Gold has a claim of sorts on the

Heart, because of the sinking of *Lucre*. They've pursued it openly for many years. They can argue that their search for it is a matter of honor. Ualtar has no such claim; if they sought Yacoura, their only reason could be to break the peace, and . . ."

"And that just makes them look bad?"

"Don't act superior. Beatrice tells me that public opinion drives policy in the outlands, too," Annela said.

"The two nations need each other, but they won't want to admit it," Bram said. "Like a secret marriage."

"Yes," Annela said. "The Golden also won't wish to concede that they needed help to get the Heart . . . We might use their pride against them."

"So how many people are we going to be addressing?" Sophie said.

"The minimum for an emergency Convene is twelve representatives. According to tradition, we need equal representation from the port and starboard sides of the government," Annela said.

Twelve people. That didn't sound so bad. Sophie stepped out onto the main deck of *Constitution*, taking in a deep breath of the clean, cold air. "We can do that."

Annela gave her a look that bespoke grave doubts.

"It's session break." Beatrice spoke for the first time. "Won't they be hard put to scrape up a dozen Convenors?"

"Normally, yes. But it's graduation."

"Is it?" Something complicated passed over Parrish's face. Unhappiness? Ten or twelve people.

*It's time I got over the weird stage fright,* Sophie told herself. *If I can do this, going home and defending my thesis should be easy.*

Bram squeezed her hand, as if he knew what she was thinking.

"I'll do what I can to prepare you," Annela said. "But first, I've got to see who I can find for a session. Stay on *Constitution*. Parrish, keep them in order, will you?"

With that, she vanished back down into the bowels of the ship, leaving Sophie with Bram, Parrish, Beatrice, and Verena.

Verena elbowed their mother, who gritted her teeth.

Then she asked: "Sophie. Why are you limping?"

"I had some trouble retrieving the Heart. And . . . your octopus died. I'm sorry." She fumbled in her things, coming up with the flute, offering it back.

Beatrice took it, looking it over with a fond eye. "I expect if I called, we'd rustle up another one."

"Is that what'll happen, if we get Yacoura back? You'll call another octopus and it'll make off with it again?"

"No, probably not. The Legend about its disappearance came to a natural close when you retrieved it. The Fleet will take custody."

Sophie bit her lip. "Listen, I'm sorry about the . . . about the whole legal mess."

"About my being arrested?" A bitter half smile. "Verena's been trying to convince me I made my own bed there. She says you're fundamentally softhearted, that if I'd told you my neck was on the line instead of 'screeching like a banshee . . .'—that is how you put it?"

Verena stared at the floor, clearly embarrassed at being quoted.

"She says you'd have left well enough alone."

"Uh . . ." She was at once grateful for Verena's support and unsure that it was true that she could have been dissuaded so easily from looking into her background. "I don't suppose there's any chance you and Cly talked out your issues?"

At the mention of Cly's name, Beatrice stiffened.

"I'll take that as a no."

"How would you have felt," Beatrice asked, "if you'd found your parents in . . . back in the outlands, and your father had turned out to be the guy who pushes the button in the gas chamber?"

"I—" *He's a lawyer. A judge,* Sophie thought, but she remembered again, his voice: *Do you fight?* And there was what he'd said to the pirate, too: *I'm reckoned by some ill-tempered.*

What did you say to that?

Beatrice continued: "What if his title was Lord High Executioner, rather than Duelist-Adjudicator? Wouldn't that bring you up short? Give you a bit of a chill?"

"This is . . . a different place," Sophie said. "I don't know if that's a fair comparison."

"The Dueling Deck is where the Fleet shunts its—" Beatrice broke off abruptly, her gaze drawn over Sophie's shoulder.

Cly was there, standing in a shaft of moonlight, beaming at Sophie.

Its what? Its fighters? Its killers?

Beatrice turned away.

"Sophie, is this your brother?"

"Uh . . . yes. Bram, this is Clydon Banning. Cly, my brother Bramwell Hansa."

Cly bowed. "Your sister is devoted to you. This tells me you are a man of great worth."

"Thanks," said Bram. He didn't quite bow back, but he bobbed his head, the way Tonio sometimes did.

"Cly, is Lais okay?" Sophie said.

"Your dissolute spider breeder? Shattered pate. I've transferred him to Allium's primary hospital ship," he said. "If he's to live, they'll have to scrip him. Sophie, I'd like to escort you to the Fleet Graduation."

"Uh—"

"Unless, that is, your mother would like to complete her analysis of my character."

Whatever it was, Beatrice wasn't prepared to say it to his face.

*Okay, they're under stress, it's exactly the kind of situation where people are gonna be acting like jerks. Cut them some slack.* "I can't believe you guys were ever married."

"It was a source of wonder to two nations and all who knew us," Cly said, with every appearance of good humor, as he offered her his arm.

"You're injured," he said, as they made their way toward the bow.

"Pulled some muscles. It's healing." *Constitution* was coming up behind *Temperance*, closing the distance between them.

"So that's the pirate-sinker," she said, changing the subject. "Its hull—is that skin? It looks like there's a healed scar."

"Very perceptive. It's sharkskin over stone wood," Cly said. Unlike the other ships, *Temperance* had smokestacks instead of sails. It had what looked like a cannon deck, too.

"The Tallon designer who built her had lost her parents and husband to the Piracy," Cly said. "The ugliness of the ship, I've always thought, bespeaks the fundamental nature of revenge."

"That's poetic of you."

"What's odd is that so much good came of it." He gestured at the Fleet. "She's a brute instrument, and yet the Cessation has been of indisputable benefit."

The Cessation. That was what was at stake now. "A hundred years of peace, right?"

"One hundred and nine." He nodded. "The tales from the century before describe a world at the height of savagery. Nations wiped off their home islands, populations eliminated to the last child, by better-armed raiders. No ship sailing alone was safe, and when they were taken . . . well, anything might happen to the people aboard. The seas bear silent witness, we sometimes say."

"All at risk, now."

"I have faith in you, child," he said. "In the future of the Fleet, too."

They were looking down upon the main deck now. There were uniformed kids down there, perhaps sixty of them. The youngest was about twelve, Sophie guessed, the eldest maybe eighteen. They wore red jackets and white gloves and most of them had brought dates, some of whom were dressed in civilian clothes from, presumably, a variety of nations. The variety of clothing designs gave the sight a TV science fiction feel: as if this were *Star Trek*'s idea of a senior prom in space. All that was missing was a few people with latex forehead prosthetics.

Waiters in livery moved among them; they were the oldest people there. Otherwise, the deck was entirely clear of adults. The gathering nearly sizzled with an air of anticipation. The kids kept casting looks over the bow. Sophie paused, following their gaze into blackness. Seeing nothing, she scanned the upper decks. Bram and Parrish were on a higher deck, overlooking the same scene amid a crowd of gray-haired officers.

Parrish's handsome face had that carved and closed look, as if he were more statue than man, as he took in the gathering. Then he looked out over the bow, his attention snapping forward like a cat's, watching for the same thing they were.

A burst of light. A flare, Sophie supposed at first, but it had wings and a sparking fan of a tail. Flapping upward, expanding, it cast blue-green light on a raft crowded with figures, perhaps a half kilometer away. Eight people . . . ten? The lightbird rose, growing ever brighter, and then shrieked as it began to fade. The cry was a signal, like a starter's pistol. The figures dove into the water.

The uniformed kids on *Constitution*'s foredeck began shouting and cheering.

*A race.* Sophie checked her watch. If the distance was five hundred meters and *Constitution* was the finish line, they'd be at least five or six minutes.

"This is the graduating class of the Fleet Universitat," Cly said. "The officer candidates."

"And the swimmers?"

"The ten of them out there, racing to *Constitution*, are at the top of the class. The tradition is to finish out the year with this race, and a dance. Then they're each posted to a ship."

"If it's a graduation, shouldn't their instructors be down there?"

"Officially, the Slosh—the race—isn't allowed. Now and then someone does drown," Cly said. "Any instructor on deck would be obliged to forbid it."

*Another faintly uncivilized custom,* she thought. They were casual about death here in a way she just couldn't like.

Her thoughts turned to Beatrice's unfinished statement about Cly. What if she'd discovered her father was an executioner, she'd asked. The Judiciary was where the Fleet kept its . . . what? Warriors?

"Adults only step on deck after it's too late to prevent the race. Which is now. Shall we?" He offered her his arm, nodded to a guard, and escorted her past the rope.

"I'm not dressed for a ball, Cly," she said, thinking momentarily of the white gown the Conto had given her, and the use she'd been putting it to.

"No one will care unless you do."

She concentrated on not falling down and, when they reached the bottom of the staircase, she glanced back up at Bram. He conferred with Parrish briefly, then set off down the stairs on his own.

"Parrish won the Slosh in his year, back when he was a rising star," Cly said.

"Your Honor, Your Honor!" Dazzled-looking graduates were bowing at them as they progressed through the throng.

He replied with affable greetings and handshakes: "Congratulations! Well done. Good for you, Kir." He seemed to know all their names.

It was oddly like going out with a celebrity, to a movie premiere or some other grand Hollywood event.

"Do you dance, Sophie?" He indicated a quartet of musicians with string instruments, who were setting up on a small bandstand.

"That depends," she said.

"On?"

"If it's something waltzy or more *Pride and Prejudice*."

He smiled. "I don't know what that means."

"I can fake a waltz. If it's two lines of people passing each other back and forth—" She pantomimed what she imagined was a Regency dance move.

"The first dance usually takes that form."

"I've never done that . . . but I'm good at picking things up. If I watched for a few minutes I'd probably be okay." She hesitated, and her imagination helpfully supplied footage of the two of them dancing, birth father and daughter. A swell of difficult-to-identify emotions assailed her. Was this sadness? Relief? Gratitude?

If Cly saw her struggling, he didn't acknowledge it. "If you'd grown up at home, as you should, you'd have had a dancing instructor."

She clung to a little thread of outrage and used it to pull herself free of the morass. "And someone to teach me pianoforte? And embroidery?"

He frowned at her crutch. "Fencing, in any case."

"I don't think a bit of sword instruction could have prevented this."

"There's more to fighting spirit than knowing how to slap a weapon about."

"I don't want to learn fighting spirit. Knifing that sea monster was way up there on the list of yuck experiences of my life."

"You have a compassionate heart," he said. "The oddity would have drowned you."

"Well," she said, trying to lighten the mood, "dancing's probably out, at least for now."

"No matter. What I truly wanted was privacy, or what passes for it," he said. "I've been looking into the matter of your inheritance. You should consider claiming it."

"It's not mine, it's Verena's."

He waved off this statement, as though it were a gnat. "Your mother was the one who inherited the courier position and the material wealth of her mother line. Gale Feliachild was merely her designated agent. There's no reason why Verena cannot be yours."

"Why would I do that?" She pushed away the thought of *Nightjar*, the prospect of sailing her anywhere.

"For the sake of the daughters you may have one day."

"I've known you a week and you're lobbying for grandchildren? Holy crap, Cly—"

"Mind your language," he said.

"You are *so* getting ahead of yourself."

He flashed that wolfish grin. "Quite right, my dear. Focus on the discussion at hand. The Feliachild estate."

"Me snatching the inheritance would be a slap in Verena's face, Cly. Gale didn't want that, Beatrice doesn't want it. And you're just advising me to hand it over to her anyway, so what's the difference?"

"You might yet become a woman of Verdanii. That's a significant position in this society. Vastly more important than their trinket of a government job or that appalling scow *Nightjar*."

"Hey!" she objected.

"After all you've done for the Cessation these past weeks, you're entitled to something."

"I'm not entitled to Verena's life."

"It's not right. You shouldn't be nobody."

"I'm not nobody!"

Like that, the hint of fury vanished. "No, of course not. Forgive me."

She wobbled on her unsteady leg so that she was facing him, balancing by leaning on his upper arms, almost a dance position after all. "Listen, Cly. I don't know the Verdanii, but what I've observed about their society, so far, makes it seem kind of . . . bizarrely screwed up."

He pealed laughter, startled.

"This primogeniture thing is a case in point. And the whole tough woman thing . . . Annela reamed Beatrice out for crying over Gale, and they apparently treat their men badly. But that's a side issue. I'm just not gonna do it. There may be all kinds of advantages and I understand that Beatrice broke the law, and that what she did to you was very hurtful—"

"What she did to us." That steel and coldness again.

"Yeah. If she'd made different choices, everything would be different. But we can't punish Verena for that. I'm not ripping her life out from under her, I'm just not. Get it?"

He was statue-still for a painfully long stretch of time. His smile, when it came, was tight. "You have an admirable sense of honor."

She could feel an answering smile breaking over her face. "I'll take that over pianoforte and fighting spirit any day."

"I respect your position," he said. "But it is a shame. It would give your assertions more weight in Convene if you weren't an outlander."

A flutter of nerves. "What about your nation? Can't I say I'm yours?"

"Oh, Sophie Hansa." He wrapped her in a sudden hug, an almost shocking burst of warmth. "I will be honored to claim you as a child of Sylvanna, but that can't be done overnight. There's a paternity assertion, a formality, obviously—"

"Hang on. Sylvanna? You're Sylvanner? Isn't that the big pharma island?"

"The . . . Big Farm?"

"Sorry. The Stele Islanders told me that Sylvanners are . . . well, patent thieves, I guess."

"The wealthy and industrious are always envied by the less fortunate," he said. "But—"

"Swimmers ahoy!" shouted several of the kids.

The musicians struck up a suspenseful riff, the low strings of their instruments humming like something from a horror movie soundtrack.

"Here they come," Cly said.

The dance dissolved as the young officers rushed to the rail to cheer their classmates.

"This is the part where we elders look officially disapproving," Cly said. A dimple quivered in his cheek.

"Elders. I'm elder?"

"Just don't cheer."

The students hurled a sturdy net over the rail, transforming it into an improvised rope ladder. Shouting cadets obscured it, leaning over, shouting in a dozen languages, who knew how many variations on "Go!" and "Swim!"

"There's a woman I've requested for the Judiciary," Cly said. "I'm hoping she . . . ah, no such luck."

A young man, lithe, muscled and shivering, hurled himself onto the deck.

"One!" roared the cadets.

A teenaged girl—the one Cly had been rooting for, from his expression—was perhaps five seconds behind.

"Two!"

Maybe half a minute later: "Three!" The bronze went to a magically altered, moon-pale cadet with fish scales and fins, who had climbed the rope ladder—and had presumably swum—with a net full of stones tied to its belt.

Sophie said, "So your girl came second?"

"The odds that she'd beat Fessler were never that good," Cly replied. He waved the young woman over. She came, wrapped in a heavy towel, and bowed deeply.

"Nicely done, Kir Zita," Cly said.

"Thank you, Your Honor!" She was shivering, but his praise clearly meant the world.

"Four! Five!" The cadets shouted, as two more of their classmates came over the side.

"May I present my daughter? Kir Sophie Hansa."

The young woman—Zita—waited a beat, as if she expected something more, one more bit of information, before dipping her head again. "Honored, Kir."

"Um, likewise, Kir." *Where I'm from. It should have been Sophie Hansa of somewhere. That's what he means by position.* "You made good time," she added.

"The Slosh isn't much of a race in weather like this," Zita said.

"Count yourself lucky, child," Cly said. He had somehow made one of the waitstaff appear with a hot bready thing and a tray of what smelled like brandies. "You'll have plenty of chances to risk yourself if you're called to the bar."

"Yes, Your Honor."

"Six!"

The music began anew.

"Please, join your friends," Cly said. "I'll make an opportunity to talk with you later."

Zita bowed, toweling her hair briskly, and trotted over to a waiting girl in a garment like a sari, kissing her roundly on the lips before pulling her out onto the dance floor.

*No "don't ask, don't tell" here,* Sophie thought, pleased. *And Cly likes her, so he's not some big-time homophobe.* She scanned the crowd for Bram. He was doing the same math as her, for once—he tipped her a pleased-looking salute. The cadets and their dates began the dance, the youngest of them looking adorable and oh-so-young in their grown-up clothes.

Socializing and chitchat. This was what Beatrice couldn't handle, if Cly was telling the truth: night after night of polite, shallow conversation. She leaned on the rail. The strained muscles in her thigh twinged.

*Dancing's definitely out,* she thought. *And I need to sneak away and look up Sylvanna in the big book of Stormwrack nations, too . . . oh, it's still on* Nightjar, *well, I guess I can ask Beatrice and Verena . . .*

*Yeah, because they won't be biased.*

"Seven!" Some of the swimmers were still coming in.

A few cries of consternation. Was someone hurt?

"Sofe, watch out!"

That was Bram.

She didn't have time to absorb his words. Cly thrust her behind him, practically tossed her, a shove so abrupt she fell on her butt on the deck. His sword whisked out of its scabbard with a rasp. Its cutting edge seemed to be made of a slick, blood-colored stone, and there were bone-white letters, in spellscrip, on its haft.

He squared off against two men, both dressed as waiters. One, Sophie saw with an ugly jolt, was John Coine. He looked worn out, older than she remembered; there were dark circles under his eyes and age spots on his hands. His hair had a dried-out, burnt look to it.

The other fake waiter was a stranger, a shortish man, square of face, and faintly swollen-looking. He had a sword out, too, clutched in a hand whose thumb was tightly bandaged.

If Cly stepped back, he'd trample her. Sophie slid backward, clearing some space, and looked 'round for something blunt she could swing, if needed.

In his left hand, Coine held a tray of canapes, shrimp on crackers.

In his right was a pistol—big, modern and black.

*Tech from home, like the grenade that almost killed Lais,* thought Sophie.

The cadets on deck had cleared away from the stand-off. Some looked curious, as though they thought this was some bit of performance art in honor of their graduation. Others, including the boy who'd won the Slosh, were casting about for weapons. A gray-haired waiter with the bearing of an admiral was directing the celebrants and their civilian escorts up to a higher deck, sending the youngest up first. The circle around Cly, Sophie, Coine, and the fourth man was getting bigger.

"Nobody need die here," Cly said. "You can't hope to achieve your goal now that you've been spotted."

Coine looked past Cly to Sophie. "What about this? She agrees to keep her silence, Kir, or I'll blast out your heart."

"I will not be used in such a way," Cly said, tone careless. "Fire the musket, Kir."

"Very brave."

"Cly," Sophie objected. "Unless you're bulletproof—"

"My child will not give in to blackmail." Cly's words rang like hammer blows; the man with the cutlass stepped back.

John Coine wasn't as easily impressed. "She did before, didn't she?"

"Shoot, Coine, if you must. Bramwell, collect your sister and return her to your family." Cly took two steps forward, stepping so close to Coine that the gun was mere inches from his chest. He knocked the canape tray away. "Go ahead. Assassinate me. See what becomes of you."

"No!" Sophie shouted. Bram was at her side now, helping her regain her feet.

"Sofe—"

"He'll get shot!"

"This is all about stopping you from talking to the Convene," he said. "Cly's right. If you're gone, their threat won't—"

A blur, from above. Coine had been about to say something and then he was—what had happened? Clumsiness and her injury slowed Sophie as she wrestled Bram, fighting to see.

It was Parrish. He'd leapt on John Coine from the upper deck, or the sail—

Was he hurt?

No, the gun hadn't gone off. He had the pistol, in fact, and was wrestling Coine.

The guy with the cutlass had taken two healthy steps back from Cly, toward the rail. His expression and body language said he was terrified . . . and yet he didn't drop the weapon.

Cly advanced, sweeping his arm up and around, seeming to try to catch the other blade, to disarm his opponent.

The guy screamed . . . but then parried the swing easily. He stared at Cly across the X of their crossed weapons, and his expression was one of sheer surprise.

"Interesting," Cly murmured. He thrust again, and was again blocked. The swordsman was sweating heavily; his face was greasy, but the color of his skin, which was ruddy, did not change in the slightest.

"John Coine," Parrish said, voice carrying over the clash of swords, "you will be confined by the Watch and examined by same, on my authority as a—"

A cacophony of shouts interrupted him. *Warnings,* Sophie thought. *Warning who?*

"Sofe, we're going. You're not safe," Bram repeated.

"Stop!" someone yelled. One of the graduates?

"Stay there!"

"Wait, just wait—ah, no!"

A young officer candidate in wet breeches climbed up on deck, more or less stumbling right into the swordfight.

"Nine," he called, surveying the scene in confusion. "What's going on?"

The swordsman lunged for the kid. To use him as a human shield?

He didn't make it that far. Cly attacked again. As the swordsman came 'round to block the swing, he slipped in close, caught his opponent's wrist, and snapped the whole of his arm, elbow first, down against *Constitution*'s rail.

The shock of the crunch, as the arm broke backward at the elbow, was so intense that Sophie felt the impact through the deck.

With a moan, the man dropped his weapon and curled up at Cly's feet.

By now, Parrish had John Coine bound and was searching his pockets. His eyes searched the deck for her. "You're all right, Sophie?"

"Not a scratch on me."

Bram gave up tugging her arm. He pointed at the shaking, disabled swordsman. "That's the guy you saw on Erinth."

"No, it isn't," Sophie said.

"It—" he frowned, looking again. "It looks like him."

"I'm the one who broke his nose back home, and I say it's not."

"His nose is recently broken," Parrish observed.

"Is that why his face looks puffy?"

Sophie shook off Bram's grip, picked a linen napkin off the deck, and limped to Cly's side.

"What is it, child?"

"Cly, please stop calling me child. I'm checking for concealer. Makeup." She reached for the man's face, then balked when he whimpered. "Sorry, I'm sorry, but—"

Cly whisked the napkin out of her hand and rubbed it over the oily-looking skin of his nose, none too gently. The bound man wailed.

"Stop, it's hurting him!"

"You're right," Cly said. Pinkish smears covered the cloth, and now the bruising on the swordsman's nose was obvious.

"See?" Bram said. "It is him. It's the other guy who attacked Gale."

"It's *not*," Sophie said.

Parrish interrupted. "Let's discuss it somewhere secure. You're too exposed here."

"He's right," Cly began, but before they could bundle her away, John Coine and the other man both coughed once, in peculiar unison. As one, they let out a long breath, a shaking hack of air torn from raw throats.

Their bodies went rigid, spines curving like bows. The skin of Coine's forearms bulged against the neat loops of ropes Parrish had tied around them. The swordsman's eyes streamed tears, further streaking his greasepaint, cutting tracks across his cheeks and revealing more bruised flesh.

Their eyes rolled up in their skulls, and then their bodies went slack as they died.

## CHAPTER 25

"Okay, I know this is an obvious question and I'm only asking because I'm hoping to be wrong, so wrong, but did those two guys just drop . . ."

"Dead? Yes." Cly scanned the dance floor, then reached out to draw Parrish back to Sophie's side, sandwiching her between him and Bram.

"How? I mean, they just keeled!" How many people had died since she had been here? The innocent fishers on Stele Island, the *Estrel* crew . . .

"They've been scripped to death," Parrish said. "To keep them from talking, one assumes."

"Return Sophie to Convenor Gracechild, Bramwell," Cly said. "Now, please."

"Okay. Come on, Sofe."

"You can just do that, just write a spell and make someone die? You, Verena, anyone, they can just . . . Bram, you said you didn't give them your middle name, right?"

"It's you whose name is out there, remember?" Bram and Parrish were obeying Cly, half supporting her weight as they dragged her back amidships.

"Deathscrips are rarities, Sophie, if it helps," Parrish said. "Writing one is a capital offense."

"Why would that make it any better? This is a terrible, stupid, horrible place! And anyway, why come after me at this Slosh-thing if they could just zap me remotely?"

"The Watch might find and destroy the inscription, for one thing."

"Pardon?" she stopped in her tracks, sending jolts of pain shooting from her injured leg.

"What you saw works like any other inscription. If it were to be destroyed, Coine would revert."

"Revert. Be alive again. Poof!"

"Yes."

"So then he and the other guy they sent to attack me—"

"Sands," Bram said.

"It wasn't Sands," Sophie and Parrish said simultaneously.

Cly, who had caught up with them by now, frowned.

"Nobody's going to turn the Fleet inside out looking for deathscrips for two would-be murderers," Parrish said.

"No? They threatened Cly. He's a big shot, isn't he? Couldn't we call it an assassination attempt and get this supposedly all-powerful Watch off its butt—"

"Mind your tongue," Cly said, and it was obvious he was biting off another "child."

She planted her feet against the three men's apparently relentless urge to haul her off to an armored panic room. "You see my point, though, don't you? If ripping up the inscriptions that killed them would bring John Coine and the other guy back, we could get them to tell the Convene what they know."

"I'll bring pressure to bear for a search," Cly said. "But you, Sophie, must promise to return to Annela immediately."

She nodded. "Fair deal."

Cly turned on his heel, heading back the way he'd come.

"They really could be alive again?" Bram asked.

"They will be. No inscription lasts forever," Parrish said. "One day, inevitably, they will revert. But it makes no sense that they would try to kill Sophie."

"No?"

"Convenor Gracechild asked the Watch to stipulate that if she was unable to testify, her assertions would be read into the record as uncontested fact."

"Then what was their game plan?" Bram demanded.

"I don't know."

"Can we hope they were just dumb?"

"No," he said. "There would have been a purpose."

"Be pleased that whatever they wanted, the attack on you failed." That was Annela, attended by a trio of burly types who could only be cops, or the local equivalent of palace guards. "Come, children. The hearing's at dawn."

"You said we'd have time to prepare," Sophie said.

"You do—you have until dawn. Isle of Gold has demanded that the Fleet entire make a penitential cruise to the site of the *Lucre* sinking. If we sail north, we won't be able to aid the Tiladenes before Ualtar's had time to raid them."

"But people believe us, right? That they're in cahoots?"

"No," Annela said. "We need to convince the Convene that this isn't simply a matter of the Piracy achieving its long-cherished dream of revenge on *Temperance*. You'll have to show them the Ualtarites and the Isle of Gold are in league."

"When's morning?"

"Four hours," said Parrish, with a glance at the stars.

"Come to my rooms. We'll go over your testimony."

Annela's rooms were almost as sumptuous as the Conto's guest quarters had been, though on the cramped scale typical of oceangoing vessels, and in a completely different style. Everything was draped in fabric: thick velvets, heavy cushions, sturdy nailed-down couches. She favored moss greens and dark browns, the colors of the forest.

"You need not worry about what to say. Simply tell the truth. The thing to remember is this: Whenever something you wish to say touches on Erstwhile, you'll both need to say 'my home nation' instead. Got it?"

With that, they began to go over all the facts and observations they'd accumulated in their weeks at sea, one tiny piece at a time.

"I need to stop," Sophie said, after a couple hours. "At this point either we know it or we're gonna get more muddled, not less."

"All right, let's move on," Annela said. "I've gone through your trunk—"

"My trunk's locked."

"It wasn't a very good lock."

"You had no right!"

"I had every right. You've eraglided to Stormwrack illegally, twice. You broke your promise not to tell anyone about us, when you confided in your brother. And the trunk is full of espionage equipment—"

"Espionage equipment?"

"But that's not the point."

Sophie tried to wait her out, and failed. "Okay, I'll bite. What's the point?"

Annela turned, producing one of the gifts from the Conto—the full-length ball gown.

*Busted!* Sophie's heart sank.

Instead of castigating her, Annela said: "I think you should wear this to the hearing."

Was this a trap?

*Don't throw me in the briar patch!* The thought had an edge of hysteria, the hint of a laughing fit that could turn into a crying jag. "Don't you have a smaller version of one of those wraps?" She gestured at the vivid green and brown sarong Annela was wearing. "It looks a lot more comfortable."

"Given the ambiguity surrounding your citizenship, a Verdanii garment is out of the question."

"We can't even dress me like I might belong to Beatrice?"

"Self-pity doesn't become you, child."

"Annela, this is practically a wedding dress."

"Not here in the civilized world, it's not. It merely indicates you have the support of the Erinthian crown. Your current . . . ensemble . . . will raise questions."

"It'll take me two hours to put that thing on. It's not bad, as neck to floor princess dresses go, but . . ."

"The Erinthians do go for foolishly confining garments, considering their warm climate." Annela shook it out. A dried flower fell out of the skirt. Sophie tensed, but she didn't react. "Step in; I'll lace you."

"Just so long as we understand that nobody's touching my hair," she said. But she'd protested enough. She let Annela gather the skirts to her waist, and held it there until the waist was cinched. Then she pulled her shirt over her head, so she had her arms and the fabric crossed over her chest. "It probably won't even . . ."

But it did fit, exactly.

"I don't understand. It's like it's tailored."

"Conto's seamstress would only have needed a look at you."

"You expect me to testify looking like the cover of *Bride*?"

"Whatever that means, I want you to look respectable," Annela said.

"I don't even know why he gave me this thing," she grumbled.

"I imagine he thought well of you." Annela finished fastening the bodice. "It's a flattering garment. You have swimmers' shoulders. A true child of the sea."

"I have no idea what to do with a comment like that."

"Of course. Forgive me." She took a step back, evaluating, a slow examination that did nothing to ease Sophie's nerves.

"You look like that movie princess who fell in the garbage pile," Bram murmured.

"Thanks a lot."

"Maybe you should reconsider about the hair."

She ran a finger through her curls—they hadn't gotten too shaggy, she supposed. What had it been? Four weeks, since her last haircut? "I'll brush it out."

"Can you even sit?"

She perched on a cushion, briefly, then stood again. "It's pretty comf, actually. I guess the Erinthians, since they bind up their old people in these things . . ."

Annela glazed, visibly bored. "I'll give you some time alone."

"About the rest of my trunk," Sophie said.

"The data-gathering equipment will be confiscated."

"That stuff wasn't free, you know."

"Verena can reimburse you."

"I wouldn't have shown the files to anyone."

Bram said. "Some of that hardware is mine . . . does that make a difference?"

"You may both count yourselves lucky that nobody's charging you with mischief or spying."

"Spying for who?" Bram said.

Rather than answer, Annela treated him to a withering glare and she swept out of the room.

"Oh!" Sophie said. "I wish I had a princess shoe so I could stamp my foot in style!"

Bram had no such reservations and hurled a cushion in the direction Annela had taken. His aim was decent; it caught Parrish coming in, knocking off his silly bicorne captain's hat.

"Ah. Am I—" He had bent to fetch the hat and as he rose and took in the sight of Sophie in the white frock—

"Don't say anything," she said. "It wasn't my idea." Damned magic Erinthian seamstress anyway, she had to engineer a dress with a padded bodice and an open collar . . . she felt like she was heaving out at him. In 3D.

*Get a good look, Captain Tasty. It's all going back to San Francisco in a few days.*

Parrish raised his eyes to her face and kept them there. "It's a good strategic choice."

"If everyone's dressing up, I suppose I'd better at least throw some water on my face." Bram scooped his backpack off the floor and vanished into the head.

Parrish *was* turned out neatly, in a fitted pair of black breeches and a white linen shirt and suspenders. He had the long black officer's frock coat draped over his arm, and Sophie saw that he'd had the button replaced. He was freshly shaved, and had done something to tame his lamb's-wool curls.

It made her feel better; she wasn't the only one gussied up. And he was certainly easy on the eye. No wonder Verena was smitten.

"So . . . what, you've been at the salon all this time?"

"I oversaw your attackers' bodies when they transferred to the Watch, and alerted *Sackcloth* to their situation."

"Any luck finding the inscriptions that killed them?"

"I'm afraid not. After this is all over, they'll be taken to Issle Morta to await the breaking of the spells."

"Because that's what your people do," she said.

He set the coat and hat on a low table and she saw he had a small satchel in his hand. "I am a child of Issle Morta, but I'm not truly of that nation."

"Does that mean you're from nowhere, too?"

"My home has been *Nightjar* since I was eighteen."

"It's complicated?" she said.

"Only lately."

"Since Gale's death."

"Yes."

"Did I tell you I'm sorry she died?"

He inclined his head in thanks. "Dawn's not for an hour. Will you not sleep?"

"Not a chance."

"In that case, I've brought something," he said, opening the satchel and making room on a low table.

"What is it?"

He laid a green seed case the size of two doubled fists on the table. "It's called a lifeboat," he said.

Sophie took it in both hands, feeling the soft hairs on its seed coat, like those on wisteria, taking in the variations in hue: a darkening almost to purple where the stem had been attached. At the tip it was still bright green, despite being dried.

Near the tip, the two sides of the seed case gaped in an opening like a pair of pursed lips.

"You can open it," Parrish said.

"Seriously?"

He handed her what looked like a steak knife.

Working the point of the knife into the opening, she cut gently along the top seam of the pod. It was leathery and resistant.

Inside, she found a treasure trove of fly wings. A large, dead, half-pupated insect was squeezed into the bottom like a balloon, resting on a clutch of small barbed seeds. A few undeveloped seeds hung from the upper portion of the pod, embedded as tightly as pomegranates but with tiny hooks.

A faint smell of honey or beeswax exhaled from the thing, an undercurrent to the rot of dead bugs.

"What do you think?" Parrish said.

She sifted through the pod, examining everything.

"The pod's probably closed while the seeds are developing," she ventured.

He nodded.

"Once they're ready, the pod opens. Insects come in . . . there's nectar down here at the bottom, a lure. Some of them hook a seed and carry it off. Others probably get caught and can't dislodge themselves. So they'd die."

"Yes." He touched the pupa with the handle of a fork. "And this?"

"I'd say the plant this comes from has evolved a relationship with something like a wasp," she said. "It lays a grub in the bottom of the pod. As the bugs come in for the nectar, baby hoovers them up. As it grows and pupates . . . do the seeds get incorporated into its body? I've never seen that before."

Smiling, he produced a small jar containing a pickled wasp, about half as big as her fist. Its thorax was studded with hard beads, popcornlike kernels. "It's called a jeweler's wasp."

"Huge wings," she said, pinching one of the seeds. "They'd have to be— these things are pretty heavy."

"It sheds the seeds after about a month."

"Huge stinger, too."

"They're aggressive."

"Where does this pod grow?"

"Craven Reach, Larchrock, Cabrialle Island. Southern edge of the Sea of Bounty. They're used in spells for battening livestock, and sometimes for sickly children."

"Where did you get it?"

"The seed pod? It had imperfections, so it's no good for magic. Sub-optimal, Bram would say. I traded for it."

"Today?"

"No," Parrish said. "I pick up bits and pieces on our travels. This adult—" He swirled the wasp in the jar. "—it got into Gale's cabin, a couple years ago. She managed to catch it for me."

"Thank you, Parrish."

He ducked his head, then rose. "I have to send for Tonio."

"That reminds me," she said. "Can you get him to bring that little tube of polystyrene peas—"

He raised his eyebrows in a question.

"Small white . . . beads, sort of. They're soft. They were in my cabin, unless Annela got them, too."

"I remember," he said. Then, with a bow, he was gone.

She grinned at the pod. A little dissection was just what the doctor ordered; she was calmer now. "He might be infuriating, but he sure knows his job," she muttered, hiking up the outer skirt of the wedding dress and snagging a few of the barbed seeds within the quilted pockets.

"Awww," said Bram, startling her; she hadn't heard him return. "Did somebody bwing ooh a buggie?"

"Shut up. It's the least he can do after being consistently annoying for a month."

"Yeah, he *annoys* you."

"Change the subject, Bramble."

He handed her a comb. "Sofe, are you sure the guy with the busted nose isn't the one we saw on Erinth? He was a couple hundred feet away, across a crowded market."

"I saw him from a distance of two feet when he tried to stab Gale, remember? There's a strong resemblance, between Erinth guy and our dead swordsman, but no. They aren't one and the same."

"You have to be sure. This is all getting to be kind of a big deal."

"A big deal," she scoffed.

"If they don't believe us, there's going to be an invasion and their hundred years of peace are toast."

A renewed thrill of nerves, jittering performance anxiety, crawled through her. "I'm sure, Bram. It's another guy."

Bram looked into the pickled wasp's jar with an expression that said, basically, *Ewww, gross*. To spare his sensibilities, she pocketed it.

"Sofe, you never defended your master's because you like gathering information more than you do presenting results . . ."

"I didn't defend my thesis because I had a chance to film narwals."

"You've always been happy to coauthor bio papers with your advisors—"

"Bram, this isn't the time."

"You can climb a rock face with your fingertips, but you've never been able to deal with having your conclusions questioned."

She started combing out her hair. "Not listening."

Bram kept psychoanalyzing. "You're afraid of coming up short. Of being told you did it wrong, or you don't belong, or it doesn't count."

"Know why you don't understand that? Because you don't get what it's like to be fallible," she said.

"You're not wrong about this invasion," he said.

"Are you trying to make me nervous? If you are, keep it up."

"I'm trying to remind you—"

"It's too damned early for amateur therapy hour," she interrupted.

"None of this is on us," he said. "It's their war. You didn't start it."

"They've had world peace for a hundred and nine years."

"If these Convene guys aren't bright enough to see what's going on—"

"If I choke and can't convince them, you mean?"

"You've been amazing," Bram said. "I'm proud. Remember that, okay?

Try to can the stage fright and just give them the facts. Tell them the truth, let them make their own choices, good or bad, and we'll go home."

It was good advice, and it should have helped.

It only made her more nervous.

## CHAPTER 26

When dawn came, Annela appeared, escorting them wordlessly to the heart of the government.

The Convene ran the Fleet and kept the peace from the depths of *Constitution*, within a long chamber that, in most ships, would have been the hold. It was an imposing, somber room, illuminated by an array of lanterns that resembled giant pearls, nacreous globes with hints of gray and rose, within which firelight wavered and danced.

The space used the curvature of the ship's hull to provide a natural rake for the seats arrayed in rows on both sides. They were made of a dark, oaky hardwood, amply cushioned, and provisioned with little writing tables. A narrow strip of polished floor divided the port seats from those to starboard, creating what Sophie thought of—perhaps erroneously—as government and opposition.

The head of the room boasted a colorful tapestry, a grid eight wide and thirty high depicting the various islands' national flags. There was a big podium, complete with bell and gavel, and tucked to one side she saw a desk for clerks. Screened viewers' galleries were above on a mezzanine.

"Pomp and circumstance," Bram said in English, and Sophie nodded. It all reminded her of what she'd seen of the British House of Commons on TV, except that an assortment of crates, nets, and rope was piled high right beside the entrance.

Annela saw her looking at the stacked ropeworks. "Convene goes out of session for the southwinter break, right after graduation. The ship's logistics officer usually takes the opportunity to shift around the stores while the government is resting up."

"Sometimes it's a storage room, sometimes it's where you run an international government," Bram said, choosing his words slowly, speaking in a thick Fleet accent.

"Down with the bilge and the ballast," Annela said.

It was obviously an old joke, so Sophie tried to make herself smile.

"Wear these," Annela said, handing out wrist corsages, pomegranate-colored sprays of small lilies. "In memory of Gale."

Sophie fiddled, one-handed, trying to affix it to her wrist.

"Right hand," Annela said.

"I'll help—" Bram said, and in the same instant Parrish said "Allow me."

The men's eyes met, and then Parrish stepped back. Sophie thrust her arm out and Bram slid the catch into place and tightened it.

"You're ready for your closeup, Ducks," he said.

"Don't be a jerk, Bramble," she whispered.

"Over there is the petitioner's loft," Annela said. "You'll wait there."

"Don't go! Tell us what to expect," Sophie said.

"The first mate of *Constitution* acts as chair or speaker. He'll grant you permission to address the Fleet." She looked as though she might have something more to say to Parrish, but he had turned away to greet Tonio, who was just arriving. The two of them seemed extra upright and respectable in their starchy officer uniforms.

*Protective camouflage,* thought Sophie. She asked, "Where's Verena?"

"Unavailable," Annela said, pointing at the visitors' loft. "I'm hoping to keep the Convene from getting sidetracked into the question of Gale's position, and why you're holding it."

"Great," Sophie sighed. *Hiding all the embarrassing Verdanii gossip,* she thought.

"Good luck," Annela said, sweeping over to the starboard side of the room and taking her place among the other government officials.

"Isn't this grand?" Tonio bowed in greeting before handing Sophie the tube full of polystyrene peas. "I've never seen the Convene before."

"Very grand," Sophie agreed. She had been surprised and delighted to discover the princess dress had a couple of little pockets—they were probably for lipstick or similar grooming tools. Now, as she tucked the jar into one of them, it clinked against something glass already there.

It was the pickled jeweler's wasp Parrish had given her. She was smiling as she switched the peas to the other side of her skirt.

"Gonna stand there daydreaming, or are you gonna sit?" Bram asked.

Reluctantly, she crunched her backside down onto the cushioned seat.

She'd never expected to wear the dress, and in the past few weeks she'd tucked enough bits and pieces into the quilting of the skirt—shells, seeds, wrapped leaves, a few bones—that it made for lumpy seating. *Wish I'd gotten the data card for the camera in here,* she thought, mourning her sea raft footage.

Then again, if Verena noticed the chip was missing, they might search her closely enough to find the rest of her stash.

Convenors were filing in now, skirting the pile of crates and murmuring. They looked like they were mostly in their fifties and sixties, and many glowed with the confidence and charisma Sophie associated with Hollywood actors and rock stars. One stood out—a fragile, sylphlike maiden with a walking stick, in Erinthian dress. She blew Sophie a kiss, mouthing the words "illa Conto," before joining Annela.

"This isn't ten people," Sophie whispered to Bram.

"It's more than all of our fingers and all of our toes," he said gravely. It was something they'd said as kids; he was trying to make her laugh.

"The room's filling up."

"Breathe, Sofe."

"It looks like the whole government's here!" She strained to draw breath, imagining the dress was cinched corset-tight. "I can't—"

"You can," he insisted.

"There's hundreds of them." She felt a flash of panic. With it came that unsettling sensation she'd picked up back on *Estrel*—imagining the grenade, imagining her hand exploding.

"Meditate?"

She shook her head.

"Come on . . . distract yourself. Make some observations."

"Okay," she said. Her heart was racing. "Yeah. Plenty to see here, right?"

"Always. What *do* you see?"

"Um . . ." She scanned the room. "A number of the folks on the starboard side of the room are wearing the same lily corsage Annela gave us. Show of solidarity, maybe?"

"Maybe."

"No sign of Lais," she said.

"What else?"

She looked at the Convenors filling the seats. They looked rumpled and grumpy, the way anyone might if they'd been called in to work on the first day of vacation. A few cast dark looks in Parrish's direction.

"Whatever you did to alienate the Fleet oligarchy, it must have been apocalyptic," she blurted, regretting it instantly when the expression drained from his face.

"Memory runs long here," was all he said.

She grasped for the first change of subject that came to mind. "Where's Cly?"

"He'll be up there," Parrish replied, indicating the viewing gallery.

"Doesn't he have to testify—to say he saw the blockade?" Bram asked.

*Testify.* Sophie felt her shoulders clenching.

"His Honor is an adjudicator. If he says there's a blockade, it can be read into the record as fact."

"Just like that? I suppose if he says pale pink rhinoceroses are dancing on the beaches of Tiladene in tutus it can be read into the record as fact."

"Yes," Parrish said, with just a trace of a smile. His words were barely audible; even so, a few of the gathered Convenors glared at them.

Conversation petered out entirely as Tanta Maray, the woman from Ualtar, joined them in the petitioner's loft. She was in a gown too, a gold shift with long, trailing tatters of fabric.

"Kir Hansa," she said, and as her one-eyed gaze took in first Tonio and then Bram, something glinted there—revulsion. "You seem to go out of your way to surround yourself with vilemen."

"Funny," Sophie said. "I was just gonna say that for a raging homophobe, you have stunningly accurate gaydar. Where do you get off—"

"Shhh!" someone hissed from above. The speaker was taking his place. Maray favored them with a smile that could have frozen the sun, then sat daintily down next to Sophie.

They were a bit crowded on the bench; Sophie could feel the other woman's body heat through the layers of their skirts, warming as the formalities of getting started dragged on for what seemed like forever.

Parliamentary process was long and chewy, like cold gum: There was a head count, and then a formal protest from someone about being called back from break. The scribes had to attest that they were reliable, rested, and sober before they could sit down and start scribbling, super fast, taking in every word uttered.

Then each of them: Sophie, Parrish, Tanta Maray, and Bram had to petition for speaking rights and swear to tell the truth.

*At this rate we'll break for lunch without doing anything,* Sophie thought. She'd beaten back the panic attack, but only just.

But the speaker said, "The matter before us is the Isle of Gold's request that the Fleet make a penitential cruise to Harrow's Bay, as reparation for the sinking of *Lucre* in the final days of the Raiders' War. The Convene recognizes Kir Brawn."

"Thank ye, Speaker." An old man rose from the portside ranks. Unlike John Coine, who'd always been dressed in those tailored smocks that looked like medical scrubs, this gentleman was dressed in a way that pretty much screamed "pirate." His longcoat was bloodred velvet, embroidered in gold and bound with a crimson sash on which stylized skulls had been silkscreened, also in gold. He wore a skullcap studded with rubies. He stood about seven feet tall, sun-leathered and bald, and his fingernails were long—almost as long as his fingers themselves, and straight as stilettos.

*Do they straighten those using magic, or technology?* Sophie wondered. Either way, they flashed with the fire of opals.

Brawn launched into a long rant, the gist of which was the Fleet had kept kicking the Piracy long after they were down, back in the latter days of what he called the Raiders' War. He concluded: "The days when the threat of *Temperance* was needed to enforce the Cessation are long behind us. We're all tame and civil folk now."

"Once a rogue, always a rogue!" came a call from the starboard gallery. The speaker banged his gavel.

Brawn reacted with indignation. "If our claim cannot be respected, Kirs, we maintain that the threat of *Temperance* cannot be allowed to persist. 'Tis no mere symbol, and power must be used responsibly . . ."

The hoots were louder this time.

"We of the Isle of Gold have ever maintained that we have a transcendent moral right to seek and destroy the inscription that enfangs *Temperance*," said Brawn. "If the Fleet will not make amends to the dead of *Lucre*, we will put an end to that threat."

"Are you saying that you have recovered the lost inscription known as Yacoura?" asked the speaker. "And that you mean to destroy it?"

"The Heart may have been recovered, but not by anyone from Isle of

Gold," Brawn purred. "You have my word that it rests not in the possession of the Golden, nor has it passed through our hands."

It was as Parrish had predicted: They'd handed it over to the Ualtarites to cover their butts.

*Good,* Sophie thought, *he guessed right.*

"If nothing's changed," bellowed a starboard Convenor, "why are we here?"

"You're out of order, Kir," the speaker said. The mood of the room had turned ugly.

Brawn raised his hand, spreading his fingers so his opal-toned claws flashed in the lantern light. "If I seek that inscription, I will put my hands on it. I hereby vow to break Yacoura *Tempranza* within the day. Ye all know I am a man of my word."

Worried murmurs.

*He says he doesn't have it, so they can't just compel him to give it up. But he can get it, if he wants it.*

Word games and loopholes, Sophie thought. Everyone here was playing lawyer.

"Does that complete your petition, Kir Brawn?" asked the speaker.

"For now." Radiating satisfaction, the Isle of Gold's representative took his seat.

"Rebuttal?"

Annela rose.

"The Convene recognizes Kir Gracechild of Verdanii."

"Thank you, Speaker. First, I will note that the matter of redress for the tragedy at Harrow's Bay is in the courts."

"And has been for the length of the Cessation! How long must the dead wait?"

"You've had your chance to address, Kir Brawn."

Brawn fluttered his long nails, almost as though they were a fan. "My most heartfelt apologies, Speaker."

"Since when does the Convene interfere in Judiciary affairs?" Annela continued, as if there had been no interruption. "At this time, the Fleet's presence is urgently required to calm the waters between two member nations. The following Ualtar warships have been seen by the Duelist-Adjudicator, taking up positions around Tiladene and effectively enforcing a blockade: *Loftbridge, Righteous, Dictum—*"

"Excuse me, Speaker, but what has this to do with the matter at hand?" asked Brawn. "My business is nothing to Ualtar, nor theirs to me. And 'tis *me* holds the question."

Sophie shifted in her seat. They all already knew this; they had to. This was either theater or an exercise in getting the situation into the record.

"Speaker, I believe there has been collusion between Ualtar and the Isle of Gold. The former has lent assistance to the Isle of Gold's petition for this penitential cruise to Harrow's Bay. I charge that it is Ualtar who keeps the Heart for the Isle of Gold."

"To what end, Kir Gracechild?"

"Ualtar means to invade Tiladene. They want to break the peace."

The air was charged now; everyone was sitting up, straight and tense.

Annela continued. "What's more, they murdered Fleet Courier Gale Feliachild of Verdanii in their quest for Yacoura."

Tanta Maray was on her feet. "These are specious accusations!"

"They're certainly very bold," the speaker said. "Can you prove them, Kir Gracehild?"

"My argument is built upon the following facts," she said. "First, that Gale Feliachild was set upon twenty-nine days ago, by two men who caused her life-threatening injuries."

"Who says so?"

"Feliachild reported the tale to the Watch and confided in the herbalist and chieftain of Stele Island."

"Accepted as fact, then. Read it into the record."

"Next: The two assassins were John Coine of Isle of Gold and Hugh Sands of Ualtar, the latter presently assigned to the Erinth diplomatic mission."

"Who says so?"

"Sophie Hansa, natural daughter of Beatrice Feliachild, natural niece of Gale."

Tanta Maray rose. "Permission to address the Assembly?"

Sophie felt her breath catch.

"Granted," said the speaker.

"In the absence of the Ualtar representative, I must assert citizen's rights to speak for my nation."

"You are recognized. What have you to say?"

Maray bowed. "Ualtar reserves the right to contest Kir Hansa's asser-tions, Speaker. It is our position that she is not unimpeachable."

The speaker looked to Annela. "Is there nobody else to confirm the sighting of Coine and Sands, Convenor Gracechild?"

"No, Speaker."

"Record as unproved. We'll revisit it later."

*They'll impeach Bram, too,* Sophie thought, by way of quelling another flutter of anxiety. *This is just a big game of Constitutional Chicken.*

Annela continued, laying out *Nightjar*'s various discoveries and conclu-sions, starting with Lais Dariach and his spider-breeding program, then the first attempt on his life. She told the Convene about the mezmer attack on Gale, John Coine's threats against Sophie in the market, their sail to Tallon and Bram's abduction. The dry facts of the second assault on Lais Dariach and the blockade around Tiladene were accepted on Cly's say-so.

Whenever Annela mentioned some fact or another that rested wholly on Sophie's testimony, Maray hopped up and registered another inten-tion to challenge.

*Sophie Hansa is not unimpeachable.* The words chattered around in her skull.

Finally Annela put out both arms, a gesture that looked as though she were about to draw someone into a hug, and dropped her head before saying: "This concludes my submission."

They hadn't challenged Bram, or Parrish.

The speaker clanged the brass bell on the podium. The peals echoed in the vast chamber. His gaze swept over the galleries, coming to rest on the petitioner's loft and Tanta Maray. "Verdanii makes a highly persuasive case. What has Ualtar to say?"

Maray swept out onto the floor, taking a position in the center of the room, where the light was brightest, heightening the anticipation with a long silence. She looked supremely confident, in complete control of her-self. Sophie was reminded, fleetingly, of a flamenco dancer. The tattered fringes of her golden gown trailed behind her on the floor, and her milk-white eyepatch had been polished to a high gleam: "Convenor Grace-child's chain of logic, it seems to me, is strung together by a few crucial facts, all of which are supported by a single witness. I beg the Convene's permission to examine Sophie Hansa."

*Weak link, she thinks I'm the weak link, if I choke there's gonna be a war and people will die, more people . . .*

"Approach the lectern, Kir Hansa."

Bram squeezed her hand.

Sophie got to her feet. She felt small as she walked to the middle of the great theater, past Maray, all the way to the lectern. Her knees were quaking. The hundreds of Convenors looked down at her, their expressions schooled to blankness.

*It's truth, all I'm going to do is tell the truth. Bram knows it, Verena knows it.* She clung to the lectern for support.

The speaker addressed her: "Kir Hansa, your credibility has been challenged. Kir Maray's position is that you are mistaken or malicious. Will you recant?"

"I'm not lying," she said.

"Speak up, girl!" An anonymous and hostile bellow, from starboard, loud and sudden enough to make her startle.

"Everything I've said is true." Her voice was louder. It also shook.

"If you were to reconsider now, or withdraw your assertions, there would be no honor lost," the speaker continued.

She looked across the floor at Bram. *Breathe,* he mouthed.

"Kir Hansa?"

*Breathe, right. You* stand up here. "Kir Maray can cross-examine me to her heart's content," she managed.

Maray didn't give her time to gather herself. "Your assertions are these: first, that one of the individuals who attacked Gale Feliachild near her sister's home twenty-nine days past was Kir Hugh Sands, whom you later learned was a member of the Ualtar diplomatic mission on Erinth. Second, that you saw a lantern belonging to Captain Layna Dracy, first aboard *Estrel* and then on *Ascension*."

"In your office," she said.

"Third, that the *Estrel* crew and no others knew your identity, and that on Erinth John Coine revealed that he knew your full name. From this, you conclude that Coine and I were involved in the accident which befell *Estrel*."

She met Maray's cold, one-eyed gaze. "That's about the size of it."

"This is the entirety of your evidence of collusion between my people and the Isle of Gold?"

It sounded like so little. Sophie wanted to protest that there was more, that she knew *lots* of other things, but of course Annela had stripped out the rest. The fact that Lais had almost met his death by grenade couldn't go into the record because her home was a secret . . .

*. . . and Coine had a gun last night. He'd all but flaunted it . . .*

That seemed important somehow.

"Is that a question?" Sophie said, to buy herself time.

Why *had* they attacked her? And why make such a public display of it?

"I'm asking you to confirm that these are your assertions."

She nodded. "The spellscribe on Stele Island also knew my name, as did Lais Dariach. Otherwise . . . yes, that's all true."

"You're certain it was Hugh Sands that you saw . . . where was it?"

"Near Beatrice Feliachild's home," she said, as Annela had instructed her.

"Which is where?"

"I can't say, Kir. What matters is I'm sure it was him."

"The lantern: You examined it closely on both occasions?"

"I used it on a dive," she said. "I held it. I'd never seen anything like it before, so I took a good look."

"Isn't it true that Gale Feliachild asked the Conto of Erinth to claim you as an illegitimate child, to give you a false position as an Erinthian?"

"What?" Jolted by the change in direction, Sophie had to take a second to search her memories. "Yes, I think so. I mean, the Conto told me they'd discussed something like that."

"A small fraud, perhaps, but a telling one," Maray said. "Who must you be if the prospect of posing as an Erinthian bastard is considered a better identity?"

She could hear the Convenors whispering. "I can't talk about my background."

"If I call upon John Coine to relate the details of your conversation on Erinth, what will he say?"

Another change of direction. *She's trying to rattle me by jumping around.* "John Coine's dead."

Gasps ran up and down the galleries.

Maray affected shock. "Dead, Kir Hansa?"

"Yeah, right. Tell me, honestly, you didn't know?"

"You're the one under question." Maray glided past her, more shark than spider. "Coine told the Watch, yesterday, that you begged him to help supplant your half sister Thorna Feliachild, in the matter of a certain inheritance."

"That's not true!" Sophie said. The response sounded, to her ears, forceless. But part of her was stirring. This wasn't going to be some matter of defending her interpretation of the facts. This wasn't about her being dumb, or coming to the wrong conclusions.

She'd thought they would say she'd misinterpreted, that her chain of logic was erroneous, that her analysis was lacking. That she wasn't bright enough, or good enough. That she'd been a sloppy thinker.

But they were just going to lie.

*Maray's taking me seriously, even if nobody else is.*

She bit her lip, suppressing a giggle. Was it wrong that somehow that made it all a bit easier?

The speaker interrupted. "Can you produce any witnesses to this conversation, Tanta?"

"There is a shell vendor from Erinth about three days' sail away," Maray said.

"Three days. By then those ships of yours will have rolled right over Tiladene, am I right?" Sophie demanded.

Maray whipped around, turning so sharply that for a moment the dragging train of her robe looked like it might entangle her legs. She kicked it aside with practiced grace, and Sophie saw a speck of bone-white within the sun-colored tatters at its hem. "It is only you, Kir Hansa, who says we mean to engage in hostilities."

"So? You've got me saying one thing and John Coine saying another. He says I'm lying, I say he is. It's my word versus his."

"Not exactly." Maray gave her an almost pitying smile. "The assertions of John Coine cannot be contested now that he's dead."

Her mind whirled. "So he . . . he attacks me last night, and he dies, and then his saying I tried to rip off Verena goes into the record?"

"Oh! He died in an altercation with you?"

"You're gonna make it out that I had him . . . what was it? Death-scripped?"

"Did you, by chance, know his full name?"

"Yes, he gave it to Cly, but—"

*Oh! They killed him on purpose, had him feed the Watch a pack of lies and he went to his death, must have been in on it, would someone die just to make me look bad? Sure he would, people sacrifice themselves for their countries all the time, and he was getting so ragged from all the magic they worked on him anyway . . .*

"Given that you held his name," Maray continued, "it would have been easy enough to hire someone to inscribe his death, using the ill-gotten resources of your estate."

"I wouldn't know how," Sophie said. Her voice rose, despite her attempt to keep it even. She was becoming furious.

"You had another motive. Coine abducted your brother, didn't he? And tortured him?"

Across the chamber, Bram was tapping the rail of the petitioner's loft with his finger, a signal. Meaning what?

*Get back on point,* she thought. It was a good reminder. "Coine wasn't acting alone."

"Ah yes, that brings us handily back to your insistence that it was also Hugh Sands who attacked your aunt." Maray gestured, and the great doors creaked open—only to bang against the piles of stored crates. Two guards hurriedly rearranged the piles of nets so they could be swung wide.

Eight brown-robed men who could only be monks bore in two draped stretchers, and carried them past Maray amid a rising murmur from the Convenors. They laid them on either side of the podium, on the floor, and pulled back the shrouds, revealing the bodies of John Coine and the terrified swordsman from the night before.

For the barest of moments Sophie braced to see the contorted expressions the men had worn just before they died, but the bodies were still, calm. The concealing makeup had been wiped from the swordsman's face, revealing livid bruising.

Sophie looked from the bodies to the Convene, scanning first the portside, then the starboard. The assembly was rapt; people leaned forward in their seats, as if they were afraid they might miss a whisper. Did they expect her to swoon at the sight of the bodies?

Instead, she took the opportunity to look at them closely. *Now I know why they attacked Graduation last night. They wanted Coine's accusations about me wanting help to steal Verena's estate to be ironclad. They'd made sure I had Coine's name. But the other guy . . . why's he here?*

Calm descended. Suddenly she might have been fifty feet underwater with a failing tank. She looked back at the bodies, at Maray.

Maray gestured. "This is John Coine, who you say attacked Gale Feliachild twenty-nine days past?"

"It sure is."

"This other gentleman?"

"I don't know him."

"His name is Arlo Shank, also of Isle of Gold."

"Okay."

"Do you recognize Kir Shank?"

"He attacked me last night."

"Is he not the other gentleman who attacked your aunt?"

"No."

Of course. That's why he'd been busted in the face.

*Theater*, she thought. *Make up the lie and then sell, sell, sell it.*

"Are you certain, Kir Hansa?"

"I'm positive."

"Would you agree that he bears a strong resemblance to the diplomat you saw on Erinth?"

"He does," Sophie said, "But he's not the man I saw in Bernal."

"You contend you struck your aunt's attacker in the face? This man—"

"He's not the one. It's not him."

"Last night, during the altercation, your brother was overheard saying he *was* that man."

"My brother wasn't around when Gale was attacked."

"Still, there's disagreement?"

"Bram never saw him. I did."

"Once again we come to the question of your reliability. Who are you, Sophie Hansa? Of what people?"

"Does that really matter?"

"Why is it nobody can vouch for you?"

"My lack of . . . social connections, I guess? . . . shouldn't have any bearing on your assessment of my honesty."

"You're not merely ill-connected. You were discarded by your blood relations at birth, were you not?"

"Discarded . . ." The Convenors' eyes were pitiless, and everyone was staring. Sophie knew that, within the tight sleeve of the white dress, she was red right down to her cleavage. "Yes. I was adopted."

"By whom?"

"What matters is they want me." She looked at Bram.

"While that's touching, I take it to mean your adopted kin can't lend weight to your assertions, either. I put it to you again: How can this gathering accept your word?"

"What does my origin have to do with it?" Sophie pointed at the tapestry depicting the flags of all the nations. "Can you name me one of those countries whose entire population is truthful? Or one where everyone's a liar? I mean, the pirates are considered legit, aren't they?"

A chuckle from the starboard side of the gallery.

"We need not impugn an entire nation, Kir Hansa." Maray seemed to accept the point graciously. "Let's move closer to home. Isn't it true that your natural mother stands accused of bigamy and fraud?"

"I—" She swallowed an urge to defend Beatrice. *Where did that even come from?* "Yes."

"And it was your mother who had hidden Yacoura for so many years, your mother who's now accused of a serious crime against a prominent member of the Judiciary?"

"Yes."

"And it was, in fact, you who retrieved the Heart of *Temperance* and turned it over to persons unknown."

"True," Sophie said.

"Nobody but you has seen Yacoura, and yet you come here and accuse others of intent to commit an unforgivable act of vandalism against *Temperance,* the most cherished symbol of the Cessation."

"Before you go any further, Convenor Brawn up there explicitly said he'd smash the thing by day's end. Everyone here heard that. You don't have to take my word for that one."

Maray paused in mid-breath, caught out, and there was a ripple of quiet laughter from the starboard side. Sophie looked down at the fringes of Maray's robe again.

*Did I really see . . . ? Yes, there it is.*

"Kir Hansa makes an excellent point, Speaker," said Annela Gracechild.

Maray recovered quickly. "Since we're speaking of banditry, isn't it true that you have taken steps to usurp your sister's intended position among the Verdanii?"

Sophie bit her lip. "Are you going to challenge me on the facts? Or are you just going to make me out to be dishonest?"

"There's no point in cross-examining you if you can't be relied upon," Maray said.

"If there's no point in cross-examining me, you've been wasting everyone's time for a while now. Come on. Can't all you people see this is all about making me look bad enough that everyone will forget that her people have a blockade around Tiladene?"

"Have you or haven't you tried to assume your sister's rightful place in Fleet society?"

"I have *not*," Sophie said. "There's been confusion with Gale Feliachild's . . . estate, but Verena and I have always agreed that it all goes to her. The rest is paperwork."

"This confusion . . . did it originate with you?"

*No getting out of that, is there?*

"Yes," Sophie said. *Don't look guilty, you didn't do anything wrong, it's not your fault . . .*

"Might you be *confused* about some of your other assertions? Can we really believe, for example, that you saw Hugh Sands? Here lies a dead Golder, known to be violent, in the company of John Coine, with the injuries you describe."

"A dead Golder who conveniently resembles him, yes," she said.

"If you can get confused about something as enormous as the adjudication of a great Verdanii estate . . ."

"Now you're calling me stupid," Sophie said. She kept her eyes on Maray, trying to forget the hundreds of strangers in the room, hanging on their every word. "I'm not stupid."

"Your tale is outlandish. You must either be actively deceitful or grievously mistaken."

"Is that a question?"

"Active deceit seems most likely. I put to the Assembly that the closest relation you can produce stands accused of fraud. You yourself are tarnished with this inheritance 'confusion.' Honored Kirs, Sophie Hansa has a documented tendency to lay claim to things that aren't hers, and she has no heritage to offer us but her mother's criminal behavior."

"Cly Banning—" Sophie began, but then she saw a little gleam of triumph in Maray's face.

*Oh,* she thought, *this is where you want this to go. You want me to claim I am Sylvanner now, and then you're gonna say I'm out for whatever I can get, that nobody's proved Cly's paternity anyway, and then you'll stomp all over me some more for stealing the magic purse.*

Instead she said: "Okay, true, I'm not Verdanii. Beatrice slammed the door on that possibility when she didn't present me to the Everymom—"

A faint shock of nervous laughter met this and across the gallery, she saw Tonio flinch.

*Oh good, way to start, Sofe.*

"I met Beatrice for the first time about four weeks ago and she rejected me utterly: She wants nothing to do with me. I am not Verdanii. I never was, never said I was. And—since you're so interested—I don't particularly want to be. My sister Verena is Beatrice's heir: she gets the purse and the job and the ship and crew and . . ." She fought an urge to look at Parrish, keeping her eyes on Maray. ". . . and all the trappings."

The trappings seemed to be looking down, fighting to hide a grin.

Annela rose. "I believe Kir Hansa is formally declaring an intention to relinquish her claim on Verdanii citizenship and the Feliachild estate, Speaker."

"Well?" he asked. "Is that true?"

Was it?

"That stuff was never mine," Sophie said.

A murmur from the assembly: Apparently this had made an impact.

"There you go," Annela said, "This dispenses with the intimation that Kir Hansa is engaged in some grandiose form of estate theft."

"All it shows is she knows when to cut her losses," Maray said. "The question remains: if she's not Verdanii, who is Sophie Hansa?"

"The people who raised me are from . . . what's your phrase? No great nation. From your point of view, they're nobodies."

Over in the petitioner's loft, Parrish was definitely smiling.

"I'm nobody," she repeated, as if she was saying it to him alone, but it wasn't true.

"Then you've made my case for me," Maray said. "Speaker, Honored Kirs, I submit that Sophie Hansa has no national honor to fall back on, no pedigree, and nobody stainless to vouch for her. Perhaps she's been obliged to give up her flimsy attempt to usurp her sister's inheritance, but her history remains tarnished by her natural mother's fraud. You cannot accept her word on matters so damning to my people."

"I am inclined to agree," said the speaker. "Sophie Hansa, this Convene cannot accept your unsupported assertions. They cannot be read into the record. Resume your seat in the petitioner's loft—"

"Wait!" she said. "Don't I get a turn?"

"To do what?" Maray said. "Make more questionable assertions?"

"To prove what I've said is true," Sophie said.

"Your word—" the speaker said again.

"I said *prove,* not bluster," Sophie said. "If I can catch these guys in a lie or two, it changes the whole game, doesn't it?"

The speaker's face darkened. "This is no game."

"Oh, believe me, I'm taking it more seriously than any of you seem to be." She'd had enough with playing the nice girl in a pretty dress, holding her emotions in and wearing the social mask. She should have told Annela to bag the ball gown; she should be wearing a true skin, like her wetsuit. "You spent all this time and energy just to hash over the possibility that I might lie? Anyone might lie. Why would you take my uncorroborated word? Why would you take anyone's?"

The speaker gaped at her . . . as did everyone in the room. "I beg your pardon, young woman—"

*Don't give them a chance to shut you up.* Being brazen seemed to be setting them all back on their heels, so she limped out from behind the podium toward the monks. "Is any of you a doctor? Anyone here?"

Looking nervous, one of the monks raised a hand.

"He's not authorized to speak to the Convene," Maray objected.

"I was the ship's medic aboard *Starbright,*" said one of the starboard Convenors.

"Come on down here. Kir. Your Honor. Please." Sophie bent close to the dead man, the fake Hugh, and pulled the sheet farther down. His arm, the one Cly had busted so casually, had been realigned and laid at his side. "This arm's broken, right?"

The Convenor felt his way up both sides of the joint and said, clearly, "Yes."

"It looks pretty okay. It's not swollen or anything. Why is that?"

He looked closely. "Death occurred so shortly after the fracture that swelling was minimal."

"Okay. But his face is swollen."

"Yes," he said. "That injury occurred perhaps a few days ago."

"A few days," she said. "You sure?"

A murmur ran through the room as the quickest of the Convenors saw her point. Maray flushed, ever so slightly.

*You people don't even have basic forensics. A* CSI *fan could do this.*

"Yes, a few days, a week at most—"

"Not a month?"

"Oh." The Convenor looked startled. "No, the bruising would have healed considerably in a month."

"Okay. The attack on Gale was last month. Nobody's contesting this. Maray's saying I broke this man's nose a month ago. So are you sure?"

He took a careful look. "This is not a month-old injury."

*Point for me,* Sophie thought. She gave the Convene time to absorb the discrepancy of timing before she continued. "Now, what about this raw patch here, around his wrist?"

"The man was clearly bonded," the doctor said.

"A slave?"

More murmurs.

"Suggestive as this may be," Maray said, "I fail to see how it proves anything."

Sophie took a moment to cover the corpse, checking Maray's robe-tatters one last time. Still playing to the crowd, she took the doctor's hand, letting him help her up, like some kind of great lady. "What if I could prove the Ualtarites have Yacoura?"

You could almost hear the whole room snap to attention.

"Excuse me?" the speaker said.

Maray was staring as though she'd gone mad. "There is no such proof, Kirs."

"Says you?"

"It's not me who's been declared unreliable."

"Why don't I put some evidence up against your unimpeachable word and see who comes out ahead?"

This caused a sustained babble among the Convenors. It rose until they were on the verge of shouting.

Finally, the speaker hammered his gavel, eventually silencing the hubbub. "What could you possibly have to indicate the Ualtarites are in possession of the Heart?"

Sophie limped to Maray's side. She picked the white fleck out of the fringes of her long golden robe.

*All a show,* she thought, raising it high. *Constitutional chicken. Take your time.* Pacing out her steps with deliberation, she crossed the floor, finally dropping it in the speaker's palm.

"And so?"

She fished in her skirt, groping for the sealed tube full of packing peas. She rubbed the glass on her princess skirt to build up a bit of static, uncorked it, and flung the peas out on the scribes' table. They did what they always did: bounced everywhere and stuck to things. Those that didn't cling to the inside of the jar scattered, some lodging on the papers. A few spilled onto the carpet and rolled under the desks.

Suddenly Maray looked disturbed.

The speaker was, visibly, puzzled. "And these are?"

"These? I call them packing peas. They're polystyrene—"

"Are they inscribed?"

"Nope. They're ordinary everyday technology. And I'm betting you've never seen anything like them," she said.

The speaker squeezed the foam experimentally. "They fall outside my experience. Anyone?"

"They are mundane gadgetry from the outlands," Annela said. "Not commonly available within the Fleet."

"So recorded. What's the point of these packing peas, Kir Hansa?"

Sophie said. "Before I turned Yacoura over to the pirates—"

"Point of fact: nobody from my nation has laid hands on the Heart," said Convenor Brawn.

"Whatever. I packed the Heart in these things before I gave it up."

"Who says so?" Maray was looking uneasy. "You? We've established that your word is worthless—"

"Captain Garland Parrish—"

"Ah! Parrish!"

"—and Tonio Capodoccio, the first mate of *Nightjar,* saw me do it. Think you can impeach their honor too? They're right over there."

Maray flinched, ever so slightly. "Kirs, she could easily have concealed that item in her hand before seeming to take it from my garment. She might have dropped it on me in the petitioner's loft."

"Ah, but they don't travel alone, do they?" Sophie addressed the speaker again. "You search Maray's rooms on *Ascension.* I guarantee you'll find packing peas there. She may be honorable, but she is messy. That place was an absolute junk warren, and there'd be no cleaning the peas out once she opened up the bag. See how far two tablespoons of them have gone in thirty seconds? There's one under that guy's—that Convenor, sorry—his foot. Garbage spreads."

Maray was trying—and failing—to hold onto a derisive expression. "This is a child's gambit."

Sophie decided not to give her a chance to get the wind back in her sails. Instead she pointed across the floor at Parrish's satchel, as though it were her own.

*Theater,* she thought again.

"While we're talking about weird mummer garbage from my insignificant nation, I've been making pictures of everything I could since I got here. I'm curious, which you guys seem to hate. I've been asking questions and noting answers and even taking the occasional name."

"Kirs—" Maray protested. "This woman has no standing."

"Sophie," said Annela Gracechild. "The materials you've gathered—"

*Oh, don't go telling them you had Verena erase them all . . .*

"No, no, no," she said. "Explaining where my information comes from is your problem, Convenor. Maray says I'm a liar. If I've figured out anything about all this—" She waved a hand at the big room. "—it's that that's a huge insult. Am I allowed to prove my honesty or not?"

This raised a small spontaneous cheer, led by the little sylph from Erinth.

She couldn't quite wait until the speaker reestablished order. "I'm not sitting here with my mouth shut like a mouse and letting her label me a liar and a thief."

"Your documents are no substitute for your good name," Maray said.

"You just made it, like, the word of law that I don't have a good name,"

Sophie said. "But you know what? Keep it. I have more to back up my words than just hot air and dead slaves. What did you do, enchant him so he could swing a sword? What happens if we look for polystyrene peas aboard your ship? Will we find them? Yes or no?"

"Consider your answer, Maray." The speaker raised his hand; the Styrofoam pea lay in his palm, a nonbiodegradable pearl. "If *Ascension* were to be searched and any sign of the Heart's having been there were found, your people would face significant loss of face. If *you* were proved to have lied to the Watch and this Convene, I need hardly tell you how serious that would be."

Maray swallowed. "Yes, Speaker."

Annela wasn't one to ignore an advantage: "Kirs, the penalty for attempting to break the Fleet Compact is a sinking. If *Ascension* has Yacoura—if it were to be found there—I would move that the captain of *Temperance* be ordered to speak that ship's name."

Complete silence spilled from that. The tension in the room ratcheted up, up, so high it felt like Sophie's eyes might start bleeding.

"Leave that for now, Convenor Gracechild," the speaker said. "Well, Tanta? Do you wish to answer Kir Hansa's question? Has Yacoura been in your keeping? Shall we put your word to the test with a search?"

Maray was now the color of cottage cheese. "What if the inscription were to turn up by . . . say, sundown?"

Snap. The tension broke.

"Say noon. The blockade of Tiladene is to be withdrawn. I believe we'll be tasking a body of warships to return Kir Lais Dariach to his homeland and inspect the region."

"The naval maneuvers that were so lately misunderstood by the Duelist-Adjudicator are coming to a close," Maray said, bowing her head. "The ships will embark for our capital within two days."

There were shouts from the starboard side of the galley, but the speaker waved them down. "Acceptable. Now, to the matter of spiritual reparations to Isle of Gold for the sinking of the *Lucre*. This is an active case and the Convene will continue to await a Judicial ruling."

"We must protest," said the old Isle of Gold Convenor, Brawn, but he seemed almost bored now. He knew it was over.

"So recorded. Kirs Hansa and Maray, unless either of you has something to add, why don't you surrender the floor?"

Sophie gathered her skirts, fought down an urge to make a rude gesture at Maray, and made her way back to the petitioner's bench.

Bram nudged her with an elbow. "I think you won."

Sophie nodded, a little breathless. They'd bought it: a whole world's government, and she'd got them with an empty satchel and some litter. "Chalk one up for the girl with no poker face."

"You were angry," Bram said. "Hides a lot."

"Are you still with us, Kir Hansa?"

She leapt to her feet, cheeks flaming.

"Kir Gracechild informs us you have violated the terms of your travel visa. You are ordered home as soon as is practicably possible, and if you wish to return to the Fleet, you must convince the Passage Office that you can keep your agreements. Bramwell Hansa, you are likewise deported, but without prejudice."

Ouch.

"You win, thanks much, get the hell out," Bram murmured.

"Excuse me?"

"Nothing," he said. "Thank you, Speaker."

"This emergency session of the Convene is closed." He clanged his hand bell.

Sophie managed to emulate Parrish's bow and leave the Convene with her head high.

## CHAPTER 27

Annela's reward to Sophie for a job well done was to more or less put her under house arrest.

"I confess you had me worried, but you did well," she said, after she'd marched them back up to the suite of rooms she occupied on *Constitution* and had ordered a host of clerks and other assistant types to pack up the few remnants she was allowing her and Bram to take home. "We'll have Yacoura in government hands by dinnertime, and we've dispatched battleships to Tiladene. With Lais Dariach secured and restored to health, the Ualtarites' pretext for the invasion has been undermined."

"So war's gonna fizzle out before it begins?" Sophie asked.

"That's the likely outcome," she said. "It's not an exaggeration to say you've prevented a catastrophe."

"You're welcome. Will the Tiladenes succeed in breaking Ualtar's silk monopoly?"

"Hard to say. The Ualtarites will file for an order of restraint, in all probability."

"Why didn't they just do that in the first place?"

"They preferred to invade, primarily—they regard the Tiladenes as thoroughgoing perverts, not to mention easy prey. They're part of the bloc that resents the Cessation and would like to resume hostilities. We can wager they didn't hatch this plan in a vacuum. That aside, they had no reasonable proof of what Lais was up to. Now it's been discussed in the Convene; it's a matter of record. They can use the transcripts of this morning's session as grounds to file a suit."

"Loopholes and paperwork," Sophie said. "You guys seem to have an excess of legal maneuvering and a shortage of common sense."

"Sofe—" Bram said.

"It's a fair point. It's also the price of the peace," Annela said. "Bureaucratic warfare. Less bloody than the real thing."

As she said the words, her eyes fell on the lily wristlet, the mourning corsage. She pulled it off, letting her thumb roll over one of the petals.

"I don't suppose Gale's life was much like this," Sophie said. "Sailing madly from place to place, uncovering plots?"

"It was, actually. Though there weren't as many formal inquisitions. Her word had got to be almost as good as an adjudicator's." Annela looked at her sideways. "You're suited to it. You have the right spirit."

"I can't fight."

"That's one thing Parrish is good for."

"Are you saying I should snatch Verena's life out from under her?"

"Merely wondering if you're having second thoughts."

*Am I?* No. When Sophie thought of what Stormwrack offered her, she thought of Cly, of the otters and the sea raft and exploring, all the things she could see and learn. A passport to a weird matriarchy and *Nightjar*'s pink slip weren't on the list. "What do I do to have to sort out the inheritance?"

"I could challenge you," Verena said. "It'd delay your leaving, but—"

It was a bit of a test. "I know you guys don't have much use for Cly, and I can't say I understand the problem there."

"Yeah," Bram said. "What's the deal?"

Annela drew herself up. "I can't comment on the Duelist-Adjudicator's personality, but his reputation is impeccable."

"You don't want to get sued," Sophie said.

"You're franker than you should be, child."

"I'll grant you this much about Cly," Sophie said. "I don't quite trust him not to insist on a dueling proxy for me . . . especially since I'm injured."

Annela said. "You told the Convene you meant to repudiate your Verdanii citizenship."

"And you jumped all over that offer, didn't you?" Bram said.

"It's okay, Bram."

*I'm being tossed out of a party I didn't know was happening*, Sophie thought. The thought lacked its usual sting. Whatever she'd been looking for, it wasn't a seal of approval from some far-off politician who called herself the Allmother. "What'll that take?"

"Sincere intentions and a few signatures." Annela produced a sheaf of documents.

Sophie looked over the pages. They were densely written, in tiny script, all Fleetspeak. "I'm not agreeing to anything else here, am I? Not to give up eating meat or never talk to Verena again or, I dunno, move to Oakland?"

"The document says you relinquish any claim on the blessings of the Allmother, and the property, talents, and entitlements of the Feliachild family. It specifies that your offspring and heirs are likewise without entitlement, and that you won't show up on Verdanii territory uninvited, except in the case of shipwreck, imminent starvation, serious injury, or other extreme hazard."

"Oh, is that all?"

"It's a standard clause."

Damn. She'd have to read it from start to finish.

"Want me to go over it?" That was Bram.

"You barely speak Fleet, Bramble," she said.

"I'm making out okay."

"I'd help," Verena said.

"What if we three wade through the mumbo jumbo together?" she said.

Annela looked as though she approved of that. "I'll leave you to it. Please don't go anywhere, Kirs. Verena, when's the next opportunity to get them home?"

"The sun's angle should be right in about two and a half hours."

"Fair winds, then."

It took them about an hour to read through the document. When they'd done so, Sophie put her name on it. "What's the date?"

"Fifteenth day, third month, hundred and ninth year of the Fleet Compact," said Verena. "Thanks, Sophie."

"Bram? Can you witness this?"

He took the pen and scrawled his first and last names across the bottom.

Sophie took out Gale's courier purse, holding it over the contract as if it could see it. "You got that, magic handbag? Break-up time. You're so over me."

Then she tried to unlace it.

Nothing happened.

She handed it to Verena. "I'm yesterday's news."

Verena drew a finger across the join. The purse, after a pause that was just long enough to seem insulting, somehow, gaped.

"Congratulations," Bram said.

"Thank you," she said, sounding relieved. "Seriously, Sophie—thank you."

"No problem. Oh, hey—my phone's in there," Sophie said, keeping her eyes on the documents she'd just signed, folding them.

Verena pulled out Sophie's smartphone, and instead of handing it over she started tapping on the screen. "Sorry, but I've gotta wipe this."

*Damn.* "I know."

"I'll take you home as soon as—"

There was a tap at the door. "May I interrupt?"

It was Lais Dariach.

Lais had an ugly scar on his scalp, a pink line like an earthworm just below his hairline, and the same expression of mischief she remembered. He let his eye roam over Bram and Verena.

"These are my siblings," Sophie said.

"What a beautiful family you have," Lais said.

She giggled. "Shut up."

Bram took that as a cue to get lost. "We'll go pack up. Come on, Verena."

When the door shut behind them, Sophie said to Lais. "So . . . are you okay?"

"Thanks to the Duelist-Adjudicator," he said. "I'd got my skull cracked. You heard?"

"They don't have magic healers on Tiladene?"

"It's the rainy season and there was some trouble with a foal on the other side of the island," he said. "Both of them had been marooned."

"Convenient."

"All carefully orchestrated, I'm sure. Makes me feel terribly important. So much fuss over a few spiders." He put an arm around her waist, laying the crease of his scar against her forehead, flirting. "Princess Zophie—"

"I'm no princess."

"That boobie dress you're bursting out of begs to differ."

She gestured at the paper. "It's official. I'm not Verdanii."

"As I hear it, you're a Sylvanner heiress instead. That makes us pepper and chocolate, darling. Sweetness and spice—"

"All that's pending a paternity test. And me finding out something about Sylvanna. Which isn't happening anytime soon."

"Mmm. Is this Convenor Gracechild's desk? Looks . . . what was that Anglay word of yours? Comfy."

"Did the magical healing leave you more determined than ever to live up to the Tiladene reputation for randiness?"

"Ah, Kir Sophie, I believe it's an accepted truth that a brush with death tends to make a gentleman—" He fluffed her skirts. "—energetic."

"That's a hard effect to measure when the test subject apparently never thinks of anything but sex."

"You malign me, Kir. I also think about horses and spiders."

"Which you breed."

"Fair point." He kissed her. "But I didn't come here solely to raise your voluminous skirts."

"Could've fooled me."

He leaned against the desk. "Sophie, you've done a great thing. For me and my people, but also for the peace. And not only are you stripped of rights on Verdanii, it's my understanding that you're being sent into exile."

"I do have to go home," she said. "Bram too. I'm hoping to wangle permission to come back."

"If need arises—" He produced a heavy envelope. "This might help."

"What is it?"

"A summons, actually. Requires you to appear in court."

"Just what I need, more court. Appear for what?"

"The phrasing is vague. I'll come up with something legitimate, I promise. It's our way of thanking you."

"That's an even weirder present than your spider collection, Lais. Weird, but sweet."

"I'm all about the sweetness." He caressed the edge of Annela's desk again.

She felt a little surge of heat. Did she want this? The shipboard affair had been pretty nice, but . . .

*But what?*

By way of buying time, she asked: "Aren't you weakened?"

"Magically restored, or so they say. I haven't had a chance to assess my potency yet. Don't you want to help?"

She chortled, and he took that as a yes, sweeping her into his arms, dragging the weight of the skirt with him.

But—

"Actually, Lais."

"Mmm?"

"I don't know if anything will come of it. I don't know if he's even noticed me, in the romantic sense of 'noticed,' but—"

"But someone's caught that roving eye of yours?"

She nodded.

"Ah," he said, and he didn't seem at all put out. "Someone is in for a treat, then."

"What do you say to that? Thank you?"

"It *is* a compliment," he purred, rubbing her nose companionably.

The door opened before he could release her.

It was Parrish. He had a couple of cups of steaming tea on a tray and a faintly stricken look on his face.

*Oh come on,* Sophie thought. *It's not as if he'd got my bodice unlaced.* The thought was bolder than she felt; blushing, she disentangled herself.

"Lais Dariach, this is Captain Garland Parrish."

"Kir Dariach." He was flustered, enough so that when he bowed, he almost dropped the tea things on the floor. "I—ah—of course. I didn't mean to interrupt."

*I suppose, being raised by monks, it was inevitable he'd be prudish.*

"Lais has given me a summons," Sophie said, waving it.

*What am I doing?*

"Ah. That's very . . . a summons?"

"It's a legal excuse to come back, Parrish."

Since Sophie's attempt to smooth over the awkwardness was dead in the water, Lais gave it a try. "Tiladene owes you a debt too, Captain. If you ever need—"

"Ah. No. And I'm intruding. Kir Hansa—" He bowed. "I came to wish you fair winds."

"Call me Sophie, Parrish. And maybe I'll see you when—"

But he was gone—the hatch closed with a click.

"—when I come back," she said.

"Flailers," Lais said. He flung himself onto one of Annela's plush couches, grinning. "Don't worry. He'll head straight to the medic for some eyewash, I imagine."

"Yeah," Sophie said, feeling suddenly downcast—abandoned, almost. "I suppose he will."

## CHAPTER 28

She almost didn't get to say good-bye to Cly.

After Lais left, she and Bram found themselves confined to Annela's rooms, checking on the remains of their stuff. She'd had to give up both cameras; Bram lost his scientific equipment. She'd willingly left the diving supplies, all but the tank. "Keep it on *Nightjar*," she said. "Maybe I'll be lucky enough to need it again."

"Sounds good," Verena said. "It'll be waiting if you manage to return."

A harassed-looking clerk cracked the door and said, "His Honor the Duelist-Adjudicator would like a word, Kir."

Sophie glanced at Verena.

"Be back in seven minutes," she said, handing her back her phone. It had been wiped, set back to its factory presets. "Time it on this."

"Okay." She followed the clerk to a small audience room.

Cly enfolded her in a hug as soon as she walked in the door. "You should assume that someone's listening," he whispered, before saying in a normal tone, "You look lovely, my dear."

"I look like a little girl dressed in her mommy's clothes."

"You sell yourself short. Sophie, your presentation to the Convene was . . ." He paused, searching for the right word.

In the past she'd have quailed, expecting something like "substandard."

"Innovative. Revolutionary, perhaps," he said. "You may have set a precedent by which those with tarnished honor may regain some capacity for addressing the courts and government."

"You really don't have a standard of proof here?"

"Oh, court cases occasionally revolve around evidentiary matters, when there are no good witnesses. It's easier to duel them out," he said. "But what you've done is raise the question of whether a person's word should be the first line . . . but I'm wasting our precious time on constitutional minutia. Forgive me."

She found herself smiling a bit, at the quaintness of his manners. "It sucks we didn't get more time together!"

"Must you go?"

"For a while," she said. "I've got a—sort of a ticket back."

He nodded, as if this was what he'd expected. "With your permission, I'd like to take steps to establish our familial relationship by the time you do return."

"What do you need for that—DNA?"

He looked at her blankly.

"A biosample? A few hairs?"

"I have your name." He circled the room, brushing the walls with his long fingers, with restless energy. "And I expect Beatrice will swear she honored our marriage vows."

"Will that make me Sylvanner?"

"It's a first step. There would be others. You can decide later."

"About Beatrice . . . I wish you'd go easy on her."

He made that gesture, the waving away of an airborne pest, and she thought that she could get tired of that fast. "Twenty-four years," he said. "Almost your entire childhood. I can't but feel robbed of something so fundamental . . ."

"I know, but—"

The clerk tapped at the door. "Two minutes, Kir."

"Okay." Had five minutes already elapsed? "Would you think about it?"

"For you, of course." Cly's smile was easy and gracious. Was it sincere?

"I have to go."

"You must, you must. But come back to me, child, as soon as you can." His eyes were alight. Whatever his flaws, Cly Banning wanted to know her—wanted it badly. And that was irresistible.

"Count on it," Sophie said.

He walked her back to the others and kissed her forehead. "Good-bye, remarkable one," he said gravely. "Go with my blessings and know that I am proud."

She was tearing up. "Bye, Cly."

The clerk ushered him away and Verena took out the big pewter time-piece again. The switch home was much like the transit to Erinth—there was a gust of wind, a sense of her vision blurring, and suddenly they were in a bare room with old wallpaper, a thin carpet, and a loudly ticking grandfather clock.

The floor beneath her feet was still; they were on dry land.

"Is this Beatrice's place?" Bram said.

"Yes. We're in Bernal." Verena opened the curtains, letting in the light. Through the window was a thick, familiar wash of San Francisco summer fog. Telegraph Hill was barely visible in the distance. Car engines hummed at them from the mist.

Home. Despite everything, her heart lifted.

Bram's phone beeped.

He dug it out, glancing at it.

"You texted me even when we were *both* there?"

"It made me feel better when you were kidnapped."

"And people think *I'm* a geek."

Sophie brushed that off, turning to Verena. "So . . . we're okay, you and I?"

"Yeah. I'll be on Stormwrack a lot, especially until Mom gets home, but I'll call when I'm in town. I thought maybe the three of us could all . . . get to know each other a bit?"

"Of course," Bram said. "But you and Sophie might also want—"

"Right. Alone time. Sister time." Verena blushed.

"It's okay, guys," Sophie said. "There's something about the idea of us becoming a weird sibling trio that seems . . ."

"Optimal?" Verena said, with a ghost of a smile.

"Super-duper-optimal, even. I'd love it if we could all hang."

"Okay," Verena said. She seemed to struggle with something before saying, "Listen, I'm sorry you had to write off being Verdanii."

"I barely know what I gave up."

"I'll try and spell it out one day."

"Sure. And Beatrice? She won't really go to jail?"

"Banning must want to be divorced. He's got to let her off the hook, doesn't he?"

"Does he?" She thought fleetingly of how pleased he had seemed when he told her there was an arrest warrant out on their mother.

*I'm reckoned by some an ill-tempered and vengeful fellow.* Was it true, or had he been posturing to scare John Coine?

"I know what Mom did was wrong. And she more or less went out of her way to make a bad impression on you," Verena said. "It's like a gift she has. But give her a chance, okay?"

"I'll give her one if she gives me one," Sophie said.

"It takes her time to get used to change," she said.

"Okay. Thanks."

There was a moment of awkward flapping.

"This is the part where you hug, idiots," Bram said, and then he folded them into a three-way squeeze.

*Sister,* Sophie thought. She found herself beaming into Verena's face. "I got a little sister out of all this!"

"Okay," Verena said, turning pink. "I have to get back before the Fleet moves. Um . . . this . . ." She handed them each a long sheaf of pages. "It's your copy of the repudiation of citizenship, and also the paperwork on traveling from the Fleet to here."

"It's longer than the last visa."

"Annela felt it necessary to go into exhaustive detail about how Stormwrack's a secret. Tell anyone else and you're seriously toast."

"What can they do?"

"The whole world's got your name, remember?" She opened the sliding doors to the sidewalk. "Don't tempt Annela to scrip you forgetful or something."

"Would she?"

"In a heartbeat."

"Thanks for the warning."

"I'll have what's left of your trunk sent to your place as soon as I have another look for video files," Verena said. "And—I'll call you?"

"Yes, please."

Bram's phone chirped again.

*Dammit,* Sophie thought. "Come on, Bramble," she said cheerily, catching his arm and strolling out.

"Don't let them know how smart you are?" he asked, reading another of the texts she'd sent while the Golden had him.

"They'd grind you up for genius powder and put it into inscriptions."

"Eye of newt, toe of Bram." He rubbed his forehead. "Friggin' magic."

"I know." They were at the fence, through the gate. She was listening for footsteps, but no—they were clear, standing on an ordinary sidewalk in a familiar American neighborhood. Pigeons clucked at her from the awning of a corner grocery down the road.

"So," he said. "What now?"

"I don't know where to start. You never figured out the landmass thing."

"You're already planning a trip back?"

"Gotta. I have to get another look at those otter rafts."

"Even if you got data, you couldn't publish here."

"Maybe they have a scientific journal or two on Stormwrack. Besides, I want to get to know Cly."

"Right."

"I'll have to make the most of Lais's summons, or get some kind of permit out of Annela to come and go." She'd never felt so full of plans . . . of direction.

Bram's phone beeped. "Hang on, I am going to get you out of this. It will all be okay. I'm sorry, I'm sorry— Seriously, Sofe, how many times did you text me?"

"I was *upset!*"

The jingle of a streetcar made them pick up the pace. They climbed aboard, heading for downtown. There wasn't much to see. The fog was thick enough to make shadows of everyone on the street, to turn the buildings gray.

Another beep, from both their phones this time.

"Oh Emm Gee," Bram said. "It's the fourteenth. The parents are coming back today. Their flight lands in ninety minutes."

Suddenly the prospect of seeing their lovely, sane, low-drama parents was the best idea in the world. "We should go pick them up!"

"Sofe, look at yourself. You're dressed like Bridezilla."

"Can we make it to your place and back again?"

"Are you kidding? We'll ditch the dress at the nearest mall."

"Can't ditch it," she said.

"You'd keep *that* as a souvenir?"

She tried to maintain an innocent expression.

"What have you done?"

"Done? Me?"

"Ducks."

"If it turns out a few seeds and bits of shell got caught in the weird damned petticoat, that's not my fault. Oh! And did you see that Erinthian princess dresses have pockets?" She produced the glass jar with the repulsive jeweler's wasp.

He covered it with his hand. "You smuggled samples home. If anyone finds out—"

"I could have forgotten it was there."

"I wondered why you weren't mourning your data trove." He frowned suspiciously. "Still, how much could you have shoved down your petticoat? A few seeds and a pickled bug . . ."

She couldn't help bouncing in her seat.

"You got video? But Annela ordered you not to smuggle any data out."

"Yeah. She ordered me twenty-four hours ago," she said.

"But you've sent me texts." He took her smartphone, looking suspicious, looking for files. Verena had deleted everything, setting the thing back to its factory presets and confiscating the data chip for good measure. "Nothing here . . . what did you do?"

"I sent the phone home in the pouch, with Verena, when she came back here for Beatrice. I told her I'd sent Mom and Dad an e-mail so they wouldn't report us missing. Which I did, incidentally."

"So Verena brought it here, the phone sent those texts and synced all your files up to that point to the cloud, and . . . Sofe, what if *she* gets into trouble?"

"Haha! Thought of that. She couldn't get into the courier pouch. Even if she'd realized what I was up to, she couldn't have done anything about it."

"Maybe you are a lawyer's daughter after all."

"See?" By now she'd gotten the phone online and accessed her cloud storage. "Here are my video files up to the point where she went to get Beatrice. And here's the stuff you filmed in Erinth, all those books from the library, and some of your measurements."

She saw the relief on his face.

"Your otter raft . . . that stuff's gone?"

"I need to go back and dive it properly anyway. With a partner and a plan and no damned monsters! And at least a week to look at everything. But in the meantime, we have pink narwals and the Tallon shipyards and the Erinthian market and a respectable chunk of the Conto's library and John Coine being a creepy, threatening ass."

"Sneaky," Bram said. "You're learning to hide your cards."

"Is that a compliment or an insult? Oh!" She pointed as a shopping center loomed out of the mist. "I know what we'll do. You can buy me a normal outfit somewhere, so I can go to the airport, and we'll get a gym bag for the dress."

"I can buy?"

"I maxed out my credit card buying cameras."

They hopped off at the next stop.

"Mall air," said Bram as they stepped through the doors. "Air-conditioning and French fries. I thought we were never gonna get home."

"Dry land, and the smell of pizza baking under heat lamps," she said, raising her skirt above the food court floor. A gust of breeze—air-conditioning, or a current from the open doors, caught the skirt, tugging her forward and in, pressing it and her samples against the backs of her legs.

*Wind in my sails,* she thought, and that was exactly it. Even though she didn't know anything—how she was going to get a toehold into Storm-wrack, what Cly was truly like, whether things would work out with Verena—she felt, perhaps for the first time, like her life was on course.

"Princess!" A little girl bounded up and down in a booth, waving a hot dog. "Mommy, look! Princess!"

"Princess Sophie," Bram said. "Of Sylvanna?"

"Of no great nation," Sophie corrected, feeling strangely cheerful. Sketching a curtsy at the kid, she locked arms with her brother, sweeping into the familiar fluorescent-lit world of the mall.

# ABOUT THE AUTHOR

A. M. Dellamonica is a recent transplant to Toronto, Ontario, having moved there in 2013 with her wife, Kelly Robson, after twenty-two years in Vancouver. She has been publishing short fiction since the early nineties in venues like *Asimov's*, *Strange Horizons*, and Tor.com, as well as numerous anthologies. Her 2005 alternate history of Joan of Arc, "A Key to the Illuminated Heretic," was short-listed for the Sidewise Award and the Nebula.

Her first novel, *Indigo Springs*, won the 2010 Sunburst Award for Canadian Literature of the Fantastic; she is also a Canada Council grant recipient.

Dellamonica teaches writing courses through the UCLA Extension Writers' Program. *Child of a Hidden Sea* is her third novel.